WARRIOR QUEEN

He entered her tent and fell to one knee. "My queen," he murmured, his voice soft and strong.

She came to him and felt the shock as their eyes met. She trembled, warmed by his presence, and for one sweet instant they forgot the battle they would fight on the morrow.

There was a tremor in her voice as she spoke: "Stand, dear Canis, for I hope you are not only my general, but my friend, too."

And then they were in each other's arms, answering with hungry kisses the questions that had gone so long unasked . . .

Warrior Queen

JAMES SINCLAIR

A BERKLEY BOOK
published by
BERKLEY PUBLISHING CORPORATION

St. Martin's Press
175 Fifth Avenue
New York, N.Y. 10010

SBN 425-03947-1

BERKLEY MEDALLION BOOKS are published by
Berkley Publishing Corporation
200 Madison Avenue
New York, N.Y. 10016

BERKLEY MEDALLION BOOK® TM 757,375

Printed in the United States of America

Berkley Edition, JANUARY, 1979

**To
Joanna and Kate**

BOADICEA'S CAMPAIGN

Battle sites ✗

Ninth Legion 9

Paullinus ▯▯

CORITANI

ICENI

VENTA ICENORUM
Caistor by Norwich

GLEVODURUM

TRINOVANTES

DOBUNI

CORINIUM
Cirencester

AQUAE SULIS
Bath

CAMULODUNUM
Colchester

VERULAMIUM
St Albans

LONDINIUM

CALLEVA ATREBATUM
Silchester

DUROVERNUM
Canterbury

DUBRAE
Dover

BELGAE

CANTII

VENTA BELGARUM
Winchester

DUROTRIGES

VECTIS
I. of Wight

N

PLACE NAMES

Calleva Atrebatum	—	Silchester
Camulodunum	—	Colchester
Glevodurum	—	A site between Colchester and Caister St. Edmunds
Glevum	—	Gloucester
Lindum	—	Lincoln
Londinium	—	London
Mona	—	Anglesey
Venta Icenorum	—	Caister St. Edmunds
Verulamium	—	St. Albans

AUTHOR'S NOTE

The story of Queen Boadicea is one of great love and great tragedy, a single blaze of colour in the intermingled tapestry of Ancient Britain and Ancient Rome. Regrettably, historians have been comparatively brief about it and only Tacitus and Dio Cassius, scribes of Rome, give us more than an outline. Even then they do not agree, for whereas Tacitus implies that the Romans won a miraculously quick victory in the final battle against the Iceni queen, Cassius tells us that the conflict raged all day. In view of the strength of each army, the latter is far the likelier.

By reason of the historians' brevity, Boadicea comes down to us as more of a legend than a fact, but in both legend and fact she stands a rich and colourful figure of her time.

She was a woman of majesty and magnetism, a queen greatly loved by her people. On her behalf they rose to challenge the might of Rome. It was an entirely impulsive gesture that burdened them with a task of Herculean proportions, for in weapons and armour they were vastly inferior to the enemy. Yet they almost succeeded.

If, during Boadicea's campaign, the Britons gave cruel death to many Romans and collaborators, this was something the vanquished suffered in most wars of those times. Students of history who deprecate the way in which Boadicea revenged herself for wrongs done to her and her people do so with an obsessive pro-Romanism common to many classical scholars, forgetting that there was little any nation could teach Rome about cruelty. There are those who write angrily or bitterly about Boadicea's destruction of the temple of Claudius at Camulodunum (Colchester), but the modern parallel is Cassino.

There are also those who, studying the conduct of the queen's campaign, have concluded that it was masterminded by a man of great tactical ability. This could have been none other than her general, Canis (*Kay-nuss*), also known as the Wolfhead. Apropos the final battle, historians have been puzzled as to why Boadicea, after so many great victories, virtually threw away her chance of ultimate triumph by the reckless manner in which she committed her army against

Paullinus. My own conjecture is the one I have written into
the narrative.

In Celtic story and legend, Boadicea is more strictly and ac-
curately known as Boudicca, meaning Victory, but I have
kept to the modern version of her name throughout, as this is
how most of us now refer to her. Although it is still not certain that the chief city of the Iceni was Venta Icenorum
(Caister St. Edmunds), I have made this the queen's city
because no other lends itself more suitably.

Boadicea and her Iceni, as well as her allies the Trinovantes,
were true Celtic Britons, and were neither woad-painted
savages nor uncultured barbarians. Their customs were
civilised and untouched by the sensuous degeneracy of Rome.
Their arts were numerous and their concept of godheads
superior to the grosser idolatry of the Mediterranean peoples.

Put aside any Victorian impression you have of Boadicea as
a muscular, matronly Britannia, for this she was not. She was
still in her thirties at the time of her rebellion and like many
Celtic women of this era she was slim, supple and active. She
was also beautiful. Dio Cassius waxes lyrical when writing of
her vivid blue eyes. Imagine Boadicea as she raced her light
sporting chariot and picture a hulking figure of a woman if
you dare. You cannot. She was as lithe and quick as all the
women warriors of her time, and the army she led
against Rome was full of them. She was like Hippolyte, the
tall swift queen of the Amazons: she loved to hunt, she loved
life, the summer sun and the crisp winter, and in her courage,
pride and final heroism there have been few queens to match
her.

And the story of Canis the Briton, who was her great and
beloved general, and also her life and her death, is indivisible
from her own.

                                                    J.S.

1

THEY TRAVELLED BY way of the ancient road, one that had been rebuilt in recent years by the Romans, the hard stone surface striking sparks from the iron-shod wheels of their chariot.

They were brother and sister, Julian and Lydia Osirus. She was nineteen, he was six years older. They were on their way to Venta Icenorum, chief town of the kingdom of the Iceni, and had ridden steadily in company with their friend, Paulus until a short while back, when Lydia had wagered that she and Julian could outride him to the last stone marker. Now, with Julian running the pair at a blood-tingling gallop, they were already leaving Paulus well behind.

Although the March day was unseasonably warm the wind was brisk. It tugged at her dark hair and girdled cloak of blue. She clung with one hand to the brass rail and the other to the studded belt around her brother's waist, and they laughed together, exhilarated by the speed of the gallop.

The road bore straight and true. In the crisp sunlight it was like a bright arrow aimed at the heart of Venta Icenorum. On each side the green earth softly awaited the kiss of spring. Grass and trees whispered in the wind and the only sign of man's intrusion on nature was the paved highway which bore the speeding chariot.

"Faster, Julian," cried Lydia, eyes sparkling, "give them the whip."

"Let them be, they're doing well enough," said Julian above the rush and clatter. The pair were running bravely.

"They can do better, said Lydia, "and with a taste of the leather will run Paulus clean out of sight."

"Why, do you think he can catch us now, faint-heart?" mocked her brother.

"Faintheart? That from a softheart?" she taunted. "Give me the whip."

She snatched it from him, planted her sandalled feet firmly on the jolting floor and struck boldly. The leather whistled and bit at the wet flanks of the sweating horses.

She glanced back, but the dust of Paulus, which had been receding into a disc of grey peppered with gold, was no longer visible. It was impossible for him to over-take them now, but because Lydia, wilful and spoiled, preferred a complete victory to a comfortable one, she lashed the horses in spiteful exultation.

The chariot rocked and clattered, the whip sang and smote, brother and sister sped on. They were Romans. They could not think what it must be like not to be Romans, and although Julian would have accepted an alternative philosophically, Lydia would have said that were she not Roman she would rather be dead. They had been in Roman Britain almost twelve years, their father, Marcus Osirus, having brought them to this island of Celts and barbarians in the eighth year of the reign of illustrious Claudius. True, Claudius had gone. But there was another in his place. Nero.

Julian was on his way, at the request of his father, to observe events in Venta Icenorum, where King Prasutagus lay gravely ill. Marcus Osirus, who knew the Iceni well and considered their queen, Boadicea, a woman who would not suffer injustice gladly, did not trust Catus Decianus, Imperial Procurator of Roman Britain. The Imperial Governor, Suetonius Paullinus, was campaigning against Druids in the far west, and in his absence Catus Decianus was likely to commit every kind of greedy indiscretion should King Prasutagus die.

Lydia, for a whim, decided to accompany her

brother. She was always more likely to be moved by whims than reasons.

There was just a league now between the running chariot and the Iceni town. The stone marker came into view. Lydia laughed. Sluggish Paulus had indeed been outpaced but she continued plying the whip, stinging the now labouring horses.

They reached the marker where they were to wait for Paulus to come up with them, their servants and baggage following on. Julian strove to quieten the distressed horses. They were in sweating, foaming exhaustion, flanks heaving, nostrils and mouths spattering white flecks. Julian, seeing them so winded, turned angrily on his sister.

"Do you confuse strength with brutality, worshipper of trumpets?" he shouted.

Theirs was a love-hate relationship, typical of brothers and sisters. They were more often quarelling than not, and they quarrelled now. Lydia was taunting and shrewish, Julian angry and bitter. Not far from the roadside stood a wattle hut, dilapidated and ancient. From the doorway a man observed them and listened to them. Tall, leanly hard of muscle, he wore the short kilted tunic of a Briton. His legs were bound with leather to the calves, his sandals worn and dusty. His coppery-brown hair was long and thickly grown, and tied at the nape of his neck with a strip of leather, Gaulish fashion. His cloak folded, was slung, and on the ground was his pack.

He came towards them. Lydia, seeing he was only a barbarian and therefore very little in the sight of the gods (or herself), regarded his approach without interest, although there did slip into her mind the thought that there might be sport to be had at his expense until Paulus arrived. The Briton halted, looking at the sweating horses, than up at Lydia and Julian. His smile was friendly.

Lydia saw a face strong and hard, and brown from a

thousand suns. Grey eyes held a knowledge of life and people, and even impudent knowledge of herself because of the way she ill-used horses. She saw a wide mouth where humour slyly lurked, but there was a hardness there too, and of a kind that might make a barbarian maid gasp in pain from his kiss. She found herself staring intently, almost compulsively, and disliked exceedingly the fact that he should disturb her in a way that was uncomfortable.

Julian saw the stranger differently. He saw a tall man with eyes clear and direct, with features that were surely carved by the strong but subtle hands of Celtic forebears. Lydia would have said his look was devious, not subtle, and whereas Julian thought his smile frank and friendly, she thought it held the impudence of a barbarian daring to be in sly reproof of her. Abruptly she turned her head to look back for signs of Paulus. She saw none. The Briton placed his hand on the shivering neck of the nearer horse. The animal quietened under the caress.

"Are you bound for Venta Icenorum?" asked the Briton in a deep and pleasant voice.

"We are," said Julian cheerfully, liking the look of the man.

"I thought to ask you to take me up with you," said the Briton, "but your pair are in such reduced circumstances that I had better not add my weight to the pole."

"That," said Julian with a smile, "makes you a more considerate person than my sister, who is out of all consideration when she has a whip in her hand."

"Ah well," observed the Briton, "the sensitivity of a horse, being unknown, is not to be put on as high a plane as the infectious exuberance of a man's sister."

Insolence! Lydia's blood ran hot. The Briton stroked soft noses. The pair nuzzled. She compelled his glance, showing him her anger. He gave her back look for look. Lydia, black-haired and green-eyed, was cast in a mould of spoiled petulance, her mouth at once maliciously spiteful and redly beautiful. He did not seem impressed, only curious.

"If you have anything else to say," she said, "then say it only to yourself."

"To myself I say, then," he smiled, "that it is better to come to one's destination in good time than to run the means of conveyance to a standstill. These two will not recover their wind for some time."

"Barbarian," said Lydia, showing white teeth, "you will lose your tongue in a moment and never recover it."

"Come," he said pleasantly, "you should not take my point churlishly. You are Romans and because of your civilisation must look for truth before offence."

"Myself, I agree," said Julian just as pleasantly, "but I cannot speak for my sister. Lydia has never been known to agree with anyone."

"That is an endearing trait in some sisters," said the Briton. Lydia felt again the rush of angry blood.

"You are a dog," she hissed.

"Ah," said the Briton as if she had spoken in monumental wisdom. Such mockery she found unbearable.

Julian, who had been whistling softly between his teeth, said, "Carefully, my friend. I take no offence myself but I warn you for your own good not to provoke my sister without thought for the consequences. She has a most unfriendly way of returning a jest. Though she may lack a sense of humour she does not lack aggression."

"I believe you," said the Briton. He smiled up at Lydia as if she had been a wayward, amusing child. Rushing blood suffused her face. She smote the rail of the chariot with a passionate hand.

"This for your belief and your insolence!" she shouted, and smote at him with the whip she still held. Adroitly he brought up his arm and the leather snapped harmlessly around his wrist. Lydia, unyielding,

wrenched and pulled as his hand closed over the thong.
He shook his head chidingly. Because he was only a barbarian she spat into his upturned face. He did not move
but for a moment his features were like brown, carved
stone.

"You are a child who will take a long time to grow
into a woman," he said and loosened his hold on the
whip.

"For that," hissed Lydia, "you shall choke to death
in the dust at my feet!"

And she spat on him again, jerked the whip free and
sprang like a she-cat from the chariot. The breeze
tugged at her cloak, moulding it to the curving lines of
her body, and the glitter in her eyes was venomous.

"Temper your spirit, Lydia," laughed Julian, leaning
on the rail in amused interest. It was always sport to see
his sister in a fury with others. "Temper it, I say, or you
might in reckless impetuosity indeed be his death, and
he has, after all, only given you jest for petulance."

"Julian," she said, coiling the whip purposefully, "I
swear there is a dullness in your blood that comes not
from my spirited father."

"And there is a lack of gentleness in yours," returned
Julian amiably, "that forswears the memory of my
sweet mother."

"Wait, only wait," she cried, while the Briton regarded her in curiosity, "and when I've dealt with this
dog I will deal with you!"

"My friend," said Julian to the Briton, "you see the
tigress you have roused. Deal with her temper as you
must to defend yourself, but if you so much as touch her
with your littlest finger then, alas, I will have your head.
This I must swear, it is no less than I must for the
honour of my house and Rome."

"Swear not so finely on so small a matter as a child in
temper," said the Briton.

Lydia could hate. She did not know she could hate as
much as this. In new fury she ran at the man and struck

viciously. The whip cracked but again he threw up his
arm, and again the leather anchored itself around his
wrist. With a dextrous sally he jerked the handle from
Lydia's grasp. She heard Julian's laugh, she saw the
mockery on the face of the barbarian and tigerishly she
sprang to claw and scratch.

But he retreated swiftly, his folded cloak falling, and
then so quickly and effectively did he use the whip that
before Lydia was aware of his intent the thin leather
wound around her to bind her. He jerked and the result
was devastating. Lydia screamed, for she was spun like
a top. She staggered and fell in the dust.

From the ground she gazed up at him, her hair wild,
her face livid. "Oh, Rome, Rome," cried her mind,
"can you look on this and turn your face? Oh, Diana,
great goddess, smite him, blind him, pierce him with a
thousand burning arrows!"

But Rome looked elsewhere and Diana seemed deaf.
Lydia came to her knees. The Briton extended a helping
hand. She struck it viciously away. She rose to her feet
and thrust back her tumbled hair.

"Look well on me, Briton," she hissed, "for I swear I
will be your death, if not now then on another day, I
will see it done even if I have to wait a thousand years!"

Julian shook his head at her foolishness. It was
seldom he saw his wilful sister bested. It had not happened since the day she first learned to use her tongue
and green eyes. He would not have put her in the dust
himself, for he could not have treated any woman that
way, but it was intriguing to meet a man who could,
who would and who had.

"I did not conceive you would put her down," he said
to the Briton, "but since you did not lay any finger on
her, I will not argue the point. Give me your hand, then.
You have drawn her teeth and without hurt."

Without hurt? Lydia could have killed her brother.
What of her pride, her humilation? Did he not understand the enormity of the barbarian's act? Ap-

parently not, for to her almost unendurable rage he came down from the chariot and clasped hands with the Briton, each with his right hand around the other's wrist. The Briton was more than half a head taller than the dark, wiry Roman.

"I am Canis," he said, "of the Iceni nation. My father is Callupus, chieftain and lord of the northern forests."

"Aye, mangy offspring of mangy father," cried Lydia, "and will stink when you lie dead! Which will be soon, for here at last comes Paulus." She pointed a triumphant finger. Canis turned to see a chariot glinting and swaying in the distance. "Stay, I beg you, bold beater of women, try your valour on a man who is a better Roman than my dear brother. If Julian lacks pride and courage, Paulus does not."

"I will stay," said Canis, "for I've been travelling for days on my feet and as I am in haste to reach Venta Icenorum perhaps your friend will take me up with him."

"My friend will kill you," said Lydia softly, letting each word linger. "So will you not run, brutaliser of women?"

"Not yet," said Canis, watching the oncoming vehicle.

With a harsh grinding of iron wheels, with creak of axle and vibration of brass, the chariot of Paulus pulled up beside them. Paulus, broad and stout-limbed, dismounted heavily. He was dusty, had a smear of blood on his arm, sweat on his skin and a vexed smile on his face. Blue-eyed and blue-chinned, he wiped his forehead with a leather-strapped wrist.

"I've been accursed by weak-legged asses and a clumsy tumble," he said.

"And I by a fury who whipped the wind from my pair," said Julian. "Let Lydia claim the victory, not I. It will console her for her own tumble."

"Lydia took a tumble?" said Paulus, aware of the tall Briton close by.

"Paulus," said Lydia, "a barbarian dog has barked out of turn."

Paulus saw the dust on her cloak, the glitter in her eyes and the whip idle in the Briton's hand. Puzzled and suspicious, he gave her the protection of his arm as she put her shoulder to his. Her smile was softly spiteful.

"My friend," said Julian to Canis, "I should not linger if I were you, for Lydia will yet do you a most violent mischief."

Canis acknowledged the friendly warning with a smile. In a flash Lydia, drawing a dagger from the belt of Paulus, leapt at the Briton. She was pantherlike, the dagger's blade bright in the sunshine, her red mouth drawn back in a grimace of hate and triumph, but as she struck her hand was caught by fingers of iron. The iron squeezed so that bones and flesh were numbed before pain burst. She screamed and smote with her free hand in blind rage. The Briton parried the blows and smiled at her

"You are not as tender and gentle a child as some I have known," he said. He released her pain-racked hand. Paulus, thunderclouds riding his brow, stared in disbelief at a barbarian who had dared to lay so outrageous a grip on the daughter of Marcus Osirus. Lydia, fingers lifeless, the dagger on the ground, had tears of violated pride in her eyes.

"Monster, wolf, jackal!" she cried. "I will dance one day on your carcase!"

Gently but resolutely Paulus put her aside and looked grimly at the inactive Julian. Julian merely raised an eyebrow.

"I think you are smiling," said Paulus heavily, "and this I do not understand."

"That, friend Paulus," said Julian, "is because you have no gift for discerning the subtleties that turn drama into comedy. You have come late to the play and have missed the better part of it. Lydia has not received worse than she has earned, and having been bested still burns to redeem herself. Our friend has raised no hand that Lydia herself has not provoked. Will you take him up with you to Venta Icenorum?''

"Are you mad?" Paulus was grimmer. "I am going to despatch the dog.''

"Paulus," said Lydia thickly, "you are the only man here.''

Paulus stepped forward to face Canis.

"Barbarian," he said, "I must indeed kill you, for you have laid your godless hand on a Roman lady of noble birth.''

"The Roman lady of noble birth," said Canis, "has indiscretion enough for fifty ladies of lesser birth and mistakes a loud voice for a compelling one. So go your way, Roman, and let neither of us hurt the other for the sake of so inconsequential a matter as this.''

"Kill him, Paulus," sobbed Lydia, "kill him!''

"I must," sighed Paulus. He was not a vindictive man, only a single-minded one, his attitude towards barbarians implacably governed by the infallibility of Rome. He drew his short Roman sword.

"Paulus," said Julian, "don't be a fool.''

"Stand aside," said Paulus obdurately, "while I take the burden of your honour on my own shoulders.''

"Lydia, not I, shall mend your bones," said Julian, shrewd in his assessment of the qualities of men.

Paulus advanced. The fact that the Briton had no weapon, only the whip, did not disturb him. One did not have to concede equality to any barbarian, least of all one as offensive as this. Canis retreated two paces. Paulus, an officer of the reserve, stamped his right foot forward and thrust. Canis side-stepped and slipped the double-edged blade. Quickly, Paulus swivelled and thrust again. Canis, as elusive as a thin shadow, swayed and as the sword slipped by once more he smiled regretfully at the Roman, then came under his elbow with an arm. He dropped the whip and struck downwards. Paulus drew his lips back at the sharp agony, he felt the wrench of bone and sinew, then the paralysing grip of a hand, the lever of a leg and the impetus that rushed his body earthwards. Lying numbed, helpless and inert, he saw the point of his own sword descending to tickle his chin.

"Did I not say it was an inconsequential matter?" said Canis mildly, and withdrew the threatening point.

Lydia, beside herself to see Paulus grounded so cruelly, snatched up the fallen dagger and launched herself in new frenzy at the Briton's back. He turned and knocked the weapon from her hand.

"Surely only the elephants of Hannibal charge more loudly than you," he said. "If you wish to murder a man you must come at his back softly and quietly. Let be now. Life has pleasanter pursuits to offer a child than brawling."

"Have you broken his back?" asked Julian, looking down in some concern at the heavily-breathing Paulus.

"He is only winded and bruised," saiid Canis, "and also has a wrenched elbow. He might have persisted otherwise."

"I'm relieved," said Julian, "for it might have gone hard with you had it been serious. Even so, you were a little rash in besting him so roughly. He is a proud man and will not find it easy to either forgive or forget."

"Nor will I," said Lydia, her face pale amid her disordered raven hair, her voice bitter and vindictive. "My time will come, barbarian."

"Come, little sister of sweet mercy," said Canis as Paulus began to groan, "is not this suffering man your friend? Don't waste your prattle on my ears, but lend your tender care to one in need. Get water. There's a spring beyond the hut. Sit your friend upright and pour the water generously over his head. When he is better than he is now, let him do you a similar favour. In your own way you are as much in need of it as he is."

"On the day your barbarian gods forsake you," whispered Lydia, "on that day I will come for you, I swear."

"Farewell, friend," said Julian, interposing tactfully. "Although you have not endeared yourself to either Lydia or Paulus, I have no quarrel with you."

"Nor I with you," smiled Canis. "Now, because you must bear your bruised friend along with you, I will favour him by taking his chariot into my care. I will leave it beyond the gate where, when his aches have gone, he may take it up again."

"That is not a favour which will commend itself to Paulus," said Julian drily.

The Briton smiled again. He took up his cloak and pack and mounted Paulus's chariot. Julian lifted his hand but Lydia was rigid, her eyes reflecting the burning obsession of a vengeance that was to eat into her soul. Canis called farewell, then whipped up the horses and sped down the road to Venta Icenorum.

"I knew you for a fool, Julian," said Lydia bitterly, "but I did not know you for a coward too."

"I am neither," said Julian as Paulus sat up and groaned. "Know your own self, Lydia. Wit and resourcefulness are not exclusive to Romans. Neither is culture, nor honour, nor bravery. You are like so many others, blind to the virtues of all who are not Roman."

"He is a stinking jackal," said Lydia, "and one day I will kill him. And you are an offence to Rome as well as to me. Is it your wish to become more of a Briton than the Britons themselves?"

"I wish only to make good Romans of all Britons," said Julian, and knelt to do what he could for the groaning Paulus.

2

THE AFTERNOON SHADOWS were lengthening and his own stretched obliquely behind the Briton as he came to the royal house in Venta Icenorum. It was a great, square edifice built of huge, mellowed timbers, with a roof of warm shingles. The oak doors opened into the clemency transit, the small area designed to insulate the large, spacious hall against the direct impact of winter's winds and chills. Behind the east and west walls of the hall were apartments for the resident elders and nobles of the royal household, and kitchens lay beyond the vast stone fireplace at the north end. The whole bore witness within and without to the wealth and power of Prasutagus, Iceni client-king under the protection of Nero, great Caesar.

But Prasutagus, who in his wealth and power stood between his people and Nero, was direly sick, and in the busy streets about the palace the women walked with mournful faces half-covered. Inside the palace the hunting dogs and the guard dogs, the mastiffs of Britain, lay with noses thrust forlornly between paws.

An Iceni warrior, a captain of the royal bodyguard, with proud moustache, fearless eyes but soft voice, opposed the entry of Canis.

"You have come quietly," he said, "and must go quietly, without argument. The king today can give no audience, nor hear any petitioners."

"I am aware of that," said Canis, "but will you be a friendly fellow and ask among the queen's men if there are any who might remember Canis, son of Callupus?"

In the light of the quick-dying March sun, reflected faintly by the great studded doors of iron-bound oak, the captain peered anew at the tall one.

13

"Are you Canis in truth?" he asked in some interest. "I've heard of you, and your father. I've heard you forsook the Iceni to find fortune with the Gauls and fight for them against Rome."

"Much good it did them," said Canis, "for in the end they came to the same conclusions as all others who have opposed Rome. Friend, I did not forsake the Iceni, for I am here. Will you send word I am home again?"

The Iceni captain smiled. He was as lean as Canis and just as agreeable.

"I'll do more than send word," he said, "I'll take you to the queen myself. Bograt, you scum-dipper, come here."

At the call another warrior appeared, a palace guard, clad in homespun fustian and leather breastpiece studded with metal. He carried a spear. By Roman decree, arms were forbidden to all Britons except those who served as guards to native kings and princes.

"Bograt," said the captain, "give entry to none until I return." Bograt smiled and chewed the point of his spear. The captain turned to Canis. "I am Cophistus of the queen's own guard."

Canis followed on as Cophistus parted a hanging curtain of soft, handsome skins and entered the great hall of the royal house. At the far end a large fire burned and the dogs lay before it, stretched on the stone floor. They rumbled in hairy throats at the intrusion but did not move from their warm comfort. At long oaken tables, which Canis remembered crowded with laughing men and women, there sat only a few this afternoon. They turned curious eyes on him. The light from the fire reddened their faces and softened the stone and timbers. The flames threw black shadows distorted and dancing. Invisible women keened softly.

Following Cophistus down a timbered aisle, Canis spoke quietly.

"Can you tell me of the king, Cophistus?"

"I can tell you he's sick," said Cophistus, halting to

whisper. "I cannot tell you more. If the queen will receive you then perhaps she will know what truth to tell you and what to keep to herself. I have heard about you, as I said, and for the sake of your physical comfort at least I hope the queen will look kindly on your return, although she is not likely to be influenced by any mood but her own in the matter. This is a time of stress for her."

Cophistus went on until he reached a certain door. He smote it lightly and it was opened by a woman. A soft linen headdress shadowed her face. Cophistus asked for audience and she let him in, Canis following. Cophistus disappeared with the woman into another room, leaving Canis in surroundings dim but well-remembered. His mind recaptured images and pictures, and in the light that thinly pierced the narrow slot serving as a window his eyes grew reflective.

Cophistus reappeared, smiled at him and went. The woman in the headdress came through, looked at Canis from out of her shadows, then turned on swift feet and hastened back into the inner room.

Canis waited. He could smell the living aroma of the palace, its timbers, its warmth, its food and its wine. Here he had known strong men and supple-limbed women. Here he had found the strengths and the weaknesses, the wild tears and shouted laughter of the Iceni, and the living with the pain of life sharper in the mind than the body, for what was physical hurt compared with the cry of the mind if you were Iceni and Celtic?

"Canis."

The voice low, rich, strong, sweet. He turned.

She was tall, nearly as tall as he was, and robed in blue. Not the blue of the foolish, childish Roman girl, but the blue of her eyes, if there were a blue that could match their changeable shades. It was the blue that shone from the silver coat of a wolf in winter, the blue of a mountain peak, the blue of the river when the summer sky kissed each ripple of water. It was the blue of cornflowers when the warm sun softened every tiny petal. And sometimes it was the blue of ice. She had wide, magical eyes, mirroring her every mood of coolness or warmth, tenderness or anger, and yet retaining the mysticism of the Celt and the subtlety of woman, so that a man knew he could never wholly discover her.

In the light, such as it was, her hair flowed golden-bronze. Her features were dominated by fine cheekbones that gave her a handsome, enduring beauty, and by her remarkable eyes. Her mouth was wide, mobile and shapely.

Such was Boadicea, Queen of the Iceni, lover of life and freedom, and for all her willowy grace the mother of two daughters, one sixteen, the other seventeen.

Canis spoke very quietly.

"My lady." He dropped to one knee and took her right hand, touching it to his forehead to signify his fealty. Her fingers trembled, were instantly stilled.

"Canis, you rogue, are you returned at last?"

He rose. She looked up at him with the air of a woman who never found it easy to look up to any. But on her mouth, which had both sweetness and strength, a strange smile came and went.

"My lady, I am returned," he said, "and without your leave."

"Indeed," she said softly, "you are here where you swore to tread no more."

"Is a man who can forswear a foolish oath a more foolish man or a wiser one?"

"A wiser one, Canis, and more of a man. You went from us in stubborn pride and we have missed you. Seven years." She shook her head. "It has been a long time, Wolfhead."

He looked carefully at her and remembered how it had been seven years ago.

*   *   *

King Prasutagus had vigorous health then as well as great riches. He was a wily and thoughtful ruler. He had made a pact with the Romans when they invaded Britain under Claudius. He preferred to live in amity with Rome rather than in conflict with the powerful Belgic tribes of southern Britain, and accordingly stood aside while the Romans destroyed them. In return Rome accepted the Iceni as allies, and Prasutagus and his queen, Boadicea, retained a nominal independence as client-monarchs of their nation under Caesar. Boadicea, not yet eighteen at this time, spiritedly opposed the pact, but Prasutagus, using specious argument mixed with unassailable logic, had his way.

Ten years later Callupus the Wolf, lord of the northern forests, sent his son Canis to serve the house of Boadicea, which was not quite the same as the house of Prasutagus. Only by marriage to Boadicea when she was a young princess had Prasutagus, a wealthy and influential noble, come to be consort and then king.

"You shall know whom we serve first," said Callupus to his son, "an that is the queen."

Boadicea had some reservations about Canis, whom she found a little lacking in humility. Prasutagus found him stimulating, much more so than the greybeards around the court. Canis was personable and articulate. Although a natural warrior, he was also a scholar. He could read and write. This made him distinctive, and Prasutagus, addicted to lively argument and informative discussion, found his distinctiveness very agreeable.

Canis had a thirst for knowledge and a curiosity about people. The Iceni had their art and culture and considered those which other people possessed to be inferior to theirs. Canis thought this fancy, not fact. No one could produce proof that all other people were idiots. Prasutagus liked this particular argument, he liked the man himself and in his feeling for what was right allowed Canis the privilege of arguing on equal terms. Which meant that sometimes he allowed Canis to disagree with him.

Not so Boadicea. She did not encourage this in any man. She knew that if she did most of them would soon be telling her how to rule. When she first saw Canis her eyes clouded a little. He was taller than any other man there, which compelled her to raise her eyes to him. Nor did she like what Prasutagus liked, the gift Canis had for wagging his tongue. She did not mind a little argument or discussion, but she minded considerably if it went on and on. There was too much of it among Celts as it was.

She was, in fact, a restless woman. She could not sit too long by the fireside in winter or stay dreaming by a window in summer. She loved the outdoors, the earth and the sky. And she loved to hunt. But perversely, when she discovered that Canis excelled in this sport she did not seem to like that, either. The ease with which he trapped the prey and made the kill provoked her. So did the manner in which he confessed his prowess on one occasion.

"My lady," he said as he watched the wild pig snapping and clawing at the javelin between its ribs, "I have the art. It is one gifted to me as a babe."

"Then you were a damnably overblown babe," she retorted.

Once, when she herself, with joyful laugh, with golden-bronze head poised and graceful body arched, launched her own javelin and saw it strike a tree instead of a disappearing buck, he shook his head sympathetically and said, "My lady, you have the art but not the timing."

She turned furious blue eyes on him. He rubbed his mouth and chin. She knew this was to hide his smile.

"Aye," she said, "hide your impudence, you villain, for if I see so much as a twitch of it I'll have you bound to that tree and try both my art and my timing on you. You will end up looking like a dead porcupine."

Yet she wanted him among her other hunting companions, boisterous men and long-legged, quicksilver women, whenever she was in the mood. Despite his conceits, his skill and cunning could not be denied.

One morning the company was ready, the men and women eager to go, the horses spirited and Canis not yet to be seen. Boadicea despatched a servant to fetch him. "By the nose, if necessary," she said. When the laggard arrived she latched on to his dilatoriness with quite biting sarcasm.

"Forgive me, my lady," he said as soon as she paused for breath, "but my lord the king hooked me by the ear. And since, in a manner of speaking, he still retains his majestic hold I beg you to excuse me from your sport today."

"You may beg until the sky turns black," she said imperiously, "but will not be excused. Overnight I commanded your attendance today, therefore what my lord Prasutagus wishes to do with your ear does not signify. The king will understand this. You are to ride with us. We shall have good sport in weather such as this, providing you spare us your conceit in your accomplishments."

"Well, since my ear is only a trifle and the king—"

"It is a trifle you will lose, jester, if you do not mount immediately."

He mounted and rode with them. Boadicea kept her haughty blue eyes on him all day but deafened herself to his tongue by putting her fingers in her ears whenever he opened his mouth.

In addition to hunting, she had a great enthusiasm for her speedy chariot, a vehicle of grace and beauty. Its body was of wickerwork, the wheels and pole and chassis carved triumphs of Celtic craftsmen, embossed with brass, bronze and gold. It was not a war chariot but a racing one. She drove it with immense skill, so much so that, certain she could shatter the self-esteem of Canis, she commanded him to race against her. On a bright April day, with Canis driving one of the king's chariots, they engaged in their contest along the broad bank of the river. Venta Icenorum, a town of stone and timber dwellings and grassy escarpments, nestled in the soft green valley of the Wensum, whose waters flowed misty grey in winter and sparkling blue in summer.

Amid the cheers of her people, who loved her as they loved Andrasta, their goddess of victory, the queen drove her chariot fiercely and fearlessly. With her bright hair streaming, her strong white teeth gleaming, her breeze-blown cloak whipping around her swaying body, she won by the length of her pair.

Laughing, exultant, she wheeled and rode up to Canis, who greeted her triumph with a smile.

"I salute you, my lady," he said, "you are swifter on two wheels than a spear launched from a mountain top."

"Do you not have the art of this sport?" she asked.

"It is the heart I lack," he said, "the heart to run ahead of you."

"Braggart, either you have cheated me or are denying me. Well, then, we will ride again."

The course was cleared and once more Boadicea flew in her bright, bouncing chariot over the broad, grassy level. The skilful way Britons handled every type of chariot was something the Romans generously admired, and their chroniclers did not deny Boadicea's own prowess. She went at Canis like a woman with demons at her heels. To the drumming beat of galloping horses she raced side by side with him, and did not shirk the risk of dangerously edging him to obtain the better going. To the Romans present the goddess Diana herself would have made no more exhilarating spectacle. The people shouted as she drew ahead, then in different key as Canis boldly caught her and thrust his nose in front. But how they roared as Boadicea plucked the race from him with reckless abandon, whipping up her pair to beat him by the length of their heads. She ran on, she wheeled and pulled up. She waited for Canis to come to her this time. Her face was glowing, her eyes alight. She was challenging rather than triumphant, and her teeth showed as he bowed his head. She distrusted the gesture. It hid his face.

"My lady," he said, "whatever art I have in this sport is inferior to yours. I did the best I could. It was not enough. Happily I concede."

"Happily?" she said. "Let me see your face, then, you sly fox. How else shall I discover the true mood of your concession?"

Canis lifted his head and smiled at her, his eyes frank and clear.

"My lady?"

"Oh, you disarming dog," she said and rode away, leaving him to follow.

In these and other pleasant ways, Canis spent many months at the court of Boadicea and Prasutagus. He intrigued Prasutagus in his facility for debate, so much so that the king thought it would do no harm to keep a mild eye on him. He only seemed to put Boadicea out of patience, particularly when he began to fraternise with Romans, of whom there were many in the city, all of them ostensibly protective guests. But, as he said to the queen, his interest in Romans was to suck from them knowledge of things common to them but not to him.

"Flummery," said Boadicea. "It is said you go among them not to find out what is in the minds of their men but what is in the arms of their strumpets. I will tell you, Wolfhead, if your fondness for Roman ways and Roman women is above your fondness for Iceni ways and Iceni women, you are a man in confusion."

'Any man who cannot distingush between that which is gaudy and that which is beautiful," said Canis, "is in the sorriest confusion."

Her daughters, Cea aged ten and Dilwys aged nine, loved Canis with all the fervour of children who found utter delight in the tales he told them of forest maids, spellbinding wood-witches, warrior Britons and one-eyed Romans. And of fair princesses and heroic princes. Cea thought him more heroic than a hundred princes. He taught her to play the lyre and this put her in more delight.

As the summer advanced Canis came to know Boadicea and she to know him. Because she was intelligent and had a hunger for life in all its facets, she came to understand something of his thirst for knowledge. He was interested in everything that motivated, influenced and afflicted people. She realised how in his gift for words and his recounting of tales he passed on much of what he knew. So she summoned him one day and told him that she desired him to teach her and her daughters all the subtleties of the written word.

At this time Boadicea was twenty-eight and Canis twenty-seven. If she looked younger it was because of her grace and handsomeness, and if he looked older it was because of his leanness and maturity.

He did not express any great enthusiasm for her suggestion. Instead he pointed out that she was already able to read the written word.

"I am indeed, but not as well as you," she said, regarding him from her stone seat on the escarpment outside the palace. A cluster of her bright-eyed women looked on from a distance. Canis was an intriguing fox. "And Cea is eager to be taught," added Boadicea.

He said cautiously, "In your house and service, my lady, each day brings a new interest. I am your very contented subject at the moment."

At the moment? What a dog he was.

"Ah," she said softly, "you are expecting a small disaster, perhaps? My roof to fall on you? Your food to be poisoned?"

"I meant," he said, "that I may be a disappointing teacher. There are learned Romans in your city who are practised teachers of the written word, and while they would be competent to instruct you I would very likely be very incompetent.''

Boadicea's eyes darkened to night blue.

"Romans? Romans in my house? Teaching me? Instructing my daughters? You graceless villain, to commend those acquisitive leeches to me!''

"But it is not unrewarding to know the ways of others,'' said Canis persuasively, "whether they are for you or against you. Pluck from any man his knowledge and you are more than his equal, for you have above him your own knowledge.''

"Do not school me in something which is obvious even to a babe,'' she said.

"Aye, but since you have been a busy queen for years, harassed by all manner of things, I thought you might not remember the simple philosophies that engaged your infancy.

Myself, I do not remember what was obvious to me as a babe, saving only the comfort of my mother's breast.''

She turned on her seat, averting her face. It would never do to show the artful wolf that she was in amusement. But when she faced him again there was laughter in her eyes.

"Jester,'' she said, "you twist every word I speak. Attend me. I say to you, you have a gift for learning. Therefore, learn the art of teaching and learn it quickly. For you are to teach your queen and her daughters how to fully interpret the written word and how to clearly inscribe it. It is more than my wish, it is my command.''

"Ah,'' said Canis. He rubbed his chin. She frowned. Was her command not good enough for any man? He looked at her. She was at her most bewitching. Her hair, bound and fastened by fillets of gold, crowned her in burnished majesty. Because of her love of the open air she was coloured by the sun and wind to golden-brown, yet there was a delicacy to her skin by reason of the touch of soft, misty mornings. To look at her in any mood was to sense a magic she had. Proud of her lineage and her race, not even the great north wind could bend her, she could face it as straight and slim as a spear of polished bronze but for the arching curve of her breast. She was a true Celt, quick in anger and joy, a woman of temperament, pride and spirit, and such tears as sprang to her eyes were only of pride and spirit, for no one had ever seen her weep.

A little anger began to show now. Canis in such unresponsive silence was not to be endured for ever.

"Answer me, scholar," she said, "or has a witch tied your tongue?"

"My lady, I will teach you and the princesses to read and to inscribe as best I can," he said, "but I have been considering the frustrations you will suffer. You have a high spirit, my lady. It may make you too restless to be a patient pupil."

Oh, the knave, the impudence. And she the queen.

"I tell you," she said, "you are a man to vex the gentlest gods. You impute to me the fault of impatience so that if you fail to teach me what I wish you to, you will lay the blame on me. This is deviousness of the craftiest kind."

"My lady," said Canis with his disarming smile, "when have you sat for longer than the space of a meal? When have you dallied in patience over a problem?"

"I am dallying here in great patience with you," she retorted, "and you are a more provoking problem than any, with your answers all outrageous questions. Some there are, Canis, who can solve problems only by resting by the hour on their rumps. I am not of these."

"But learning cannot be acquired by rushing here and there, fine Queen, only by resting by the hour on your own rump."

"Oh, you saucy fox!" she cried. She looked as if she were about to leap and smite him. Instead she took a deep breath, then shook her head and laughed.

"Oh, Canis," she said, "there is so much impudence

about you that I tremble for you. You are more likely to die from the kisses of my women than from my anger. They ask me each day, how long does Canis stay? Let him stay long, they beg, bind him to your house, O Boadicea, for though he is a sly wolf who smiles falsely on most women, yet he is handsomer than a red fox. Do you know what this means, Canis? It means that all women are foolish and none more so than my own. I have seen you with them, flattering them all, yet favouring none. Or do you favour one, perhaps? Which woman do you love, Canis?''

"Only the queen, my lady, as do all men.''

Boadicea smiled.

"Tongue tattle,'' she said. She mused for a moment, her eyes holding his, then abruptly she said, "I cannot sit longer. We will speak again about the written word when the summer has gone. The winter will be a good time for teaching and learning. If I am not the best of pupils, you will find no fault in Cea, or in Dilwys.'' She rose and walked with her long-limbed supple grace towards the rim of the escarpment, which was walled in part and overlooked the Wensum and the rich green forests beyond. On the banks of the river children played, laughing and shouting. She joined the group of women. Canis followed on. The women, colourful in their mantles, were animated in the sunshine and more so at the appearance of Canis, also called the Wolfhead. The escarpment became alive with chatter.

"By the sweetest gods,'' said Boadicea after a while, "never have I heard such inconsequential absurdities, and all to impress a man whose deviousness is far above all his virtues.''

"As you see, Bodulga,'' said Canis, taking the hand of a sleek and glossy young woman, "I am in high regard with the queen today.''

The summer sped. She seemed to become more mettlesome, quicker to be irritated. She could not brook his tendency to make a jest of everything. If he disagreed with her, which no one else dared to, he did so with a lightness that was more irritating than the disagreement itself. On the other hand, he might have said that nothing he did was right in her eyes. But he only smiled each time she found fault with him, although sometimes she felt he had a pride he considered as inviolable as her own. That, if true, was something she would never tolerate.

Also, he so endeared himself to her daughters, especially to auburn-haired Cea, that they sought his company more often than anybody else's, even more often than hers.

The queen's women were used to her temperament, her moods, her ups and her downs. They were what made her the kind of spirited queen she was. But she was always so generous and so softly handsome after every anger that she was wholly irresistible. But the women were not used to seeing her irritable. Was she perhaps with child after a lapse of so many years? No. She and Prasutagus were companions now, not lovers, they had their separate apartments.

Prasutagus and Boadicea had a civilised relationship. They pursued their own interests quite happily, but were one in standing between Rome and the Iceni people, and in their regard for their daughters. Prasutagus, however, was not unobservant of the interests and activities of Boadicea. Her increasing irritability did not affect him too much but he knew about it.

He smiled, he shrugged. He was a philosophical man.

At the first rise of autumn mists Boadicea called Canis to her apartments. He came, a warm cloak over his tunic. She wore a loose white robe. Her hair, unbound, was spilling and she pushed it back as he was ushered in. She looked soft, informal and quite beautiful. He bent his knee, took her hand and touched it to his forehead.

"My lady?"

"Canis, are you off to ride with Romans?"

"No, with the king, my lady."

"I see." She lifted her eyes to his. "You ride willingly enough with the king, with Romans and with others. You only argue with me."

He stared a little.

"But those," he said, "those, I thought, were the moments we enjoy. I would not argue any pursuit with others, where would be the pleasure? It is different to be in sweet argument with the queen."

"You confess it, you enjoy provoking me?"

"I enjoy seeing you smile," he said.

That, when she knew she smiled less for him than anyone, made her laugh a little ruefully.

"Canis," she said, "soon we shall have to spend more time in than out. When the weather does that to us you shall have my promise to sit quietly and patiently in company with the princesses, so that you may teach the three of us all that you can about the written word."

Canis sighed. He knew that of all things Boadicea would not sit quietly. She was flowing movement, restless grace. Her intelligence was instinctive, not academic, and she learned not from scrolls but life. As a student she would be irked each time he corrected her, she would throw the parchments in his face and call him an upstart pedagogue.

Boadicea, seeing his reluctance, turned from sweet humour to quick affront. Why so many of his reactions irked her she did not know. Or perhaps she did.

"My lady—"

"Oh, you stubborn, long-shanked villain," she said, "will you still stand against me in this my especial wish?"

"Only with quaking feet," he smiled.

It was one jest too many. Boadicea, in a mighty passion, turned on him.

"You have mocked the queen you say you love once too often," she said and clapped her hands. A woman appeared. Boadicea told her to summon Apha, master of her domestic household. Apha came on quick, obedient legs. "Apha," she commanded, "take this unmannerly rascal Canis, have him stripped and flung into a bed of nettles. A thousand stings will prick his arrogance and bring him to humility." She swung round, her eyes stormy, her handsome face unmerciful. "What say you to that, jester?"

"I say," said Canis, with a sigh of regret for misreading his queen's temper, "that I wish I had as much gift for discretion as you have for being a queen. It is very queenly to have a man thrown naked into a bed of nettles."

This was unbearable. Boadicea's eyes darkened to the angriest blue. She smote a bronze cylinder with a wooden cudgel. This brought Gwyndu, the captain of her guard. Apha stood blinking.

"Gwyndu," she said fiercely, "I give into your charge one Canis, arrogant beyond all tolerance. Take him and see that he is given twenty lashes."

Gwyndu blinked too. He thought Canis held in high regard by the royal family, but seeing the look on Boadicea's face he said quickly, "Aye, my lady." He took Canis by the arm. Canis glanced at Boadicea. There was a little smile on his face, a whimsical acknowledgement of her ability to be very queenly indeed. She bit her lip.

"Now what is on your impudent tongue?" she asked.

"I am wondering," he said, "if after the count of twenty lashes I am also to be thrown into the nettles."

"Out with you," she stormed, "take the villain, Gwyndu."

Fifteen minutes later Princess Cea, ten years old and as pretty as an auburn-haired Celtic elf, came running in tears to the queen.

"Oh, my mother," she sobbed, "they are whipping Canis—stay them, oh please stay them."

"Cea," said Boadicea in a quiet voice as she cradled

the tearful face against her soft robe, "Canis this day has been guilty of arrogance."

"But to have him whipped," the girl cried, "this I cannot bear."

"What is a whipping to a man except a step towards humility?"

"But you are the queen and did command it," wept Cea, "and I hate you for it, I hate you!"

"Hush, my little wood elf, it is none so bad," said Boadicea gently, stroking Cea's bright hair. "By this whipping, Canis, who is a man, will be a better one and I a better queen."

Cea lifted dark wet eyes of anguish to her mother.

"But why are you doing this? Canis is not like other men, you cannot make him humble. Oh, my mother, why do you punish him for what he says when he only means you to smile on him?"

Boadicea gazed into the eyes of childish wisdom and sighed.

"He mocked me, little one, and showed me a pride that was insolent. So he had to be whipped."

"I cannot bear it," cried Cea, "and if you break his pride you will break my heart. I shall be the only princess in Britain with a broken heart. Bodulga is crying too."

"It will not break his pride, Cea, only cure his arrogance, and Bodulga is but one more of my foolish young women. Where is the king your father?"

Sobs racked the slim body of Princess Cea as she hid her face.

"He is watching Canis being whipped. Mother, he is smiling."

"Canis is smiling?" said Boadicea in a strange voice.

"No, my mother, our father is smiling."

Prasutagus had a word for Canis some days later.

"I tell you, Wolfhead," he said, "that in your wisdom, such as it is, you have overlooked one simple tenet that quite ignorant men have an instinctive knowledge of. It is that women cannot brook a tongue sharper than their own.''

''I am not like to overlook it again, my lord,'' said Canis, ''since it was more painfully brought to me than everything else I have learned.''

Boadicea intended to have a word with Canis herself. On a day when autumn sought a return to summer she was with her women on a paved way above the grassy escarpment. She loved the place for the view it gave her of river, forest and sky. Golden-russet light caressed the waters and the trees, and near the river's edge children acted out their noisy games, boys and girls all with their warrior spears of wood in mimicry of war, their bows and arrows in mimicry of the hunt. The girls were as fearless in these pursuits as the boys. They were taught from their wooden cradles that their survival lay in the skill and strength of every arm. The Iceni, fiercely independent, cultivated an insularity that kept them free of extraneous influences. They had their gods but were not steeped in the mysticism of the Druids as were peoples to the west of them.

''Go, find Canis and bring him to me,'' said Boadicea to Bodulga, one of her young women.

Gladly Bodulga sped in search of the tall one and after some time returned with him. Despite his still stiff back he bent his knee to the queen. She gave him a forgiving smile.

''I have seen little of you recently, Canis,'' she said.

''Is it so?'' He was a little wary. ''In truth, I have a daily wager with Tarsus Pelia, the centurion. It is to do with out-running him by chariot.''

''If you take a full day every day to outrun that Roman tortoise,'' said Boadicea, ''you are only another tortoise yourself. I could outrun him at the first turn, for he has no talent for turning a tight wheel.''

''Your talents, my Queen, are monumental.''

Oh, he was a dog. She had forgiven him, he had not forgiven her. He had not come to humility. His pride was monstrous.

"So you desert my house to find favour in Roman villas?"

"My lady," he said evenly, "you know that is not true."

Oh, twice a dog! What did it matter whether it was true or not? Was she, the queen, to be named a liar in front of every curious man and woman there? She glimpsed Bodulga hovering close by, the daughter of Cacchus, chief Iceni elder. She was glossily fair, as were many of the original Celts of Britain, her hair flowing in rich abundance to her shoulders, her robe complex in its graceful folds. She had felt every stroke of the lash that had burnt the skin from the shoulders and back of Canis some days ago. Boadicea knew her heart but never discussed the matter with her. Now the queen made a gesture and Bodulga, aware that she was too close, moved reluctantly away.

"Canis," said Boadicea, "you are still stiff with pride. I had you marked because of it and never did any man deserve it more. But I did not think you a man to sulk over it."

"I do not sulk, my lady, I only smart," said Canis, "and in trying to outrun Tarsus Pelia each day I smart the more. This is my daily reminder that you are a better teacher of life than I could be of scrolls."

"If that were so," said Boadicea, "you would not be more often away from my house than in it. Nor would you take such pains to avoid me as you have. Do you feel you have stayed too long among us?"

Canis looked in surprise at her. He saw a strange hurt he had in some way given her.

"My lady," he said, "when I came to your house ice lay on the river. Now they have gathered the wheat from the fields and driven horses westward to trade. In all that time each day in its pleasure has passed all too swiftly for me. Is it you yourself who feel I have been here too long?"

There, he had turned her question upside-down. It was always the same. He was the slyest of villains. They called his father the Wolf. They called him Wolfhead. But she would best him yet.

"I have no such feeling," she said. "Your father sent you here to serve me, and indifferent though you are in your regard for me, you shall remain here. But you have been too long unwed, and because of this you make my young women restless. Go to Cacchus and speak for the hand of his daughter, sweet Bodulga."

Canis looked at her in frank dismay. Her response was an aloofness.

"My lady," he said, "Bodulga is a prize for a better man."

"There are a thousand better men, no doubt," she said coldly, "but it is my wish that she weds you."

"If you love her," said Canis, "treat her not so ill."

"Ill?" Her coldness turned into quick anger. "Dare you answer me so! It is in her sweetest interest that I do this, for she has eyes for no one but you."

"Sweet as she is, I do not wish her for wife and because of this the union would in the end be unkind to her."

"You will do as I say!"

Her lack of all reason, her touch of wildness, disturbed him.

"I cannot," he said obstinately, "for I am promised elsewhere."

She froze. It was a moment or two before storm swept the ice aside.

"What, you fox," she hissed, "you dare to tell me this! You dare to say you have bemused one of my women behind my back! Which of them is it? Who is this paragon of beauty to whom you are promised in love so great that you have kept it secret?"

He looked at the sky, he looked at her feet, he looked everywhere but into her stormy blue eyes. Her desire to smite him made her tremble.

"My lady," he said, "I am promised in the sight and hearing of the king."

"To whom? To whom?"

"To Princess Cea."

Stunned, she could not believe she had heard alright. Then incredulity burst into outrage.

"Princess Cea! Oh, you infamous dog, you dare to use her name in this way!"

"Believe me, my lady, I would not have spoken at all had you not been so firmly resolved in the matter of Bodulga," he said.

"Better a hundred times for you if you had kept a still tongue and taken Bodulga," said the furious queen. "Princess Cea, promised to you! With the consent of the king! What lying villainy is this? Come with me!"

She swept towards broad stone steps in such tempestuous anger that it seemed as if her sandalled feet flew. Into the great hall she came like a robed goddess in pursuit of dark and offending phantoms. Elders and counsellors, seeing storm about her, receded in haste from her path. In her wake walked Canis, his long stride tying him to her rapid progress.

A whisper reached his ears.

"Think on philosophy, Wolfhead, the pain is not so sharp then."

His response was a rueful smile. The queen entered the king's apartments. He followed on. Prasutagus raised his eyes from a shining bronze mirror as Boadicea rushed in. He let the mirror droop in his hand, its burnished surface matching the lustre of the queen's hair. It flashed for a second in reflection of her golden neckchain. Prasutagus saw her wrath, saw Canis behind her, and sighed.

"My lord, I am sorely affronted," began Boadicea.

"Again?" said Prasutagus. He looked at Canis.

"Have there been more foolish words?"

"There has been a lack of words," said Boadicea. Her hands were clenched, her robe whispering around her angry body. Prasutagus tugged at his beard, smoothed it and beheld the result in his mirror. He had the reasonable vanity of a man who, despite his years, still possessed physical virility and handsome beard. His wiliness was hidden by mild eyes and mild smile. The same height as Boadicea, nevertheless because of her proud, erect stature she always seemed the taller. She turned and turned before him, pacing the floor, the soft skins that covered it, and spoke quickly, passionately. "I had not thought you would keep from me a matter that touches me as dearly as you. Have I become of small account in this house? Is it the Romans who counsel you not to confide in me? Are Britons to make chattels of their women as Romans do of theirs?"

"What is this matter?" asked Prasutagus.

"Why," she said, "you have shamed me by making secret pact with Canis."

"Have I?" Prasutagus blew on the mirror, then polished it. "What pact is this?"

"You promised him the hand of Princess Cea," said Boadicea angrily, "which is a shameful thing in itself, she being only an innocent child, and then charged him to say nothing of it, even to me, which is more shameful."

Prasutagus looked puzzled. He rasped his bearded cheek with a thoughtful hand, then raised his eyes to Canis. Canis was looking at the ceiling, his expression patently that of a man who wished himself anywhere but where he was.

"Canis told you this?" said Prasutagus, placing the mirror on a couch.

"Aye, he did," said Boadicea, "the secretive fox made everything of it when I commanded him to speak for the hand of Bodulga."

"Ah, Bodulga." Prasutagus sighed again. "So, you

would have him wed Bodulga? And he cried off and told you he was promised to Cea? Canis, you have stirred up a nest of hornets with a stick of grass. You had better give the queen the truth of the matter.''

"My lord," ventured Canis, "I—"

"Speak to the queen, not to me, unwise one."

"My lady," said Canis, and Boadicea gazed into eyes that seemed contrite but which, she was sure, meant to disarm her. "It was this way. I was about to meet Tarsus Pelia yesterday. The king was enjoining me to race less carelessly than on the previous day, when Princess Cea came up to us and said, 'Canis, my sister Dilwys and I are lonely, for we have not seen you for several days. My lord father,' she said, 'Canis has no more love for me.' And the king said, 'Before you go, Canis, tell my missel thrush you love her dearly.' So I told her I loved her very dearly. At which Princess Cea said, 'Since you have no wife, Canis, and love me very dearly, will you wait until I am a grown maid and then wed me?' To please her, as would any man, I said I would. She clapped her hands and said, 'So now you are promised to me and shall wed only me, it shall be our secret and we will tell no one of it yet.' My lady, the king laughed and said this should be so, and I also said it should be so, but I did not laugh, for although she understood her father's laughter she may not have understood mine. The heart of a child is a tender and delicate morsel.''

Boadicea turned pale, then red blood leapt to turn her honeyed skin dusky.

"So this is it," she breathed, "this mockery! This was no great secret, this was a game with a child and no more than that. In a month it will be forgotten by you and by Cea too. Yet you dared to speak of it as if it stood between you and Bodulga. Infamous villain, you have put one more mock upon me! I will break your arrogance for good, you shall wed Bodulga as I command!''

"That would destroy the game for Princess Cea," said Canis quietly, "and bring no real happiness to Bodulga."

"Concern yourself with what I command, not with speciousness," said Boadicea furiously. A new thought struck her and put her into passion. "Oh, you scheming dog, are you so puffed up that you think you will have Princess Cea in time? Ah, now I see it, you have bewitched my little one, you have trapped the heart of the child, thinking to use her to advance your status when she is old enough."

"I should like to know what my Lord Prasutagus advises," said Canis.

"It is the queen you have offended," said Prasutagus, perching himself on the fence, "and hers must be the ruling."

"Canis, if you oppose me further," said Boadicea palely, "you shall go from this house and this land, never to return except by my leave! You will wed Bodulga!"

"I cannot," said Canis, his eyes dark, "for I do not love her as she needs to be loved. So I will go, my lady, and in going will carry with me the consoling thought that my absence will recompense you for the irksomeness of my presence."

Prasutagus from veiled eyes saw the look on the face of Boadicea. He smiled thinly and plucked another hair more deliberately from his beard. Boadicea, hand to her breast, stared palely at Canis and whiteness pinched her mouth.

"Oh, you fling your barbs bitterly, Canis," she breathed, "and it is vile of you to be in such stubborn, cruel pride."

Canis bowed his head to hide that which was not pride.

"I beg your forgiveness for all I have said that hurt or offended you," he said, "but I will take my choice and go."

"Are you so out of love with us that you are as eager to go as this?" she cried.

"Boadicea," said Prasutagus, in mild irritation at what were now useless words, "are you now pleading with him to stay?"

"I do not plead with any man," said Boadicea, rounding angrily on the king. "I am only asking him to properly consider his decision. Anyone who makes a decision in a mood of ungovernable pride and arrogance wakes at dawn sadder and wiser. Myself, I will be generous, I will give him until tomorrow's sunset to decide."

"My lord," said Canis, touching his forehead to Prasutagus.

"Aye, think on it," said Prasutagus with a sigh.

"My lady," said Canis, looking at his queen. The mist of winter seemed to stand between them. She was in pale but unbreaking resolution. So, it appeared, was he. "This in true fealty and with all my heart," he said, and he bent his knee, took her stiff hand and touched it to his forehead. Then he went. He was gone from the palace within an hour. Few were aware of it, however, for he went unobtrusively and without fuss.

Boadicea, having gone straight to her own apartments, dismissed her curious women and sat alone. Later she recalled one of them.

"Gwydna," she said carelessly, "go and find Canis. Tell him to attend on me. He has been obstinate but I have not been as temperate as I might. I will argue a little more generously with him."

"My lady, he has gone," said Gwydna, "he went a little while ago."

"Gone? Where has he gone?" she asked in a voice Gwydna had not heard before.

"I do not know, my lady, only that he told Bodulga, who saw him and ran after him, that he hoped to discover the world, for he said that vast though it is he had all the time a man might need."

Gwydna slipped out. Boadicea looked at the white robe she had meaninglessly picked up.

"Oh, Canis," she whispered, "to have as little regard as this for me. I did not think you would go, I did not think you could."

When Princess Cea heard that Canis had gone and without saying farewell to her, she was a child stricken. She sat by herself above the escarpment for day after day. She sought the company of no one, not even Dilwys, for all the mists of weeping autumn were in her eyes and it was not to be borne that any princess should show a broken heart to her playmates.

*   *   *

To travellers who afterwards visited Venta Icenorum from distant lands and were given the hospitality of her table, Boadicea ofter said a casual word or two.

"Have you in your journeyings seen anything of an Iceni warrior who is also a scholar? A man with grey eyes and a sly, disarming smile? His name is Canis, he is very tall and also known as the Wolfhead. He is promised to my daughter Cea, and although this was only in jest, yet the rogue is likely to eschew his playful promise unless he is reminded of it or sends word. But since he is an arrogant and ungrateful knave and is, moreover, old enough to be her father, it matters not, except to Cea's childish heart. I have no regard for the villain."

At which Prasutagus would smile thinly within his rapidly greying beard.

3

THAT HAD ALL been seven years ago. He did not think she was any less handsome, any less disturbing. The shadows were there, softening, haunting, illusory. Hers was a changeless beauty, born of quick life, majestic grace and peerless bone.

"Cea has wept for you, Canis."

"And I've thought often of both your fledglings."

"Fledglings?" She smiled. "They're a little older now." She might have asked him a hundred questions but did not. She wondered. He had changed? Perhaps. He was harder, leaner, more worldly. But less in pride and conceit? Perhaps. He looked as if he had been travelling long and far. "I could have wept myself to have you desert us as you did," she said, "but tears do not become queens. Canis, I cannot pretend, I am glad to see you again, I am glad you are here. You shall rest and not until tomorrow will I ask you to tell us of all you found that you could not find here. For the moment I will only ask you to see the king."

"I came because of this."

"Only because of this?"

"Because of the king," he said, "and because, after all, I belong here and hoped you would agree I had served my time. I have seen as much of the world as I wish to, but all I have learnt of different peoples is that nowhere have I been able to say I would rather have been born of these or those than of the Iceni."

"You have returned alone, Canis? You are not wed?"

"Some women are foolish," he smiled, "but not as foolish as that."

"As to wed you?" She laughed softly. "Oh, the gods

protect us all from modesty such as this. My women will smother you anew. Canis, you are changed yet unchanged. I will find out the subtle difference in time. But now you shall see the king. You will find he himself is sadly changed, and desperately sick. The Romans have sent their physicians, but they only murmur and mutter. My own physician does not mutter but he will not look me in the eye. If the gods of life withdraw and the gods of darkness claim my lord Prasutagus, what are physicians but onlookers? I am not afraid of the truth, Canis, I am only concerned that the eagles are beginning to hover like vultures and I must be ready for them. Perhaps you can give me the truth, for if you have discovered the world you may also have discovered what there is about a sick man that can say whether he will live or die.''

As they reached the door of the king's chamber, she turned to Canis and whispered softly, ''You have returned to lend me strength and comfort, not to provoke me, is this not so?''

''My lady, in spite of my conceits it was always so.''

They entered the room. The smell of sickness was malodorous and although servants continually tended the burning of herbs the scented fumes could not prevail. Prasutagus lay on his back, covered with rich drapes of red and blue, with skins at the foot of his couch and under him. Canis looked down at him and saw the old, darkening face of an aged, dying king. Sweat stood out from each pore and the beard that had once been thick and glossy was now white and starved. Grey was the skin, stretched tightly over cheekbones, and though the fevered eyes gazed upwards they saw neither Boadicea nor Canis. The way of his last journey was hard for Prasutagus, and his noisy breathing as he fought the dark spirits of eternal night was harsh and tortured.

''See,'' whispered the queen to Canis, ''there is no light in his eyes, only fever.''

"When a man is looking into darkness there can be no light," said Canis.

He touched the heavy lids, damp with perspiration. Gently he closed them. They moved under his fingers like loose, dead skin. Prasutagus in the shortness of his breath groaned from straining lungs and his tongue reared in his open mouth. His breath whistled, then became harsh and heavy again.

Quietly Boadicea went from the room. Canis followed. In her own quarters she dismissed two women there and then said to Canis in some sadness, "There, you have seen. Now tell me what you think and look me in the eye as you do so."

He asked her how long Prasutagus had lain like this. Many days. He asked how it had come about. She said the king had been at the supper table when suddenly he had fallen. He had not spoken then or since. He had not been in good health for a year or more and had lately been obviously unwell and troubled by a band of pain around his head.

"Will he die, Canis? Tell me." She was earnestly in search of the truth, the tenor of her words an implication that he could tell her what the physicians could not or would not.

Because he had learnt that truth was sometimes bitter but false hope made the final reckoning more bitter, Canis spoke his mind.

"Aye, my lady. His death is in his head."

There was no anguish in her expression, only a soft sadness. She had shared more than seventeen years with Prasutagus.

"That is more than the truth, I feel," she said, "that is fact. Well, the gods of darkness must reap what the gods of life sow. Prasutagus will not complain. And I shall not be bitter." She smiled her acceptance of what was to be, then said, "You are weary. We will see to it." She clapped her hands and her two women returned. "Go with Canis," said Boadicea, "take him to Apha and command Apha to give him food and wine and then to house him in comfort. He has been a long time returning to us and it has wearied his bones a little. I am not surprised, are you? But he would do it, he was that kind of man when he went, obstinate in his desire to march over the world. We shall discover whether it improved him, shall we not?''

"Improve him, my lady?" said the second woman. "Who can make a lamb out of a sly fox?"

"That," said Boadicea, "is another truth. Go with them, Canis. You and I will talk again tomorrow, but now and for much of this evening I must sit with the king and do what I can for him."

* * *

The morning was soft and hazy, promising another unseasonably warm day. He emerged from a side door of the royal house with dogs bounding and yelping at his heels while, except for servants early at their work, the men and women of the palace still slept. The sun was no more than a yawning, misty ball of pale gold, although with each passing minute it became stronger and brighter, sprinkling the haze above the river with glimmering yellow. The sweet smell of dewy grass was a fragrance that came to the nostrils as it did in no other land. He caught also the faint sting of drifting wispy wood smoke.

Canis leaned with elbows on the wall and let his troubled thoughts come slowly to his mind. Prasutagus was dying and this meant that Boadicea would soon be sole ruler of the Iceni under the patronage of Nero, if Nero had a mind to it. No more majestic monarch than Boadicea had ever ruled the Iceni, no crueller Caesar than Nero had ever ruled the Empire. To Nero, who was Boadicea and what were the Iceni? Scratches on a wall would mean more to him.

"Canis?"

The soft voice startled him. In the misty golden air of early morning, when the shadows of birds wheeling over the river had not yet made their mark on the water, the sound of his own name hung for a moment. He turned. A girl, quite young and beautiful, with rich auburn hair and summer-brown eyes, stood regarding him. She was robed in white, the red of wild berries stung her lips and the darkness of her lashes was like the soft blackness of bees. She was young, breathless, laughing, a wood elf grown to lovely maid.

"Canis?" she said again and her cheeks mantled with pink at the look in his eyes.

Canis had seen thirty-four winters, most of them cold and sharp, and he felt suddenly old. But his smile was warm and the little wrinkles that gathered around his eyes were dancing. Her heart sang, he had come back to them.

"Princess Cea," he said and the song was louder then because he remembered her, recognised her. But she was embarrassed when he bent his knee, took her hand and touched it to her forehead.

"Canis, that is not necessary," she said in confusion.

"Princess, that is your due as your mother's daughter."

"Perhaps from others," conceded Cea, "but you are different."

"Oh?" he said, and that and his smile put her in confusion again.

"Well, have you not seen the world?" she said. If he had, he was still the same, still a man with teasing laughter in his eyes and still the man for whom, as a child, she had conceived an unchildlike love. "Oh," she said breathlessly, "how glad I am that you have come back to us. And you haven't changed, which means the queen my mother has been much mistaken about you."

"How so?" asked Canis, in a little wonder at her warm, young loveliness.

"Why," laughed Cea, "she has said many times that

if you ever did come back you would have grown a bushy tail, sharp ears and pointed teeth, and that you would slink in on all fours."

"I prowl at night like that," he said, "but am more acceptable by day."

"Oh," said Cea, clapping her hands together in delight, "you are very acceptable, Canis. Never desert us again, it is not to be thought of. All the fireside tales have been quite dull while you've been away. Where have you been and why did you send no word to us?"

"Ah, now where?" he said, looking thoughtfully at the sky. "Well, to Gaul and to Rome, to Greece and to other lands. I have fought for Rome and against Rome. I have learnt the art of war, the art of survival and the art of going from one place to another without losing my way. What more is expected of a man?"

"Why, a mind for those he loves," she said firmly. In a way that reminded him of Boadicea in a queenly mood she went on, "And I did not ask you what you had learnt, I did not think there was anything you needed to learn. Indeed, the queen my mother has often said you already knew more than was good for you. I asked you why you sent no word."

"I suppose," he said, "that what with this and what with that I never caught up with other things. But I forgot none of you, Princess."

"When I was a child," said Cea (which was to remind him she was that no longer), "it always made me merry to listen to you. Now as a grown maid I do not know if your tongue, which some think says everything but tells nothing, will make me merry or sad. Why is this, Canis?"

"A child knows only laughter," said Canis, "for all its tears are quickly forgotten. But a maid knows sweetness and pain. Have you seen the king your father this morning?"

Cea's brightness suddenly dimmed.

"He is only worse this morning," she said, "and I am so afraid."

"Cea," said Canis, "fear is not for queens or princesses. They must show only compassion for their people and pride in their house." He smiled. "The queen your mother is not afraid."

"She is always herself," said Cea. "She told Dilwys and me last night that you had returned. I was very happy, and then I was vexed that you did not come to see us."

"Alas," he said, "I was no sooner housed than I fell asleep. I did not know, of course, how bewitchingly you had grown." Cea turned rosy. "Which of the young men here do you make eyes at?"

Cea put her nose in the air.

"None of them," she said. Her smile peeped. "There is only one man I would look at in that way, but if I did he would laugh at me, I know."

"Then he's a dull dog for all his laughing," said Canis. "Tell me of him and perhaps we can decide if his dullness can be cured by a blow on his hard head."

"Oh, one day," she laughed, "you may discover how you have just tripped over your own tongue."

"How have I done this? Is it to do with my being so ancient?"

"Oh, no!" She was swift and earnest in her response to that, seeing him with his head and shoulders outlined by the hazy sky, his hardness tempered by soft light and his eyes full of laughter. "Canis, never miscall your age, never! Always you bring summer with you, and you will never be an ancient greybeard in the way that others become. You were born to be a great man, I have felt this since you first came to our house. Everyone remembers you." For a moment her heart showed as she said, "And I have never forgotten you, never."

He felt concern for her earnest wistfulness. Then he laughed it all away and said, "Come, enough of talk, for you are young and no doubt always hungry, and I need food from the habit of it. Let us go and find what they are putting before us, and later perhaps I may see the queen and discover how your father is.'' He put out a hand and she took it, as she had so often as a child, and went happily enough with him then.

The meal was served in the high, spacious hall, one long table crowded with those in service to the royal household. Queen Boadicea presided with her daughters. The table talk was quiet, its usual boisterousness muted because of the sickness of the king. Canis sat among the younger nobles, listening to the talk around him. He did not attempt to catch the queen's eye, nor she his. She and her daughters conversed as quietly as the rest. Even Princess Dilwys, gay and precocious, was moderate in voice. But sad as she was for her father she was intrigued by the return of Canis.

''It's scarcely to be borne,'' she said, ''he has neither looked at me nor addressed me yet. Has he come back only to eat and talk with others?''

''If he sees you in sulks,'' said Boadicea, ''he will speak to you only briefly and escape you swiftly.''

''But why did he not come to see us last evening?'' asked Dilwys who, at sixteen, had hair the colour of ripe corn and eyes of hazel.

''Because he had travelled far and arrived weary.''

''From where had he travelled?'' asked Cea.

''I cannot think why you should ask that,'' said Dilwys, speaking to her sister across her mother, ''for you spent enough time at sunrise with him to discover the answers to all questions.''

Cea affected not to hear but pinkness betrayed her.

''Kindest mother, may I speak with him now?'' asked Dilwys. ''I have finished my food and cannot wait to hear of all the marvels he must have seen.''

''He will tell us later,'' said Boadicea, ''so although you cannot wait, child, you must.''

Dilwys said in amazement to herself, ''Child? I?

What has come over her? I have not been a child for years."

Cea glanced under dipping lashes. Canis was listening to table companions. They were speaking of the king. One man said that it would be a sad thing if so wily a monarch as Prasutagus went, but that Boadicea had a royal competence and would not make hard work of being sole ruler. Another said that although the guile of Prasutagus would be missed, Boadicea had a more majestic spirit.

"Aye," said a third, "Prasutagus has been a great merchant warrior who has ruled like one, but Boadicea has the courage to leave Romans with fleas in their ears. They will not deny her right to be sole ruler. She was royal when Prasutagus was still a merchant. I'll swear on both my eyes it will go hard with Caesar's jackals if they attempt to deny her. They will not risk another rising, for this time it would not be put down."

It was Cywmryn, husband of Bodulga, who spoke, and the rising he mentioned was one that had taken place some years before. He looked at Canis, curious about the man who had not spoken yet, only listened. "What do you say about it, friend?"

"Only that it is uncomfortable for the king to be placed in his barrow before he is cold," said Canis.

"True, true," said Cywmryn, a man of thirty, with red-gold hair, "but he is direly sick and men must discuss eventualities. By the way, I have not seen your face before."

"Nor I yours," said Canis, "but I do not hold it against you."

A man laughed softly and leaned to catch the ear of Cywmryn. "Did I not tell you? This is Canis, son of the old Wolf of the North."

"Ah." Cywmryn ran a hand through his hair and his boldly bright eyes regarded the returned wanderer with interest. A chuckle sounded in his throat. "I have heard of you and the trouble your tongue caused you. I thought you permanently banished. But you are back."

"Well, I cannot deny I am here," said Canis.

"Make yourself heard on Romans, then," said Cywmryn in cheerful invitation.

"Romans? All men speak of challenging them," said Canis, "but it is not always advisable to go beyond talking about it."

"By all the gods, have you spent these many years nesting with doves?" said Cywmryn. "We are no doves, friend, Caesar has not conquered us. We are his allies by reason of the king's pact with him. The queen has a mind to renounce this pact in time, when we will be quit of Caesar and all his Romans."

"When wolves are in a man's kitchen," said Canis, "it is easier to shut the door on them than toss them out."

"True, true," said Cywmryn again and generously.

The dogs came rumbling for table tidbits. The fire crackled hugely in the hearth and servants had faces shining with heat. Boadicea, eating little, seemed abstracted. It was strange, thought some, that she should be so indifferent to the return of a man who must have offended her mightily. However, she did have other worries.

After the meal, when the dogs were licking the stone floor clean, she sat with the king for a while. Subsequently, in her own apartments, she summoned Canis. When he appeared she bit her lip a little. She had just left an old and shrunken man who was wasting away, and the lean hardness and latent strength of Canis seemed, by contrast, to be indestructible.

But she welcomed him with a smile, shaking her head a little as he took her hand and touched it to his forehead. It was as if he had never left, had never put his pride above hers. Her blue eyes were summer soft, her blue robe caressing her supple body as she sat on a richly-covered couch and spoke of the king. He was in a coma, had taken no food for days, only a little wine she and the physicians had forced him to swallow, and looked ready to go his final way.

"As to those Roman physicians," she said, "what is it to them whether he lives or dies? What are they but head-shaking, mouth-mumbling apostles of Roman medicine? They mutter incantations to gods who sound more arrogant than Romans themselves. What do you know of Roman gods, Canis?"

"I only know that most arrogant gods give discomfort rather than dispensation to suffering kings," said Canis.

"Do gods envy kings, then?"

"Venus, the Roman goddess of love, might be jealous of some queens."

Boadicea fixed him with a look but could discern no slyness in his smile.

"Canis," she said, "you cannot, no, you cannot possibly be trying to pay this queen a compliment, can you?"

"It is a habit not even seven years could break," he said.

"A habit? What habit? Why, you smooth tonguester, not once—" She broke off and laughed. "Oh, we will forget our sadness for a while. You are promised to tell us what you have been doing to improve the mighty world. Be seated, Canis, and when the princesses are here you shall entertain us, and I shall make allowances for all conceits and exaggerations even if they do not."

So Cea and Dilwys came to sit with their mother and listen. Canis spoke at length of his travels, of the Belgic tribes under the heel of Rome in southern Britain, of Gaul across the narrow sea and Gaulish arts similar to those of the Iceni. He spoke of Greece and of Rome, of the great stone temples and buildings of that proud and ancient city. Dilwys listened in wonder, Cea breathlessly and Boadicea with a smile on her mouth.

It was Boadicea who eventually said, "But in all this you say little of yourself, you speak of all kinds of people but tell us nothing of what you did when you were among them.''

"Nor does he tell us of women," said Dilwys artfully.

"So we know, do we not," said Boadicea, "that he has much to hide of them."

"No, he could not," said Cea, a little perturbed, "or he would have said."

"My little ones," said the queen, "he must have, which is why he has not said."

Dilwys thought, little ones? Little ones? What *has* come over her?

"I can only tell you," said Canis, rubbing his chin (so that Boadicea knew he was going to lie), "that wherever a man goes he cannot escape women. This would be diverting if it were not so alarming. It is alarming, princesses, because as the queen your mother will have told you, women are not to be understood by men, nor argued with. Now—"

"I have not been told that at all," burst out Dilwys in laughter.

"Nor is it true, but only his way of taking our minds off his dissembling," said Boadicea.

"Now I learnt," continued Canis, "that because of the complexities of women a wise man, by engaging only at a distance with them, keeps himself in peace and out of trouble."

"Dear my mother," said Dilwys, "is he not fiendish? He has told us nothing at all!"

"But, Canis," said Cea, who had to know despite not wanting to know, "tell us if you met any beautiful women, tell us if you fell in love."

He looked at the painted ceiling. He fingered an eyebrow. This time he was surely going to lie, thought Boadicea.

"I cannot lie," he confessed, at which the queen, for some reason, laughed at herself. "The truth is I fell in love with many women."

"But all at a distance, of course," said Boadicea.

"At various distances," said Canis, "for though, as we have agreed, women are far too complex to be understood or argued with, some are very finely shaped, others have beguiling eyes and others virtues or assets which a man in his weakness can neither discount nor resist. However, in my wisdom and despite my weakness, I kept my various distances from all of them and loved them from afar, as it were."

"But that is nothing again," protested Dilwys. "At least tell us if you found the women of Greece beautiful."

"Alas," said Canis, "I was so taken up with the other wonders of Greece that I scarcely noticed the women at all and could not say even now whether they had one eye or two. What I can say is that no women are fairer than the Iceni, no eyes softer and brighter than those I see now."

They were a little dumb at this. They all remembered how he rarely said anything that did not have a jest to it. He did not seem to be in any kind of jest now. Cea turned pink with pleasure.

"Canis," said Boadicea, "you have at least discovered how to put us in the sweetest of tempers. I also feel that because you have been to Rome and fought with their legions, you know Romans better than any of us now. Therefore, as we are in council this afternoon I wish you to join us. The local procurator and his jackals are treading hard on the heels of stricken Prasutagus, and I need your advice and counsel."

4

LATER THAT DAY Canis walked with Cywmryn through the crowded streets of Venta Icenorum, where soldiers of the newly-strengthened Roman garrison rubbed shoulders with Roman civilians and Iceni townsfolk. To all intents and purposes shoulders were rubbed equally, since the Iceni were not a vanquished people but, by the pact, allies of Rome.

There was trading in the market streets and slaves of both Roman and Iceni nobles scurried briskly about on errands for their houses. Here and there were seen the litters of Roman women or the equipage of busy financiers, for the money-lenders of the time found business in Roman Britain profitable. Many Iceni aristocrats had borrowed money to build Roman-style villas and adopt the Roman way of living. Slaves accompanying masters or mistresses made way for them with loud cries and punishing staves, much to the rage and fury of townsfolk too proud to withdraw in haste.

Although there was general grief at the illness of Prasutagus there was no sense that the people were worried. What was there to worry about when Boadicea was still young and brave? There was a queen for you, bold enough to keep off Caesar himself. So the Iceni talked briskly and optimistically wherever they gathered. Celtic, they were great talkers. Mellow was the sound of men's voices, liquid the women's.

Like a thirsty traveller parched from too long a time in lands arid and harsh, Canis imbibed the sights and sounds of the fair, clean city of Venta Icenorum. They were the patterns of forgotten life renewed. He paused with Cywmryn here and there to listen to discussion and

Lydia, eyes glittering, said contemptuously, "If this barbarian rides I will walk."

"Walk, then," said Julian carelessly.

"You would not dare to set me down in favour of a long-shanked Briton."

"I would only set you down at your own request."

"I will not suffer it," she said fiercely. "Take up the uncouth braggart, then, I will bear his stink as best as I can."

Julian said quietly, "Hold your disgusting tongue." To Canis he said, "Up with you, friend, and we will come apace to our conversation."

Canis rode with them. He stood behind brother and sister, the rail to hand on either side. Julian let the pair go, the chariot bucketed forward and clattered away. Lydia's hair began to whip in the wind, flicking back at Canis. Julian ran the horses at a fast trot and Lydia kept a back as stiff as a board to the Briton. They came to the villa of Pablus Vitellius on the outskirts of the town. It was set well back from the road, as were other villas, and its flowering garden was beginning to show colour. Without a word Lydia alighted catlike from the chariot and vanished, leaving Julian and Canis to enter the large, red-tiled villa together.

Canis grimaced a little when taken into a large room full of inviting couches. It was not the furniture he disliked but the heat. He found most Romans unable to dissociate civilised living from extreme warmth. Pablus Vitellius was not at home, nor was his wife, and Julian played host, dispensing wine. Canis took the proffered silver cup in which the wine glimmered redly.

"To Caesar?" he suggested drily.

"On this occasion," said Julian, "not Caesar but King Prasutagus and Queen Boadicea. My father has a respect for your king and a regard for your queen."

"To Prasutagus and Boadicea, then," smiled Canis, "and then perhaps to your discerning father."

They drank. The wine was warm and full-bodied.

Julian, a reservist officer, looked dark and handsome in his uniform. He looked with interest at the Briton clad in his kilted tunic and a cloak of fustian grey, which had seen its best days long since. Julian sensed a strength of purpose that might be far crueller than that which had made him put Lydia in the dust.

"Prasutagus is dying, I think," said Julian.

"And Nero is emperor," said Canis.

"Do you have fears, Canis?"

Canis sat on a couch, musing on the sensuous ripple that disturbed the surface of his wine. He said, "Not for myself, Roman, for a people."

"I am called Julian by my friends."

"Is a man who ill-uses your sister a friend?"

"Not of my sister," smiled Julian, sipping his wine. "Lydia feels I am in honour bound to avenge her, but if I were to avenge her for every slight she imagines put upon her, I should be full of sword pricks. Lydia brooks no ridicule from any man, Roman or Briton. Her goddess is Diana, especial deity of women. She is wilful and stiff-necked."

"Diana?" said Canis, smiling.

"Lydia. There are others with the same complaint."

"Romans or Britons?"

"Both," said Julian. "They might manage to lead all of us into folly. Britain is fertile, and rich in its people, it can become a great province of the Empire. I do not wish it to be lost to us. Let us be frank, Canis, we are here and here we will stay."

"You are here, aye," said Canis, setting his wine aside, disliking its effect in the artificial heat of the room. "That is frank and also a fact. You will stay? That is also frank, but is a wish, not a fact."

"My friend," said Julian, "everything is done in the name of Rome and the world in which we live is Roman. I will agree that what will come after is in the hands of other men, but you and I are bound to Britain as it exists under Rome."

"What is Britain to you?" asked Canis.

"My home and my life," said Julian. "I have lived here eleven years among Romans I know and Britons who are my friends. True, I represent Rome as my father's deputy, but in my lifetime I doubt to see Rome itself more than once every ten years and when my days are done my bones will lie in Britain."

"But where will lie your heart?" asked Canis.

"It is each to his own after death. These are things for old men and philosophers to discuss. You and I are concerned with what we are to be in life, and I must speak plain. My father fears that Nero will be counselled to end the pact between Rome and the Iceni if Prasutagus dies. Boadicea will lose her throne, for the precedent is that when a client-ruler dies the succession shall pass to the government of Rome."

Perceptibly the Briton's expression hardened.

"There are joint client-rulers here," he said, "and the precedent should not be invoked until both die."

"Nero, we fear, will be counselled otherwise," said Julian, "as well as being persuaded to confiscate the full wealth of Prasutagus. Boadicea will be left with nothing."

"Who will so counsel Caesar?"

"At the source will be Catus Decianus, the Imperial Procurator of Britain. He will say that all rights are vested in Prasutagus, none in Boadicea. He will use Caesar's name to take all from Prasutagus and disinherit Boadicea."

"I would not then be Catus Decianus," said Canis, "for he will find, when he is pulling the teeth of the dead tiger, that the tigress is on his back."

"For the gold-filled teeth of Prasutagus," said Julian, "Catus Decianus will risk being the worst kind of fool to become the richest. Aye, he will take his share and more. Canis, will you do your best for Queen Boadicea?"

There was a bitterness about Canis as he said, "Am I

to go to her, advise her of what Caesar might do and
counsel her to hold her peace should Nero take not only
her throne but everything else? You do not know
Boadicea.''

''No, I have never met her,'' admitted Julian, ''but I
do know she has need of wise and cautious counsel.
Neither my father nor I could influence Catus Decianus,
and he will rend her and destroy her if she defies Rome.
My father and others have a regard for Boadicea—''

''Boadicea is nothing.''

The disdainful interruption came from Lydia. They
turned. She had changed her robe for one of white
hemmed and girdled by blue. Her hair was up and over
it she wore an open-work coif of fine gold. Her nose
stood high above her scornful mouth and she regarded
them as if they were even less than nothing.

''In your mouth, Lydia,'' said Julian, ''there is a net-
tle of folly which will one day turn and sting you into
such knowledge of your foolish self that the pain will be
nothing to the self-contempt you will feel.''

''I spit on you, doting brother,'' said Lydia, ''I spit
on you for making welcome in another's house a barbarian dog who has despoiled your own sister.''

''Oh, get you gone, petulance,'' said Julian irritably,
''or I will have Canis slit your tongue so neatly you will
not know it has happened until you find yourself
dumb.''

Lydia could have killed him.

''Oh, I will have my day!'' she hissed. ''The wheel
will turn!''

Canis regarded her pityingly.

''Will you know when it has turned?'' he asked.

''I will know, offal!''

''But unless you grow up,'' he said, ''you will miss
the passage of life itself.''

''I shall not miss your death!'' she cried, and ran
from the room. Julian spread his hands.

"What can a reasonable man do with such an unreasonable sister?" he said.

"Be deaf to her," said Canis briefly. He thanked Julian for his hospitality, and Julian urged him to press caution on Boadicea and offered to drive him back to the queen's house. Canis preferred to walk.

How to counsel Boadicea? Caution to her meant timidity. Years ago as a young queen she would have preferred to fight the invading Romans. Prasutagus had preferred collaboration, thinking to link his people with the Romans and eventually absorb them.

"When you and I are but scarred bones, Wolfhead," he had said to Canis, as he had to others, "one man will say to another, 'Are you a Roman?' And the other will reply, 'My father's father was of Rome but I am of Britain.' And both will be content with the reply."

But where Prasutagus was a hopeful pacifist Boadicea was an uncompromising realist. She knew that a man who nested with eagles was liable to awake one morning to find himself being torn and devoured. Prasutagus cooperated with Romans. Boadicea watched them. The Romans did not play the part of friendly guests too well. They acted all too frequently as if the Iceni, together with their neighbours the Trinovantes, were subject peoples. Prasutagus and Boadicea stood as a bulwark between Roman arrogance and their people, and had held in check to some extent Roman greed for Iceni land. The Trinovantes had suffered ferociously from this, immense tracts being parcelled out by Roman authorities to officials and retired veterans who wished to stay in Britain.

Canis, in his contact with the ramifications of Roman power in various lands, had come to realise that for all her intolerance in some things, Rome brought systems of good government and wise administration to backward peoples. Unfortunately, like so many powerful empires, Rome suffered from the actions of individuals, from arrogant or greedy officials. And her Caesars were, for all their self-deification, the most susceptible of all individuals to corruption by absolute power. Promising well as a young man, Nero was now on the way to becoming the most corrupt of all. It was to this neurotic degenerate that Boadicea would have to look for justice, and Canis knew she was unlikely to get it.

He had noticed an increased number of Romans in the city. Today they seemed everywhere, even about the great fore-court of the palace. Often Caesar's officials came and went, but it was unusual to see so many soldiers present. If Prasutagus was breathing his last, it seemed the Romans would be the first to count his gold.

Canis made his way to the studded doors. A Roman decurion, placing himself in the path of the Briton, said, "What is your business here, fellow?"

"I am a guest in this house," said Canis pleasantly, "and so I come and go as custom allows."

"What is this?" Cophistus, deceptively soft of voice, was there. "Who are you to stand in the way of a queen's counsellor?" he asked the decurion.

The decurion, immaculate in cloth, leather and burnished armour, obviously considered the question could have been put in a friendlier way.

"You have a soft voice," he said coldly to Cophistus, "but not an agreeable one."

"Well, as I do not like the shape of your nose," said Cophistus, "we are at evens. As for you, friend," he said to Canis, "the queen has been asking for you."

As Canis moved forward his elbow touched the decurion. Instantly his arm was gripped by a strong hand.

"Here or anywhere is no place to push me, fellow," said the Roman.

"Normally," said Canis, "I am dainty in my tread and avoid all my neighbours as neatly as a nymph." Easily he plucked free the detaining hand. "But if I did collide a little with you it was not meant and nor do I think you were at fault, either.''

The decurion, unable to decide whether this was convincing or confusing, did what any other man might have done. He found a friend to go and talk to.

"What has kept you?" asked Cophistus, going through the palace with Canis. "The queen has been at my throat on your account, although she knows I am not your keeper.''

The council chamber was crowded. Boadicea was seated in a gaunt, carved chair. As Canis was ushered in she looked up, her blue eyes cold.

"So," she said, "you are here at last and with the smell of Romans about you.''

Canis, seeing Cywmryn there, guessed who her informant was, and plainly her expression told him that after seven years she did not expect he would run after Romans as soon as this.

"I am sorry, my lady," he said, "but I did not know you were meeting so early.''

"You would have had you not strayed too far.''

Cacchus, chief elder, tugged at his beard and said, "I was not aware that Canis had been appointed to council.''

"You do not have to know everything before it happens," said Boadicea. "Canis is the son of the old Wolf, he is qualified and, moreover, he is to be the captain of my city.''

Cacchus said, "It is not the custom—" "It is my custom, my way and my city," said Boadicea.

"My lady," said Canis, "this appointment does me honour, but—"

"But?" she interrupted darkly, and turned to Cacchus. "Canis would not be himself if he did not argue, yet would you not have thought that seven years of discovery would have rid him of the habit of at least arguing with his queen?''

Canis could not restrain a smile.

"My lady." He began again, more persuasively. "I would not be so ungracious as to argue with you from habit. I only meant that the appointment must not be official. By decree of Caesar we may not bear arms or create any unit of arms, except that which constitutes your bodyguard. Any man appointed captain of the city has the responsibility of organising your major unit of defence. There has been no such appointment since Caesar's decree was published many years ago. It would be open defiance of his law. And there is a less specific but more earnest point to consider."

"Which is?" She was still dark.

"The Romans must have no suspicion, if they intend moving against you, that you are seeking to anticipate them. They would crush us while we were still digging up our rusty weapons."

"We must dig them up quickly and silently," said Cacchus, no longer disposed, by virtue of his beard and his standing, to have his voice overlooked. "When the Romans come to take what we suspect they might, our strength will ensure they only take what we are willing to give."

"What is our strength?" asked Canis. "How many warriors in the city, how many spears?"

"We will find more than enough warriors, more than enough spears," smiled Cwymryn.

"How many?" persisted Canis. Boadicea viewed him, impatience at his caution vying with understanding of the need for it. "We shall not contain Romans by boldly waving a few weapons. Our real strength is not here but in the country, in the Iceni tribes. They must be prepared, administration centralised, and everything linked to plan and method without alarming or alerting Romans."

There were mutterings. He looked around. He knew some of them, others were unfamiliar. He understood those who muttered. He had chosen to leave the Iceni and now, after seven years, why should his be the voice to listen to? Boadicea understood too.

"You have been away a long time, Canis," she said, "and so there are some here who do not know what a man of finely acquired knowledge you are." Her blue eyes danced at his little smile. "Although you may not be wiser than Cacchus, however, or more venerable than Lygulf, yet you must know Roman methods in war better than any of us, for you have served with the eagles."

"And has perhaps been turned into an eaglet," said a young noble, Dumunus. "That is," he added, as the Queen turned cold eyes on him, "he has nested in clandestine fashion, my lady."

"So have you," said Boadicea, for the promiscuity of Dumunus was a byword, "and already your lions are as empty as your head."

Laughter was interrupted as the king's own physician hastened in. He whispered to the queen. She paled and rose to her feet. She swept towards the door. Canis caught the fragrance of the scent she used.

"Prasutagus is near his end," she said stiffly and the chamber hushed. "Come with me, Cacchus," she said, "and you too, Canis, for you were the only one who gave me the truth."

In his bed the king lay ravaged and old, his breath rattling in his throat, his face blue, his eyes staring, his body an almost fleshless waste around thin bones. The Roman physicians were there, and with a fierce gesture Boadicea had them out of the place. She knelt beside the couch of her dying husband and took his hand.

"Be at peace, Prasutagus," she whispered, "be at peace."

Gradually the throat rattle died and the blue face paled. Suddenly the paleness turned crimson with haemorrhage and Boadicea, in quick pity, covered the face with a cloth of soft linen, which turned wetly red in seconds. And so Prasutagus died with his blood gushing and Cacchus whispering to the gods on behalf of his royal master.

Boadicea drew the drapes over the body and came to her feet.

"Leave me for a while that I may remember him," she said quietly. "He served the Iceni well. Canis, go to the princesses and speak to them gently, as I know you can, and tell them I will come later. They are not to see their father yet, and glad I am that they did not see him die. And you, good Cacchus, go and acquaint all others that Prasutagus, our king, has gone from life."

Canis went to the apartments of the young princesses. He was admitted by one of their women. Cea and Dilwys were at the window, talking. Cea turned, saw him and the pink of quick pleasure tinted her face.

"Why, Canis," she said and came in laughter to greet him. Dilwys, knowing her sister's heart, looked on mischievously. Cea, remarking how sober Canis looked, said, "What has turned you so glum? Do you not see the sun? It is the sweetest day."

"It is not as sweet as that," he said. He went to the window, Cea by his side, and he put his arm around the slim shoulders of Dilwys, who eyed her sister slyly at this. But Cea was looking up at Canis and thinking how life quickened for her at his nearness. She had never forgotten him, never forgotten how the sound of his voice had always made her feel warm, safe and happy.

From the window they could see only peace and beauty. It was all in the silver-blue glitter of the river, the green of the land, the dark softness of forest coming to leaf, the sun-sharpened colour of distant villas and the mellow brown timbers of huts and houses. Surely in all the world there was no land like that of the Iceni. Was that what he had discovered? Was that why he had returned? If so, why did he look so sad?

Canis turned his head, she saw the truth in his eyes and Cea's breath stopped.

"Canis?" A little gasp. "Is it the king my father?"

"Aye," said Canis gently, "he has run his life to its end. The queen your mother asked me to bring you the news as tenderly as I could, but there is no way I know of to ease the grief for you and Dilwys."

Dilwys ran to her couch, threw herself down and wept. Cea sought the comfort of a strong, warm hand. But she could not hold back her tears. They magnified, spilled and ran.

"Aye, weep, Princess," he said, "for it is not the sun but the tears of those who belonged to the king which can enrich a day like this."

"You do not weep," she said brokenly.

"Yet I grieve," he said, but his grief was not so much for the death of her father as for what he felt would follow.

"Oh, Canis, now we do have need of you in this house—"

"Not so," he said gently, "for it is the queen your mother who gives this house all it needs. By her strength and love you will receive greater comfort than anyone else could give you. She will never fail you. Nor will you ever fail her. You are her first-born."

But Cea wept, for how could she tell him that only he could give her the comfort she really wanted?

5

THERE FOLLOWED DAYS of mourning. The great barrow was prepared to receive the body of the Iceni king, with all that was personal to him, his regalia, shield, sword and spear, rings and jewels, drinking cups and many other things. He was buried outside the city, on high ground overlooking the river, and the barrow closed. And when all was finished the tumulus of Prasutagus was a black, silent hump against the purple radiance of the evening sky.

Within the house of the widowed queen an uneasiness disturbed the quiet mourning. The eagles were poised to swoop. Boadicea was like a watchful, suspicious tigress whose distrust of Rome was constant. The Romans had withdrawn from the palace precincts and their quietness was ominous. Canis, sure that this meant that Catus Decianus, the Imperial Procurator, was only awaiting official word from Rome, went unobtrusively about certain very practical matters. Only Cophistus, who assisted him, knew what he was about.

The queen listened to the greybeards each day, enduring their wordiness with thinly-disguised impatience. Eventually she summoned Canis to her apartments.

"Canis, what am I to do in the event of Rome denying me?"

"Nothing, my lady."

"Nothing?" The light of battle leapt. "I am to sit meekly doing nothing while they dispossess me?"

"It must seem so," he said, "for the worst thing would be to have Rome say the Iceni struck the first blow. This would be Caesar's excuse to crush us."

"So, then," said Boadicea witheringly, "let us be

mice. Let us be dumb mice and not raise even a squeak.''

He was aware of her readiness to challenge the will of Caesar if she disliked it enough. In her pride she could provoke the destruction of herself and the Iceni nation.

"Let us only be cautious," he said.

"Aye, let us be mice," she said again. She regarded him beneath lowered lids, wondering about the advisability of caution. It was not really what she wanted from him and he knew it was not. "Canis," she said, "most of my counsellors think I am threatened. Yet you are the only one who advises me to do nothing. You have not returned to me a timid man, have you?"

"No, only an older one," he said. She paced the floor. The day outside was wild with rain and cloud as April drowned the crispness of March. "My lady, do not fight Rome until it is unavoidable, until it is the only alternative."

"Canis, I shall not quietly suffer injustice."

"I know you will not, but I should not like to see injustice fathering indiscretion—"

"By all the gods," said Boadicea heatedly, "if injustice is the father of indiscretion, then scholars are the children of timidity! Where are all your bold conceits, where is your pride, your arrogance? These are what I want from you now, or have you come back to be the agent of my submission?"

"Submission? To Romans? Queen Boadicea?" Canis shook his head and laughed. "Before any man can contrive that the sun will fall from the sky. My lady, there will be no submission, only a play for time. We will procrastinate and argue, we will use words until their ears are numb and their reasoning at odds with their purpose."

She was not convinced.

"Canis, do you say we can defeat Romans by words? You are trying to make me believe what you do not believe yourself. But seven years have not changed me, I have never wanted false comfort and do not want it now."

"I know you have not changed—"

"Ah, this is it!" She pounced. "You mistrust me, you think I do not have the patience to properly consider my problems, you think me impulsive enough to commit the rashest acts. I am not a child. Oh, you upstart, I am your queen!"

"Indeed you are," said Canis soberly, "and no man would deal with you as less. I only ask you not to let injustice make you venture your fortunes too high-spiritedly, for the chief concern of all who love you is not the spilled blood of acquisitive Romans but the survival of yourself and your family."

Her anger slipped away. She smiled and said very softly, "Do you too love me, Canis?"

"I share this with all your subjects, my lady."

"Oh, that love is courteous but dull," she said. She was tall and regal in her robe, her hair a piled crown, but still had to look up to meet his eye. "And if my caution and discretion mean I am to live in a hut of turf and tread muddy ground, what then?"

"That is not to be endured," he said, "none of us would have you surrender all you have to live no better than a slave. Only do not run with your head down, do not let your spirit rush in advance of your reasoning."

Boadicea smiled again. The conceited rogue was quite unchanged. He was still the only man presumptuous enough to challenge her regal infallibility. He still argued with her, and now he commanded her—aye, as good as!—to do nothing when her whole being cried out for her to arm every man in the city. Even so, she smiled.

"You are still something of a fox, Canis," she said, "but no one could say you are not a man. As to Caesar and the hope that he will uphold my claim, tell me, has he ever been known to uphold any claim but his own?"

And Canis knew the queen had no illusions. She was certain the Romans intended to deprive her of power, throne and wealth, and she would fight them.

"There is no need to be so serious," said Cophistus to Canis later that day, "I and many others will cheerfully die for her."

"It would be better," said Canis, "if you all contrived to stay alive. What good to any harassed queen is an army of smiling corpses?"

*   *   *

The day when the will of Prasutagus was to be made public coincided with the arrival in Venta Icenorum of a detachment of Roman soldiers and veterans from Camulodunum. They added considerably to the strength of the armed Roman faction already in the city, and had been sent by Catus Decianus, the Imperial Procurator, to impress on Boadicea that whatever the will of Prasutagus entailed it was the will of Caesar that was to be implemented. These soldiers and veterans were among many who had terrorised the Trinovantes for years, and the people of Venta Icenorum viewed their arrival with hostility, hands itching to feel weapons long since buried and hidden.

There were crowds about the palace, braving the wind and the rain, including soldiers, servants, civilians and officials of Rome, all certain that this day would see the end of the reign of Boadicea. One retired Roman veteran, Tybus, who had settled in Iceni territory, was there with his friend Aurelius.

"The widow, they say," said Aurelius, "is more in arrogance than grief, but there you are, she is a barbarian for all that she calls herself queen."

"Let be," said Tybus uncomfortably, "Boadicea has the spirit of her kind and would not show her grief publicly in any event."

"She will by the time this day is over," said Aurelius.

"I have lived here many years," said Tybus, "I have fought with the legions against the Belgae, the Cantii, the Druids and others, and been rewarded with so many gashes that my wine runs out of me like water from a cracked pitcher. I hope, therefore, to take no more gashes but live my remaining years here in peace."

"So you will," said Aurelius as they shouldered their way through townspeople, "and more richly, for what Boadicea has and what Prasutagus left will all belong to the Empire and we shall have our share of land, you and I."

"In that event," said Tybus, "I will sharpen my sword, which I put aside, and plug the holes in my shield, since if I am to enrich myself at the expense of Boadicea I must be brave enough to fight her. You had better sharpen your own sword, for I tell you she will not meekly surrender that which she holds and that which she considers her due. Time has a strange way with some of us and I confess I would rather not see injustice done to her. She is too fine a queen to be deposed."

Aurelius shrugged. Tybus was getting soft in the head.

The will of Prasutagus was promulgated in the presence of the queen and her court, with Roman officials, civilians and soldiers also present. Outside the palace large numbers of people awaited the outcome. Boadicea, seated on a huge, ancient chair carved with dragons and other Celtic symbols, was in the simplest majesty, wearing no jewellery other than a gold ring and her white robe waisted by a girdle of brown wool. She seemed detached, introspective, her daughters seated one on each side of her.

Catus Decianus had himself disdained to attend. The man who stood in for him was the fiscal procurator of the Iceni province, Septimus Cato, a languid, fattish man, but carnal. He lounged in a chair opposite

Boadicea, his face looking like pastry left long in the
dark. Boredom was his main contribution to the occasion, except that occasionally his dull eyes took in the
warm youthful loveliness of Princess Cea.

Prasutagus, the wily one, had done his best. He had
appointed Nero co-heir with Boadicea and the princesses. All his land and wealth he left jointly to his
family and Nero. Thus, by making Nero an extensive
beneficiary Prasutagus had thought to secure for his
queen and his daughters inheritance of throne and
property. Couched in simple terms his wishes and hopes
were made clear. They were just to his family and
generous to Nero.

At the end Septimus Cato lifted an indolent hand. He
was a man who favoured indolence except when a
woman was involved. His servants loudly commanded
silence for Caesar's representative. Septimus began to
speak, his voice in keeping with his boredom, his attention given more to his appearance than his address as
he adjusted the fashion of his toga.

"To Boadicea, widow of client-king Prasutagus,
greetings from Catus Decianus, Imperial Procurator in
the name of Caesar."

Boadicea's eyes flashed beneath drawn brows at the
omission of her title.

"I have listened in some surprise," said Septimus,
"to this public advice of the testament of the late client-
king Prasutagus, since the reading and hearing of such
testament is legal only in a Roman-convened court of
properly appointed magistrates. As to the testament itself, this shows an even more provocative ignorance of
Caesar's law. I will dispel such ignorance by making
known to you, as others have before, that the law is this.
On the death or abdication or removal of a client-
monarch a provincial government will be established
under the authority of the imperial governor. Caesar's
law does not permit any other course and the testament

of Prasutagus is thereby invalid."

"But this law concerns only conquered nations," said Cacchus the elder, "and—"

"Who asked you to speak?" said Septimus.

Angry rumblings stirred the chests and beards of Cacchus and other elders. Boadicea watched with veiled eyes and Canis, behind Cea, watched Boadicea.

"Bandy-legged lackey," said Cacchus to Septimus, "what have you said so far that does not proclaim your own ignorance?"

Septimus lifted a lazy hand.

"Seize this whiskered idiot and bind him," he said, and at once two Roman soldiers took hold of the aged Cacchus. Boadicea leaned forward, her hands gripping the carved arms of her chair.

"Unhand him, Romans," she said quietly, "he will hold his tongue. Do him no mischief, Septimus, for he spoke in a moment of indiscretion, as we all do at times."

Canis, aware of Cophistus and others of the queen's guard showing restiveness, shook his head at them. Despite Boadicea's quiet manner he knew she seethed, and it had been costly to her pride to ask indulgence of Romans.

Septimus gave a nod. The soldiers thrust Cacchus backwards and the proud old man tumbled and sprawled. A dozen Iceni leapt forward, shouting in fury. Cea and Dilwys looked on with dilated eyes.

"Stay!" Boadicea was on her feet, hand lifted. "There is to be no brawling, my people. Cacchus, stand up, turn your eyes to me and say no more."

"There is a little more," said Septimus. Boadicea resumed her throne, and he looked into icy blue eyes. In his malice he went on, "Widow, you represent a subject people, I represent Caesar. You may not sit in my presence unless I give you leave. So stand before me, and your daughters also."

Boadicea contemplated him as she would vermin, her nostrils twitching at the odour.

"I am the rightful queen of the Iceni," she said clearly, "and you only the mouthpiece of your master, Catus Decianus. You cannot take my right from me by words whose origin I do not know. If they are Caesar's words, then show them to me above his seal."

This was what Canis had advised her to say if the need arose. It brought a frown to the muddy face of Septimus and a murmur of approval from the Iceni.

"In clemency," said Septimus, "I will say I did not hear what you have just said. But stand to me, widow, or my soldiers will have you first on your feet, then on your knees."

Canis saw the tremor that shook her. Her teeth clenched and her honey-brown knuckles turned white from the grip she put on her chair. He spoke over the head of Cea.

"Stand, I beg you, my lady," he whispered above the angry waves of sound from the Iceni, "for if they lay their hands on you I will surely kill them."

Boadicea paled. Then she came to her feet. Cea and Dilwys, fearful in their apprehension of worse indignities, shivered. Canis turned his eyes on them, his look commanded them, gave them courage. They too rose to their feet. The Romans present thought to smile on Boadicea's humiliation but in some way could not. In her tall, regal grace, her golden-bronze hair crowning her with brightness, she was not in any humiliation. Her expression was cold, contemptuous, her bearing undiminished. She brought a burning to the eyes of her people there and strange discomfort to some Romans, especially to the man Tybus and to Julian Osirus, who was present with his sister Lydia.

"Roman dog!" A Celtic voice spoke in anger and passion. "Are you so uncivilised you cannot respect a rightful monarch or understand dignity?"

Septimus merely lifted a flaccid hand to enjoin silence.

"Mark the owner of that loud tongue," he said, "we will deal with it anon. Hear me, barbarians, and know the will of Caesar concerning you and your land. Caesar has shown you tolerance for many years, but now your client-king has gone and therefore that which obtained in his lifetime is no longer so. This land and all within it are subject to Caesar and his laws. All that you had you have no more, it is confiscated by imperial decree. There is no king, no queen. The Imperial Governor rules by authority of Caesar. So go from this place and in what wisdom you have make no commotion."

"I will speak without making a commotion," said Canis and went forward to look into the indifferent eyes of the fiscal procurator. Septimus, despite his instinctive desire to have the tall Iceni thrown down, let curiosity flicker as he beheld the wordly eyes that fixed his own.

"Speak, then," he said, "but softly, and within the law."

"It is said and you have said," observed Canis, "that the law is as I quote. On the death of a client-monarch a provincial government will be established under the authority of the Imperial Governor. Where is the Imperial Governor?"

Boadicea drew a deep breath. Septimus smiled coldly, derisively.

"Do you consider in your high majesty," he said, "that it is necessary for Caesar's general to pronounce on this matter in person?"

"I will answer your question with another," said Canis. "Do you not consider it would be politic and commendable for him to do so?"

"Carefully, barbarian, or there will be a commotion," said Septimus, but the hall was in tense silence. The Iceni were looking to Canis, the Romans, except for Lydia, attending on Septimus. Lydia in her hatred could attend only on Canis, the while she willed Septimus to destroy him in some way.

"It would be politic in that the Imperial Governor lends more authority to a decree than a fiscal procurator," said Canis reasonably, "and it would be commendable in that he would have the might of his army to ensure conclusion of the matter. But is he not with his army in the west, hunting Druids? And the conclusion must be as peaceful as Caesar would wish."

The derisiveness became a muddy scowl on the face of Septimus. Disregarding Iceni murmurs of approval he asked, "What name do you go by?"

"Canis," said a loud voice, "it is Canis who gives you sweet reason, Roman!"

"Canis," murmured Septimus, "it is not within the law to defy me or to question my authority."

"Excellency," said Canis, "I only counsel you. You must know that Caesar will not thank you to handle the matter in such a way as to turn it into expensive and disagreeable trouble. Caesar did not commend Publius Ostorius Scapula when he discounted Iceni arguments that led to the rising ten years ago. If we argue the testament of Prasutagus with you it is because, as the queen has said, you have only given us words. How are we to know they are Caesar's words unless you show us Caesar's deed and seal? That is why we think it better for both Romans and Iceni to invoke the arbitration of the Imperial Governor in the matter, which no one can say is of less importance to us than to you."

This was sharp-edged procrastination. Septimus did not like losing his temper, it made him perspire. But the airs this barbarian gave himself were enough to make the gods loose thunderbolts.

"When I gave you leave to speak," he said, "did I not caution you? In what you have said you have defied great Caesar himself. Do you know the penalty for this?"

"Heed him, procurator." Julian spoke. "What he has said is fair and reasonable. The implementation of this matter is for the Imperial Governor."

But he was shouted down by his countrymen. Septimus waited for the noise to die, then in his languid malice he pointed a finger at Canis.

"Take this man," he said, "and also the other we marked earlier. Take them and rip out their tongues, so that though we may not be spared sight of their faces we shall at least be spared the sound of their insolent voices."

Cea screamed as soldiers swarmed to take Canis and the other man. Iceni men drew weapons but were immediately surrounded by Romans and beaten to the ground by flat, heavy swords. Boadicea burst from frozen immobility. Plucking the dagger from her girdle she leapt. Everyone thought her about to strike at the soldiers who were at confused sixes and sevens in their efforts to hold Canis. Instead she swivelled and came at the throat of Septimus, dagger posed for the thrust. Her lips were drawn back from her white teeth and Septimus sat paralysed. Before any could move to prevent her she thrust her knee into his groin. As he shrieked in agony she rammed her left arm under his chin. The pressure against his fat throat was hideously unbearable, it brought his tongue out, while the point of her dagger pricked the very skin of his left eyelid. He gurgled and his face turned blue. Romans stood aghast as they saw their fiscal procurator only a sharp thrust from death.

"Let no one move," hissed Boadicea, "let no one take a step or I will lodge this dog's eyeball in his brain. Roman," she said to his purpling face, her arm and knee savage, "release my friends permanently from all threats or you will die in agony!"

A Roman officer held back soldiers who might have moved, for seeing the look on Boadicea's face he knew she would kill Septimus fiendishly indeed. Septimus was choking, his hands clawing at her robe in frenzied effort to secure relief, but Boadicea, supple and strong, never wavered. Neither did her dagger's point.

"Quickly, corruption," she hissed, "command your Romans to leave my house, instruct them there is to be no seizing of mine, and do so by raising your right hand in token of order given and promise to be kept."

He jerked up his right hand, his tortured wheezing reaching every ear. The soldiers released Canis and the other man. Boadicea stepped back from Septimus. The shoulder of her robe was torn, smooth flesh gleamed. Romans came storming and shouting at her, and Boadicea flung her dagger at their feet.

"Has he not given his word? Is his not a Roman word? Are you not Romans? Or are you not even men?" And she turned her back on them, walked to her throne, faced them all and sat down. One Roman in his fury picked up her dagger and ran at her. It was Dilwys who screamed this time and Canis who smote. He took the Roman in the neck with the side of his fist. The man dropped senseless.

Other Romans swore in suppressed fury, but their soldiers accepted, as soldiers will, the order Boadicea had wrested from Septimus. Their officer marched them out, avoiding looking at Septimus, who was beyond anything but a desire to suck in air. Sick with disgust he shuddered, gestured feebly towards the door and let his servants bring him to his feet and help him out. The rest of the Romans trod on his heels, then there were only the Iceni left. Boadicea's clear voice carried to every ear.

"It has been a little hazardous, but they have not robbed us yet."

She rose and led Cea and Dilwys from the hall. The Iceni bent their heads in homage, in admiration.

Some time later, in composure, she summoned her advisers.

"Is it to be war, then?" she asked.

"If," said Cacchus, speaking first because of the infallibility of his beard, "if you give up your wealth, your heritage and even your house, and if we give up all that we have too, then it is not war. It is only dishonour. Are there any who can accept this, who do not mind begging sustenance from Romans such as these?"

"It will not end there," said Cophistus, "they will beggar us and then enslave us, take us into their houses to sweep their dirt or into their legions to fight their battles. I would rather fight them, for I have seen what I would agreeably die for, I have seen Queen Boadicea turn Septimus Cato into palsied putty."

"It was bravely done, and saved the life of Canis," smiled Cywmryn.

"It was only his tongue," said Boadicea. Canis was silent, abstracted.

"Aye, my lady," said Cywmryn, "but if a man like Canis loses his tongue he is as good as dead."

"True, he has a tongue that makes him run ahead when he should be walking behind," said Cacchus, "but he used it well enough today."

"He ran ahead of Septimus Cato indeed," said Lygulf, who was apt to blow on the beard of Cacchus, "and that thieving rascal did not know how to catch him up."

"As our problems are so light," said Boadicea in fine sarcasm, "let us also talk about how trees grow leaf and bees gather honey. What, after all, is Caesar's threat compared with the pleasure we have in our own voices?"

Cacchus said ponderously, "Let us first consider whether the Romans will wait for their Imperial Governor to return and offer arbitration."

"Never," said Cywmryn. "Septimus Cato has blood in his eye now and will attempt enforcement. Let him. We will be ready this time for his jackals."

"Aye," said several, but Canis said nothing, and

Boadicea looked at him a little impatiently.

"Why are you so dumb?" she asked. "Have they taken your tongue, after all?"

"No, my lady," he said and smiled at her. "I thank you for my tongue." She brushed that aside with a gesture. "It is certain," he said, "that the Romans know we are for argument. They also know we can raise a spear or two. That will not worry them, for they think our strength is only here. But it is in the whole nation. It is the nation we must rouse and it is warriors from every tribe we must assemble if we are to fight a war. But it cannot be done today or even tomorrow."

"If you cannot fight today or tomorrow," said Cywmryn, "I can and will."

"And I," said another man, and others supported Cywmryn's bold aggressiveness.

"Do not blow the horns of war until you can command the battle," said Canis. "First, every tribal chief or prince must be told that Rome intends to disinherit the queen and make beggars of us all. Most will march on Venta Icenorum with every warrior they have then. Until they come we must argue peaceably with Romans."

"Do you mean that if they so command me, I must leave my house?" asked Boadicea.

"Even that," said Canis. "Why provoke them by pointing a few hundred weapons at them when, with patience, we can show them thousands? Suetonius Paullinus himself would elect to parley with you if you had an army at your back, for a bitter and bloody war would cost Nero as much gold as he could have by peaceful means. Moreover, the preferred policy of Rome is to absorb client-kingdoms without strife."

"Why, Canis," she said, brilliant with delight and approval "who can deny argument like this? I cannot. Nor, surely, can anyone else here."

If they could not deny, some could mutter, and they did. But Cacchus, stroking his beard said, "Canis

speaks my own thoughts in that although he advises
caution he does not discount the necessity of ultimate
defiance. Aye, the Romans will have to come to terms
with us and that bandy-legged lackey will have to eat his
own tongue.''

''Perhaps,'' said Cywmryn, ''but I still say we should
smite before we are smitten.''

''There are not enough men of the warrior class in the
city,'' said Canis, ''and not enough weapons. I have had
stock taken. The Romans have already anticipated an
uprising here by strengthening their garrison. Let us
follow their example, but less loudly, less con-
spicuously. When we can open the gates and bring in no
more than two thousand armed warriors we shall have
sufficient strength to parley with. When we can bring in
thirty thousand we shall be able to do more than
parley.''

''Thirty thousand?'' said Boadicea.

''Canis,'' said Cywmryn, ''you have the speech of a
man afraid to die.''

''Thirty thousand?'' said Boadicea again.

''Cywmryn,'' said Canis, ''I do not want to die to no
purpose. If it comes to war with Rome it will not be
enough to free our land alone. They will come at us
again and again. Romans do not willingly cry quits. We
must do more than defeat them here, we must sweep
them into the sea, disgorge them from all Britain.''

Cywmryn shrugged. The Queen fixed Canis with a
compelling eye.

''Thirty thousand?'' she said for the third time.
''How come you by that precise number?''

''By this way, my lady,'' he said and told her how
with the help of others messages had been despatched to
every tribe. Every chief and prince had been advised of
the possible disinheritance of the queen so that he might
make ready in the event of possibility becoming fact.
Each had also been asked to state how many warriors
the queen could command if it came to war. So far the

count had reached thirty thousand.

Boadicea, seated, advanced one sandalled foot so that her fine-boned ankle thrust honey-brown from beneath her robe, and leaned forward to smile sweetly and dangerously.

"Why, this was commendable, Canis. But," very softly, "why was I not told? What else have you done and kept me ignorant of?"

"Indeed, nothing, my lady," said Canis, his brown face disarming in its sobriety, "except that I did, as captain of your city, order every weapon in the kingdom to be unearthed—"

"Captain of my city? This was an appointment which, at your own request, I did not confirm."

"My lady?" He seemed mildly surprised, then said, "This slipped my mind. To be frank—"

"Frank? Oh, the gods," said Boadicea.

"To be frank," said Canis, "until today there was always hope, I thought, and this hope I could not take from you by telling you I was certain Caesar would take everything from you. So I went about the matter of advising the tribes and assessing their warriors without troubling you, for you already had trouble enough. Today, as soon as Septimus Cato had gone with that pain in his belly, I despatched news to the chiefs and princes that possibility had indeed become fact. I asked them, in your name, to be ready to march on Icenorum as soon as possible."

"Canis," said Lygulf, "you are a man of forethought and action."

"Silence!" Boadicea turned on Lygulf. "Is an unconfirmed captain above me?"

"If he is unconfirmed, why is he here in council?" asked Cacchus.

"Will you raise that old bone again?" she said stormily. "We are here to chew on other things. Aye, on the fact that this upstart has usurped my authority, has done what he has done without consulting with me over any of it. I will have no man setting himself above me or show me I must let him think for me.''

"My lady," said Canis, "I did not want you to worry about the worst that might happen, and in acting in some secrecy I—''

"Oh, you are in fine conceit of yourself," she said bitterly, "and I will not excuse you for it, I will not." She turned from him to listen to her council in argument and counter-argument. They analysed pros and cons, ways and means, but returned always to the indisputable fact that they did need an army to back their demands for justice. In the end the queen wearily dismissed them but detained Canis. Him she regarded stonily from her chair. He was insufferably himself, and that was not the worst of it.

"Canis," she said, "I did not realise until you spoke of why you had done what you had done how much you mistrusted me."

She had struck well this time. She saw his lips come together in a hard line. His eyes flickered.

"I have never known you so mistaken, my lady."

"I am not mistaken," she said. "You kept me in ignorance because you do not trust me. But what you did was well done, so do not let your mistrust keep you from similar endeavours on my behalf. I will not detain you longer. You may go."

For a moment the cold hardness of his expression and the icy grey of his eyes numbed her. She had never seen him look at her like that. But he said nothing, only bent his knee to her and went. He did not see how she trembled and bit her lip. As he reached the door she called to him, her voice strangely unsteady.

"Canis, stay."

He turned. She was out of her chair. She came swiftly, flowing in her robe. She strove with her pride and pride yielded.

"Canis, oh I beg you, do not mistrust me. Whether I am queen or not, never mistrust me." She was flushed and in soft appeal, a warm, magical woman. He shook his head. He smiled.

"You are my queen." His voice was firm, resonant. "I would trust you if the rest of the world was in darkness." Mist came to her blue eyes. He took her hand, lifted it to his lips. He said, "I am going to old Wolf, my father."

She stiffened. "Going? To your father? Indeed you are not. I will never permit it. You are my chiefest captain, you would not dare to leave my house."

"Only for a while," he said and explained. His father's tribe dwelt north of the city and was nearer than all others. He would go this evening and return tomorrow evening, bringing with him every warrior prepared to come. His father, Callupus, would understand the urgency of the matter, for it was possible that Septimus Cato would attempt to enforce the decree without delay. This was not to say his father's warriors would contest the enforcement, only deter the Romans from committing abuses. They would count considerably in persuading Septimus to proceed with discretion. And within a few days other tribes would have sent what warriors they could.

"But you need not go yourself, Canis," said Boadicea, "send another, send Cophistus. He is swift and intelligent."

"It is my own father. He will not deny me a single warrior. We must have them here and I must be sure of getting them here, a thousand and more."

She was wholly feminine now, soft and bewitching in her anxiety. She would let him go because in her perceptiveness, perhaps, she recognised that in Canis she had the one man who might outwit and even outfight Rome. Except that it was more than that. But she was the queen and could not, would not, beg from a man that which he did not first offer.

"I will be back," he said, "by no later than tomorrow evening. Your gods keep you in peace and security until then at least.''

When he had gone Boadicea put her back against the door, leaning on it.

"I swear, Wolfhead," she whispered to the deserted chamber, "I swear you had better return or I will have you brought back in chains and keep you in chains. You will not leave my house again, whether you love me or not.''

* * *

At the close of the day, when the wind and rain had sped eastwards to the sea and the sun was a red-gold ball in the west, Canis walked with Princess Cea on the rampart above the escarpment. They could see the glint of Roman helmets as soldiers patrolled the city. Cea, in Celtic superstition, thought to read an ominous portent because the glint was red.

"It is as if fire and more than fire is to sweep our land, Canis. Oh, just a few days ago I was so happy.''

"Today has had its turn, Princess. Tomorrow you will be happy again.''

"Why do you call me princess when I have always been Cea to you? Canis, you will stay with us, you will not leave us?''

"I am too old to take up more wandering.''

"That is not the right answer," she said. "You were meant to say you could not leave us because you love us. I would die if you did go.''

Perhaps because he sensed that events would place him in no ordinary position, and that this might be the last day for many days when Iceni men and women could freely give each other love, he took her hand and smiled down into her lustrous eyes.

"Not so long ago you were a fair child," he said, "and now you are a maid as fair as the first flower of spring.''

Cea, deeply pink, said breathlessly, "I cannot be

more fair than other maids or you would surely not be able to resist a bold urge to kiss me."

"Ah, but I am twice your age," he said lightly, "and therefore, like all men of thin blood and ancient bones, can resist all that young men cannot."

Cea, being a true princess despite her sweetness, stamped her foot.

"That is a sly twist," she said imperiously, "and I can play some of my own. You call me Princess. Therefore, as that, I might command you to kiss me."

"Might you? Would you?"

"Aye, I would." Then she was in confusion. "But I would not. Would I? Oh, only if you wished it as much as I did. I wish it beyond anything."

He felt tender, compassionate. He thought of Rome, of possible war. It was unlikely that he himself would survive such a war. He could not do anything to mortify her and only an insensitive man would deny her some happiness now. He kissed her and Cea melted in his arms.

As a happy child she had loved him, as an adolescent she had kept him in her heart, as a maid she yearned for his return, and as a woman, born so in this moment, she loved him for all time. Her slim strong arms encircled his neck, she gave him kiss for kiss in impulsive delight. Then she threw back her auburn head and laughed in joy.

"Oh, Canis, I have kissed no man before now, but however many women you have kissed you shall kiss no others, only me."

"Cea," he began, but in her bliss she could not be prevented from leaping into more.

"Do not foolishly say I am too young and you too old," she breathed, "for I will not listen. You will speak for me, beg my hand from the queen my mother?"

"The queen will wish for you a man more royal than a chieftain's son, Cea."

"But you are the son of Callupus, a prince of the

North," protested Cea, "and I will not wed any man but you, I will not. Canis, if you do not speak for me, if you do not wish to, what is to happen to me?"

Unable to hurt or shame her, he said gently, "I will speak for you, Cea, but not yet, not while the queen is so beset. We will wait for a better day."

She was happy enough with that.

"Oh, do you not recall you were promised in secret to me even when I was a child? I did not forget that, now it obtains again. Canis, I did not know how sweet it was to kiss. Do you think we might again?"

She was the loveliest and warmest of maids, and daughter of her mother.

"I cannot resist again, after all," said Canis, and if she saw only his smile and not the clouds in his eyes, it was because she looked only for a reflection of her own happiness. She held to him for a moment, for her knees were treacherously weak. Then when he told her he had to go, to make his way to his father and for what reason, a different weakness took hold of her.

"Oh, I know what this means," she whispered, "and I know I must be as strong as you, but you are so dear to me that if you were slain I should be lifeless too. Oh, carry my caution with you—but see, if it comes to the worst, I will bear my own spear and we will fight Romans together. Do not shake your head, for I can bear a spear and will."

"You are too precious to your house and to me to do that," he said, "although when the gods can show me Romans able to stand undefeated against the warrior maids of Britain in such a cause as this, then they will show me invincibles. Now, sweet one, I must go. Let the night and the day keep you in quiet peace."

"I love you dearly, dearly," whispered Cea and wept as he left her. She stayed there for a while until the fire of the sinking sun had gone from the land and the kingdom lay shrouded in strange half-light.

6

DUSK WAS SOFT over the land as Canis slipped from
Venta Icenorum to secure his father's help and his
father's warriors. He followed in the steps of the
messenger sent to alert old Wolf to the immediacy of the
queen's need. Canis did not doubt that because of
previous warnings hidden weapons were being unearthed, sharpened and polished throughout the
kingdom. Boadicea was no mere figurehead. She commanded awe and induced affection. Every tribe gave her
loyalty and paid all dues. Now she needed their armed
warriors.

Years ago the Roman commander, Publius Ostorius
Scapula, had ordered disarmament of Britons in all occupied and client kingdoms. But he neglected to set up
machinery adequate to properly enforce the order.
Disarmament in the Iceni kingdom existed only on the
surface. Nearly every man and woman could lay their
hands on a weapon or two somewhere. Perhaps the
Romans would not have been unduly worried at
knowing this. The Britons generally were regarded by
Caesar's soldiers as an undisciplined people, with no
real skill in the art of waging war. Individually they
could be courageous, their handling of chariots incomparable, but collectively in the eyes of Romans they
were an ineffective rabble.

The night passed with the city in uneasy, fitful sleep.
But Septimus Cato did not retire until late. For hours he
had been unable to set aside his venom. He dwelt vin-
dictively on how he would repay Boadicea for what she
had done to him. Then he turned to business of a different kind. Muddy of soul, corrupted by self-
indulgence and petty power, he considered personal

87

gain a natural perquisite of his office. Catus Decianus had instructed him to enforce Caesar's decree concerning dispossession of Boadicea and confiscation of Iceni land, property and wealth. Septimus did not properly know if it was Caesar's decree or not. Catus Decianus had said it was, however. So it must be.

Septimus, with the aid of his steward Dixtus, made calculations and worked out the permitted percentage. Nero would receive the lion's share, Catus Decianus would obviously grow fat, but no one would go entirely unrewarded. It would begin in the morning. Appropriation and confiscation. It would be carried on throughout the kingdom. It would include the pleasure of reducing and punishing that accursed widow.

His work done, Septimus gave orders to his servants and to the commander of the Roman garrison. They were to be ready at daybreak. Only then did he retire to his couch, where the thick, slow tide of hatred rolled over him once more and he gave himself up not to sleep but to vengeance.

Not long after daybreak the servants of the fiscal procurator, backed by troops, commenced their work. They went out and raped the helpless city.

A boy called Cwentus and his sister Cyllwa suffered.

Bundled with their father from their house, to the door of which a soldier was hammering the seal of Caesar, they ran to Dixtus the steward. They knew him well and Cwentus was known to Romans—he had joined with them in their sport, their activities.

"This cannot be," he cried, "I am a friend to Rome and so are my father and sister. There is some terrible mistake here, Dixtus."

"There is no mistake, yours is one of the properties decreed to Caesar," said Dixtus uncaringly, inscribing the act on his tablet.

"How can this be?" begged Cyllwa. "We have done nothing to offend Caesar and my father is blind. Is he not to live within the only walls he knows?"

"This is your father's misfortune," said Dixtus, "or do you expect Caesar to appear and lead him by the hand?"

"This cannot be," cried Cwentus again. He was pale and trembling, no more than a youth.

"Cannot?" Dixtus spoke haughtily. "It is."

"Then," said Cyllwa, seeing only ruin and slavery in front of them, "then I say that Caesar is no Caesar, but a thief and an offence in the eyes of all true men."

Dixtus raised his staff and smote her. She staggered and fell. Townsfolk being herded into the streets by soldiers spat in the direction of Dixtus and were beaten themselves by the troops. The pale April morning was a cold, thin cruelty.

"Insolent whore," shouted Dixtus, "if you thought this day hard for you in the beginning, you will find you have made it doubly hard now."

Cwentus, eyes horrified as he saw his bruised sister come dizzily to her knees, turned on Dixtus.

"Monster," he whispered and leapt at the steward. But two soldiers pinned him and laughed at him as he vainly sought to break free. Cyllwa, still dazed from the blow, uttered a cry and ran blindly at the soldiers. Dixtus interposed with his staff, thrusting it brutally into her stomach, and Cyllwa, mouthing agonised gasps, went reeling back into the arms of other soldiers.

"Take her for your sport," said Dixtus, "for though it is Caesar she has insulted I doubt he has the time or fancy for such ninny wenches himself."

They jerked Cyllwa's robe and shift from her shoulders. Cyllwa, round breasts agleam, screamed. They laughed at the pretty baggage, picked her up and carried her into a nearby house. Her blind father, hearing the nature of her screams, turned white and dropped senseless. Cwentus tore himself free and ran frenziedly to help his screaming sister. He was thrown aside by soldiers and kicked to the ground. He rose, a redness in his eyes, flung himself at one man and staggered him with a wild fist. The soldier did what the law entitled him to do. He drew his sword and effortlessly despatched Cwentus.

Not long after, Cyllwa found a merciful dagger to hand and stabbed herself to death.

In a brutal charade of might and pomp, which intoxicated the perpetrators as the morning wore on, the Romans heaped every kind of terror and indignity on the Britons of Venta Icenorum. Men and women who found weapons with which to resist the plunderers were slain out of hand. The Romans had had more than enough of playing the part of uninvited guests, more than enough of hearing Iceni demand the rights of an unconquered people.

Septimus Cato, with servants and troops, came to the palace. To depose Boadicea. On her account he had not closed his eyes all night, he had lain sleepless, waiting for the morning. He permitted himself a smile as he approached the palace and his tongue ran over his anaemic lips.

Many Romans, including minor officials and whole families, followed Septimus. The spectacle of an arrogant widow receiving her just dues was not to be missed. There were only two troubled Romans, one a veteran called Tybus, the other Julian. Lydia was there, her green eyes alight, her smile secretive, her dark beauty marred by the sickness that ate into her soul. She looked everywhere in search of one man, Canis the Briton.

Lydia savoured the coming events. Almost she could be heard purring.

At the entrance to the large courtyard of the palace the Romans were halted by an officer of the queen's guard, six warriors at his back. Septimus gestured and his soldiers advanced with precision and purpose, led by a centurion.

"I smell the makings of a commotion," said the Iceni officer in grim mockery. "Or do you come in peace?"

"We come for the widow," said the centurion.

The seven Iceni barred the way with spears and swords. Boadicea had not commanded her guard to keep Romans out, but neither had she told them to let the dogs in. The Iceni officer did not like the look of them. Therefore he would not let them in.

"Iceni knave," said the centurion, regarding the point of a sword that threatened him, "do you know that is a dire offence?" The odds were impossible but Boadicea's guards resisted so fiercely that it became a bloodier affray than the Romans had expected. But they were at the studded doors eventually, which for once were closed and barred. They were battered until they broke open and hung askew.

"Boadicea, where are you, hag?" they shouted. Two servants appeared, protesting. The Romans hacked them down, and the entrance to the hall itself was suddenly full of armoured soldiers with their heavy feet in blood. "Boadicea! Show yourself! Caesar has a score to settle with you!"

There was little need to bellow for her. She was there, standing before her throne. With her were her elders and the rest of her bodyguard, including Cophistus and Cywmryn. There were also other men and women of the court and household, all silent and in fear for the queen. They were aware of what was happening in the city. Boadicea had resisted all pleas to set up a militant defence. All aggression must come from Romans. She knew seven of her guard lay dead outside and that two of her servants had been cut down at her doors.

She was pale but composed. She was dressed in a girdled blue robe, fastened at one shoulder by a Celtic brooch of gold inlaid with stones. Her tawny hair was richly bright but her blue eyes were like frozen sapphires as she surveyed the Roman soldiers. They moved towards her but halted as she spoke.

"What need was there for murder?" Her voice was clear but bitter. "I did not think, since I have received no declaration of war from Rome, that the soldiers of Caesar would enter my house over the bodies of my servants.''

They laughed at the airs she gave herself. Septimus appeared, stepping mincingly over the bodies, and the blood. He lifted his pale, muddy eyes to her.

Boadicea's smile was cold, wintry, chilling.

''You have come to dispossess me, Septimus,'' she said.

''I have come for that and for you yourself, madam,'' he said, ''I have come to put the mark of Caesar's anger on your unholy, insolent body.''

From the courtyard came the sound of dull, heavy hammering.

''I have a captain,'' said Boadicea, tall and fearless, ''whose name is Canis. He has travelled far, even to Rome itself. I have heard from him that Caesar in anger has been known to crucify people, that in a land of dark bearded men Caesar even crucified one they called King. Will he now crucify a queen?''

The Roman let his thick hate consume him as he said, ''I have not come to crucify you, widow, but to have you scourged. You are no queen and do not merit more than a knotted whip. You will be scourged like any common miscreant.''

A groan of mingled fury and agony came from the Iceni and a quiver shook Boadicea. Her eyes blazed and some said afterwards that to see her at this moment was to see all that was terrifying in a proud queen. Every violent emotion ran nakedly over her face, then receded to leave her deathly pale.

''This you would not dare,'' she whispered.

''Take her,'' said Septimus to his soldiers. They stepped forward. The Iceni swarmed to protect her, whipping out daggers. Boadicea shook her head.

''My friends,'' she said quietly, ''put them away. There is to be no more blood spilt in my house. Cophistus, I command you.''

Cywmryn buried his face in his hands, Cacchus wept into his beard. Cophistus looked at the face of every soldier and etched them into his memory. Septimus languidly addressed the queen's court.

"Iceni, you have drawn weapons in my presence and this is an offence which the law says is punishable by death. But I will overlook the capital aspect and for the moment you are free to witness this woman being publicly scourged. However, when this has been done, you will all be taken from this house, some to serve in the legions of Rome, others to be sold as slaves. Be in gratitude that your lives are spared. Centurion, bring the widow."

Boadicea would have gone quietly with the soldiers but because of her calmness and pride they had to lay hands on her. It was too much for one Iceni man. He ran at the soldiers with his dagger. They slew him in front of his queen.

"Oh, foolish man," she whispered, "it was bravely attempted but needless. No more," she said to the other Iceni. "Let be, let be."

The soldiers hurried her. Outside the Romans laughed and jeered as she was thrust forward to the whipping post which had been set up in the centre of the courtyard. The place was crowded and the Iceni who followed the queen were squeezed behind a barrier of soldiers. Julian, who had been waiting unhappily, saw the look on the queen's face and went angrily forward to confront Septimus.

"Procurator," he said, "think twice, think a third time before you do this outrageous thing. This is not Caèsar's will, this is not Roman justice, this is your own act. If you scourge Queen Boadicea it will shame and hurt her, but the greater shame and greater hurt will be ours, and the Britons will forgive neither you nor the rest of us. Therefore, think well on it and do not do it."

Septimus regarded Julian irritably.

"Who are you to speak so boldly out of turn?" he asked.

"You know me well enough. My father is Marcus Osirus of Calleva Atrebatum, and he would tell you, as I do, that this is not the way the Imperial Governor would wish you to deal with Queen Boadicea and her people. There is outrage here and in the city. I protest it."

"You are here, not in Calleva Atrebatum," said Septimus, "and here you are no more than a fly in the wind. You are not of this municipality, so get back to your doghole and speak no more insolence to your betters."

He turned his back on Julian and gestured to the soldiers around Boadicea. Julian said to himself, "Toad, serpent, infirmity, may Jupiter strike you dumb, blind and palsied." He looked on in bitter shame as they bound Boadicea's wrists high up to the crosspiece on the solid stake so that her supple body was stretched tautly. Onlookers were thrust back by troops to make way for Bilbo the scourger, a vast and mountainous man of blubber and muscle, yet neat and light on tiny feet. His black beady eyes twinkled jovially, like bright buttons of merriment in the fleshy moon of his face. Stripped to the waist, his round arms and round torso gleamed in the sunlight. He seemed like a huge pumpkin the colour of shining yellow cheese. In his hand he held the knotted whip.

Septimus, standing forward, gave a nod. Bilbo, quick and active for all his size, put out a hand and ripped the queen's robe as if it were no more than a cobweb over her back. The assembled Romans sighed, the Iceni groaned. A woman cried out as Bilbo ripped the queen's shift. Robe and shift, sundered, drooped around her waist as the queen's straight back showed naked. She made no sound but a rigidity took hold of her body, and she pressed her bare curving breasts to the post to hide herself from the eyes of men. Her lips moved but no one heard her whispered words.

"Oh, Canis, I did not wish you to go but glad I am that you are not here to see me so ill-used."

The jeering laughter of Julian's own people shamed and nauseated him. His own sister was among those who jeered. In reckless impulse he strode beyond Septimus to take up a stand between Bilbo and the queen. He looked in loathing at the mountain of a man.

"If you are a Roman or a servant of Rome, will you willingly do this vile thing?" he asked.

Bilbo, his little eyes twinkling, his nimble feet dancing, said with a smile, "Aye, I will, that is what I am paid for."

"Then you must strike me down first, fat corruption, and even then should you lay so much as one lash on the queen's back you will enjoy delight in it only for as long as the gods take time to draw back in horror, then reach to destroy you."

"Julian, you are mad!" Lydia shouted at her brother in panic. "Noble Septimus, pay him no heed, he has gone from his mind."

Septimus had not moved. The interruption only extended the pleasurable prelude to the satisfying act. He smiled his dead smile, nodded his head and saw his soldiers drag Julian away. Julian was beaten into the dust. A savage blow caught his head and stunned him. Lydia, furious with him, let him lie. She did not want to provoke Septimus, who had favoured her by letting her purchase a certain Iceni man.

Bilbo, in his affability, was without impatience. Only when there was silence would he commence his work. There must be nothing that would distract attention from his artistry and skill. And so he waited until the silence was absolute. He passed the knotted whip through his hand when the absolute was a breathless expectancy, he viewed the naked back of the Iceni queen with a sweetly fat smile, and with graceful dexterity he struck.

With hissing malice the first lash whipped across the

white back to mark it with a pitted red line. Romans smiled and Iceni winced to see Boadicea shiver, but no cry came from her lips, which were tightly compressed over her teeth, and she did no more than turn her face into the couch of her uplifted arms.

Bilbo struck again. The knotted scourge whistled and bit. She made no sound. Bilbo was not a common exponent of the whip, he was a virtuoso. He scourged Boadicea with twenty finely-biting lashes, laying each one on with an interval of sadistic deliberation between all. The pitted marks criss-crossed with geometrical exactitude. Her blood ran to seep into the ripped folds of the clothing around her waist, but throughout she uttered no cry, only a shuddering gasp as Bilbo struck the final lash. The heartbroken Iceni wept and amid their tears called silently on their gods to avenge this their bitterest day. Not in all their history, in all their mystic legends, had so great a humiliation, so unspeakable an outrage, been inflicted on their royal house. Fire kindled in their hearts and leapt into flames of hatred.

When her bound wrists were cut free Boadicea, eyes blinded from pain and torment, momentarily sagged. Romans waited to see her collapse in the dust. But she lifted her head and drew herself upright, crossing numbed arms over her naked breasts. Fighting the monstrous pain that ravaged her back, she turned her pale face on Septimus Cato. There was the dull glow of pleasure in his eyes. She spoke slowly and with effort, her bottom lip stained with blood where her teeth had bitten, but each word was clear and distinct.

"You have done your bravest deed, Roman, for which Caesar in his nobility will surely commend you."

Septimus smiled sourly. She was arrogant yet. Well, she would change her tune by the end of the day. All she would own then would be twenty stripes.

"Widow," he said, "you will leave your house by noon tomorrow, for your house and all it contains now belong to Caesar."

If she heard him through her thick red mist of pain she gave no sign. She turned slowly from him and he saw her again the bloody lines wetly criss-crossing her back. Her sundered robe and shift, stained red at the waist, drooped. She spoke quietly to Romans pressing forward to mock her.

"Is there no one here who will cover me? I should like to return in modesty to my house."

It was Bilbo who danced close to her on his twinkling feet.

"Have I not covered you with a sufficiency already, widow?" he chuckled, his merriment like the sound of warm, bubbling oil. Romans wanting to cap his quip began to toss trifles at Boadicea's feet.

"There," cried one of these clowns, "bend your royal knees, O Queen of nothing, and you will find all you need to cover your sore hide and stick most prettily to it."

At this the man Tybus contrived to jab his knee so violently into the jester's stomach that he fell shrieking and writhing to the ground, where he was heedlessly trampled by people pushing to get closer to Boadicea. But his wit had made even Septimus smile and Lydia, wanting to keep his favour, stepped forward.

She spat on Boadicea.

"You are viler than a harlot!" It was Julian's voice at her ear. He thrust her aside to stand before the queen, buffeting back those who sought to hem her in. He was almost of her height and he looked directly into her pale, drawn face and her eyes. Their blueness was clouded by mists of intense pain, but he could not see either defeat or broken spirit. For her part she perceived a great shame and a warm compassion in him. His jaw was bruised, his temple bloody and his uniform dusty. His red cloak he held in his hands.

"I am a Roman, Queen Boadicea," he said, "and am in bitterness and shame for what has been done to you. If you would let me put my cloak around you it would not ease your hurt but it would cover you. I beg you, take my cloak.''

Despite all her pain, all her humiliation, Boadicea smiled.

''It is not a man's birthright that makes him a man, it is his own self,'' she said. ''I heard you speak bravely in my defence. So put your cloak about me, friend.''

He would never forget the mists that were in her blue eyes. He put his cloak over her shoulders and drew it carefully and gently around her, wincing to see the whiteness that pinched her mouth as the cloth touched her wounds.

''Go in courage and dignity, Queen Boadicea,'' he said, ''you have lost nothing this day but we have lost all.'' She moved forward and he held back jeerers who sought to impede her. Tybus drew a deep breath, then tossed away all favours he might have had from Septimus Cato by coming forward to help Julian keep a passage clear for her. Julian could have wept to see how stiffly and painfully she moved, but she held her head high and went in quiet disregard of those who mocked her. As she reached the battered doors of her palace the jeers grew louder. Unable to stomach more of his country-men's malice Julian went bitterly from the place.

At her doors Boadicea became surrounded by her weeping women.

''Widow.'' Septimus was like something unnameable in his sadistic reluctance to cease tormenting her. ''Did you hear my command that you will leave this house?''

''I heard you, Roman.'' She answered through stiff lips. ''I will remember all your commands and forget none of your deeds.''

She walked into her palace. Septimus turned to his servants and soldiers, dull blood suffusing his eyes. He had had her scourged for all to see but in some way his worms still felt cheated, hungry. ''We will come at the insufferable whore in other ways,'' he said, and his men poured into the palace. The Iceni turned on them. Cophistus and Cywmryn, unable any longer to do nothing, led the queen's bodyguard against the de-spoilers while the queen herself was taken to her apart-ments by her women.

The fighting in the hall was savage. Five Iceni were slaughtered, several Romans were hacked to death, but the outcome was inevitable. Surviving Iceni, including Cophistus and Cywmryn, were battered senseless and dragged away.

Septimus, the palace won for him, entered the hall. One of his servants was roughly bundling a young woman out. She shook off his grip, her lithe body fierce with hatred. The lackey struck her. She fell, twisted, came up on one knee and spat at him. Septimus, seeing the curving suppleness outlined by her robe, passed a wet tongue over his lips.

"Where are the brats of the widow?" he asked.

"There are no brats in this house," she said.

Septimus smiled. "Take this creature to my house," he said to the servant, "where we shall find out if she is worth a small price or a large one. Woman," he said to her, "it is not an offence to be spirited but it is very much an offence to spit on those who are the servants of Caesar."

She screamed as she was dragged to her feet. They muffled her mouth, her face and her head with her own robe and shift so that her nakedness was a shame to her; then she was carried out writhing and frantic over a man's shoulders.

"This house," said Septimus to his followers, "is to be sacked from corner to corner. Convey all you find to the municipal storehouse with inventory of every item. Remove everything—no, leave the widow and her brats their couches. No one need say they spent their last night here in complete discomfort. If any of the women give you trouble you may do what you wish with them."

The sack of the palace began. Septimus went with two servants and four soldiers to find the quarters of the princesses. Their door was guarded by two Iceni, the only men now left in the palace. The queen, throughout

the morning, had confined Cea and Dilwys to their
apartments, hoping to keep them out of all trouble and
ignorant of the worst of it. The two Iceni warriors
defended the door bravely. One died, the other was
beaten unconscious. The door was broken open and
Septimus walked in. The princesses were there, pale-
faced because of so much commotion, and two women
with them. The women put themselves courageously
between Septimus and the princesses. He had the
soldiers drag them away, kicking and screaming.

Muddy eyes speculative between lazy lids, he looked
at the first-born of Boadicea. A quiver shook Cea and
intuitive apprehension froze the blood of Dilwys.

"This house belongs to Caesar," said Septimus, his
slow blood heating at Cea's warm loveliness, "and you
and everything else here are his property."

"Until Caesar himself says this I will not believe it,"
said Cea bravely, "and if he should say it then he is
without generosity, tenderness or mercy."

"Who are you to defame him so, daughter of an
arrogant, barbarian whore?" said Septimus, and
because of the way he looked at her a sudden horrifying
awareness of the unbearable took hold of Cea.

"What have you done with the queen my mother?"
she cried in anguish.

"She has been scourged," said Septimus, and felt a
little content.

Dilwys uttered a moaning cry and fell across her
couch.

"Oh, sweet dear mother," she gasped, "oh, Roman,
you are wicked and cruel beyond forgiveness."

"I would, if I were you," whispered pale, stricken
Cea to Septimus, "hide from all the gods for all time."

"Take that doleful songstress where you will," said
Septimus to the soldiers, gesturing towards the moaning
Dilwys, "for she is miserably out of tune. Teach her a
livelier song. Leave the other to my tuition."

Dilwys, swooning, was plucked from her couch and
borne away to another chamber. Cea was left frenzied

in the clutches of Septimus who, seeing the wild despair on her face, smiled in the way of a man capable of all perversions but soullessly incapable of any love. His smile put every kind of fear on her. She screamed, then sank her teeth into his arm. Septimus hated any kind of pain. Livid, he struck her. She fought him, her whole being in horror, her mind an anguished cry for Canis, and Septimus found her supple, desperate strength more than a match for his own. He shouted for his servants, the door opened and they hastened to him.

"Strip this harlot," he spat, "and bind her wrists behind her."

They seized her. She screamed again, she fought again. Her fierce nails scored the men, her knees jabbed and her feet kicked, but they threw her onto her couch and they stripped her. She writhed naked, suffused and in unbearable shame. They bound her wrists and left her to Septimus Cato.

He came out after a while. His muddy face was flushed but his worms were appeased. "Enjoy her if you wish," he said to his waiting servants.

Grinning, the two servants went in.

Septimus stood outside the door for a while, fingering scratches on his face. He heard Dilwys screaming somewhere but Cea did not scream at all.

In her apartments Boadicea, kneeling before her couch so that her crying women could attend to her wounded back, heard the screaming herself. It rose in frightening anguish above the sounds of Romans sacking the palace, and the pain of her back was nothing then compared with her fear.

"Go quickly," she said, "find out what is being done, who is screaming and why. Go. Go!"

Her drawn face was haggard as two women ran from the room. She tried to rise, but the other women could not bear to see the agony this caused her and made her stay still. On the floor a bronze bowl full of vinegar wine was cloudy with blood as they dipped the linen they were using to cleanse her scourged flesh. A helmeted soldier strode unceremoniously in. He stared at the kneeling queen whose arms were over her breasts and whose back showed her wet red scars.

"Aye," he said in an everyday way, "you are sore, widow, but will be sorer tomorrow. It's always like that with the knotted whip. Make way."

He stalked through the women and around them, gathering up furs and skins and coverlets, tossing them to a second soldier at the door. Boadicea said nothing, she was waiting in terrible torment for the two women to return. The other women looked with fierce hatred at the soldiers, who took all there was to take, all but the bloody clouts of linen and the queen's couch. They even emptied the bronze bowl of its contents and took that too, as well as pots containing salves.

"See, I plead with you," said one of the women, "leave us the salves."

"Let him take them," whispered Boadicea. She was shivering. The man took them, departed with them. One of the women returned. Her robe was torn, there was a smear of blood on her arm, a bruise on her face, and she reeled against the wall, as white as the chalk of the southern cliffs. She whimpered and hid her eyes, unable to look at the queen. Boadicea, fighting her physical agony, rose to her feet, the darkness of worse agony closing her in.

"Speak, Gwynda," she breathed.

"My lady, I cannot," sobbed Gwynda, groping to find support for mind and body, "I cannot. Oh, that you should see a day as evil as this—and they have taken Blangwen who went with me—they have taken her also—"

"Also?" Boadicea's voice was drowning in her sea of anguished pain.

"My lady—the Princess Cea—sweet Dilwys—oh, my lady."

That was how Boadicea of the Iceni came to know there was nothing Roman she did not hate with an intensity that would never die.

7

CANIS, IMPELLED BY a consuming urgency, returned at
dusk with a thousand warrior men and women from his
father's tribe, others to follow as soon as ready. Leaving
them deployed in the forest beyond the river, he came to
the city with only his father, Callupus the Wolf.
Callupus, lord of the northern forests, was a man of
iron grey, not as tall as Canis but with an oak-like
strength.

On their journey they had met scattered Iceni who
had managed to escape the city, and the tale each one
told turned Canis paler than snow which had lain long
on frozen ground, and made the light in his father's eyes
leap into flame.

Canis had expected dispossession in all its greedy,
grasping ungenerosity, he had expected the queen and
her daughters to be beggared and humbled, but he had
not expected outrage. Some blood had been bound to
flow, some death to strike, and there had always been
the risk that Boadicea herself might in her spirited
majesty have provoked Septimus into dangerous malice.
But never had he thought of the unthinkable.

Boadicea. Scourged. The princesses violated.

Ice encased him and his blood took on the bitterness
of water that sluiced iron.

He and his father did not attempt to enter through the
city gates. They climbed the escarpment and the wall of
the palace, by a way Canis knew, avoiding patrolling
soldiers. They reached the courtyard, and a Roman sen-
tinel, emerging from the gloom, alertly challenged
them.

"Who are you who walk like free Iceni this night?"
he asked.

"Death," said Canis in a harsh, terrible voice, and smote the Roman in the mouth with his fist. The man's teeth and jaw broke, his mouth gushed blood. He fell. Callupus drew his sword and swiftly gutted him. They entered the brooding palace where carnage, grim and eerie in the feeble light of a single, flickering torch, stared at them with fixed, grinning eyes. Bodies of slain Iceni, including a woman, were still where they had fallen.

There was no sound, no life, only a palace sacked, plundered and outraged.

Canis ran swiftly, silently, his father close behind him. He ran to Boadicea. Only her couch had been left her and this was bare of coverings. One small oil lamp lightened the darkness of horror and pain. She sat on the couch, looking blindly before her, her cheekbones thrusting against frozen flesh, her eyes like clouded blue stones. Her rent garments hung loosely around her tortured body. Two women, old, with wild grey hair and bony faces, spared because they had nothing at all that Caesar wanted, attended her.

She was not aware of him at first, he came so silently. Then she saw him and a shuddering sigh broke. He knew her agony was far more of the mind than body, her look was of inconsolable anguish, her eyes enormous in her white face.

"My lady, my sweet lady," he whispered, "was I so accursed as to leave you on this your most unbearable day?"

"Canis," she said in pain, "you are here at last? I have waited so long, even longer than before, and I know now that the length of a single day may outspan even the length of seven years."

"I am here and I am not alone." He did not know how to comfort her, he did not think she could be comforted at this moment. "My lady, I have heard what they did and all they did, and I have also heard how you endured. I am in bitterness that I left you on a day when all your gods, even Andrasta, forsook you. Are you so much in hurt?"

"Canis." She put her hand on his shoulder, he was down on one knee before her. "Canis, lift your head so that I may look at you, for I am haunted by the unspeakable face of Rome." He raised his head and she saw in his tormented harshness a reflection of her own bitter pain. "Oh, glad I am that you are back," she whispered.

"I am back and I am done with words. We have all done with words. I will say no more of what the dogs have done to you and yours. There is work to do and I will do it, I swear. Give me leave to act this night. My father is here, and he is not alone."

She turned her eyes to the dark doorway and saw the shadowy figure of sorrowing, brooding Callupus.

"So there you are, old Wolf," she said, "you have never come empty-handed to my house and years ago you gave me your son. What do you bring me now?"

Callupus came forward and showed her the brightness of his cleansed sword.

"This and my spear, Boadicea. This and a thousand more." He spoke fiercely, for the tears of a strong man had him cruelly by the throat. "And with them the love and fealty of all my people who are yours before they are mine." He knelt and brought her hand to his forehead, then his lips. "We will show the dogs the right way of men. That is my oath and promise, rest you on it."

"In an hour we will bring in our thousand," said Canis.

"Lord," quavered one of the old women, "there are twice a thousand armed Romans in this city tonight."

"Then twice a thousand will die," said Canis. He could not speak of Cea and Dilwys, not yet. He looked at Boadicea. Her arms encompassed her body to compress the area of pain and he saw the whiteness constant around her mouth. "Is the hurt so much? Let me see what has been done to ease you.''

She shivered and even that gave her pain. Canis had a sudden realisation of why it was that she sat so still. The plundered room, except for the lamp and the couch, contained nothing. Nothing. ''What has been done for you? Let me see,'' he insisted.

''Canis, do not look,'' she said wildly, for she could not bear to show him the savage ugliness Bilbo had put on her flesh. But Canis went to the other side of the couch and came behind her. She bowed her head and held the sorry robe and shift to her breasts as he parted the ripped garments at her back. And Canis, a scholar and a warrior, a man of facile mind and hard muscle, who had seen much of suffering, caught his breath at the hideous mark of Caesar on her back.

He turned fiercely on the old women.

''Is this all you have done for the queen? You have only washed her wounds with vinegar wine and left even the odour of that on her. Where are the salves, the clean linen? Go, hags, find what is necessary or I will have your heads.''

''Lord, there is nought but what you see here,'' wailed one of them, ''the Romans took all, even the linen, even the salves.''

''They speak true,'' whispered Boadicea.

''I will fetch a surgeon while there is still time,'' said Canis. ''We might have waited for Grud, my father's physician, but not now. You have suffered enough.''

''I will stay, I will look to her,'' said Callupus, ''but be quick.''

''Canis, do not go,'' said Boadicea faintly. ''I will bear this, you need not go. You may be taken and then you will never return.''

''I shall return.'' He touched the hair that fell about her face and shoulders. It was the lightest of caresses. ''I am in bitter blame for so much. Was there no one among them to speak for you?''

''One man,'' she said, ''who was the only man of

them all. One Julian, who spoke for me and gave me his cloak. If you find him, spare him.''

"I know Julian and I thank you for his name," said Canis, and slipped away. He passed swiftly through the hall but was stopped before he reached the sagging doors by a dark-haired young woman. She came out of the shadows and in the light of the flickering torch her green eyes shone like a cat's.

"I have waited all day for you, barbarian," she said sibilantly and mockingly. "I have looked everywhere for you and have found you at last. Diana is all, she has delivered you into my hands as I knew she would."

It was Lydia, her face within its frame of unbound black hair bright with triumph and greedy with possession. But she saw him as she had not seen him before. His face was hard, hewn out of bitter ice, his eyes greyly chilling.

"I am here to take you, barbarian. You are my property. Yesterday you threatened Septimus Cato and defied Caesar, for which offences you were today condemned to be sold as a slave. It has since been inscribed by the fiscal procurator that you, one Canis of Venta Icenorum, belong to Lydia, daughter of Marcus Osirus. I have paid gold for you."

Two armed lictors, broad and muscular, stepped grinning from the shadows, where Lydia had had them wait. Confidently they advanced to take the Briton. He went to meet them, meekly extending long arms to be bound. But as they came within reach he caught each man by the throat and squeezed. Agony attacked their windpipes, their breath turned back and their tongues protruded. Then Canis brought them violently together and the sound of head breaking against head was like the crack of a whip in the vast, empty hall. He let them drop to the ground.

Lydia stared incredulous. They had been brawny men, picked by herself to take the Briton, and now they lay broken.

"But for your generous brother, one light in the blackness of Rome," said Canis in an icy voice, "I would put you into a cold embrace with them. Thank him for your life."

He disappeared noiselessly. Lydia stared into the darkness that swallowed him. Then, as the torch flung its eerie light and shadow over the still, broken lictors, a strange terror clamped itself about her. She fled into the night, searching hysterically for her servant and litter. In the morning, she would go to Septimus Cato in the morning and tell him all. But in the morning. The night was a terror to her and she could not get to Julian too soon.

Canis reached the house of a Roman surgeon, broke silently into the villa and came upon the man and his wife at supper.

Canis planted a dagger at the throat of the woman, and the surgeon, because of the fear on the face of his petrified wife, did as the Briton commanded him, gathering up salves and soft linen and making his way to the palace. Canis followed at his heels, in company with the terrified woman. They were not accosted or questioned. The Romans were celebrating in their homes, not in the dark streets.

"To whom do you bring us?" The surgeon spoke at last as they entered the desecrated palace.

"To a queen," said Canis and brought them to Boadicea, whose stiff mouth softened in relief to see him. He instructed the surgeon to do all he could, then said to her, "I must go again."

A spasm twisted her lips, it was not of pain.

"You go, you come, you go and you go again," she said. "Are you ever here?"

"Go I must for a further while," he said and went abruptly. He made his way to Cea and Dilwys. Despite pressures he could not disregard them any longer. He did not know how he was going to speak to them.

They too had for company only women grey,

wrinkled and undesirable. The princesses' chambers were in black darkness, the door broken down. One weeping crone, eyes used to the lack of light, saw him, knew him and wept afresh.

"Lord," she whispered desolately, "you are the only Iceni man in this unhappy house, but man you are and they cannot look at you, not even in this blackness."

"This I know, old mother," he said gently, "but let me speak to them."

"Canis." A grasping, broken voice reached from a dark, tragic couch. He went to her. She had no drapes to cover her, only her torn robe, and she lay palely. On the other couch Dilwys was inert, her body horrified, her faith in sweet life shattered.

"Light no light," gasped Cea, "do not look at me—oh, Canis, they have made a harlot of me."

"They have not." He put aside bitterness to speak with firm tenderness. "You are still as sweet as you have always been, as if the sun alone has kissed you."

"Canis, it can never again be as it was between us."

"I neither believe that nor accept it. You are yourself, which is unchangeable."

"I shall lie always with a Roman on me, I shall never be clean again. And I must talk no more of love. Canis, will you do me the sweetest mercy, oh will you? Will you kill me?"

"I will not." His voice was gentle but uncompromising.

"I would have done it myself, but I waited for you."

"I could never kill those I love, least of all so sweet a maid as you." He was in infinite compassion for her. "Do not tell me you are no longer a maid. This is not true. You were grievously hurt, as Dilwys was too, but theirs is the impurity, not yours. All of them will die, Cea, this I swear."

"How might this be?" She spoke differently, in a quicker voice.

"It will be. They will not see the light of another day."

She sat up, holding her robe close around her.

"Give me your dagger, Canis, and take me with you."

He understood her but he would not place the dagger in her hand yet.

"I will return for you when I have fired a beacon, if you truly wish it," he said.

"I do," she said, "so come for me when you are ready and do not fail me. I will wait for you."

Wait. They had all waited. He alone had been absent. If he lived until his hair turned white he would never forgive himself this absence.

He left her and took from its iron cradle the torch in the hall. Outside the palace he climbed over the rampart to the corner of the north wall. There he put the torch within the friendly lee of a stone buttress so that its flicker was hidden from the city. He could neither see nor hear any sentries, yet caution fingered every nerve. He gathered dry grass and twigs, piled them and with the torch ignited the heap. It burst into flame. He let it flare for no longer than a minute, then stamped it out.

He returned to Boadicea. The surgeon and his wife had done what they could to ease the worst of her pain, her wounds had been liberally salved and covered. Some of the whiteness had gone from her mouth and Canis felt his heart wrenched by the smile she gave him. His father stood silently suffering for her, his eyes never leaving the surgeon and his wife.

"It is a little better now?" said Canis.

"No more than discomfort," said Boadicea. She knew where he had been. "You have seen Cea and Dilwys? I went to them and stayed so long trying to do what I could, but in the end I could bear no more and they begged only to be left to themselves. Oh, Canis, my sweet children."

"My lady, they will smile again. They can be shamed by such men, they cannot be corrupted."

The surgeon looked uncomfortable, his wife unhappy. The surgeon said, "If you will let me, I will gladly do what I can for them."

"Could I bring a Roman to them?" said Canis and his voice made the woman shiver again. He turned to his father. "Look to the queen a while more, I must go and bring in your wolves."

"Gladly," said Callupus, "but I warn you, Wolfhead, do not begin the work without me. I am part of it and will not be denied. Go now."

"Aye," said Boadicea tiredly, "go, as he says, before your new habit of trying to be in two places at once provokes me to put a chain on you."

"See to her," said Canis to his father in a way that made the oaken one tug at his long moustache and wonder what sons were coming to. "See to her, get her to rest."

Boadicea drew a deep breath when Canis had gone and said, "Callupus, do you remark the conceit of your first-born? He would command his queen if he could."

He stooped, she put her hands on his shoulders and gently he helped her to rise. Her teeth clenched and despite old Wolf's care a spasm of acute pain flamed through her back. But she persisted, and with his help she lay face down on the bare couch. As Callupus straightened up, the surgeon's wife, spurred by fear and dread, ran for the door. Like a leaping old stag still king of the forest, Callupus came at her back, caught her and flung her to the floor. The surgeon, who did not understand the inhumanity of men, only how to minister to those damaged by it, went courageously to comfort her, but Callupus barred his way.

"Let her whimper, Roman," he said, "better that than to have your brains and hers dapple the queen's walls."

Boadicea lay there in her pain, her face hidden, her lips moving.

Cea—Dilwys—oh, my sweet ones.

Do not be long, Canis, do not be long.

8

PRINCESS CEA, the dagger of Canis thrust into her girdle, her torn robe fastened securely around her, went silently with him to the escarpment. There they lay to watch the dark wall. There was no sound except the night whispers of furry creatures preying on other creatures and, occasionally, the sudden agonised squeaks of sharp, cruel death. They waited, saying nothing, Cea with her hand around the hilt of the dagger, caressing it, her outraged body forgotten for the moment in the anticipation of vengeance. A warm and affectionate person, she was still as much a warrior maid as any of her kind. And not for nothing was she the daughter of Boadicea.

They waited. The stars studded the black sky with tiny diamonds of light. At last Canis, as soundless as a fox, rose to his feet.

"Wait here and do not move," he whispered and was gone into the darkness. Cea heard then what had made him move, the distant tread of a solitary sentry. There were few on patrol this night and this one considered himself miserably done by when so many of his comrades were celebrating in the barracks. He was miserably done by indeed. Death smote him when he least expected it.

The way was clear as the Iceni climbed upwards and slipped over the rampart wall. They were the strong, wiry warriors of Callupus, maids and women among them. These, in their short, belted tunics were a joyously fierce breed of fighters, with long flowing hair of red or gold, brown or tawny, born of the original Celts of Britain. They climbed silently, effortlessly.

"Are they all following, Hadwa?" asked Canis of the man who appeared first.

"All, lord," whispered Hadwa, a huge-shouldered warrior. "A thousand and more, each of us ready to do whatever is necessary. You left us when the air was foul and stinking with tales and rumours. What is the truth?"

Canis watched others springing over the wall, filling the darkness with moving shadows. They crowded the rampart but made no noise, despite the weapons they bore. Canis gave the truth to Hadwa and others, and what he gave them was relayed to the rest. The warriors of Callupus were incredulous. The queen scourged? Her daughters outraged? It could not be true.

A thousand warriors spilled around the ramparts and the dark, grassy ground adjacent the palace. Incredulity became horror, and horror turned into fury. When they could no longer repress their feelings the silence was broken by a low exhalation of breath that was like the first sigh of a mighty wind.

"Lord," said a young warrior woman called Cerdwa, eyeing the tallness of Canis against the black sky, "bring us to Romans, bring us to those who did these things."

They followed him, all of them, and he took up Cea on the way. Leaving the bulk of the warriors in the great courtyard, he took into the palace a company of fifty and enjoined them to keep it secure for the queen. In charge he placed Hadwa, quick and versatile for all his size, and Hadwa said, "Go about your other work, lord, we shall not fail you here. This is a stout place to defend, where fifty men can take off the heads of a thousand."

To Boadicea, Canis took a man called Grud, an ageless mystic with bow legs and round eyes like those of an innocent. Boadicea, resting face down on her couch, turned her head and sighed to see Canis back again. He sent the surgeon and his wife out, placing them under the supervision of Hadwa's men.

"My lady," he said, "you are in discomfort, I know, but at least you will be undisturbed. Also, here is a man called Grud."

Boadicea, restive because of her physical weakness, her back on fire, turned dark eyes on Grud. He looked innocuous rather than impressive in the dim light.

"I cannot say you are seeing your queen at her best, Grud," she said.

"There are many who would say I am, majestic one," said Grud, "and as to what they have done to you, I will lift the worst of the pain from you without too much fuss. I have a little art in such matters."

"I would commend Grud into your service, my lady," said Canis, "for I have known him all my days. He has seen me grow from babe to boy, from boy to man. He has taught me the ways of forests and waters, the meaning of men and the pain of women. He will give you remarkable service and be a boon in his own way."

She looked again at the bow-legged, round-eyed one. He was neither young nor old, yet he was both. Her eyes were smudged with pain and weariness as she said, "Is your own way as elusive as his?"

"My own way," said Grud, "will be to serve you so adroitly, O Queen, that you will not even notice me. First, you shall have a potion that will bring you to peace and hold your lids fast until daybreak."

"Well, mix your potion, then. And you, Canis, when your work is done bring me instant word of it. And then remember, there are to be no more of your comings and goings, your hopping about like a restless flea."

Involuntary, fleeting, the smile that touched the mouth of Canis was a compulsive acknowledgement of her spirit. On his way out with his father he said, "Grud, put Princess Dilwys to sleep as well, and in the gentlest way you can."

Outside they rejoined the waiting army of silent warriors.

"Canis," said old Wolf, "you shall lead us. You have the way of this city and while I have the way of command I cannot exercise it as well as I think you can tonight. I am bedevilled by so much anger that there is fire in my brain and blood in my eyes."

So Canis took command, as he would have contrived anyway. He gave orders to the old Wolf's captains. First and foremost the barracks, where the Romans had their main strength, must be invested and the garrison destroyed. Units of troops elsewhere in the city could then be easily dealt with.

"Until you are at them," he said, "make no sound above the pad of your feet. If I hear any warrior so much as whisper a war cry, I will kill him for the sake of the rest of us. Pay no attention to any call but that of the blackbird."

He gave other orders, other instructions, and then he led them into the city, Cea at his side. Still she said nothing, nor did she look at him or any other man there, only at her inner self. She touched the dagger often.

They swarmed silent indeed, swift scouting parties running ahead. They were impalpable shadows in the darkness, their blood hot, their nerves strung. Where a light peeped they skirted it unseen, like invisible death. There were no Iceni abroad, only Romans, soldiers patrolling in pairs. The invisible death whispered, smote. The patrols died by dagger, by shortened spear, by sharp sword, and given only time enough to gasp or gurgle.

The Iceni split into groups, flitting through the city like gigantic black spiders, and at the head of the largest group of seven hundred Canis reached the barracks. There his warriors spread to speedily invade the perimeter and encircle the clustered buildings. Sentries died with a merciful swiftness. Leaving any to die in loud and prolonged agony was a luxury the Iceni could not afford at the moment.

Every barrack-room was surrounded. Quietly Canis entered the first. It housed fifty men, of whom there were about forty present, lolling, whistling, gambling. Their armour was hung, their weapons racked. They looked up to see the tall, hard-faced Briton in the light of lamps, and they smiled at the boldness of a barbarian inviting himself to their sport.

"Join us," said one soldier amiably. "You have not mistaken your way, this is indeed a bawdy house and beneath our beds we hide the lustier wenches, letting them out to any with an Iceni gold crown in his purse. Only say which you prefer, long or short, full in the breast or round in the belly, and we will produce her for you."

They all laughed uproariously. Canis waited for quiet, then said, "Were you at the palace today?"

"Aye," said the amiable one, "and found royal sport among the widow's women. Have you lost your pretty wife, Iceni? If so, go find another, for the one you had will have discovered not one man better to bed with but several. She will take no more joy in you now that she has been favoured by Romans."

There was louder laughter.

"You speak like a man still warm from a bed," said Canis. His voice was quiet but his look had some of them gawping. Had he been Caesar and not a presumptuous Iceni who had in some way escaped their net, they would have thought his look spoke of death. "Are there any here who favoured the daughters of Boadicea today?"

"Aye," said a man, smiling reminiscently. "I favoured the straw-haired one." Dilwys had hair the colour of ripe corn. "Caspus here also had her in joy." He thumbed at a lolling, grinning comrade. "Why, is the sweet wench outside, then? Is she hot to be favoured again?"

They roared at this sally, which was not a bad thing under the circumstances, since men who laugh heartily in the presence of death may enter the presence of their dark gods with mirth still about them, inclining the immortals to believe they are pleasant fellows on the whole.

Canis whistled softly, like a blackbird. His father, standing unseen just outside the door, took up the whistle and relayed it. Within seconds the soundless shadows were leaping into every barrack-room. Startled Romans were still staring as hideous death struck.

In the first barrack-room the Romans gaped for brief moments, brief moments that were fatal. Too late they scrambled for their weapons. There was a gurgling, ghastly sound of Romans dying, pitching like wheat under a multitude of knives, the sound fearsomely accentuated by the unnatural silence of the Iceni, men and women warriors biting on bits of leather thrust between their teeth to help them suppress their war cries.

As terrible as the sinewy Iceni men were the long-limbed warrior maids with long tossing hair, who slew expeditiously with short stabbing spears or slim biting daggers. Romans died with astonishment glazing their eyes. Fiercest of all, because of the ecstasy with which she struck, was Cerdwa, the warrior maid who had begged Canis to bring them to Romans. A swift, beautifully supple creature, she stood apart from the others because of her lustrous black hair and wild violet eyes, and also because she struck not with spear or dagger but a hunting axe of glittering, sharpened iron. She slew one man in a trice, then smashed in the face of his comrade.

Canis took the amiable man and strangled him. He separated from death for the moment only two. These were those who had spoken of Dilwys. All others lay dead or dying within minutes, the long room cluttered with bodies and shimmering with blood. Cerdwa of the axe eyed Caspus and the other man hungrily, then came

at them. Canis thrust her roughly back. Eyes of ice encompassed her and denied her. She would have laughed
it off, for laughter and joy were her soulmates, but sudden strange heat took hold of her and she stood back to
hide her face in shadows.

"These are not for you," said Canis and her ears
tingled. "Bring Princess Cea," he ordered a warrior,
and the man went and brought the princess.

"These are for you, Cea, if you wish," said Canis, indicating the two Romans who stood ashen-faced in the
hands of warriors. "By their lust Dilwys suffered. Do
you want them?"

"Bring them," said Cea and went outside. The
warriors brought the stark-eyed Romans to her. They
were held with their backs to the wall and in the
darkness Cea drew her dagger and put them to death,
first one and then the other, and each died in agony,
their screams muffled by fierce hands.

The Roman garrison was bereft of Roman life.
Within no more time than a crow takes to peck out the
eyes of a dead sheep, every occupant had been
slaughtered, every officer, every man. By surprise, silence and fury the chief Roman strength in Venta
Icenorum had been destroyed without a single official in
the city being aware of it. Detachments elsewhere could
now be isolated, attacked and destroyed in their turn.
Romans in their villas wondered as they lay down to
sleep whether the small sounds beginning to disturb the
night were anything to do with revellers.

By the light of warm, golden lamps Septimus Cato
was reckoning with his steward Dixtus the count of the
day's gain. He was pleasantly tired but could not leave
this satisfying atmosphere of profit. When he did, part
of his own profit would await him in the person of a
shapely young woman from the palace. She would not
scratch. She was very sweetly drunk from wine his servants had forced on her.

Outside the city was full of the gliding shadows as

Canis despatched his arms of vengeance. One of the
warrior captains said to him, "We shall come at all
Romans, young and old as well. What are we to do
should we be in doubt?"

Canis, who had rejected all gods, answered, "Take
the youngest children and send them to the northern
forests, where they can make pots and pans for the
women. Take all the young women and send them to the
men of the eastern marshlands. All others you need be
in no doubt about, for all of them stood to see the queen
suffer, all of them laughed at her. Go with them, old
Wolf," he said to his father, "and command their
work, while I take Cea and twelve warriors to lift the
fiscal procurator. If you find a man called Bilbo, who
scourged the queen, bring him to me alive."

Callupus took a mass of warriors and they flowed like
a dark tide through the streets. Canis, with Cea and
twelve warriors, one of them Cerdwa, went to the house
of Septimus Cato. The guards died in the same fashion
as others before them, swiftly and cleanly, which was
not an unkindness, considering everything.

And so it was that Septimus Cato suddenly looked up
to see the long, lean figure of death, and by his side a
pale, auburn-haired girl, who also was death. Septimus
stared bemused for a moment, then because he had a
Roman's disdain for all that was not Roman he coldly
removed from his mind the image that had first entered.
He recognised both insolent intruders. They were not
death, only negligible appendages of the widow. They
were also alone and outside were his soldiers and inside
were his servants. He himself need not address these
two. He raised his dull eyes to Dixtus and Dixtus addressed Canis peremptorily.

"By all the gods," he said, taking up his master's
cudgel, "you are impudent to the point of folly. You
have entered without leave the house of the fiscal
procurator. Out with you, you long-jawed knave, and
with you take your baggage here. Deliver yourselves to

the guards or it will be the worse for you.''

Canis smiled, looking not at Dixtus but Septimus.
The pale lips of Septimus writhed and his eyes began to
glow with malice. He would have deigned to speak, after all, and viciously, but at that moment a dozen Iceni
warriors entered the room, cleaning red-stained
weapons with leather. One of them was a glossy-haired
young woman with laughing violet eyes and wild
beauty. She bore a glittering axe.

Canis smiled again, his lips drawing back so that Septimus saw his white teeth. Cea did not smile, she only
looked fixedly and burningly on the muddy pallor of
Septimus. Canis turned bleak eyes on Dixtus, then
spoke to the warriors.

''Take this Roman who has been guilty of unwise
speech in the presence of a princess of Britain,'' he said,
''take him and rip out his tongue. Then, so that we may
be spared the sight of his face as well as the sound of his
voice, give him to Cerdwa.''

In this way Canis mocked Septimus Cato at the
terrible expense of Dixtus. It put the fear of all the gods
into Dixtus, for he did not need to be told that Cerdwa
was the maid with the axe. Two warriors took him and
Cerdwa, smiling delightedly, went with them. Dixtus
screamed. He remembered a young Iceni girl who had
begged for clemency that day and he had shown her
none. The house stirred at the sound of his screams and
servants came in haste to enquire into the cause. The
Iceni pounced, the servants ran, taking refuge behind
the chair of Septimus, now pallid with fear. Outside
Dixtus screamed again. The sound died horribly to a
bubbling gurgle. A few moments later came the sound
of the axe, sharp and beautiful to the Iceni, hideous to
Septimus.

Cerdwa returned, her slim legs shamelessly agleam
below her short, belted tunic, her smile vivid and the
blade of her axe red. The steward lay outside, dying in
appalling agony.

Canis, his voice disarmingly quiet, said to Septimus, "I have heard you had much sport today, Roman."

Septimus untied his stricken tongue and drew a long breath. Sweat stood on his forehead and his skin was like glistening mud.

"If you will go now," he said, "I will overlook the sport you yourselves had this moment with my steward Dixtus. I will agree that it came about because of his own indiscretion, since he should not, of course, have said what he did say about your princess." He swallowed as he glimpsed Cea's face, but he went on as he had to go on. "But if you do not go at once I will summon all my servants and guards. Then you will wish you had departed as I advised."

"Roman," said Canis, "your teeth are rattling. And if I do not follow your advice, remember that you did not follow mine of yesterday. Roman," he continued softly, "I have heard you smiled as Bilbo scourged the queen. I have also heard you violated an innocent, one who could give no man offence, and that you countenanced a similar evil in the matter of another innocent, her sister. You are an unseeing man, Septimus, and so you shall go blind to your grave tonight."

Septimus, his sweat a clamminess, shouted in a hoarse voice for his guards and rang a tiny brass bell like a man gone mad. Canis let him shout and ring. More servants arrived, but no guards. The servants, seeing the armed warriors, fell back and joined the others behind Septimus. They pushed and bunched together. Cerdwa smiled and cleaned her axe.

"Dogs!" screamed Septimus, twisting in his chair to show his servants fearful rage. "Do you not see how I am beset? Fall on them, I say! I am reviled and threatened—what, will none of you strike in defence of your master?"

The servants might have fallen on lesser men, but they saw all too clearly the dire consequences of falling on the fierce Iceni. And work of that kind was for the guards, not for them. Where were the guards? Their absence was putting their master in palsied terror of the bitter-faced Briton and the pale, silent girl by his side.

"Roman," said Canis chillingly, "there were servants of yours who followed you in your sport. Who were they?"

Cea spoke then.

"After him," she said, pointing to Septimus, "it was this one and then that one." And she indicated two of the cowering servants, all of whom were now blocked from escape by the Iceni.

"Take all three, Princess, for all three are yours," said Canis.

But suddenly Cea laid the dagger in his hand.

"Let Cerdwa have them" she said.

"Let Cerdwa have those two," he said, "for I will take Septimus."

The two servants were in terrified alarm. Cerdwa of the axe gazed wonderingly on Canis, who had so confused her joyful blood. Cea raised her eyes and for the first time this night looked at him.

"Aye," she said quietly, "because of what he has done he is rightfully yours. So take him."

Septimus chewed frantically on his lip. Loud in his ears was the dull, heavy thumping of his heart.

"I will wait for you outside," said Cea to Canis, and he had two warriors escort her from the house. He turned again to Septimus.

"Finally, Roman," he said, "where is your servant Bilbo who scourged the queen?"

"Here, here!" The voice was like the squeak of a merry mouse as in bounded a vast and fleshy Bilbo. Clad in a white kirtle he was, for all his blubbery obesity, as nimble as ever. His little eyes beamed in his round, jovial face. "What, what," he wheezed playfully, scattering the crowded servants with a twitch of his blubber, "is my master at odds with devils? Out, rabble, out," he flapped fatly at Canis and the Iceni, "or I will break your heads all together or one by one."

"Defend me, Bilbo," cried Septimus and rose to hide himself behind the propitious mountain. "Defend me, I say!"

Cerdwa laughed like Circe, joyful to see so huge a man as Bilbo.

"Come, O fat one," she said, "let my blade be the first to kiss your belly."

"Wench," said Canis coldly, "to be hungry is excusable, to be greedy is not. These two are mine, so keep the pale one intact for me while I kill the fat one."

Septimus was mumbling and chewing. Only Bilbo seemed happy. There was no man who could best him. He was destined to go peacefully to his gods in his old age. Or so he thought.

"Try me, lean and stringy one," he invited Canis, "and I will eat you first, then I will devour the woman and her toy, then swallow all others."

He flexed his white plump fingers, danced forward on light, quick feet and reached confidently to lay a cunning hand on Canis. But Canis, well-taught by a Greek wrestler in Rome, took the hand, bent the plump fingers back and with far more cunning than Bilbo had ever known he advanced his right leg and turned the mountain upside-down. Bilbo, gasping, was aloft and neither his hands nor his feet could find purchase. And suddenly he was borne down into unbearable pain, bent backwards over the right knee of Canis, whose other knee was firm on the floor. Cerdwa watched enthralled as the Briton set the little eyes of the Roman lardbag starting from their fat bed.

A wrist of iron pressed Bilbo's fleshy throat, an arm of iron pinned his plump knees and singing torture afflicted his ears. Slowly, mercilessly, Canis applied pressure with both arms until the pink wet tongue of the agonised scourger protruded from his wheezing mouth. His beady eyes bulged and his fat chin pointed upwards.

"Bilbo," said Canis, "this day, without pity and

without mercy, you flogged a queen. Here you only obeyed the orders of your corrupt master, so you shall not die for that alone. You shall die because you were in pleasure while she was in pain. You are unfit to live amongst men, you are unfit to live at all. You are a fat-bellied river rat and shall die in such agony that you will squeak like one.''

With terrifying deliberation, Canis began to break the scourger's back. Bilbo's convex obesity arched like a fat bow. With the Briton's knee in the small of his back, with iron pressure on his throat and knees, the Roman's screams of agony were so squeezed that they did indeed emerge from his gaping pink mouth like the squeaks of a tortured rat. His tiny eyes popped from their sockets like brightly suffused marbles seeking frantic escape from horror.

"Bilbo," whispered Canis from between his teeth, "now you shall feel the agony of all men and women in torment, now you shall remember Boadicea and all others whose pain has given you joy."

And he thrust sharply downwards with both arms. Bilbo screamed. Not all his vast covering of flesh could protect his spine from this. It snapped. His screams became whistling expulsions of gasping sound, which turned into bubbling agony. Canis let the ponderous heap of quivering flesh slide to the floor. The bubbles whistled and gurgled.

Septimus mouthed and shook, Canis rose to his feet.

"Take them," he said to his warriors. He indicated the servants. "But only Cerdwa is to have the two whom Princess Cēa pointed out. And I will deal with Septimus Cato."

The servants, howling, broke and ran. But there was nowhere to run to and death struck them like violent rain striking helpless grain. Cerdwa took the two who had outraged Cea and each man screamed for a long time.

Then Septimus Cato, foaming and hysterical, was

hustled out into the darkness of his own garden. There by the light of a torch they made him mark out his own grave, the sweat glistening on his grey face, the anticipation of fearful death a screaming madness in his mind. When he had finished, the Iceni quickly dug the pit. Then Canis gouged out those eyes of wet mud, bound the fiscal procurator and threw him into the grave. The warriors covered him with loose earth and they left him. Only the worms knew how long Septimus Cato, blind and mad and demented, took to die.

The Iceni brought from the house a young woman drugged with wine, covering her nakedness with drapes. Then the only thing that stirred in that place of death was a weighty mass of tormented flesh which emitted bubbles and gurgles.

Sometimes it emitted a thin, shrill scream.

A man with a broken back and all that flesh does not always die immediately.

The city was full of noise and light now, the torches of hunting warriors flickering and dancing. There was something else Canis had to do. It concerned the only Roman who had spoken in defence of Boadicea. But first there was Cea. He told his twelve warriors to escort her safely back to the palace.

"I will stay with you, lord," said Cerdwa, "for you are a great warrior and one for Cerdwa to stand with against Caesar himself."

"Caesar would eat us," said Canis, "so go with the others."

"They are enough," said Cerdwa, "I will hunt Romans with you, lord."

"Go with the others," he said and Cerdwa, crestfallen, drew back. Canis turned to Cea, silent in the darkness. "Cea, you will find the palace warmer and better now. You will also find a man called Grud there. He has a special understanding of maids and women. Do not be too sensitive, let him do what he can for you."

Cea said nothing. He watched her disappear with the
warriors, then went to the stables of the fiscal
procurator, slapped one horse into wakefulness and
mounted the snorting, resentful animal. He headed it in
the direction of a certain villa outside the city, galloping
past scenes of carnage. The warriors of old Wolf were
taking bloody vengeance. Here and there flames leapt
from Roman property, scorching the night. Outside the
south gate Canis caught up with advancing Iceni. They
turned fiercely to see who rode a black horse at them. In
the light of their torches they saw him, and he saw them,
fierce and exuberant.

He left them shouting their war cries as they battered
at gates and doors of villas. He rode furiously and
found the household of Pablus Vitellius in fleeing turmoil. Sobbing, panic-stricken women were running
down the dark road to the south. A man, desperate to
kill before he was killed himself, came at the dismounted Briton with a frenzied sword. Canis kicked
him in the stomach, then slew him with his dagger. He
went swiftly into the villa and saw Julian and Lydia,
Lydia bearing a casket.

"Go," he said to Julian, "and quickly. Take the
horse outside before someone else does."

"Since Pablus and his family have taken my
animals," said Julian, "I am—"

"Go," said Canis harshly, and left the villa. They
followed him, Lydia's eyes full of liquid hate. Julian,
about to mount, took Canis by the arm.

"You are mending the wrong done to your queen,"
he said, "but it is going to be a bitter business, both for
you and for us."

"Go," said Canis again, "or it will end for you
now."

The Iceni were closer, speeding from villa to villa, and
the night was on fire. Julian wasted no more time. He
mounted and turned to help Lydia mount behind him.

She delayed a compulsive second to fling a taunting farewell at the Briton.

"I will return and claim you yet, slave!" Then she was up and they were away, galloping into the darkness and heading south.

*   *   *

More than twice a thousand armed Romans, as Canis had promised, died that night. And with them, those who had mocked, those who had tormented, usurped, robbed and violated, were slain by people who had sworn to avenge their bitterest day.

Romans were slain in the streets, in their houses and in their gardens, young and old, healthy and ailing, men, women and adolescents. Many of them died bravely, for from the time the first stone was laid on the Seven Hills, no nation had called them cowards. There was Tybus. He had been as surprised as any at the speed with which the Iceni had struck. He had guessed they would be in fury at the scourging of Boadicea but thought it would take them days to mount any real attack. He remembered a trench his servants had recently dug in the garden, and in this trench he put his wife and two children and lightly covered them with the cut turf. And that was all he could do for them.

He ran from his house, alone, to lead the foraging Iceni in the dance they loved well this night. They saw him, and their singing cries chilled his blood, but he ran on, leading them away from his house and his family until he could run no more. He turned, faced them and drew his sword. He was a hardy veteran, he hoped only for a clean death. With a torch and spear a warrior leapt at him. Tybus smashed the torch with his sword and the warrior fell back from the flying sparks. But a laughing-eyed young woman with wild black hair came at him with an axe, slipping his thrust with cat-like grace, and

so Tybus, who respected Boadicea and would have been
a friend to the Iceni, died sharply and cleanly at the
hands of Cerdwa.

They did not find his wife and children, however,
who with a few other survivors, fled southwards in the
night.

It was a long night. It took time and patience to locate
hidden Romans and some were not found until dawn
broke. But when all was finally done, when at last Canis
and his warriors had made the city secure for the queen,
he returned to the palace. The pale light of the chill,
misty morning put a grey, ghostly look on the streets
and he walked weary and bitter, his mind full of distorted and violent images of death, his tunic stained
with blood, his hands rustier than neglected iron.
Around the palace groups of warriors were encamped
and resting. At the doors guards stepped aside to make
way for him.

His smile was grim as he saw the oak doors were re-
hinged. And as he entered the hall that too was as he
had always known it. His other orders had been carried
out. Everything was back in place and there was even
the familiar, hospitable fire crackling and burning. All
that the Romans had taken had been taken back.

His father came to look keenly at the grey, bitter
hardness of his son.

"Wolfhead," he said, "ease yourself, it has all been
done and done well."

"It is only the beginning," said Canis.

"Still, it is a good beginning," said Callupus.

Cophistus arrived, greeting Canis as a hero when
Canis knew he had only been an instrument of grim,
cruel carnage. He was in no mood to listen to praise and
interrupted brusquely to ask if the queen still slept.
Cophistus said she was awake and spirited.

"Go to her, then," said Canis, "and tell her that all
for the moment is done."

"I had rather you went yourself," said Cophistus,

"and who has more right to carry this news than you?"

"I will go to her when I look and smell cleaner," said Canis, "she has had her fill of blood and ugliness for the moment. But, Cophistus, does she still endure?"

"Aye, with a will. She is up, she is robed. After yesterday, who could endure better than that?" And with a smile Cophistus went to the queen. Despite the sleep Grud's potion had given her, she was still pale and drawn. But she was bathed and refreshed, and Grud had applied his own herbal salves to her wounds. She sat on her couch in a fine new robe of white. Her women were there, restored to her, and although some were dark-eyed because of certain things they would not easily forget, they were in content at being with the queen again.

She greeted Cophistus without preamble.

"Well, do you bring me joy or trouble, Cophistus?"

"I bring you a message from Canis, my lady, to say that all for the moment is done."

Her long slim fingers curled, her nails bit into her palms. She was a little fierce in her satisfaction, then suddenly frowned.

"I am grateful, Cophistus, to you and all who helped in this work," she said, "but where is Canis? Why did he not bring me this, his own message, himself?"

Cophistus bent his head to think of the best answer and said, "My lady—"

"Cophistus!" Boadicea was on her feet, heedless of the wrenching pain this brought to her back. "Cophistus, do you think to bring me evil tidings cloaked by good? Do you think to sop me with your soft voice and soft words? What has happened to Canis?"

"My lady," protested Cophistus, flustered by her passion, "I myself am only here—"

"Speak, fool, speak of Canis, not of yourself," she hissed. "Why did he not come as I commanded him to? Will you tell me he is dead? Will you dare tell me that? If so, I will build a pyre higher than my house for his body, and I will build it of Romans who slew him and my Iceni captains who let them!''

Cophistus, bemused by her intensity, could only stare. The queen, for all the pain of her ravaged flesh, was much herself again.

"Indeed, my lady," Cophistus managed to stammer, "it is only that Canis thought himself too foul with blood and dirt to come yet, and so—"

"Ah," The storm subsided. She drew a deep breath. She even smiled, but not in a way to make Cophistus feel easier. "Cophistus," she said softly, "bring me Canis, this captain who thinks I cannot look on blood and dirt. Bring him now. Now."

Ruefully Cophistus delivered her command to Canis who, having emptied a cup of mead, was about to bathe himself. Without comment he went to the queen. She had dismissed her women and was on her feet, preferring in her temper to fight her pain rather than nurse it. But it put marks like blue dust around her eyes.

"So," she said, "you have come at last from your guzzling."

"My lady," he said, "why are you not resting?"

"I have rested, and you are not here to question me. All has been done, has it? Why did you not come to tell me so? Did I not command you to?"

"When all was done I thought you still asleep."

"Empty words," she said, "for if you could send Cophistus to wake me why not yourself? And since you saw Cophistus, did he not tell you I was awake?"

Canis frankly marvelled at her fine temper. She regarded him coldly. She did not want him to be other than he was, but what he was frequently piqued her. She would not let weak-minded concern for his night's travail mitigate her anger. The anger of any proud queen is not to be undermined by her tenderness.

"Forgive me," he said, "I was at fault, I know. But now I am in concern, you should not be on your feet. Sit, at least."

"I will when I will and not before, I will not be commanded!"

"Only prevailed upon. Sit, my lady." He took her hands, he felt them grip his as he seated her and knew that even this movement gave her hurt. "My lady, I tell you that all you suffered has left me bitter at my own inadequacy. But do you think in our night's work there were any of us who did not have you always in their thoughts? Despite what was done to you and yours you are still in pride and majesty, but we who let them do what they did are in bitter blame, myself more than any. That is why I did not come myself, why I sent Cophistus instead. I could look into your eyes in last night's darkness, I could not this morning."

Her anger ran from her.

"Canis, always you are ungovernable in the way you disarm me," she whispered, "but there is no blame on you, there is no blame on any of you, only on Romans."

"It was I who counselled passive argument, I who left you armed only with this argument, I who left you on your most grievous day, and I am in great blame."

She saw what she would not see before, his exhaustion, his bitterness.

"You are only in great foolishness," she said, "and passive or not, we could not have fought them without murder being done to most of us. You knew we could not and you were right. Canis, I have known you in various moods, but not in one like this. Foolishness is for others, it is never for you. See, we will speak no more about what you did not do, since it is what you did do that saved my city. And I am told you destroyed the man who scourged me and did away with Septimus Cato, and that you also put down the Roman garrison before they knew you had set foot on their ground."

"This was done by your warriors."

"This was done by you," she insisted, "and you shall put aside your gloomy pride and accept your queen's gratitude, do you hear?'' He smiled. ''That is better,'' she said. ''Now you shall rest.'' She called her women. They came and Grud appeared too. ''See to Canis,'' she said to the women, ''give him all he needs and wash him clean of Roman blood. It has been a long night for all, but longer for him. He is to sleep on the couch in my inner room. Watch him, or he will sneak away. It is a habit of his. Today he is not to leave the palace except by my leave. When he is rested there is much to discuss and he is to be here.''

''I myself am tending the queen,'' said Grud, ''and her stripes will worry her less in a few days if, like you, she heeds commands not to indulge in too many comings and goings.''

Boadicea turned eyes of outrage on Grud. His ageless countenance was innocent.

''Say you so and to me, you saucy villain!''

''Aye, I am so, my lady,'' said Grud, ''but you are in my care and must attend to my advice.''

''Great gods,'' cried Boadicea, ''am I to come to you and say I would go to my daughters and may I?''

''Aye, you must,'' said Grud placidly. ''You may look in on the princesses now, but only look. I have given them a mixture which will make them sleep all day. When you have seen them I will give you the same, for you need to sleep again too.''

9

THE DAY WAS a grimly busy one. The Iceni cleansed the city of blood and bodies, making great funeral pyres of the dead. They decapitated many of the slaughtered Romans to offer the skewered heads to Andrasta, their goddess of victory. They had drunk their fill of heady mead and Roman wine and sweated out their excesses by restoring the queen's city to proud order. Soon enough there would be more fighting to do. They had no illusions about Roman reaction.

Canis despatched new messengers, who took word of uncompromising war to the tribes and an urgent request for them to gather at Venta Icenorum. He also sent word of events to the Trinovantes, neighbours and allies of the Iceni. The Trinovantes had long been in a mood of hostility towards Rome.

With the aid of Grud's potion, vile-tasting though it was, Boadicea slept all through the day. Canis slept until the afternoon, then went to confer with his father and others. There was much to do. The tribes had to be welded into a single mighty unit. War with Rome could only mean life or death and Boadicea needed an army, not a collection of independently operating tribes. The council talked all afternoon and into the evening, but Canis doubted whether the most loquacious oratory could be more effective than the bluntest sword, providing the latter could be used skilfully. So he left the debate and went out into the city to inspect the guarded points and to talk to the captains of his tribe.

Boadicea awoke refreshed and in less pain. She summoned Cacchus, conferred with him and then asked for Canis to be called. When told he had gone into the city she flew into temper. Grud, in attendance, remarked in an innocent aside that a patient quick to be irked was slow to be cured, where-upon Boadicea turned on him and said that a bow-legged quack with an insolent tongue could be shorn of it for all his medicine.

Canis, returning, was taken to the queen. She was towering in her temper. Her women bore the marks of tears. Their foolishness in letting Canis bemuse them and slip them had brought Boadicea's wrath down on them.

"Oh, there is much in you to try all my patience," she said. "Did I not say you were to remain here, that you were to go nowhere today without my leave?"

"You did, my lady, but I thought this was yesterday."

"You villain, this was today!"

"Today?" No one could have said he did not look surprised.

"However," he went on pleasantly, as if he were only there to help a passing cloud on its way, "with so many hours in but one critical turn of the sun; and with sleep taken by day instead of by night, it is not surprising we are in confusion about where yesterday ended and today began or how one night turned into two."

The tear-marked faces of the women began to show sly smiles behind the queen's back. She only thought what a conceit he was in to imagine he could bemuse her as he did others.

"I am not in confusion, jester," she said, "nor are you. Today is yesterday, is it? Aye, and dogs fly and birds bark."

He liked that. He liked the indomitability of her spirit. He smiled. It softened his hardness. Boadicea compressed her lips, but she could not resist his smile or his artfulness. She smiled too. Her women sighed with relief.

"Well, you are more forgivable when you are smiling than when you are scowling," she said. "But I will put some kind of a chain on you. I will think about it.

Return to me when I call you.''

When he had gone she put her mind to the problem. She would curb him in some way, she would. Unless she did he would rise above her, command her, flout her. She must at least remain his equal, she must. That was more important than queenship.

"Grud," she said, "mix me your potion that imprisons the most obdurate mind and strongest will. Mix it so that it is even viler than that which I took this morning."

Grud did this and brought it to her.

"It will be as effective as you requested," he said, "and is so vile that you must pinch your nose, O Queen, when you swallow it."

"It is not for me, fool," she said, "I do not have an obdurate mind."

She had Canis brought back.

"Because your restlessness will do you no good," she said, "you shall for this night at least lie incapable of all movement. Give him the potion, Grud." She watched as Canis took the silver cup containing a liquid dark and thick. "Drink," she said, "it is my command."

He drank. His grimace at the vileness of the liquid made Boadicea smile a little. Well, that would curb his roving for the night. It did. Not long after he was in a deep, restful sleep, eased of all thoughts of bitter war. Boadicea, knowing he would awake revitalised in the morning, ready to campaign clear-headedly on her behalf, was content. There was no telling, as she remarked to Grud, what the restless dog would get up to if he were not chained in some way. To which Grud replied, innocently enough, that the dog which runs ahead of the pack is the first to scent the trap.

"Or the first to get his nose caught," said Boadicea.

*   *   *

A week passed during which time the warriors of the

nations converged on the queen's city to fight for her in her war against Rome. Thousands of them camped around the city. To the palace came chiefs and princes, fierce, shrewd and articulate men. They spent many hours designing the foundations of victory. The first necessity was how to knit the separate tribes into an indivisible host under one commander. This in itself was the very stuff of enjoyable argument, especially as it embraced the problem of deciding which man was better equipped than all others to command the host under the auspices of Boadicea. The queen herself contributed nothing to this particular point. She knew, in any case, that much of their argument was only wordiness dear to their hearts, and in the end they would leave the decision to her. They would accept the man she chose because she was the queen, although this did not mean they would unconditionally submit to his orders or agree with his battle tactics. In this or that battle he might be less convincing in strategy than any of them. The Celts were not men who lacked belief in themselves.

Canis, busy with more practical matters, spent little time in the palace. Boadicea did not cavil at his absences now, for she knew what he was about, and the necessity. Cea and Dilwys remained in pathetic seclusion in their quarters. Too sensitive to appear in public for fear of parading their shame, they kept to themselves and saw no one except their mother.

For the better part of each day Canis was to be seen on the broad plain close to the river, either educating the wild, fiery charioteers in the specific arts of harassing a Roman front or instructing infantry and cavalry in the more necessitous arts of fighting not for themselves but the whole. He had served with Roman legions and knew their classical methods of defence, their ability to present an unbreakable front of short swords and clamped shields. He sighed at the misplaced confidence the Iceni had in boisterous individualism. They grew up believing only in loud, pell-mell attack. How, they asked, could any battle be won by standing still?

The time available to turn thousands of temperamental Celts into a disciplined army was miserably
inadequate, and Canis was dealing not only with men
but with women too. If the male warriors were reckless
and impulsive, the women, especially the younger ones,
were exuberant and headstrong. And even more in-
dividualistic. To form a cohesive unit of a score was difficult enough, to bring four thousand of them into line
was to take on the father of all headaches.

The warrior maids would go joyfully enough into battle for Boadicea and expend themselves in careless rapture. Obedience to the command of their captains they
would forget as soon as battle was joined. The Iceni
were a nation whose women had equal rights with men,
who fought side by side with their men in battle. They
could love even more joyously than they could fight,
they were wild and colourful, but they did not like
discipline. Only because Canis was distinctive and
because they had heard how he slew Bilbo the scourger
did they heed him at all. Not until he put aside patience
and became ferocious or mocking did they begin to love
him. It was one thing to have him show a warrior maid
how to make a Roman uncover his guard, it was another
thing altogether to have him pick her up and toss her
into the river, or to have him seize her by her hair and
say bitingly, "Who named you a warrior maid, Glynis?
You have a spear, aye, but you could use it better
stirring a cooking-pot."

This delighted them, won them to his ways and purpose. His authority as the queen's chief captain was not
inconsiderable, but it gave him no real rights of command. A warrior's first obedience was to the tribal
chief, and each chief was answerable only to the queen.
Canis, therefore, had to impose his will and his purpose
in his own way.

One warrior maid had no reservations about his
authority. This was Cerdwa. More untamed than any of

them she nevertheless wooed his favours. She followed him wherever he went and gave him his due as the son of old Wolf by calling him lord. She had seen him break the back of a mountain and accordingly he was to her the mightiest of warriors. And his voice set her ears tingling. She listened captivated to him as, in biting irony, he addressed those slow in the head, and she never hesitated to give him velvet whispers of encouragment.

"You are right, lord, the only place for this fool is in the river. Will I toss him into the reeds for you?"

Or, "This one is so deaf to simple reason, lord, that she will understand nothing unless she first takes a buffet. I will smite her gladly for you."

It irked her at times that he seemed to hear so little of all she said. But he did respond once. He said, "Put out your tongue, Cerdwa." Because he intrigued her so much she put it out. He examined it, then said, "I have seen tongues twice as long that still could not chatter half as much."

Cerdwa flashed her violet eyes at him, then smiled and said, "You are in jest of me, lord. See, do I not have the sweetest tongue?"

And impudently she put it out again. If he was amused he did not show it. He was a bitterly hard man, yet full of subtleties, and sometimes when he smiled himself out of his grimness Cerdwa felt strange weakness take hold of her.

The week passed. Roman Britain, previously troubled only by minor uprisings and the Druids, took on the great quiet preceding a storm. The Iceni tribes were massed to march with the queen, and Boadicea had to weigh advantages against disadvantages. One great advantage was that Suetonius Paullinus, the governor, was still with his army in Mona. One formidable disadvantage was that Iceni armour and weapons were extremely inferior to Roman. And there was one unknown factor. The quality of the Iceni army as an integrated fighting whole.

News of the Iceni action in Venta Icenorum would have reached Roman towns by now, would have reached Paullinus himself. But Canis did not know whether Paullinus would halt his campaign against the Druids, despite the anger he would feel on receipt of the news. Paullinus might consider Quintus Petillius Cerialis, in command of the Ninth Legion at Lindum, well able to deal with any Iceni revolt. As yet, however, Canis had received no word from any of his agents of Roman troop movements anywhere.

His own personal burden lay in the fact that in avenging Boadicea and her daughters he had committed his queen to make war on every Roman in Britain. True, the Iceni warriors had a burning desire to plunge into battle, and it was harder for him each day to keep their restlessness in check and to feed them the stodgy stuff that for all its dullness could lift them above mere brave endeavour.

Boadicea, aware of his problems, spoke to him at the end of the ninth day. Her back was still tender but far less painful. Grud was a competent healer.

"Canis, are you weary of your task of making my many thousands fight as one?" She was soft of voice. She had forgiven him for his irritating comings and goings, for looking back she was not quite certain whether she had been too much the sensitive queen and too little the understanding woman.

"My lady, if I am some small education to your warriors they are a greater education to me. They have already taught me that you will have an army able to lift the head of Paullinus himself."

"Is this by virtue of your efforts?" she asked.

He shook his head at her smiling attempt to put him in conceit of himself.

"They will do it in spite of my efforts," he said,

"they will do it because they love you."

She was quiet for a while at that, then said, "Canis, if you are not weary, I am. While you have been coercing my warriors I have been coercing my princes. To action. If they fight as well as they debate, they will be fearsome. I am for rest. Go to your own and may Andrasta kiss your right hand this night. No, do not look sad, for like all my counsellors I do not doubt our victory. Rome has become evil and cannot prevail against you and me and mine. Sleep with a sure mind, Canis, as I shall."

He bent his knee and took her hand. It lingered for a moment against his forehead and touched the coppery thickness of his hair.

10

HE SLEPT PEACEFULLY and awoke to the soft sun of morning. He lay there, reflective, the light mellowing the oak beams. He turned his head as the door opened and saw Boadicea. She wore a patterned tunic and a grey, hard-wearing cloak. The cloak was not fastened and in the belt of her tunic he glimpsed the jewelled leather sheath and the bright hilt of her dagger. Her hair was bound by clasps of shining bronze that matched its burnished gleam. He sat up. His chest and shoulders were bare and there was a hardness about his brown flesh that even a queen might commend in a man.

"I have slept like an old one," he said, "while you are up and dressed for battle. Do you, despite your wounds, go with us, my lady?"

"Go with you?" Her smile was warm, her blue eyes bright. "I lead you. Who else should be at the head of my army?"

"Aye, who else?" he agreed. Today they would march, then. It was her decision.

"Your knowing Grud, although something of an old woman," she said, "has taken all the fire from my back, and what little soreness I still feel is a good reminder of the intolerance of Rome. Canis, you have done much for me, you must do even more from now on."

"What I have done," he said sombrely, "has led you into war against Rome."

"This war was inevitable," she insisted. "It was begun by them, by Septimus Cato, in return for which you destroyed him."

He could not see it as she did. An act of vengeance that resulted in the Iceni having to fight the might of Rome could not be construed as one of his wiser impulses, even by the most generous friend.

"My lady, perhaps what I did I could have done differently."

"Canis, do not do this," she said imperiously.

"This?"

"Argue with me, quarrel with me, for you are always attempting to, and I am always foolish enough to let you."

"My lady?" he said in some astonishment.

"Aye, despite your looks it is so," she said. She hesitated, then put aside her pride and went on, "I will not be stopped from saying what I must say. Canis, will you pardon your queen for her fault of anger?"

"Pardon you?" He was in dismay. "My lady, at least consider whether any man could be in such conceit of himself as to dare to say he had pardoned his queen."

"Yet I have been at fault," she said. "But that night was a bitter one for both of us, and for all the warriors you brought I did not know whether the morning would cry triumph or tragedy. When you did not come to me yourself I thought it was because you could not, that you were lying dead. Perhaps my anger at your disregard was unjust. Then you disobeyed me and put me in more anger. There perhaps I was more unkind that unjust. But there have been other times when I—Canis, I have shown you too much vexation and too little gratitude. It is this you must pardon me for." Her voice was low, sweet, and her eyes warm.

"I have never known you in excessive vexation," he said lightly, "only in very fine spirit."

"You are a handsome liar," she smiled. She shook her head. "No more of it, then. Yet just a little more. Canis, because of this war we do not know how we may grace the future. We shall be concerned with more serious things than courtesies and tantrums. Therefore, if I should be guilty of more vexation you are not to think it has any real significance, for I do not want your regard for me to be lessened by what will only be my peevishness.''

He had never known her in such a self-critical mood. He put a drape around himself and rose from his bed.

"My lady—"

"No, do not bend your knee to me, this is not the moment," she said. "You were born not to be my servant but my strongest shield." Again she hesitated before continuing softly, "Canis, do you not know your queen?''

Her blue eyes were as warm as the summer sky. He said quietly, "A woman is not for knowing or understanding, she is for loving and holding secure. That is the most any man, because of his limitations, can do for any woman. And a queen is for serving without question and loving without condition.''

She laughed at him.

"Oh, sweet gods," she said, "I ask only for your simplest understanding and receive instead the pretentious observations of an old greybeard. You do not know me, then, do you? You do not even know yourself. Why, you are a man who can become the scourge of Caesar himself. And you will, I swear it.''

She took his hands, turned them palms upwards and placed one over the other so that only his right palm showed. She bent her proud, shining head and he felt the pressure of cool, soft lips as she kissed his palm. She closed both his hands over the kiss and did not look up as she spoke in a low, breathless voice.

"So, Wolfhead, within your right hand you hold the mark of your queen. It is a charge on you to guard me, shield me and, aye, guide me. With it I tie you to my house and never shall you leave it. If you ever do I will either have you slain for your indifference or drag you back in chains, for what is the house of Boadicea without the heart and mind and body of her first captain?''

All which life had given Canis, the hardness, the wisdom, the experience and the pity, counted for nothing against that which this moment gave him now. He drew a deep breath.

"Do you not realise that by this you have already put me in chains for the rest of my life?"

"Which is as it should be," said Boadicea, her smile soft, "for the gods themselves decreed that you were born to belong to my house and no other. Your father knows this. I know it and will have it so. Come to me as soon as you are ready and we will speak to our army and our people."

When he was dressed and had scourged the bristles from his chin, and when he had eaten, he went to the queen. She was in the hall and so were all others of importance, elders, chieftains, captains. They greeted Canis with the generosity of men unable to deny he was no less than they were, though he was not a chieftain, only the son of one. And they looked at him as if he had something about him they should have noticed before but had not.

Outside, in a great living arc of unbroken depth to the eye, thousands of Boadicea's warriors and people were massed. The sun fired the tips of burnished weapons and as she appeared every point of light flashed high and every voice acclaimed her.

"Boadicea! Boadicea!"

And ten thousand lifted swords and spears shook as if a great wind blew rippling over a field of fiery brass and iron.

She stood there on the stone steps of her palace, clad in her battle cloak, her hair a brilliance. She smiled and despite the austere dun of her cloak, fastened now over her colourful tunic, she looked radiant and regal, so that her people laughed and cried for love of her.

"Boadicea!"

She raised her hands. The gesture induced complete silence. The bright sky and the golden sun made the scene radiant, the warrior maids in their short, picturesque tunics adding splashes of vivid colour to the concourse.

Boadicea spoke.

"You are my people all," she said, clear and proud, "I know you and love you. Your rights are life and freedom. When the Romans came we held out our hands to them, for there is room in our land for all who love it. We had thought Caesar just and noble, for this is how Romans speak of him to others. We opened our cities and our dwellings to them, and in my house I have received their emissaries, their officials and their soldiers, not thinking that behind their smiles treachery lurked. What awaits the robber who comes to speak friendship while he counts your gold?"

"Death!" shouted the warriors.

"What awaits a guest who turns on his hosts to take them in slavery?"

"Death!" shouted the people.

"What is the just reward for the spoiler who outrages a queen and violates her daughters?"

"A thousand spear thrusts!"

"Shall Caesar despoil our whole land?" cried Boadicea. "Shall we submit to a will that would make beggars or slaves of us all? Or shall we fight? Aye or no?"

"Aye!" The assent was a thunder of sound. It was repeated again and again until once more the raised hands of Boadicea commanded silence.

"Then fight we will," she cried. "Here in our city they walked in arrogance, here they vilely despoiled us and here we slew them. Today we march on their own city of Camulodunum. My people, we must destroy every Roman camp and every Roman army in Britain. The way will be hard and many of you may dance no more on days of thanksgiving, but be sure that Andrasta will go with us and the Great Father commend us. My people, I will lead. Who will follow?"

"All!" roared the warrior men.

"All!" sang the warrior maids.

"Then look to every spear and every sword," cried
Boadicea, "and we will drive Romans not from our land
alone but from all Britain! At your head to command
you I will give you a general to outmatch any Roman.
He is no stranger to you. He is a man. He is Canis the
Wolfhead. My people, look to him, follow him and
above all, obey him. Hear me now, for I charge you,
each and every warrior, to guard his life before your
own, since he belongs to my house and is not to fall to
the dogs of Rome!"

The forest of shining weapons lifted and shook again.
If the Iceni loved Boadicea, they looked upon the slayer
of Bilbo and the destroyer of Septimus Cato as a
warrior of heroic might. There, for them, was a formidable general indeed. The warrior maids leapt in
delight and ecstasy, for they loved him out of all reason
considering he was not averse to dumping any of them
in a gorse bush. This, he said, was to prick sense into
that part of their person where they kept their brains.
Their singing cries sweetened now the edge of the
roaring acclaim.

"Oh, Wolfhead," cried one, "bring us to Rome and
we will give you the head of Caesar himself!"

From the forefront of the press in the forecourt itself
sprang Cerdwa, her axe flashing as she whirled it
around her wild, black head. Her violet eyes danced in
the light of the sun. Her slim, long-legged body vibrated
as she ran forward and threw herself at Boadicea's feet.

"Lead us, O Queen! Command us, Wolfhead! And
grant me favour, O Queen!"

"What favour?" smiled Boadicea, looking down at
the strangely beautiful face.

"Let me look to your general, Majesty, let me look to
Canis, for there is a man I would stand with in battle
and keep safe from the toothiest dogs of Rome. He
broke the back of Bilbo within my sight. Give him into

my keeping, O Queen, and I will guard him for you by day and I will warm him by night. I would be virgin no longer, I would be the eyes, the shield and the comfort of my lord alone. Give him to me!''

Men and women nearby laughed to hear the untamed Cerdwa speak so boldly, but the queen lost her smile and frowned.

"Wench, what is your name?"

"Cerdwa, noble Queen."

"Do you love me, Cerdwa?"

"Aye, fiercely," said Cerdwa in her liquid voice, "for you are braver even than Canis. I am to die for you, this I know, but I cannot die a virgin. O Queen, there is the one man I would kiss not with my axe but my mouth."

Boadicea, about to deny the favour, thought again. There was a wit and a quickness about the wanton that were more than ordinary. Such a warrior might serve Canis better than well, guarding him against all hazards and treachery. She gave a small sigh.

"I will concede you this," she said. "You shall ride on his chariot, look to his weapons and see to his food. But as to the other matter, put it from your mind. His responsibility is to contrive victory, not to favour virgins."

Cerdwa glanced up at Canis, throwing back her long hair and showing eyes big, bright and unabashed.

"O Queen, if his responsibility rests at the end of each battle, might he not then be free to contrive a different—"

"Do not play at words with me," interrupted the queen coldly. "I know you now. Cannot die a virgin, you say? So, you are not a true warrior maid but a wood-witch, black of hair and immodest of mind. You can bed only with men blind to your devious ways. Canis is not such a man. In any event, he is not for you and you will serve him only as I have directed. Up with you, strumpet."

Not at all discomfited, Cerdwa kissed the queen's

foot, and laughter sprang to animate her triumph as she
went not to rejoin the warriors but to stand by Canis.

"I am here, lord," she said in velvet sweetness.

"I hear you," he said brusquely.

At a signal from Boadicea there were shouted commands and the warriors gave way to make room for the
entry of the war chariots. These were far sturdier
vehicles than the racing chariots, but graceful and glittering nonetheless, a hundred of them. The ground
before the queen was soon crowded with noisy wheels
and stamping horses. Boadicea's own chariot, built with
a high frontal guard and floor stout enough to carry
both the queen and her armour-bearer, was embossed
with gold and bronze, and the hubs of its iron-bound
wheels were bright in the sun. The ornamented bridle of
leather and brass was polished. The two black horses
quivered and blew. Grud advanced with the queen's
banner to place it secure in the chariot, where it fluttered bravely. He took the queen's ironheaded spears
from an attendant, together with her round shield made
of wood, leather and metal. He mounted her chariot.
He was bow-legged, round of eye, old in wisdom,
ageless in bearing and impervious to all things except
those which concerned his service to the queen.

Amid rejoicing Boadicea advanced down the stone
steps. Canis and her army commanders followed. She
boarded her chariot and lifted her hand. Ten thousand
warriors and a sea of flashing weapons saluted her. She
took up the reins and drove the chariot forward at a
walking pace. Warriors and people spilled back to open
an avenue for her. Behind her in his own chariot, a gift
from the queen, Canis followed on. Cerdwa stood with
him, close to him, so that her woodland smell was borne
to him as if by a warm breeze from the richness of a
deep forest. Chieftains and princes followed in other
chariots, and then came the queen's cavalry. The Iceni
were famed breeders of horses and a third of her army
was mounted. Captains, warriors and warrior women

rode in loose, easy style astride wooden saddles blanketed with wool. The column grew as it passed along the crowded way, with foot warriors breaking from the press to march behind. More cavalry took up position, more chariots and foot warriors, and the lengthening cavalcade became rich with colour and equipage.

Lifted spears and javelins saluted and acknowledged Boadicea's progress, and exhilarated warrior maids gave her joyous song before attaching themselves to the column at her back. She drove slowly, so that her people might see her as she passed from the environs of her royal house down the wide street of the palace, not knowing when she would return.

Her ten thousand fighting men and women had become more. They had arrived from the four corners of her kingdom and from other realms too. Bands of anti-Roman partisans—Cantii, Brigantes and Dobunni—hurried to attach themselves to the cause of the Iceni queen. Boadicea was loved by all Celts except the ungenerous.

Her friends and southern neighbours, the Trinovantes, were also on the move. For too long they had suffered ruthless land confiscation, heavy taxes and outrageous levies. Particularly outrageous, since they were not of the faith of Rome, had been the special levy imposed on them for the building and upkeep of the temple of Claudius in Camulodunum, the symbol to them of Roman idolatry and oppression.

Although the Trinovantes owed no direct allegiance to Boadicea, in her expressive and compelling way she appealed to their Celtic hearts. Even if Iceni ways were not quite their ways, they were linked to each other by blood. When news reached them that Boadicea had been scourged and her daughters raped, they regarded the messenger with thunder and disbelief. Some suggested that the messenger was surely a lying Iceni fox, for even Romans would not so outrage a royal family of Britain. So the messenger said, "By Romans it was ordered, by Romans it was done and by all Romans it was countenanced. This I swear by every sacred god."

At which the Trinovantes, remembering their own humiliations, united with Boadicea in declaring bloody war on Rome.

"Send word to her," said their prince, "that we will march to join with her at Camulodunum, and that where she leads we will follow."

Boadicea, leading her army from her city at this moment, rode tall in her chariot, her bearing exultant at the enthusiasm of her people. Their acclaim of her was constant.

"Boadicea! Boadicea!"

Canis, riding behind her, watched her in her pride, the sun turning the splendour of her hair into a crown of muted gold.

The warrior maids called to him, piped to him.

"Hear how they love you, lord," murmured the liquid voice in his ear.

"I hear, wood-witch."

Cerdwa smiled. From the chariot she looked down at warrior maids blowing kisses to her lord. Let them. It was she who stood with him.

The queen rode on. The spears filled her city. The iron-bound wheels of British and captured Roman chariots rolled noisily over the paved streets. Her army sang and her people changed. No Caesar ever rode through Rome with half the love that encompassed Boadicea this day. But then Caesars had only ever been symbols of power. Boadicea had the heart of her people. What difference was there between one Caesar and the next except a degree less or a degree more of autocracy?

The townspeople showered her and her warriors with bright spring flowers. A boldly handsome woman warrior, marching in the column, laughed as petals kissed her shoulder. She seized the young maid who had thrown them and sent her the colour of scarlet summer by implanting a warm kiss on her lips. Then she went on her way, still laughing, leaving the maid wide-eyed and staring. Drawing sharp breath the maid ran to catch up. Her mother called loudly after her to come back.

"I will go with her," called back the maid, "I will follow her and bear her spear for her, so that she may save the strength of her arm for battle."

Reaching the woman, a red-haired creature of joy and vitality, the breathless maid tugged at her arm.

"I go with Boadicea and you," she said, "so give me your spear to carry."

"My spear and my arm are one and cannot be divided," said the woman, "but as your eyes tell me you are not to be denied, come then, you shall cook my food and share my bed, you shall bind my wounds and keep me warm, little grey-eyed dove."

The girl went happily with the woman, and they marched together and sang together and loved together, for what Iceni maid as impressionable as this one could resist the bold kisses of any warrior, man or woman?

Behind the military cavalcade the Iceni followed in their hundreds, filling the waggons that rolled and creaked in the rear.

And so, as Boadicea began her march on Camulodunum, chief city and colony of the Romans, the Imperial Governor, Suetonius Paullinus, was in the last stages of his campaign in Mona.

11

THE FIRST REAL obstacle between Boadicea and Camulodunum was a small town called Glevodurum, garrisoned by the Romans and swelled by refugees who had fled from the Iceni uprising. Boadicea halted her army outside this town at the end of her first day's march, intending to attack it soon after daybreak.

For her comfort and privacy a large tent was pitched. It was one of many the Iceni had taken from the captured Roman depot in Venta Icenorum. Installed in it, she summoned Canis. Cerdwa, eyes glowing in the dusk, followed him from his own tent, where she had been preparing a bed of soft skins for him.

"Will I come with you, lord, to be your ears as well as your eyes?"

"You are neither my ears nor my eyes, wood-witch," said Canis, "you are at this moment the maker of my bed and the mother of my stomach, so while I am gone complete the one and look to the other."

Around them in the great camp a hundred fires flickered to receive the cooking pots. Cerdwa murmured, "Do not let the queen buzz you into confusion, lord, for she can fly fierce in a man's ear."

"I shall survive," said Canis, but smiled as he left her.

He entered the ring of watchful warriors around the queen's ground and Grud admitted him to the tent. Within the lamplit interior his eyes hardened as he saw Cea and Dilwys sitting quietly on a couch. Boadicea, observing his disapproval, set her lips.

"My lady," he said, "is this not unkind to the princesses?"

She stared at him as if her ears were deceiving her.

152

This very day she had given him sweeter words than she had given any man and appointed him commander of her army, and all this had done, it seemed, was to make him so full of himself that he was daring to push his dog's nose into another's dinner.

"Canis," she breathed, "sometimes when you open your mouth I wonder the sky itself does not retreat from the high and mighty sound you make."

"Nevertheless," he insisted, "for their own sweet sakes the princesses must return to Icenorum."

"Oh, the gods," cried the queen, "am I deaf of a sudden or did I indeed hear you say this must be and that must be?"

Dilwys spoke slowly, palely.

"We do not wish to return," she said, "nor did we wish to be left. Nor did the queen our mother say we were to do as she desired, only that we were to please ourselves. You are to fight Romans, so we wished to be with you and our people until we win or die. If we do not win and Cea and I are in Venta Icenorum, then the Romans would come for us there and give us shame as well as death."

"Never," said Canis, "never whatever happens would you be left to Romans."

"Do not be angry because we are here," said Cea wistfully.

"We have to be here, we belong together, all of us. What should we do at Venta Icenorum but die of loneliness?"

He was sombre. They were so young, so hurt, so bewildered. He looked at the queen. A woman misjudged, she was in cold pride.

"My lady," he said, "I spoke out of turn. I am a thoughtless dog and an upstart as well."

"It is for me to name you names," she said, "where is my satisfaction if you do this yourself?"

He smiled then. She frowned, then shook her head and laughed. A lamp flared higher for a moment and by its brighter light he saw the smudges under her eyes.

"I will ask Grud to see that you sleep soundly tonight—"

"There is no need," she said, "that old woman has anticipated you. His poison is already mixed. I will swallow it soon but first I would like to know how you will contrive to take Glevodurum for me tomorrow."

"Providing our warriors point themselves one way and not all ways," said Canis, "it will be taken and speedily, rest on it."

"Well, though they are wild they will obey you," she said. "They had better," she added as she moved to her couch. Cea silently brought the potion, keeping her eyes cast down as Canis took it from her. Boadicea, seated, lifted heavy lids and he brought the silver cup to her mouth. "I am not as wèak as that," she protested. She took the cup into her own hand and drank. "Merciful charity," she breathed, "if there is anything viler than this stuff old bowlegs should be served it night and day."

"I agree," said Canis.

"You have a plan for tomorrow?" She was curious.

"No, only intentions. We will see how the place looks. Rest you, my lady."

Outside he met Grud.

"She is tired," said Grud, "but will be better each day. She is a miracle of endurance."

"She is Boadicea," said Canis with a smile. He returned to his tent. Cerdwa had food ready and he ate by the fire she had built outside. But he did not speak. She knelt close by, sitting on her heels, her limbs glowing pinkly in the firelight, her violet eyes crimsoned like those of a night creature.

"Will you not speak to me, lord?" she said.

"I am taken up with speaking to myself."

"It is about the battle," she said, "but be content in your soundless observations, lord, for the Romans will not stand long against us here."

Canis chewed meditatively on his food and Cerdwa
gazed at his sombre face whereon light and shadow
danced.

"Cerdwa," he said, "it is not given to ordinary men
to win a battle before it has begun."

"Lord, did you not destroy Bilbo with your hands
and Septimus Cato with your tongue? That was not at
all ordinary."

"It was very ordinary. It is the consequences which
will be called notable."

Cerdwa sighed so that he might know she was
troubled. When he did not respond or take his eyes from
the heart of the fire, she said, "The consequences are to
be mortal for me, lord. It is writ so. But before my spirit
departs to the endless forest I will kiss many Romans to
death with my axe. I have heard that a tender man can
be loving to a maid who is soon to bravely die."

"When you are bravely dying," said Canis, "I will
wipe the blood from your lips and give you a warrior's
kiss of farewell. Thus, when life quits you, it will be love
and not war that will go with you to your forest."

"Lord," she said sweetly, "may it not be that when I
am mortally smitten the press of battle may prevent you
putting your mouth to mine?"

"Perhaps. But what of it? The warrior nearest you
will serve you just as well."

"Oh, I marvel at the ease with which you can let
careless jest replace tender compassion," said Cerdwa
burningly.

"Some of us have the gift," he said. "Close your eyes
a minute." Cerdwa closed her eyes. She pursed her
mouth. He popped a pebble between her lips. Startled,
she bit on it. Disgusted, she spat it out. Canis rose from
the fireside. He laved his face and hands with cold
water, cleaned his teeth with slivers of wood and washed
out his mouth. Then he wished Cerdwa sound sleep and
retired to his tent.

He awoke in blindness because of the pitch darkness

and sensed her there. She knelt to lean over him. Her eyes, and only her eyes, came to him out of the blackness. They were dim pools of wild violet. With them she sought to bring herself into his mind and command it. He felt lassitude chaining his body. She came closer. In her warm nakedness she brought to him the scent of the forest when the grass is damp with dew and the trees fragrant with moist leaf.

"I am Cerdwa," she whispered, her voice like wine that intoxicates at first sip, "and I have lain with no man because there is no man who could bind my body to his, except one, who is Canis. The warrior maids whisper that to look into his eyes is to feel all the pain and joy of being bedded with him."

Canis closed his eyes and took her spell from his sight and mind.

"I am not your exception, Cerdwa," he said, "for I am not so endowed that I can pleasure a woman standing ten paces from me. I doubt that of any man. Let me commend you instead to the Roman god Jupiter who, in matters of this kind, is said to be a marvel of ingenuity. Go to your bed and call on him."

"You are cruelly hard, lord," she said, "for you know I cannot and must not die a virgin."

"Aye, I have heard something of this kind," he said, "and accordingly I will do what I can to have a warrior of some account invest you and serve you."

"I would kill him at his first footfall, whoever he was," she breathed. "Truly, you are not as sweet to Cerdwa as you might be, but I would not have you different. I know that when Boadicea has gone and you have followed her, men will not see the like of either of you for a thousand years. Lord, can you be content in your denial of me?"

"Tolerably so," he murmured sleepily.

"Rest in your content, then, for I freely forgive you your lack of tenderness."

Cerdwa, teeth clenched, left the tent, took up her axe

and in the night darkness struck to lodge the blade violently in a tree. Then, naked, she sank to her knees, gripping the quivering handle and drawing hissing breath.

"He denied me and I a true virgin! But I will have him, I will, despite even the queen herself! I will not die a maid, I will not!"

So said Cerdwa to the darkness.

She did not mind dying, but she did mind dying unenraptured.

* * *

Before daybreak Canis was up and about, and as he stirred his captains so did they stir the army. The host rose from the earth, silently for the most part, without stamp of feet or clash of arms or hawking of throats. Mist that promised a day of sunshine kissed them softly and covered the town from the army and the army from the town. But each knew the other was there. Everywhere the opaque dawn, an ethereal blanket of misty light, communicated the silence of the dead, a silence always loud in the ears of those preparing for conflict.

They were all in good spirits. Although Glenvodurum was solidly Roman and partly fortified they did not doubt they would reduce it, destroy it and resume their march in the light of its flames. It was a town of Roman officials and their families, retired veterans and certain renegade Iceni who had cast aside their Celtic gods to live like Romans and worship like them. There was a small garrison of troops and large numbers of Romans who had taken refuge within its walls.

The Britons ate. Then all, except Canis, prayed to the gods of their fathers. This took time, the gods being many and varied. But it saw the lifting of the mist and the visible emergence of the town in the hazy sunlight. Boadicea, bronze war helmet on her head, rode forward in her bannered chariot. Canis, with various captains, followed. Her eyes glittered at what she saw, for the Romans had elected to meet her outside the town.

They were massed parallel with the north wall, an army of three thousand, regulars, veterans and volunteers. They seemed pleased to see Boadicea, unmistakable at this distance. Her banner fluttered and the sun fired her polished helmet. They greeted her noisily. Her eyes turned in, she felt once more the lash of the scourge, heard once more the screams of Dilwys and saw once more the muddy eyes of Septimus Cato. A hand touched hers. Canis saw the need she had to cleanse herself of Rome.

"The fools," she said bitterly, "in their arrogance they have left their lair so that they can stand and mock me!"

"Not entirely," said Canis. "Their town, though partly fortified, is not easy to defend. There are a hundred holes and they have not the means to plug half, let alone all. They would be running like rabbits from one to the other. Romans never hesitate to oppose an enemy in the field if their walls are ill-equipped. And if," he added with a slight smile, "they think little of the enemy. Although I have seen them with inferior forces and superior science destroy enemies entirely formidable. See here how they are deployed to form strength in depth, their front an arc to prevent their wings being outflanked. I am certain they do not expect us to do more than run recklessly onto their swords and shields hour after hour."

"But we are weightier by far," said Boadicea fiercely, "and can crush them against their own walls."

Having accepted the command she herself had thrust on him, it was not in the mind of Canis to let her take any part of it back. The tactics were his responsibility. He must establish that fact. She would kick at first, but accept it eventually.

"If we use only our weight," he said, thoughtfully

observing the Roman dispositions, "we are likely to climb into the town over mountains of our dead. Every warrior will happily die for you, O Queen, but I think a more conservative approach would be better than a merely happy one. We may have a score of battles to fight, so let us learn from each of them."

"Speak on, I hear you," said Boadicea, removing her eyes from the sunlit brilliance of Roman armour.

"Firstly, consider how the Romans stand," said Canis. He dismounted, leaving his chariot in Cerdwa's care, and taking up a stick began to draw in the dirt under the searching eyes of Boadicea and her war chiefs. "They are in deep phalanx, the phalanx an arc to keep their flanks glued to the wall, as here, and here. They will remain glued if they know we muster ten thousand. In standing outside the town their tactic implies an under-estimation of our numbers. If so, they will blood as many of us as they can and then retreat inside, after all. Then it may be a longer business for us."

From the Roman lines came taunting cries, provocative to the ears of the Iceni, most of whom were hidden in the woods where they had spent the night.

"Our tactics must be to ensure we lose no more warriors than we can help," continued Canis. "We will open by carrying the battle to them in numbers no greater than their own, our main purpose being not to crush their front but to bring either their left or right flank from the wall and come between them and the town." Here he looked up and thought, in some surprise, to see the queen in pride of him. "We will spread your wings artfully, my lady, with Cophistus leading your left and myself your right."

"With all good will," said Cophistus.

"Cophistus may have charge of my left," said Boadicea, "but Cywmryn shall lead my right. You, my general, shall stay back to command and direct, which is what I have appointed you to do."

"I must have your right wing," said Canis, "for the

manner in which we must manoeuvre is strong in my mind, as it is with Cophistus, with whom I have agreed it. Either he or I will bring the eagle from the wall and run under it.''

Any pride she had in him disappeared. She surveyed him coldly from her chariot.

"A word in your ear," she said. Canis approached until she was able to lean and whisper to him alone. "So," she hissed, "you are for your comings and goings again, and this time in battle. You are to fly off and flap my right wing for me, which another may do just as well if you so instruct him. Hear me, then. Immediately the success of your manoeuvre is assured, stand off from the battle. Do not argue. Obey me."

"Aye, my lady," he said, smiling up into her expressive face. Then he spoke clearly for everyone to hear. "We shall look to see you standing to inspire your centre, not rushing ahead of it, risking hurt. Grud will mark your turning point."

"So you would command me too, would you?" said Boadicea. "I am here to lead my warriors, not to be cosseted by your lackey Grud, who is a muttering old woman at times. As you are too on occasions."

Grud, beside the queen, turned ageless, innocent eyes to the sky.

"And when," continued Canis, "you hear either me or my warriors, or those of Cophistus, shout your name, then order your centre of two thousand to bear more heavily on the Roman front and signal for the rest of your army to support us all."

"The rest?" she said.

"Aye. For the moment I will lead five hundred and Cophistus the same."

"Are my wings to be so feeble they will scarcely flap?" she demanded.

"My lady," said Canis, "the bravest eagle will not swoop to lift an elephant. We must contrive to look as light and as timid as a mouse, and to engage so thriftily that at the end you will be able to say we did not lose one warrior needlessly.''

This is not battle, this is twittering,'' said Cywmryn. ''I am for the full might of our host.'' This brought all the others into the argument. Boadicea, ignoring the continuous taunts of derisive Romans, turned icy blue eyes on them all. She looked even more icily on Cywmryn.

''Who asked you to speak?'' she said as if the custom of free discussion among her captains and chiefs no longer obtained. ''Let be. If I can heed my general so can you. Are you ready, Canis?''

''Aye.''

''It is in your hands. Sound the horns.''

And amid the sound of the Iceni war horns she took the reins, with Grud bearing her shield, and rode out from the ranks of her council. A roar rose at last from the Iceni and the Romans wondered at its volume, for there did not appear to be more than three thousand Britons assembled. On the queen's left rode Cophistus, with Canis on her right, and behind them the three thousand followed. Five hundred deployed behind Cophistus, five hundred behind Canis, mostly foot.

The rest of the army, still concealed, shifted and picked their teeth, their captains urging them to stay hidden, despite their wild desire to follow Boadicea.

''Is the queen at odds with us? Aren't we to gut even one Roman today?''

''In good time,'' said a captain, ''you shall gut your full share. Meanwhile, put your trust in her and the Wolfhead. I will hang the first man who breaks his cover.''

The Romans stared as they watched Boadicea. If this was her army she was in poor straits. They saw the debouchment of small forces left and right, Boadicea herself riding tall and colourful as she led her centre. The retired veterans were quiet, but the young regulars and volunteers were noisy, mocking a queen who thought she could reduce three thousand Romans with a rabble, and that rabble full of shameless women purporting to be warriors. Confidently these Romans awaited a wild, disordered charge.

Boadicea halted a few hundred paces from the Romans. Grud took a spear from the rack and handed it to her. She lifted it. The gesture induced a sense of portent, and a quiet fell on Romans and Britons alike. The sky breathed, drew back, and the earth trembled for the blood it was about to receive. The spear-point flashed as the sun touched it with fire. The helmeted queen advanced her left foot, leaned back until her tall body was as finely taut as a strung bow, then shouted the Iceni war cry and hurled the spear forward. The heavy weapon sped in a high, curving flight, glinting and twisting as it descended to gash the ground.

Calling to her pair, she led her centre in. Chariots and cavalry thundered as the Iceni charged with the queen, foot warriors storming in their wake. The warrior maids sped with bright hair streaming, their war cries high and singing. Onward they ran, javelin or spear lightly balanced. Some clung fearlessly to chariots or to the bridles of horses, leaping like the wind to match the pace set by Boadicea. Chariot, cavalry and foot, two thousand in all, rushed at the sweeping convex of the Roman front. Boadicea, her bronze helmet a polished crown of war, raced tempestuously ahead. Her lips were curved back over her teeth, her eyes glittering and fierce.

On either side of her Canis and Cophistus swung wide to beset the Roman flanks. The Romans, silent now, awaited the impact of the thundering charge, the front rank dropping on one knee to present short swords and curved shields in close array, this manoeuvre allowing the second rank to discharge short spears, called pila, over the heads of the kneeling men.

Straight for the Roman centre Boadicea ran her chariot, other chariots rocking on either side of her. Outpaced foot warriors sped her on with shouts for her courage. She came at the Romans like their own Diana, huntress and destroyer. The veterans awaited her grimly, but elsewhere a ripple ran through the ranks as a breeze runs through tall grass. The thunder of wheels, hooves and feet shook the ground as the queen and her Iceni rushed in, the mounted warriors bending low, spears or long swords couched. A shouted command inside the Roman lines brought back the strong arms of the spear throwers and on the instant the pila leapt, but so fast did the Britons come that as the storm of short spears rushed at their heads they rode under them.

The Romans tensed, the shock and impact of violent engagement almost on them, but at the last moment, and with a skill that took the breath, the chariots and cavalry wheeled at furious speed to run sideways on against the armoured Roman front. The effect was devastating. The Romans staggered under the weighty rush of vehicles and horse, reeling and spilling back from maiming hooves and iron wheels, from the thrust of lunging spears and the cut of whirling swords.

Romans, cruelly caught by the maiming onslaught, tumbled back in agony against their comrades. This was not to be borne, this was against all the Roman rules of war. Charioteers were expected to dismount on approach, to fight on foot, a man's vehicle ready to take him speedily from the fight if it went against him. It had been Canis who, knowing so much of the fine skill with which the Iceni handled chariots, devised this crippling use of them. Boadicea, reading the confusion in the enemy lines, rejoiced in the tactic. Romans standing firm sought to bring her down with pila, but Grud took every flung weapon on the huge shield with which he covered her. The chariots ran on, staggering and battering the enemy, and the Iceni cavalry joined in this streaming, gouging gallop of iron and fury.

The earth was wet with the blood of grounded Romans. They groaned with the pain of crushed flesh, splintered bone or speared muscle. And the Britons had no sooner completed their manoeuvre and wheeled to come about, when their foot warriors rushed in. These came in exhilaration, leaping to smite with joyful ferocity, in especial the warrior maids. But at least this was offence that the Romans knew and understood.

Boadicea halted her chariot at a distance, took a spear from Grud and raised it.

"There are the dogs of Caesar!" she cried. "Oh, my brave Iceni, show them this day the strength of your arm and the fire of your vengeance!"

Her inspired force locked with the enemy for a short fierce space while the Romans were still shaken from the assault of chariot and cavalry. Then the queen's captains roared and the horns blew for withdrawal. This was how Canis had commanded it. The assaults of chariot and cavalry were to alternate with assaults by the foot warriors. On no account were one or the other to engage in any prolonged duel with an enemy well versed in such tactics.

The frightening aspect of the warrior maids was not so much in their lethal dexterity as their fierce joy. The way they laughed as they hacked at the unguarded thigh of a man made him catch his breath. It was often difficult to get them to obey the tactics of constant withdrawal, so heated became their blood as the excitement of battle grew. It was necessary to roar at them that their general would take off their heads if they did not obey his orders.

On the left Cophistus was engaged in lightly tickling the enemy flank. He mounted frequent attacks with his five hundred, but the Romans saw his obvious purpose, which was to turn their flank and come behind their centre, cutting off their contact with the town. They did not understand his lack of spirit, however, for he never allowed his warriors to properly engage. Since they were for the most part without body armour, using only light round shields, perhaps the Romans thought this accounted for their lack of valour. Indeed, after several loud inglorious rushes only one Roman lay dead, and he an unfortunately awkward volunteer whose clumsiness so offended a warrior maid that eventually she could not refrain from incontinently despatching him.

On the queen's right Canis was engaged in similar manoeuvres to Cophistus, and the Romans began to mock them. It was true that in the centre Boadicea's attacks were vigorous enough, but the Britons' endeavours on the flanks were those of warriors better suited to sitting in trees and scratching like monkeys.

Against the queen's tactics the Romans, though badly mauled, stood their ground. The resolution of the regulars and the experience of the veterans bolstered the courage of blanching volunteers. Confident, despite their losses, that they could outmatch the Britons in the end, for Boadicea's assaults could not go on for ever, Roman officers began to look for the first signs of weakness in the Iceni. They smiled at the empty threats posed by Canis and Cophistus, whose sallies all ended in tumbling, disorganised withdrawal. But suddenly Canis drove his force forward in a more salutary attack and for the first time the Romans found their left flank severely engaged. Weapons clashed and bit, iron spearheads smote iron shields, and the tumult here merged with the greater tumult at the centre as Boadicea sent her chariots and cavalry in once more.

An officer called on his men to stand firm against this unexpectedly punishing flank attack. They did. Their iron solidity had the Britons wavering, falling back again. A horn blew and Canis, wheeling and turning in his chariot, roared at them to withdraw. By his side was Cerdwa, laughter and bright anticipation in her eyes. She knew Canis was teasing the Romans, inciting them to come at him, and when they did they would be destroyed.

He indulged himself in his play, leaning to smite with the flat of his sword at warriors not retreating fast enough. "Get back, get back!" At this moment

Boadicea was compelling the withdrawal of her centre.
Seeing this and seeing the flank attack melting away in
confusion, the Roman officer in command at this point
called on his troops to pivot and re-engage with these
spiritless Britons. What a poor lot they were. He would
teach them a short, bitter lesson.

And so the Roman flank wheeled to come at the
backs of the disorderly Iceni. In their eagerness they
turned the manoeuvre into a speedy rush. Some regulars
sought to restrain the impetuosity of volunteers who
could not resist what seemed all too easy glory for them.
The movement, compact at first, spilled into untidiness,
becoming a tumultuous surge that uncovered the wall.

Canis saw the Roman counter-attack become an indiscretion. In the space of his chariot's tightest turn he
wheeled and sped to outflank them. His few cavalry
followed and foot warriors turned to stream speedily
and lustily in chase. They poured into space to cut the
Roman flank out. There was a roar, a clatter, the
pounding of hooves and the surging of feet, and then
Canis and his warriors were commanding the gap and
coming at the rear of the startled enemy to engage at last
with real and ferocious purpose.

"Boadicea! Boadicea!" His shout was taken up by
five hundred triumphant voices.

"Boadicea! We are at them!"

And Boadicea, standing off from the Roman centre,
heard the cry, seized a spear and flung it upwards.

"Oh, my general, my lovely Wolfhead," she cried,
"you have done it!"

The flung spear soared, caught the light and glittered
as it twisted in the air and fell back. It was the signal to
command the rest of her army to come in and finish the
battle. The horns blew, the waiting captains gestured
and with a howl of joy the main body of the queen's
host poured from concealment and leapt forward. Foot
warriors in their thousands followed cavalry in a roaring
onslaught.

The Romans blenched at the sight and sound, aghast
at the appearance of so many Britons. They began to
fall back but Canis had already squeezed their avenue of
retreat into the town and now he closed it. Dismounted,
with Cerdwa by his side, he led his hungry warriors in a
smiting, hacking sortie to shut the Romans from their
gates.

Slaughter began. Boadicea's warriors were ploughing
into the breaking Roman front, she herself in
exhilaration amid them. Some Romans, savage at what
they saw to be inevitable annihilation, sought to bring
her down. Javelins and pila flew dangerously around
her.

"Withdraw, my lady!" shouted Grud, knowing her
death would turn the sweets of victory into bitter ashes.
"See, the battle is won, the Romans have had their day
in this place!"

Boadicea withdrew. She was flushed, glittering. There
were splashes of blood marking her bright chariot. She
slipped off her helmet and drew a deep breath, pitilessly
watching her Iceni massacring the hated enemy. She
looked to the right, seeking to discover her general. But
she could neither see his face nor hear his voice. Warrior
maids were singing their high-pitched war cries and
Romans were screaming as they died.

Canis, with Cerdwa, fought in the van of the Iceni
surging about the gates of the doomed town. He used
his long sword and Cerdwa smote with her bright axe.
At such close quarters there was no room for a javelin
throw, it was desperate sword and dagger work and a
heady moment for a sharp, whirling axe. Rome had put
iron into the soul of Canis and he knew that if Boadicea
was to live and the Iceni survive, then every Roman in
Britain must either be slain or driven into the sea.
Exulting in the cruel, methodical destruction he
wrought, Cerdwa struck joyfully, laughing as she
greeted lunging, frenzied Romans with the kiss of iron
death. Her black hair danced and her heart sang, for

what man was there better to stand with in battle than
Canis? He and she made an indivisible, indestructible
one.

They were at the gates and there Boadicea, standing
fretfully in her chariot some way off, saw them. She
could not believe her eyes. The sounds were those of
terrible carnage and there was her general engaging in it.
She gave a shout of fury, called to milling warriors to let
her through and drove forward, her chariot lurching
and bucketing over sprawling corpses. Her Iceni
laughed and cheered as they made way for her. She
pulled up at the gates as the warriors of Canis battered
them down to pour into the unhappy town.

"Twice-damned fool!" She shouted the words.
"What do you do here? Did I not command you to
stand off once you had their measure?"

"Once here," said Canis, flicking sweat from his
forehead, "the press was so much against me that I
could not stand off."

"It was not due to any press but to your accursed in-
temperance," she raged. "Here you stand where any
Roman may spit you!" She was fiery, magnificent, her
head and shoulders outlined by the blue sky, and so
wildly compelling was her rageful beauty that Cerdwa
blinked and drew behind Canis. "You are an arrogance,
a blockhead! How shall we come at other Roman armies
if you are stupid enough to fall while doing the work of
my warriors? Am I to go against Paullinus and his
legions without my general? Aye, I am for all you
care!"

"My lady," said Canis amid the sounds of dying
battle, "I will give you my thick head later. Meanwhile,
you shall stand off, as agreed, while we take this town
and destroy it."

"Villain," hissed Boadicea, "having defied me, you
now seek to command me. Hear me, upstart. Get back
from these gates or I will have you trussed and dragged
away. My warriors need neither your conceit nor your

sword to help them destroy this poor place.''

"I do not seek to defy you, my lady," said Canis, "only to remind you it was agreed you should be where you could not take hurt."

"Oh, meat for the very dogs!" fumed Boadicea. At that moment a solitary Roman, haring from violent death, saw her, a bright target against the clear sky. Picking up a fallen spear and crying, "Die, infamous widow!" he ran at her. Grud, alert, thrust down at him, but inspired by imminent martyrdom the Roman slipped the point and lunged upwards at Boadicea. A shadow leapt to darken her as Canis swooped to fend off the spear. The weapon struck his arm and gouged a bloody line, but it was diverted from the queen. Cerdwa gave a yell to see her lord blooded, her axe flashed and the Roman dropped and died.

Canis looked up at Boadicea, she staring down at his gashed arm, her knuckles white at the grip she put on the chariot rail. But, observing his grimness, she attacked first.

"Did I not warn you?" she stormed. "Did I not say you were inviting death from dogs as desperate as these? Had he struck you as he might I should now be without a general. Is it fit for any general to venture himself in this way? Did I not caution you, did I not?"

"And did not your general caution you likewise?" said Canis grimly.

"Aye, in your conceit, you did," she flashed, "and so I told you I had come to lead my army, not to be cosseted by old women!"

Unmoved by this, which was only a woman's temper and nothing to do with majesty, Canis regarded her in frank disapproval of her waywardness. This was not to be borne by any queen, least of all Boadicea. She trembled, then with a suppressed cry of both fury and frustration she caught up the reins, wheeled her chariot and rode wildly away. Because she went as angrily as she had come, Cerdwa spoke sympathetically to Canis.

"Lord," she said as the sounds of new slaughter rose from the town, "she is our proudest queen and I do not know any man who can provoke her as you do. It is not surprising she gave you no thanks for taking the spear meant for her."

Canis smiled, his hand squeezing his arm above the dripping wound.

"What are words, wood-witch, when her spirit is so great?"

"Aye, lord, she is always in some great spirit or other, and I love her for it. There is no one like her. Come, I will bind your wound which, though it tormented her, is only a scratch."

When the town had been sacked and destroyed to the bitter satisfaction of Boadicea's general, there was only one incident that remained a sadness in his mind. He had heard screams coming from a house. There had been many screams, yet for some reason he investigated the cause of these. There was a room in disorder and a girl on a couch. There was also a triumphant Iceni warrior, intent on claiming more than his dues before he killed the wench.

The girl, naked and desperate, was in unbearable horror at the slaughter and in terror of the warrior. Then over his shoulder she saw a man like a tall shadow in the doorway. The only gleam of metal she discerned was that of his belt, Boadicea's gift to him on his appointment. But to the girl it signified that here, perhaps, was someone less defiling than the warrior.

"Oh, I beg," she cried, "in your pity do not let him do this to me, but kill me that I may go clean and unshamed from life."

The warrior did not like what he saw on the face of Boadicea's general. He released the girl and slipped voicelessly out. Canis walked to the couch. He unsheathed his shining bronze dagger. The girl did not flinch.

"I will be in debt to you for your charity," she said

simply and raised herself for the thrust.

"Charity?" His eyes were dark, pitying. "Where is your family?"

"Dead, they are all dead, all whom I loved," she whispered, "and it will be sweeter, therefore, to go with them, if your hand itself is sweet."

He looked into her eyes. They were clear of all horror and soft with relief. She saw his own eyes, dark with compassion. She smiled.

"Here is sweetness, then, child of Rome," he said, and the blow he struck was as merciful as she desired. She felt no agony, only a slight bruising shock at her heart, and she slipped instantly from tragic life into silence and peace.

It was the best he could have done for her.

When every Roman and every collaborator had been put to death, Queen Boadicea rode in triumph through the streets. Immediately behind her rode not Canis but her princes and her chieftains. Canis was at the tail of the cavalcade, for Boadicea was still so furious with him that she would not have him near her. But her warriors were in great admiration of his skill. The warrior maids danced around his chariot and sang the boldest and bawdiest love songs to him, much to the disgust and jealousy of Cerdwa. She ground her teeth as a fair-haired woman followed a bold song with even bolder gestures, and at her lord's amused response Cerdwa's disgust burst into words.

"Lord, how you can take notice of such creatures amazes me, for they are none of them true maids, as I am, only harlots."

"But companionable harlots," he said, "and I fancy the straw-haired one might make a warm bundle."

"If you mean this hump-backed one with a squint and a mole, I will kill her now."

"If you do," said Canis, as the triumphant host marched on in song, "I will take away your axe and throw you to her comrades."

"Truly," murmured Cerdwa, letting the jolting chariot carry her body closer to his, "you are a great warrior but cruel to your own comrade, lord."

He smiled. Cerdwa sighed. She had met no man like this one, so hard, so bitter and yet, in unguarded moments, so tender.

The host marched out of the destroyed town, leaving it in smoking ruins, and many were the severed Roman heads they carried on the points of their spears. Some way beyond the town they rested, fed and then marched on again, southwards. And as they marched their numbers swelled, for other Iceni joined them, as did bands of warriors from other nations, such as the Brigantes, the Coritani and the Dobunni. These nations were not at war with Rome but some of their fighting men could not resist marching with the great Iceni queen.

The road to Camulodunum was straight and long, but there were other fortified places on the way, from which Romans sought to harass or contain Boadicea. Against harassment, Canis led his cavalry with swift, wily ferocity. The fortified places he smashed and destroyed according to the threat they posed to his rear. And Boadicea, under the aegis of her general, swept triumphantly and relentlessly on.

12

FOR ALL THAT Canis accomplished as her general,
Boadicea was in no hurry to forgive him his faults as a
man.

"What has Canis done that you should be so cold to
him?" asked Cea one night when they were encamped
some leagues from another small town they had left in
flames.

"He is an upstart," said Boadicea. "I will not have
him indulge himself at my expense."

"Indulge himself?"

"Aye, child, he does indulge himself in his selfish
recklessness, and I am not going to be left with an army
that has a heart but no head. Ah, you do not understand
such a man as he is, my innocent. He is a proud,
arrogant and conceited fox. But I will bring him to heel.
He shall serve me, not master me."

"My mother, how foolish you are," sighed Cea, "it is
you who are in too much pride."

Boadicea was not in pride, she was in temper. The
rogue was so elusive and she must, according to the law,
wait a full year and a day as a widow before she could
bind him unbreakably to her and put an end to his independence. Why did the villain not help her in her impatience by being sweet to her? No, instead he must
always be defying her.

Dilwys regarded her mother and sister quietly. She
had lost her mischievous gaiety, she could not understand why men had used her so vilely. Cea was a
quieter princess too. She could not forgive the blindness
of gods who had allowed her life to be shattered at the
time of her greatest joy. Because she had been defiled
she put love from her, but her eyes would dwell

longingly on Canis whenever he was not looking her way, only for self-disgust to rise and make her turn from him.

She did not like the way her mother spoke of him and said, "Did not Canis save your life in the very first battle?"

Boadicea frowned, then smiled.

"Aye," she said softly, "rogue as he is he loves me well."

"Did you not show him some gratitude?" asked Cea.

"Oh, innocence. Do you not know the sly Wolfhead took the Roman spear to place me in his debt? Grud was there and would have used his own body to save me, but Canis in his swift artfulness was there before him, and it was only a small wound he took."

Cea could not swallow this, however sweet her mother's smile.

"I think, my mother," she said, "that sometimes your pride goes before all else and constrains you to believe what you know is not true."

Boadicea opened her eyes wide and looked the picture of surprised hurt.

"Why, Cea, to say this to me! You are still a child in all matters concerning the deviousness of men, confess it." She put her hands on the princess's shoulders and smiled lovingly. "There, I will have my disobedient general to see me, for despite all I must lend my ear to him in the matter of investing and taking Camulodunum."

At her summons Canis arrived in her tent. He smiled at Cea and Dilwys, and Cea's heart drowned. He bent his knee to Boadicea and also his head, for he perceived she was still queenly vexed with him and it would not do for her to see that his mouth twitched.

"Have you thought on my words?" she asked.

Gravely he said, "You have spoken me several words these last few days, and if I divide the days into the words there are but two words to each day. To which of these do you refer, my lady?''

The queen drew herself up to her tallest and most affronted height. She took a deep breath, would have slain him with her tongue and her eyes, but instead she suddenly laughed, and neither her daughters nor Canis had heard her so merry since her scourging.

"Canis, you are truly more of a rogue than all men," she said, "but you are a man also, as Cea has reminded me. So come, we will drink wine and I will say no more about your slippery ways. Instead you shall tell me how we will take Camulodunum tomorrow."

Cea poured the wine and they drank it from silver cups. Then Canis spoke.

"You have moved fearlessly and inspiringly in battle, my Queen, and I am still in wonder that so great a leader should have chosen me to command her army. Had it not been that my surprise was more than my modesty on that occasion, I might have pressed you to appoint a worthier man."

"A worthier man?" Boadicea was softly amused. "Oh, the gods, is there one?"

"However," went on Canis, "since the command is mine so is the responsibility for devising tactics. Therefore, my lady, I would ask you to favour me and not run headlong onto the enemy at Camulodunum as you have elsewhere."

Thus was Boadicea's good humour brought precipitately to an end by the ungrateful dog.

"Is it part of your strategy to have me lurk behind my warriors, waiting for such Roman tidbits as they care to throw me? Hear me, upstart, my warriors look to you for cunning and to me for leadership. Where I go they will follow. How shall they follow if I skulk behind them?"

"This will not be like other battles," said Canis, giving Cea another smile as she went to sit with Dilwys, "for here the Romans fight to defend their chiefest town in Britain. Paullinus, as you know, has halted his campaign in the west and is moving to bring his army against us as quickly as he can. So we must reduce Camulodunum speedily and with minimum loss, then march to take Londinium. My lady, I will let you take no risks for we cannot and must not lose you. It is said of any general that before he considers his strategy he must first consider his responsibilities. And of all my responsibilities you are the most important."

"As you are my chiefest aggravation," she said angrily, and heard Cea cry out in protest.

"Am I so?" said Canis quietly, and suddenly there was strange distress on Boadicea's face, which flushed, then turned pale.

"No, I did not mean that," she said breathlessly. "Canis, forgive me—" She broke off and Cea and Dilwys stared to see such weakness in her, the cup of wine trembling in her hand. Canis smiled, his hard face softening.

"I do not fight my demons hard enough," he said, "or I would not put such tempers upon you. My lady, we will be attacking a large town tomorrow, which will be desperately defended. We may have to prise each Roman from his stone bulwark. You still wish to lead your centre in your chariot?"

"Canis, I must," she said in some desperation.

"And to inspire your warriors from your chariot throughout the battle?"

"Aye, despite your scowls, this is my will and intent."

Canis smiled again.

"Then I will dispute the matter no more," he said, "for you cannot climb the walls of Camulodunum in your chariot. You must of necessity stand off once your warriors are on the walls and over it, to fight the fiercest part of the battle in the town itself."

Boadicea clenched her fists, ground her teeth, then

shook her head and laughed again.

"Oh, you snake," she cried, "you have deliberately trapped me!"

"I have only let you decide your own course, my Queen," he said. "Now, we shall engage our army in three parts. The greater part will be the centre, led to the walls by you. I shall lead a force on your right and the Trinovantes will make up the force on your left."

"The Trinovantes?"

"They are here, my lady, as they promised. They are encamped only a league from us."

"To whom," asked Boadicea in all sweetness, "has this news been brought?"

"By our scouts to our captains."

"My captains?" she said even more sweetly.

"Perhaps," said Canis thoughtfully, "the news came to me first."

Her sweetness dissolved and it was a sight to intrigue the gods to see the variety of new expressions passing over her handsome face.

"Ah," she breathed when she had conquered her desire to fly at him, "to you first, then, and next my captains, but to me no news at all."

"It was merely the circumstance of my being where I was when the news arrived," he said as if it were nothing she need fret about. "As to your own position, my lady, I have despatched Cywmryn and escort to the Trinovantes, asking their commander and their princes to come to you here."

Boadicea turned to speak to Cea.

"Now you have heard the rogue condemn himself. I have set him up as my general and in his conceit he has set himself up even further, even above his queen. You have heard how he has done this and commanded that and left me ignorant of all."

Cea was quite unable to understand her mother's reasoning.

"But he has not left you ignorant," she said, "he has

this moment told you everything, and you have given him the right to do this and command that. My mother, these are serious days for all of us and when so many other matters have so much import for us I do not think you should harp on the quirks and whims of those closest to us. In times of peace and happiness such frailties make us laugh or cry or vexed, and perhaps we might spend a whole day rebuking each other, but this is not a time of peace and happiness, only of war.''

More than this unexpected disloyalty, Boadicea disliked the equally unexpected maturity of her daughter's logic. The girl was still a young maid, it was manifestly absurd that she should speak like a woman and even contrive to look like one.

"Cea," she said lightly, "even though you are only a foolish child, you are still sweet and dear to me, so say no more of what you do not understand and I will say no more of what I do.''

"My lady," said Canis, heart melting at the look on Cea's face, "sweet Cea only spoke—''

"Who are you to call her so familiarly?" Boadicea's interruption was swift and jealous. "Is she not my daughter and you no more than many other men?''

"Much less than some, my lady," he said with a smile. "But think on tomorrow for the moment. When the Trinovantes have seen you and pledged their aid, then they will go and in the night form their army before the east wall of Camulodunum. My own force will take up position before the west wall, and both these manoeuvres will be completed before daybreak. But we shall lie securely hidden from the Romans, who will see only your own force, which you will lead in an hour after daybreak.''

"Wait," said Boadicea, "you are intent on sneaking away in the night? Am I to be left without my general? What of your boast that I am your chiefest care and responsibility? Am I to awake one morning and find you cold and stiff from a Roman dagger in the night?

This is not to happen, for I will see that it does not. I say and say again, Wolfhead, you belong to none but the house of Boadicea. So, in such comings and goings as I concede you, take care that you return to me, and speedily, for if you are ever again indifferent—"

Whatever might have happened next did not materialise, for at that moment Grud appeared to announce the arrival of the Trinovante leaders.

They entered the spacious tent, men of quick eyes, wiry bodies, Celtic cousins of the Iceni, but with small differences in their tunics, their helmets and their metal trappings. Their brown faces broke into extravagant smiles as they beheld Boadicea, tall and magnificently regal in a blue robe. Some knew her and the rest knew of her, and the latter gazed in a little awe at the face and form of the most redoubtable queen in Britain.

"Welcome, my friends," she said simply and extended her hand for each man to take and lift to his forehead. And each man did, for although she was not their monarch they could not deny they were ready to follow her loyally in this war. Their prince spoke.

"We rejoice that you are here in our land in your power and strength, Queen Boadicea. We give you our hands and our hearts, all our own power and strength, which are yours to command and dispose of as you will."

"For your friendship, homage and strength," said Boadicea in her sweetest, richest voice, "I cannot find words fully expressive of my thanks. But, Prince Iodemus, what are Boadicea and the Iceni in this war without the hands and hearts of the Trinovantes? I gladly accept the aid of your warriors, but in disposition and strategy I would have them look to my general, Canis, son of Callupus the Wolf. This, my lords, is Canis."

The Trinovantes turned their shrewd eyes on the tall Iceni and one said, "We have heard of Canis, we have heard the Romans would already pay a ransom for his body and twice a ransom for his cunning. We are here to follow where you lead, O Queen, and to accept that the confederated armies shall be under the sole command of your general.''

''I have no quarrel with that,'' said Prince Iodemus, a fairly equable warrior who liked pleasure more than battle and was not unwilling to surrender the responsibility of being in charge of one.

''We have heard,'' said a Trinovante chieftain, ''of many battles, we have heard that Queen Boadicea has marched on many towns and destroyed them all. We have heard that Queen Boadicea's general is a man of great guile and fierce purpose, that he has slain a thousand and more Romans with his bare hands, aided only by a formidable warrior maid who fights at his side with an axe. Or so we have heard.''

Boadicea looked down her nose a little.

''What you have heard is true,'' she said with a cool dignity that was above any false modesty (for she had no liking for saying anything which bore imperfect witness to her stature and achievements), ''except that the axe-woman is not a true warrior maid, but only a wood-witch and of little account.''

''Ah?'' said the Trinovantes and smiled questioningly at Canis, who drew a hand over his mouth and said nothing.

The visitors spoke of their own exploits, how they had marched on the fortified coastal towns of Dunwich and Walton, and destroyed them. They had choked the sea, they said, with Roman dead. Canis let them talk. They were as dissertatious as the Iceni. But eventually he took hold of their ears to explain, clearly and concisely, his plan for investing Camulodunum.

Meanwhile, Suetonius Paullinus had received news in Mona of Boadicea's uprising. It put him in cold fury, compelling him to halt his campaign against the Druids in order to move east and crush the rebellious widow. To save Camulodunum he had to move quickly. He had available part of the Twentieth Legion, the whole of the Fourteenth, and almost a full legion of auxiliaries, but governed by the necessity for haste he took only his cavalry units, leaving the infantry to follow on as quickly as possible.

As well as Camulodunum, Caesar's stronghold in Britain, there was also the Roman depot and supply base in Londinium to consider. He knew that if Boadicea took Camulodunum she would immediately move against the great trading city built on the green banks of the Tamesa. Accordingly, Paullinus despatched a galloper to Glevum, with instructions for the Second Legion there to march to Londinium and hold it, if necessary, against Boadicea.

With his cavalry he rode east to check the Iceni queen. On his way he received more news of her progress and her victories. He could hardly credit that any Britons could oppose Romans in organised battle and live to boast of success. But the Iceni, so it was said, were led by a man as wily and as bold as Caratacus, who had opposed the original invasion by the Emperor Claudius.

Amid the bad news came the hopeful. The Ninth Legion, stationed at Lindum under the command of Quintus Petillius Cerialis, was marching south to smash Boadicea's investment of Camulodunum. Quintus Cerialis, determined to destroy the deposed queen who refused to be deposed, envisaged handing her over to Paullinus in chains. The Imperial Governor would no doubt pack her off to Nero as some consolation for the damage she had done to the emperor's people and property in Britain. Nero would deal imaginatively with her. He had an artistry for such things.

It was not to be quite like that. When Quintus Cerialis, in his majestic Roman contempt for the widow and her rabble, began his march in the bright light of morning, it did not escape the notice of the spies of Canis. Before the last soldier had stepped from the Lindum fortress, news of the march was on its way to

Boadicea's general, reaching him on the night before the battle of Camulodunum.

"So," mused Canis in his tent, "this is better than I hoped, for Quintus has marched too late on the one hand and too soon on the other. We will destroy Camulodunum while he is still proudly on his way, then turn and destroy him when he has come too far to turn back."

"Lord," murmured Cerdwa as she laid herbs of early summer on the place where his head would rest that night, "will this be as you say it will?"

"Cerdwa," said Canis, "neither man nor woman can discount practical mathematics which, in this case, are based on the certainty of three fixed points. One is the point where Quintus Cerialis is now. Two is Camulodunum where we will be tomorrow. Three is the place between Lindum and Camulodunum where Quintus and Boadicea will both be together."

"Lord," said Cerdwa, "how can any one man have a brain more cunning than a fox and a body stronger than a lion?"

Canis, observing the night beauty of the wood-witch with eyes thoughtful but remote, replied with his tongue in his cheek.

"By being diligent in his study of life and people, and by not lying with harlots or wood-witches."

"You may lie happily with me, lord, for I am neither. I am the truest of virgin maids. Do you not find purity appealing?"

"I find it remarkable in some maids."

"It is said you look tenderly upon Princess Cea—"

Her voice died of strangulation, for he had her by the throat. She saw death, she felt it, and Cerdwa paled.

"Never speak that sweet name in such folly," he whispered harshly, "or I will cut out your tongue, bind your body and have the hairy ones of the forest besiege your maidenhead."

Cerdwa shuddered. The hairy ones of the dark forests

could put spells so malignant on a mere wood-witch that their secrets could not even be whispered.

"Dare to lay your chattering tongue once more on any forbidden name," he said fiercely, "and I will kill you. Do you not feel at the door of your witches' hell even now?"

Cerdwa flung back her head and her wild eyes laughed at him, though in strange, agonised fashion.

"Nay, lord," she gasped bravely, "I feel only the strength and hardness of your body and it would be joyful to die this way if only I did not die a virgin."

Canis looked at her with bitterness in his heart. Then he threw her down and turned his back on her, at which Cerdwa gave a wild cry and leapt for her axe. The blade flashed dully in the yellow glow of the oil lamps and he turned as in fury and passion, which came quickly to spurned wood-witches, she struck at him. But Canis struck too and the axe went spinning from her hand.

"Lord," she whispered in some mortification, but also in wonder, "no one has so contempted my axe before. It is as I suspected, you are no mortal man but a god of all the forests."

"There are no gods," said Canis, "only superstitions. Your axe lies where it does because of the art I have for a counter-stroke."

But Cerdwa gazed in awe and wonderment all the same.

"Truly, lord," she said breathlessly, "I did not mean to kill you, only to break your teeth or slice a little off your right ear."

"I will tell the queen of your intention. It will command her sympathy, for she has often felt similarly disposed herself."

Cerdwa's eyes became huge pools of dismay.

"Nay, I beg you, lord, do not tell the queen. I am charged to guard you, not to mark you, and she would not understand that it was only an impulsive jest on my part. She will have me dragged behind her chariot until I am dead. This would not only give me great pain but much sadness too, for she is a great queen and I love her fiercely."

"Let be," said Canis brusquely. He turned to hide his amusement at the smooth tongue she wagged so well, and left her. Whereupon Cerdwa cast herself down on his bed and dwelt mournfully on the cruelty and hardness of her lord. But she would not have had him other than he was.

13

THE ARMY OF Boadicea moved on Camulodunum with the combined might of the Iceni and Trinovantes, and of other Britons who had flocked to follow the best-loved queen in the land. If there was any monarch who could rid Britain of Romans it was Boadicea.

At this moment Paullinus was still eighty leagues away and the Ninth Legion nearly thirty. Quintus Cerialis was fretting a little, for he knew now that Boadicea was at the gates of Camulodunum.

It was said afterwards and told for many years to come that when she advanced in her chariot at the head of her host, the battle cavalcade stunned the eye. No mightier host had ever been seen or would be seen on any field of war in Roman Britain. Arrayed in her bright tunic and battle cloak, with bronze helmet polished and glittering, banners flying, Boadicea led her Britons to lay siege to Caesar's stronghold.

Camulodunum seethed with apprehension and panic. People surged from one quarter of the city to another, then another, to hear what this man or that man had to tell about the advance of the Iceni queen. Numerous in the city were time-expired veterans of the legions, for it was here that the first Roman colony in Britain had been established, and in this locality the Romans had confiscated large tracts of land at the expense of the Trinovantes. Publius Ostorius Scapula had been governor in those days, and his harshness had encouraged his landed veterans to keep the Trinovantes in subjection by acts of terrorism. Now, with Boadicea as its implacable instrument, retribution was about to catch up with the Romans of Camulodunum, and the sun that rose that fateful morning over the doomed city was the last most of them would see.

At the forest of iron and bronze spears, at the host which blotted out every blade of grass, the defenders of Camulodunum felt their blood run cold. On came Boadicea, her chariot running in moving, glittering reflection of the sun. The guide and inspiration of her warriors, she led them and swept them into the stone Roman jaws. Flights of javelins sailed from the wall. The chariots ran under them. Boadicea halted before the wall. She took a spear from Grud, who covered her with her shield, and pointing its iron head at Roman defenders she shouted, "O my people, cast down this wall built by oppressors to shelter oppressors, and put the bold mark of Britain on the infamous image of Caesar!"

Those who heard her felt fire leap, and they were the first at the escarpment and wall, snaking upwards over slanting earth and forbidding stonework, carrying their ladders of rope. From below javelins and spears soared upwards to harass defenders. The long-haired warrior maids, scorning the necessity for ladders, scaled the wall with feet and nails, daggers between strong white teeth. Romans leaned to hurl weapons at them. Some launched javelins at Boadicea, who rode up and down before the wall, encouraging her warriors.

"Smite them, my brave Iceni, they will not stand long against you, for I love you and who can contain warriors who have your courage and my love?"

She urged them in their hundreds to the assault with gestures of her spear, shouting in fury whenever one fell stabbed or pierced. She hurled her spear against the stone, her voice ringing to put fire into those who, heedless of fallen comrades, leapt to ascend and assault. Soon, from a distance, it seemed as if the whole face of the north wall teemed with quick-moving spiders.

On the ground teams of warriors brought forward great rams of oak, strengthened with bands of brass and

iron. These they ran with such shock against the huge
gates that the stone surround groaned, although the oak
rams only vibrated.

It was victory or death. She knew that. There was no
compromise for Romans, no other alternative for her.
She drove her Iceni on. Exhilarated, they responded.
They were at the top, hacking and stabbing. Blood
began to run red and thick over the stone. Romans
began to die.

The Britons, undeterred by casualties, scaled the wall
by the hundred, the war cries of the men loud and
ringing, the women's high-pitched and singing. Joy was
the keynote of this song, for the supple and fearless
Iceni women disdained Roman men. Roman men loved
neither Britain nor Britons, neither sweet rain nor soft
mists, they loved corrupt gods, gaudy gold, painted
harlots and pretty boys. So one did not shed tears at
taking their heads off.

The plain before the city trembled to the thunder of
battle and the sky flung back the echoes. With Boadicea
obviously ready to throw in her host en masse, the appalled defenders called up reserves from all other points
to help beat off the rising storm of the frontal offensive.
Only the queen's chariots and cavalry stood off. The
panic-stricken Roman officers hastened the withdrawal
of men from the east and west walls to lend aid to the
besieged men on the north.

Cophistus, from a vantage point on the north wall,
marked the manoeuvre and sent his signal. Passed from
one man to another it reached Canis on the far right and
the Trinovantes on the left, at which Canis brought his
force from concealment and the Trinovantes too broke
cover to storm the weakened walls.

Horrified, the Roman command rushed companies
back to the east and the west positions. But all too late.
Speed was the essence of every tactic as far as Canis was
concerned. It was the one thing in which they could outmatch Romans, the one thing that might bring them

ultimate victory. He knew how formidable Romans could be in defence when given time to group, regroup and manoeuvre.

His Iceni were already in, hurling aside the depleted defenders on the west wall. They carried the wall. Canis, leaving his chariot, took command of them as they swarmed into the city. Cerdwa went with him. Minutes later the Trinovantes had broken in over the east wall. The two forces began a pincer movement, and squeezed Romans tumbled and sprawled as long spears and weighty swords began their terrible work. A wild, terrified noise arose from the invaded city and Boadicea, hearing it, knew its cause and laughed in exultation.

"Oh, my sober Grud, let me see you in cheer. He has done it yet again, he has broken the Roman dogs of this place already. Did any queen ever own so quick and cunning a general as mine?"

"Never, my lady," said Grud above the noise of battle, "but do not heap your praises too thickly on his head, as you so often do, or his blown-up conceit, which you mark so readily, will take a new turn and swell him bigger than an ass that has died of too much fodder."

"Be silent, old fool," cried Boadicea, "your tongue wags with as much mockery as his, and you not even a captain."

"In truth," said Grud placidly, "I am nothing. But now let us stand well off, my lady, as Canis advised, and peacefully await the victorious outcome."

"As Canis advised?" She could not brook that. "These are my warriors, I command them and myself also!" She drove forward and her Iceni leapt clear, looking up as she shouted at them. "Break me down these gates!"

The rams went to work with greater force.

"Stand away, my lady," urged Grud, "you are a mark for a javelin yet."

"Hold your tongue," she fired.

Above them the wall was black with surging warriors and reeling Romans. Caesar's veterans paled to hear the screams of the people, for the screams were coming from within the city as the Iceni led by Canis and the swarming Trinovantes put inhabitants to the sword.

Outside the gates dead and dying Iceni lay around the chariot of Boadicea, but they were few. The rams battered. The gates fell. With yells of triumph the Iceni charged through, and except for a stout few the Romans broke and ran for the shelter of the temple of Claudius.

Boadicea, exultant, drove into the carnage of Camulodunum. Amid her warriors she raced in vengeance at the heels of fleeing Romans and hysterical citizens. Grud swayed beside her. He muttered. She took no notice. Here in Camulodunum was centred the vileness of Rome and this vileness she had come to obliterate. The city trembled to the cataclysmic roar of the brass and iron tempest.

Canis was near the centre of the city, his warriors spreading like a dark river in boiling flood. Cerdwa was by his side and the streets were full of Romans spilling from houses, running from death or standing to defy it. Savagely desperate were the latter, but dark-faced Canis was merciless and glowing-eyed Cerdwa terrifying. A veteran, experienced and muscular, sought to spit her. Lightly she evaded his thrust, crashingly she split his shield and swiftly her axe swung again. But it was the sword of Canis that took him in the throat. At which a wild-eyed Roman volunteer lunged with his spear at Canis, only to run into the path of the whistling axe. Sweetly it kissed him and sweetly it killed him, for he died instantly and without agony.

They fought as one, Canis and Cerdwa. Never had she stood side by side with so great a warrior. Romans fell like scythed corn. He seemed never to waste a stroke, he used neither feints nor slashes, only counters, taking each lunging adversary with a lightning thrust.

Suddenly all the Romans were gone, fleeing to the

temple before retreat was closed. Canis, wiping blood from his sword, watched his Iceni giving chase. The noise of conflict increased and he knew the queen had successfully invested the north wall.

"Cerdwa," he said, "go to the queen, who should be standing off outside the north gate. Tell her we have the city and are about to pull down the temple, and that I will let her know when it is safe for her to ride in."

Cerdwa looked like one who had gone deaf.

"Wood-witch—"

"Lord," she panted, "I did not hear you, I will not go. I am not to leave you in battle, it is the queen's command. Oh, I know not how you can put such a miserable choice on me, for if I disobey you will surely kill me, and if I obey the queen will put me to death for leaving you. Since, therefore, I must die in either event, then slay me here and now. I will not mind your cruelty, I will close my eyes to it, and if I show distress as you smite me it will not be because of your unkindness but because I will be worried about who will cook your food tonight."

His darkness lightened. His mouth twitched. Cerdwa's great eyes were doleful. Down the street came two Romans, beseeching their gods to deliver them from furies and fiends. They ran in terror with Iceni warrior maids behind them.

"Sybylla!"

A tawny-haired woman checked. She saw Canis and came speedily to him, her smile vivid on her reckless face, her lips as red as the blood that wetly stained the hand that carried her spear.

"Lord, am I to serve you?" she asked in delight, while Cerdwa ground her teeth and tightened the grip on her axe.

"If you will," said Canis and gave the tawny one his message.

Sybylla, laughing, said, "In this I serve both you and the queen, lord, but I will take my reward only from you." She came up on her dancing feet and kissed Canis soundly on the lips, then she went at a long-limbed run towards the north gate. Cerdwa gazed after her with rage in her eyes.

"I will kill her!" she cried and burst into tears. Canis, urgent now to reach the temple, stayed a brief moment to lift her woeful face to his.

"What is a kiss?" he said. "She is not as beguiling as you, nor is her shape half so notable."

In their thousands Romans crowded into the temple, closing the great doors in frenzied hope that they would keep out the host of the Iceni queen. When she arrived at the mighty stone edifice a score of minor conflicts were still being fought in adjacent streets, and from other parts of the city came sounds which might have made a lesser queen shudder. But there were no sounds which tormented Boadicea more than those which she had heard on the day her daughters had been outraged.

A flame sprang here, another there. It was her vow and purpose to raze this Roman capital, including the great temple erected in honour of Claudius, deified as a god for his subjugation of Britain. She saw its mighty columned height, its rich mouldings and the brilliantly alternating colours of its frieze, and she remembered how Britons had been forced to pay for its erection and its upkeep. Her smile was both sweet and bitter as she called to surging warriors.

"Destroy me this monstrous house!"

They laid siege to it, willing and able to pull it down block by stone block if necessary. Boadicea rode up and down, as they loved to see her do, and there was nothing now they could not accomplish for her. Then Canis appeared, bloody, and with him his wood-witch, even bloodier. Grimly he looked up at his queen.

"My lady, what do you play at here in the midst of inner battle?"

Oh, the gods, the airs he gave himself.

"I am with my warriors," she retorted, "and the play

is as sour as your face. I am here to see this vile temple
brought to the ground. For the moment, stand off from
this stone-breaking and bring the Trinovantes here. It
will be their especial joy to help me destroy what has
been a major offence to them. Aye, then go dip yourself
in the river for you are as usual stinking with Roman
blood, and I like your smell even less than your scowl.''

Wayward as she was, she was also irresistible. He
smiled, and she could not say whether she was sweetly
disarmed or hotly aggravated. He turned to survey the
temple. The Britons were storming it, their rams
thudding, their iron hacking at carved and sculpted
tributes to Caludius. Its magnificence did not move
him. Rome in Britain must be obliterated. Boadicea
must survive.

''My lady,'' he said, ''when we come upon Quintus
Cerialis and the Ninth Legion, we shall be so well versed
in the Roman art of destruction that we shall annihilate
his army before his eyes.''

They destroyed the temple in two days, slaying every
Roman there, and they left Camulodunum a place of
smoke and rubble. Icy rage consumed Paullinus when
he received word that Boadicea had utterly destroyed
both the city and the temple. In peace she was a proud
queen, in war a merciless one.

*   *   *

But before the temple was completely razed, Canis had
persuaded Boadicea to despatch part of her army north-
west to meet the advancing Ninth Legion. Canis headed
this force and Boadicea, escorted by cavalry, came up
with him as soon as she was able.

Quintus Cerialis had marched as quickly as he could
but by the time he realized he was too late to save
Camulodunum he was also too late to save himself. He
came face to face with Boadicea at a venue predeter-
mined by Canis, where the plains stretched unbroken on

either side of the road and the unprotectable Roman
flanks would be entirely vulnerable to the speed of the
Britons. When he saw the assembled might of the Iceni
queen, awful doubt assailed Quintus Cerialis. A hundred war chariots stood in the van, fretful horse under
the curb of restraining hands. The foot warriors made a
forest of their weapons and cavalry forged flying wings.
He observed that she commanded not an undisciplined
host but a formidable one, with an ominous quiet about
it.

In his common sense, which was not inconsiderable,
Quintus would have liked to retire rapidly in an endeavour to form on more advantageous ground, there
to coolly demonstrate the skilled Roman art of victorious defence. But Canis had chosen the field too well.
There was no terrain to which Quintus could pin his
back or use to guard his flanks, and he knew that to turn
in his tracks would bring these wolves upon him in a
matter of minutes.

They must stand resolutely. He would be served by
the incomparable courage and discipline of the Ninth
Legion, and there was also the possibility that Boadicea,
over-confident after her triumphs, would come too
recklessly at him. Supporting his massed infantry, Quintus had his redoubtable cavalry, to be used at the first
sign of the Britons in pell-mell chaos.

Boadicea attacked, leading her centre, and for a few
minutes it seemed to Quintus that she might indeed be
rushing headlong in a bunched frontal assault that
would do her no good at all if she kept it up. But then
her wings spread, the mass deployed to give every
warrior freedom of movement and action, and Quintus,
seeing the immediate envelopment threatened by her
wings, drew a hissing breath like a man in the path of a
hundred tigers.

There was a sound like a rushing, hurrying jingle,
almost melodious until it became a rising clatter of brass
and iron, this accompanied by the deep music of the

horns, the singing cries of the warrior maids and the rhythmic thunder of flying horse. It was the heady music of triumphant battle to the Britons, and Quintus, sitting his horse and his apprehensive cavalry, called on Mars to deafen the ears of his soldiers to it.

Mars or no, as the thudding, escalating shock of engagement came, the Ninth Legion visibly staggered. They recovered to fight bravely back, some wincing at the immodesty of battling with the wild warrior maids, others evincing rage that any maids or women could be so disgracefully uncivilised. It made no difference. The Romans were speedily outflanked for all their skill and discipline. Canis gave them no chance at all and the unrestrained fervour of the warriors did the rest.

Before the Ninth had time to manoeuvre in the face of the broad frontal onslaught, Canis had turned their left flank, and not long after the Trinovantes were hammering and squeezing their right. Not one Roman turned his back on the enemy, each faced the terrifying charges of the Britons with great valour, although they blinked and twitched at the fierce joy with which they were assailed by the vivid warrior maids. The main struggle lasted a pitifully short time, but the sad eyes of Quintus marked the end well before it came. He prepared to escape at the crucial moment with his cavalry.

Boadicea's centre thrust and thrust at the Roman front until it was hopelessly broken, then at the insistence of Grud she stood off. Panting but exhilarated, she watched her warriors mercilessly carrying the battle to its bloody conclusion.

She rode over the gory ground to show herself to her brave Trinovantes, many of whom had given up the pleasure of seeing the finality of the triumph at Camulodunum in order to serve her against the Ninth Legion. Now they were crushing the Roman right, hammering, bending and breaking it. Boadicea called on Iceni to attend to the Trinovante wounded and bear them to the rear. She then wheeled and sped to the right, looking to see the part Canis was playing. It took a while to pick him out, and when she did it made her blood rush. That dishonourable dog, who had given her his promise not to hazard his life, was on the fringe of a terrible melee. The men of the Ninth Legion were dying hard, taking Britons with them, and Canis, having ridden in to quell hotheads infected by the death wish, was hemmed about. Romans and Britons surged around his chariot. Boadicea caught the flash of Cerdwa's axe. In frustration and fury she struck the rail of her chariot.

"Canis! Stand off, stand off! Oh, reckless fool, I will have you cast to the wild dogs for this and throw your bones to wolves! Stand off!"

But her shouts were like whispers in a roaring wind. She looked round for any warrior who carried a horn, but saw none. There seemed only Britons and Romans in savage conflict. Canis had neither ears nor eyes for his queen in any event. He was intent on breaking through to corner Quintus Cerialis himself. He drove his chariot forward, roaring at his cavalry commander to invest the Roman horse. Weapons hacked and stabbed, Romans pitched and bodies piled. Boadicea saw his pair rear, saw the tangle of spears and swords hemming him in, then saw him topple. Above the appalling clash of battle she heard a shriek, the high wailing shriek of Cerdwa, and Boadicea turned white and lifted her face to the sky.

"Hear me, Great Father, hear me, Andrasta, do not put this upon me also, do not, for this I could not bear!"

And wildly she ran her chariot into the blood and flesh of dying conflict to come at her fallen general. Grud sought to restrain her. She thrust so savagely at him that he tumbled from the chariot to kiss the blood-stained ground. Boadicea plunged on, chariot swaying and bucketing, warriors hastily leaping aside as she drove over dead men and broken armour.

Reaching those surrounding her inert general, she leapt down. They stood aside, staring to see the wildness of her look. Cerdwa knelt beside her lord, her mouth trembling, her breathing agitated. Boadicea thrust her off, went down on one knee and seized the grounded shoulders of Canis.

"Oh, wake, Wolfhead," she cried, "wake, dearest of rogues, where stands Britain or Boadicea if you are lost to us?"

Canis opened his eyes. He saw the face of Boadicea, her blue eyes pleading, her mouth beseeching.

"Speak," she begged, "where did the Roman dogs lay wound on you?"

"I took no wound, my Queen," said Canis, sitting up and rubbing his head, "I merely fell from the gilded chariot you so generously gave me."

At this Boadicea retreated from him both in body and spirit, shocked and angered that the villain could so deceive her pitying heart.

"Then," she cried furiously, "you are a clumsy, long-legged fool fit only to ride in a litter for pregnant women. Also, you are a dishonourable fox, for you gave me false promises."

"I only promised I would not be lost to you," he said, rising to his feet. He shook his bruised head and looked around. His face darkened with anger. "What is this? Our cavalry still standing and Quintus gone with his?"

A captain leaned from his mount.

"I swear that when you fell we did not know whether to stay or go—"

"You stayed and so made the day only half a day for us. Well, we shall go now. Quintus and all his horse must be taken." He called for a mount and a warrior galloped to find the most redoubtable beast available. Boadicea, speechless, stared fiercely at her grim general, her breast heaving. Seeing her look he said, "We must take them, my lady, or they will entrench themselves at Lindum with others and cost us months to prise out."

"Go, then, since you must always follow your own reckless nose, but I shall not wait for you. We are marching south to take Londinium, you or Paullinus notwithstanding. So go, rogue, fly after your scratched birds, but if you return without the feathers of Quintus I will have you roasted."

The Ninth Legion was drowning in its own blood, but she seemed more concerned with her general's waywardness than her army's triumph. Angry, frustrated, she left him. He took the horse brought to him, abandoning his chariot to Cerdwa's care.

"Look to it until I return," he commanded her.

At which Cerdwa cried out that she would not let him go without her, the queen would not permit it and neither would she, but Canis turned a deaf ear and rode away, his cavalry following. Cerdwa, incensed, leapt at a young warrior laughing at her as he sat astride his horse. She smote him with the flat of her axe blade and pulled him senseless to the ground. She took his mount and rode it like a wild Amazon until she caught up with Canis. Her violet eyes laughed to see the look he gave her. She tossed her unruly hair and cried, "You may do without your chariot but never without Cerdwa!"

While Boadicea began burying her brave dead, he led a purposeful pursuit north-east after Quintus Cerialis and his cavalry, following trails which showed the Romans had left the road to flee across country, using wild and rugged terrain to keep the Britons guessing. Here and there Canis and his warriors caught a laggard, squeezing from each defiant and bitter captive little information except that Quintus' force was travelling in scattered formations in order to prevent being caught in a concentrated body.

The Britons rode at speed, the terrain no problem to them, and the desperate Roman cavalry left the marks of their going clear to every eye. Fording streams, galloping recklessly through wooded areas, the heat of the day clammy about them, the Britons' pursuit was relentless. But to follow the scattered bands of Romans Canis was forced to split his own warriors into groups, ordering them not to halt their chase until sunset. Through the untamed countryside the Britons hunted and distant noises of sudden sorties sweetened the ears of those who heard. Canis wanted none to escape. He rode obsessively on.

Eventually, so widely separated were the divergent bands of Britons, he and Cerdwa rode alone. Amid green bush and thicket they came unexpectedly on three labouring Romans, mounts exhausted. Two wheeled to engage Canis, but he took one man from his horse with a murderous thrust while Cerdwa, riding in skilful evasion of the thrusting weapon of the third man, leaned with supple grace to smash his helmet. The blow was so fierce that the iron blade rushed through metal and leather to cleave the man's skull. Courageous though the remaining Roman was, he blanched at the way death had overtaken his comrades and galloped for the shelter of a nearby wood. It closed redly dark around him.

Canis and Cerdwa followed, for any Roman desperate enough might bring them to Quintus himself. Quintus was an able commander and Canis knew it would be ability in command that would pose the greatest threat to Boadicea's final victory.

The wood thickened, the red-gold glow of the sun piercing it with light. Suddenly there was a rustle and a cry in front of them, and their mounts danced and skittered as they entered a clearing. There in the red light lay a grounded Roman. He was supporting himself on one elbow, his left arm bloody, his face white, his helmet gone from his dark head. Standing beside him was a woman. Nearby lay a horse with a broken heart, urged beyond endurance. Canis looked down at them, his harsh, drawn features bitter as he saw they were Julian and Lydia. She, seeing the compressed mouth and cold grey eyes of the man she hated so much, saw death also.

Fearless though she was of all things except the omnipotence of great Diana, she shuddered involuntarily. But she did not withdraw from his look. Her green eyes glittered, her hands clenched.

Cerdwa, delighted at the prospect of taking off the head of a Roman woman, leapt from her horse and ran at Lydia, swinging her axe, but Canis, leaning swiftly, sent her sprawling to the ground with a buffet that made her ears sing a wild tune of the forest.

"You are over-greedy again, wood-witch," he said.

Julian smiled painfully but philosophically from the ground, then said,

"I will accept the swift despatch I know you will grant me, Canis, and I also know you will not ill-use Lydia, despite her ill-use of you, but send her on her way. She was foolish to insist on being with us today, but she desired to see Boadicea vanquished and you taken. Let her go, she can do no harm to you or your cause—"

"Oh, the fiends," hissed Lydia, "I would rather die from the blade of this man's she-cat than have you crawl to humbly beg my life of him!"

"Cerdwa," said Canis, "go and bring some of our warriors here."

Cerdwa rose but did not go. She surveyed Lydia like a tigress robbed of its sweetest meat.

"Barbarian," said Lydia stingingly, "you will never catch Quintus Cerialis. He has the measure of your sweating dogs and darkness will further help him. Kill me if you will, but I say Rome will triumph yet, and you and your upstart widow will die not one death but a thousand. This I say and this you know, it is in your eyes. That for your presumption and folly!"

And she spat. Cerdwa let joy take hold of her, for she knew that Canis would surely strangle the harlot now. It would be sport to see, and would drive from her the strange, hot jealousy she felt. But Canis only slipped tiredly from his horse, ignoring Lydia, and told the wood-witch to heed his order and go. The sounds of scouring Britons came like harsh whispers. She was to find the nearest and bring them.

Reluctantly and with hurt in her eyes, Cerdwa remounted and went, though she paused long enough to spit at Lydia. Canis went down on one knee beside Julian, whose face was paler by the minute. The Briton turned aside a ripped, blood-soaked sleeve. The wound, a savage gash from which scarlet slowly but inexorably pulsed, was unbound.

"Bind his wound," said Canis to Lydia, "or he will bleed to death."

"I am not a fool," said Lydia bitterly, "I have bound it twice already but because of the way we have had to ride the wound will not close and what use is this?" She showed him a heap of gory, grimy linen. "You have been at our heels for a long time, Julian's horse has broken its leg and mine its heart, and—" She broke off to give Canis a vindictive look but he was oblivious, taking linen and herbal salve from the pouch that hung from his belt. He applied the salve liberally to the linen and then bound the wound.

"Tear your shift," he told Lydia harshly. She looked down at him, hating him. His icy eyes froze her. "Tear your shift," he repeated, "while I hold back his blood." The new linen was already staining but the flow was ceasing. Lydia's frozen hate was such that it was some moments before she could lift her robe and uncover her shift. Impatiently Canis seized the hem and tore it, ripping strips from the garment. She said nothing, but suffered the humiliation with burning eyes. He used the strips to augment the linen bandage and to bind Julian's arm tightly above the wound, knotting a stone into the binding and twisting the knot until it bit into the flesh and turned it white. Julian grimaced but smiled his thanks.

"You have a charitable way with some Romans," he said.

"We are all incomprehensible to our own selves at

times,'' said Canis, rising. ''You stood before your people to speak in defence of the queen, and afterwards gave her your cloak to cover herself, as I know. So because of that you are free to go. But go quickly and as best you can, for soon my thirsty Cerdwa will be back and with her some of my warriors.''

He returned to his cropping horse to lay his hand on it again and feel its strength. He did not hide his bitter weariness. He turned. Lydia was beside him. The last red light of the day touched the clearing and gave her face a dark glow.

''On a better day for Rome and for me,'' she whispered, ''I will come for you, Briton, as I have sworn to, for by all that legally obtains you are my slave and I will claim you, never doubt.''

''You are a child,'' he said tiredly, ''and think only of your childish sulks when Britain is aflame and your people dying. Go your way, chit.''

Like a child indeed she uttered a sob of rage, then suddenly her expression changed. Triumph and joy were there for a brief moment, only to founder under strangely wild apprehension. And Canis, reading it all, turned with the quickness of a sinewy wolf, despite his weariness, and caught the wrist of the brawny hand that held the Roman dagger. He looked into the face of Paulus, a haggard, begrimed Paulus who stared in a hate equal to Lydia's. Julian, who had opened heavy eyes just before Canis made his quick turn on imminent murder, spoke in a faint voice as the dagger dropped from the numbed hand of Paulus.

''Paulus—he has given us our lives—so let be—we must go, and quickly.''

''I did not speak for Paulus,'' said Canis, releasing the Roman's wrist.

''Nor did I ask you to,'' said Paulus heavily. He had separated from Lydia and Julian, staying to cover their retreat while they rode for safety on Lydia's mount. He had approached quietly, leaving his own horse tethered, on hearing voices. Now he laughed harshly. "You have gall enough for a whole race of barbarians. Do you think me timid enough to accept such a favour from you? Though you tricked me before, you will not again. Now I will surely kill you and make the world quieter and cleaner thereby, offspring of a dung-heap."

Canis was as dark as the oncoming night. Paulus had spoken with the arrogant, uncompromising voice of Rome. This was a voice that had jeered at his queen, those were the eyes that had looked unpityingly on her scourging. As Paulus drew his sword and came murderously at him, Canis slipped the lunging thrust like a lean shadow and his drawn dagger took Paulus in his unprotected throat.

Canis remounted his horse and without a word rode from the clearing to intercept Cerdwa on her return, while Lydia stared in soundless horror at the lifeless body of Paulus. Julian gazed too, but with sadness. Stiffly and painfully he walked to stand over the body.

"Aye," he said slowly to his dead friend, "you spoke obstinately and unwisely to the very last, Paulus, and so Canis had to kill you, brave stubborn fool. As for you," he said to his sister, "you would have watched Paulus slay the Briton at a moment when his generosity to us was still warm in my heart. Oh, Lydia."

"Not so," stammered Lydia, uncharacteristically agitated, "I would not have, not then. The cry to tell Paulus not to strike was on my tongue, Julian, I swear."

"You lie," said Julian and shook his head in bitter reproach. "It is you and Paulus and all others like you who have brought this war upon us. You treasure the spoils of oppression above the fruits of wisdom. You are blinder than moles cast into light. By the greed and stupidity of Catus Decianus and his kind we have reached a pass where we must destroy a proud people and a beautiful queen—"

"Beautiful! That barbaric widow!"

"Aye, beautiful. And when we destroy them we shall be the accursed of our own gods."

"I pray to Diana," she said passionately, "that I shall be the one to destroy that vile Briton."

"Pray to her to open your eyes," said Julian, "and ask her also to deliver us from the Britons, so that we may reach the army of the Imperial Governor with our heads still on our shoulders and not on enemy spears."

* * *

Canis and his cavalry took up the chase again at dawn, pursuing Quintus to the gates of Lindum, where the proud but discreet Roman commander shut himself up in the fortress and refused to budge. Canis accepted the bitter pill. He knew Boadicea could not delay her march on Londinium, but he also knew Quintus would draw to Lindum all Romans who could reach it and either emerge to become a menace again or stay and remain almost impregnable. It would all depend on the outcome of the eventual battle between Boadicea and Suetonius Paullinus himself. If she crushed him then Quintus and Lindum would be isolated.

So Canis began his return south to catch up with Boadicea.

14

BOADICEA, encamped between Camulodunum and Londinium some days after annihilating the Ninth Legion, fumed at the absence of her general. Her host was mightier than ever, a vast army that embraced not only her bold Celtic warriors but thousands of citizens as well. Men, women and children had flocked to place themselves under her protection. In all, they numbered seventy thousand.

The queen, peevish and impatient, railed at her captains and chieftains because of the disorder incumbent on so large a following of non-combatants, but Cacchus said that she was so loved by all in these momentous times that wherever she went they all wished to follow, until she had scourged their lands of every Roman and made their homes safe for them to return to.

"Have I not made the Iceni and Trinovante lands safe already?" she stormed. "I have. So tell them to return now."

"It is not as simple as that, O Queen," said Cacchus, whose bearing as a greybeard had not been impaired by the campaign's discomforts. "They are in such exhilaration over your deeds that they will not leave you until they have seen you defeat Paullinus."

"Then tell my captains to see that in their exhilaration my people do not disport themselves so obtrusively. I love them better when I am not constantly tripping over their feet. And tell them that we renew our march in an hour."

"We are still lacking the Wolfhead," said Cacchus, "and if we march so soon we are likely to reach Londinium without our battle strategy decided."

"That wilful wanderer is an irritation to my ears,"

said Boadicea angrily, "and we will march on Londinium without him and take it without him. I will decide the strategy myself and be the more competent for not having Canis bemuse me with his abominable deviousness."

Cacchus hid his smile in his beard. Boadicea marched and they halted that night close to the wide river Tamesa, not two leagues from Londinium. She was weary from all she had undergone since the death of Prasutagus, but she sat straightbacked on the couch in her tent, Cea and Dilwys with her. She summoned Grud. He came to let his ageless, innocent eyes dwell on the handsome but brooding beauty of the queen. Her hair, loosened, fell about her shoulders and glinted in the light of the lamps.

"Speak, young-old one," she said brusquely.

"On what matter, my lady?"

"On the matter of my accursed roving general," she said.

"I will not listen to such unfair words," said Cea disapprovingly and went to her own couch with Dilwys. She took up a lyre and plucked the strings in soft, haunting Celtic melody.

"On the matter of your accursed, roving general," said Grud to the queen with the wisdom of the innocent, who see light in all men, "he seems to have run exceedingly far in his accursed roving, my lady."

"Was it you who taught Canis the art of a snake's tongue?" demanded Boadicea.

"Not so, he has had the art from birth," said Grud, "and mine is an art born of a sweeter snake, O Queen."

She was about to tell him that his snake must have been another old woman when she heard the quick, challenging voice of one of her guards. Grud went to investigate. He reentered with Canis. In the flickering light of the tent lamps Canis seemed leaner, warier. Cea glanced up and though she did not smile she gave him soft, pleasant welcome. Boadicea stiffened, her blue eyes leapt into brightness and relief and then dropped to look at hands clasped tightly in her lap.

Canis advanced cautiously.

"So?" she said as he bent his knee to her.

"I have had better expeditions," confessed Canis.

"Ah," she said, "have you returned from this one to tell me, in mitigation of your conceit, that Quintus has given your high mightiness the slip?"

"He is an even more evasive dog than I am," said Canis.

"I can do nothing about him for the moment," said Boadicea, cool and serene now, "but I can about you. Your decision to go in unrewarding chase of him was worse than wilfulness. It was unlawful, for it separated you from your appointed responsibilities. So hear me. I have ordered two of my captains and twenty warriors to be always at your back and to restrain you forcibly from any further unauthorised comings and goings."

He stiffened, his mouth tightened and she knew him angry.

"I warned you," she went on quickly, "but no, you would not listen. Can you complain? You cannot. You have brought this on yourself. What is my army if its general is more often absent than present?"

"It has survived," he said and his coldness made her bite her lip. "Well, by your leave I will absent myself again, this time to talk with Cophistus and others about our investment of Londinium."

He inclined his head, wished the dismayed princesses a sound night and left the tent. Swiftly Boadicea went after him and in the darkness outside her tent caught him by the arm.

"Canis, I beg you," she said breathlessly, "do not be angry, do not scold me."

"Scold you?" he said in amazement.

"Aye, with your hurtful tongue, as you often do, and with your scowls, as you frequently do."

He could not see her expression, for she stood with

her back to the light, but he heard the distress in her voice.

"My lady," he said gently, "you are the queen, you are the protector of your people and the chastiser of Romans, and to scold you is beyond even my conceit."

Her hand was still on his arm, the pressure of her fingers warm.

"Canis," she said softly, "do you not see I must shackle you because I fear for you? Did Quintus Cerialis run at us himself, expose his head to us? He did not and would not, and so he lives to fight us again."

"Sweet Majesty," said Canis, and she drew a breath at that, "am I to run the other way? That might confuse the enemy, it would not defeat him."

"To run at his armour is the burden of battle my warriors carry gladly, it is not yours," she said. "Do you not care if I lose you?"

"You are my most beautiful queen—"

"Am I so?" Her interruption was more breathless. "That is sweet for any queen to hear."

"It is also true," he smiled. "You will not lose me, my lady. In my conceit I am well able to counter Roman tactics in battle, which are based on static shield and thrusting sword. Improvisation will always find the chink in the conventional."

"Some day," said Boadicea sweetly, "I will provide you with endless parchment and have you write a manual on the art of being superior to Roman arts, and so bring yourself renown as a scholar in military matters as well as a general."

In words she was never outmatched. But there was more than words at this moment. He caught the fragrance of the scent she used. It was heady to any man who had lately dealt in so much carnage and death. He said, to avert his weakness, "I am more likely to be renowned as a general his queen could never find."

Why would he never soften to her, why, why? She took a deep breath. The night air was warm and in the

darkness the many flickering fires of the great camp
were visible. The smell of wood smoke was faint,
elusive. He was elusive too.

"I will not shackle you, Wolfhead," she said, "I cannot. I gave no orders to anyone, I could not. Oh, you
are free to come and go as you wish. I have considered
every kind of halter for you but cannot use any of them.
You are disgraceful and disregarding, aye, but you are
dear to my house. Even more than that." She reached,
took his hands, lifted them and bent her head, as she
had once before. She laid her mouth on his right palm
and then on his left. The sweet, warm pressure of her
lips squeezed his heart. "Now will you remember,
Canis, when the heat of battle impels you to recklessness
that you are dear to me too?" Her voice was low, unsteady, and there leapt into his mind the incredible
thought that on an evening when the land was red under
the sun he had made a grievous mistake. But because it
was incredible he dismissed it and to ease the moment of
its tension he spoke lightly.

"Ah, is that why you are at your happiest when you
are miscalling me?"

Boadicea trembled. Oh, the gods, was he so much the
jester that at a moment like this it was jests alone she
could arouse in him? Surely he had some love for her.
Would he otherwise have fought and schemed so well
for her?

"As women miscall those who belong to them," she
said, "so does any queen miscall those closest to her. It
is to cover her weakness. I will rail at you many a time
yet, I fear, but Canis, what is your inconsistence and my
peevishness if they are not what obtain between two
people who belong to each other?"

She might have meant everything by that, she might
only have meant to be a forgiving woman after being a
threatening queen. It tormented him, nevertheless.
Britain was not yet free, she herself not yet secure. All
her victories would mean nothing if the last battle of all

ended in defeat. To speak of what she would like him to
be in his relationship with her house was of little importance while she was engaged in her life or death
struggle with Rome. But she was Boadicea and whether
she was indulging in high majesty or incomprehensible
vagaries, she was always inescapably herself.

"You may miscall me or command me now and
forever, my lady."

The men who had attended at her court spoke words
like that ten times a day. How dared he give her servility
when that was the last thing she had asked for? She
turned from him in frustration.

"If you are not in the mood for anything but absurdities," she said stiffly, "then I will leave you to
resolve what I cannot—how you are able to equate your
admirable perception of Romans with your total lack of
perception of me."

"Absurdities are the least of it all," he said, "but it
does grow late and while I need to speak to the chieftains you have need of rest."

"I have a need of that which in your obstinacy you
will not give me," she said in a low voice, then abruptly
returned to her tent.

Canis conferred at length with his officers and when
at last he retired to his own tent, Cerdwa had built a fire
and prepared his food. Now she brought wine as he
stood pensive by the fire. He glanced at her, her supple
limbs gleaming in the light of the flames. He thanked
her abstractedly, but the wine had no flavour, the food
no taste. He looked into the flames and saw only the red
carnage of battle. He thought of what perhaps had been
a grievous mistake, made because of tragic future and
warm brown eyes. Cerdwa crept to his side but he paid
her no attention, even when he felt the soft curve of her
breast against his arm. She sighed.

"Lord," she said, the velvet on her tongue, "we have
fought many battles and such is our might together that
none can stand against us. There are songs of Canis and

Cerdwa, do you not hear them?'' She pressed a little closer. "I am to die in the queen's last battle, as you know, but it is not writ which battle will be the last. I am only reminding you of my fate because, as you also know, I must not die a virgin. If I do I shall be numbered among the unsleeping spirits, I will be locked forever in an oak tree in a deep forest and my voice will moan in the wake of the midnight wind. That is the fate of any wood-witch who dies a virgin, unless a Druid arch-priest smites open the tree with a golden axe, when her spirit may then leap free providing she gives her virginity to the priest.''

Canis smiled. "It is an imaginative piece of lore.''

"It is also true, lord,'' sighed Cerdwa. "I do not wish to wait for a Druid who may never come. Therefore, lord, although I am so much less than you are, you will not let me die unloved, will you?''

"I will not even let you die, Cerdwa, for despite all your witchery you are a rousing warrior and Boadicea will always have need of you.''

She pressed closer yet so that he might feel the beat of her doleful heart. In some curiosity he placed his hand upon her to discover whether it was true that wood-witches had hearts whose beat cannot be felt like that of ordinary maids. What he found was warm, full-breathing roundness and Cerdwa, who had felt the touch of no man's hand there, drew a sharp breath for the confusing pleasure it gave her.

"Are you a wood-witch?'' he asked. "Your heart beats like life itself.''

"Only you can discern it,'' she whispered, "for you are no mortal man, lord, but a god, as I have long suspected.''

Canis smiled. She was silky in her night ways. The heat of the fire and the exertions of days drowsed his senses. He shook his head and took his hand from Cerdwa's roundness, but she caught it and drew it within her loosened tunic. Heedless of the fact that wherever his hand was his mind was elsewhere, her arms stole around his neck, her breath came quick and there was sweet pain within the flesh he touched. But she had chosen the wrong moment. He could not set his mind aside from his majestic and beautiful queen. He thrust Cerdwa roughly from him. The fire kindling red flame in her eyes, she breathed,

"If you were not a god and cruelly strong, lord, I would kill you."

"You will never kill me, Cerdwa," he said, "for though I might turn my back on you a hundred times, there is that in you and that in me which is like to like, and this will hold you fast from the deed. Bring me more wine."

*   *   *

The Imperial Governor, Suetonius Paullinus, was at last in Londinium, with his cavalry. The large, straggling city, its people mainly a hodgepodge of traders and merchants, contained the chief Roman supply depot, entrenched and palisaded, and held by a strong contingent of troops. But without ten thousand additional men at least, the city was utterly incapable of holding off Boadicea and her host. She now commanded nearly forty thousand fighting Britons. Paullinus reckoned, however, that if the Second Legion arrived in time from Glevum, he would have a sound bastion of defence. With his own cavalry and the resident troops to augment the Second Legion he could force her to withdraw.

It seemed to him that no sooner had he received the news of the crushing defeat of Quintus Cerialis than Boadicea's host was heard a few leagues from Londiniun. Paullinus up to then had had no first-hand knowledge of how speed dominated her campaign. Speed had its compulsive as well as its tactical element. Her warriors must return to gather the harvest. They could not conduct a winter campaign without that. And so she reached Londinium in a time that dismayed the Roman general.

And alas for all his defensive concepts, he received with horror the news that the Second Legion had refused to march from Glevum. The legate was absent, the camp prefect in charge. And the prefect was a thinking man. He thought about every pro and con, and decided in the end that if Quintus Cerialis had been foolhardy enough to leave his Lindum fortress and commit suicide, no one was going to say the Second Legion had not profited from this example. He sent Paullinus word that the Second Legion was too heavily committed to risk a march on Londinium.

Paullinus, in icy rage at this defection which left him humiliatingly helpless, destroyed his depot at Londinium and decamped with his cavalry almost as Boadicea thundered at the gates. He left terrified citizens almost completely defenceless and struck west in the hope of meeting his infantry coming from Mona.

The Romanised, cosmopolitan people of Londinium were to Boadicea as dangerous to her concepts of freedom as Romans themselves. Left alone they would admit new armies from Caesar, and assist Roman reinforcements from Gaul. So her warriors smashed the heart out of the inadequate Roman force as a whirlwind smashes standing corn, and she rode into the city in her full panoply of war, with Canis on her right hand. They came, the exhilarated host, to the sound of song, to the noise of chariots, the clatter of horses and the clash of brass and iron. They marched, they leapt, the warriors maids vivid, their naked limbs agleam, their voices joyful, and every sound and every noise melded into one melodic chorus of war. Londinium crashed in rubble and flame. Boadicea razed it as she had razed Camulodunum, and though it was rebuilt in later years someone did not forget to inscribe her deed on resurrected Roman marble.

"Here Boadicea rode in her chariot of war, and with her rode the Wolf who bore her hammer of war, and where the iron of their wheels struck stone the stone itself burst into roaring flame."

Which Canis would have said was imaginative but exaggerated.

*   *   *

She marched then, at the insistence of Canis, to engage Paullinus, who now commanded the only Roman force capable of giving her real battle. But the alarmed governor avoided her. Each time she thought she had him he skilfully slipped her. Finding the Roman town of Verulamium in her way she invested it. Canis, though not considering it important, took it for her swiftly and economically. It was Roman blood that again ran in profligate rivers.

About this time Boadicea learned that one Roman she would have given much to capture had escaped her. The Imperial Procurator, Catus Decianus, chief cause of all the outrages which had provoked the war, had not stopped running and hiding since the Iceni had risen. Panic-stricken at the consequences of his greed and cruelty he managed to slip away in a ship to Gaul, and so a man more deserving of death than most others at this time completely escaped the queen's vengeance.

Nevertheless, aside from Catus Decianus, this vengeance had almost run its full course. Only the army of Paullinus stood between Boadicea and complete victory. And she was impatient to get at Paullinus. She was dreaming of peace now, of long idyllic summer days and the crisp invigoration of frosty winter, when men and women returning from the hunt filled her house with noise and laughter. She had a great love of freedom and sport. And she had another great love, such as she had never imagined could disturb her in the way it did. So she fretted to have done with Paullinus and all Romans.

But Paullinus continued to refuse battle. He retired well to the west to build up his army. He now had all his infantry as well as other troops, and he had also augmented his Romans with levies from the Belgic tribes, ancient rivals of the Iceni. Consumed by icy hate for Boadicea, he applied himself carefully to creating a force strong enough to accept battle.

Boadicea and Canis maintained their hunt, but they refused to be drawn too far to the west. Southern Britain was their domain and where Rome might contrive to land reinforcements. And at the moment Paullinus was in a state of isolation, and if he was to prevent the Britons destroying an embarking army he would have to come to them eventually.

So Boadicea drew off for a spell to rest her host in the vicinity of Epping Forest. Here their camp, encircled by their waggons, rang to the sound of hammers on iron, to the repair of weapons and to the songs of a victorious people confident in their future. Their queen would assuredly defeat Paullinus and then lead them back to their homes in time to harvest crops sown before the rising.

Canis despatched scouts and patrols daily in search of the Romans and frequently he himself rode with Cophistus and others. He was as grimly urgent as ever. Time favoured the Romans, not the Britons.

15

IT WAS A fine day but cloudy when news at last came that Paullinus was within reach. The Roman general was moving north-east of Londinium. Boadicea broke camp and marched. She halted the following night by a small village north of the destroyed city, where Canis conjectured the queen to be in a position to dispute another retreat westwards by Paullinus. An hour after they made camp two Brigantes arrived to advise Boadicea that the Romans were indeed only a little way east of her. She sent at once for Canis.

The elder of the village had given over his dwelling for the comfort of the queen and her daughters. Because he was proud to receive her she accepted his offer, though she would have preferred her capacious tent. Cea and Dilwys, less melancholy now because of bright hopes of final victory, glanced up as Canis entered, and at last there was a fleeting smile on Cea's face. He spoke a small nonsense to her and the smile peeped again. The princesses stayed a while to talk to him, then retired to the inner room to leave him alone with the queen.

She turned with eager impatience and told him of the news brought by the Brigantes. Canis, harder and browner from the campaign, his eyes very grey because of so much death, rubbed his chin.

"I would like to speak with these Brigantes," he said, "and if they are our agents I will know them."

They were broad, weathered Brigante men and told Canis what they had told Boadicea, that Paullinus and his army were encamped to the east and could be caught and attacked by noon the following day if the queen marched at sunrise.

"You are new friends of ours," said Canis, "so I ask,

do you bring this news for gold or for love of Queen Boadicea?''

"It is brought," said one, "because Queen Boadicea is the only one who can rid Britain of Romans."

"When did you find them at this place?" asked Canis.

"At noon today, lord," said the second man.

"At noon?" Canis was not impressed. "By the horns of the great aurochs, you have taken long enough to advise us. Ten hours. Did you walk on one leg or two?''

"We were delayed by having to avoid their patrols, but they are there, lord, I swear, and look to be settled there.''

"I like it no better for your swearing," said Canis.

"What does it matter," said Boadicea impatiently, "as long as they stay long enough for us to catch them?''

"Smite them, O Queen," said one Brigante, "fall on them and smite them." He spoke boisterously. "You will have their measure."

"Will we?" said Canis. "Estimate their strength for us, it need not be exact."

"It is not inconsiderable, lord, but does not look as great as yours."

"That is a dissimulation, not an estimate," said Canis. "However, you have our thanks for coming and since you are so anxious for the Romans to be smitten you shall not be denied the joys of smiting them with us.''

The Brigantes took this jest uneasily, edging a nervous way out in the company of Grud, who put them at the disposal of the recruiting captain. Much to their amazement jest turned into reality. What reward for services rendered was it to be given sharp spears and told to throw themselves on Romans tomorrow?

Boadicea thought Canis had reacted too suspiciously and said so.

"My lady," he said, "they were not our men.

Perhaps they are in sympathy, perhaps not. They say the Romans are there. I believe that. We are to march and catch them. I question that. Do not forget that those who choose the ground govern the conditions, the circumstances and even the tactics. Paullinus knows where we are, that we have him blocked from the west, yet if the Brigantes are right he is sitting there unworried. I dislike it.''

"Oh, you are an old glumface," she said. She was robed in soft, woollen white, she was honey-brown and sweet-mouthed. "What has happened to you? Where is your smile for me? I have seen it so little of late. Is it this war? Has our campaign made me old and wrinkled? Canis, I am not a hag yet, am I?"

She spoke teasingly but teasing was not in her eyes. They were very soft and in the light of the lamps her face, with its beautifully-defined bones, was as haunting as ever.

"Am I to say again you are beautiful?" he said with the ghost of a smile.

"It would not offend me," she said. "Ah, is it Paullinus who makes you grim? Canis, tomorrow at your discretion we will fling our army around him and little help then to him will be his choice of ground."

"He is not where he is now to make the battle easy for us," said Canis, "he will not conveniently fall into our embrace. We need room to manoeuvre. He may not. We shall see."

"You are cautious before all battles and overcautious before this one." She was disappointed that he did not share her eagerness to dispose of the whole problem of Romans for good. "You are the most paradoxical of men. Cautious before every battle, you are as reckless as any as soon as the horns blow. Indeed, it is all of a mystery that you have not gone sneaking off to slay Paullinus yourself now that you know where he is. Or does he intimidate you?"

"Aye, he does," said Canis. Boadicea felt shock and

dismay. This could not be. He was the brain, the courage and the architect of her victories. He was her protector, her shield, her torment, her consolation and her staff of life. He could not fear any Roman. He must not.

"The skies will fall and the mountains sunder before I believe Paullinus a better man or a better general than you. Why, even if he had a hundred thousand Romans he could not withstand your art of being superior to every art of theirs."

Her heart lightened at the smile he gave her then.

"You have an endearing way of reducing a man's conceit," he said. "I am not in fear of Paullinus, only in fear that he may have us run into a trap."

"Oh, gloom, gloom, gloom," she said. "Canis, you will contrive victory for us, you will. You cannot fail, you have never failed. You are greater than any general of Rome."

She was at her most bewitching, in her softest of moods. Canis felt the weight of his responsibilities becoming almost unbearable. She was leaving him no room to fail, and how could he fail such a queen and such a woman as this?

"We none of us will fail, my lady," he said tenderly, "and we must contrive that Paullinus comes to us. Now I will go and speak to others."

"You will when I say so," she said, but sweetly, "and if you fidget I shall not be flattered. Canis, this is a moment when we can look forward to returning to Venta Icenorum. We shall hunt again and quarrel again, and perhaps you will even become a scholar again and teach me what I would most like to know."

His smile was a little wary. He knew how she could sometimes pose the unanswerable.

"What is that?"

"Content," said Boadicea.

"Even if we both lived to see our hundredth summer I should not be able to teach you content," he said.

"If it cannot be taught, can it not be given?" She raised her eyes. They were clear and compelling. "Canis, see me."

"I see you, my Queen," he said, acknowledging her proud, unbroken vitality.

"Queen? You see with the eyes of a servant, then." Her voice was rich with warm undertones. She drew a breath and went on, "Canis, as a widow I cannot wed or be asked to wed until my widowhood has gone a year and a day. This is the law."

"I know. It is not so much a law as a contravention of reason."

Oh, his masculine belief in his own magnanimous interpretation of arguments, his frustrating tendency to turn sweet conversation into one more argument! What did it matter except that the law was the law?

"Who are you to miscall what has obtained for centuries, what has been jealously guarded and handed down by many kings and queens?" she asked, and then bitterly reproached herself for being fool enough to let him provoke her.

"As usual, I am above myself," he said wryly.

Boadicea laughed, but at herself.

"As usual, you are yourself," she said.

"Who is it you wish to wed after a year and a day?" he asked quietly. "Is it Prince Iodemus?"

Iodemus was prince of the Trinovantes. Boadicea could not believe her ears, for that royal featherbrain's only claim to manhood was in his moustache. Canis must be mad. Oh, great Andrasta, she thought, am I in such defeat tonight?

"You have no eyes at all," she said a little wildly. "Prince Iodemus? Oh, the sweet gods, look at me and tell me, do you not see me?"

She was brilliant, compelling, entreating.

"I see Boadicea," he said, "I see pride and majesty—"

"Fool!" She flung the word passionately at him.

"What have pride and majesty to do with tenderness and love? Oh, fool, although I am in contempt of my own law for saying this, do you not know you are to be my consort? Do you not know you must be?"

Canis gazed in pain at her. Her blood leapt to put flame to her face and heat in her body. Her mouth trembled. He was engulfed, numbed. He thought of Paullinus and battle, of kingship and Cea, brown-eyed, stricken Cea, and of Boadicea who was like no other woman. And he thought of his grievous mistake. How might he take the mother without leaving the daughter more stricken? Boadicea had posed him the most unanswerable question of all and his ready tongue lay dumb. For long moments they looked at each other, the heart and the desire of the queen plain in her blue eyes, the bitter confusion of Canis on his face.

"Canis?" Her voice was anxious, appealing. "Canis, will you not answer me? I beg you, be in sweet love of me."

"Oh, the gods," he groaned, and at that moment Cea, putting aside the blanket of skins that sheltered the room she shared with Dilwys, stepped forward. She was in her long night robe, her curling hair soft and shining, and she was warm from sleep. Boadicea turned away, hiding the heat still on her face.

"I was asleep," said Cea, "but your voices woke me and I came to see why Canis was still here. There is nothing amiss, is there?" Though she spoke to her mother she was looking at Canis, her dreaminess like a smile. His heart turned over and his confusion grew worse.

"Princess," he said, "nothing is amiss except that we have been discussing how we must go against Paullinus. Sleep sweetly on my assurance that we will box him and defeat him."

Cea lost her warm glow. She paled, then said bravely, "For this I shall pray. I long for the end of this war.

Then we shall return home. Canis, you will win a great victory."

Canis saw an avenue of retreat and a chance to reflect on the unanswerable.

"Then I will go now and discover with our captains how to draw the fox from its hole and then box the animal. For that is what will give us victory. My lady," he said to the queen, "when we have victory then you and I may be able to speak more easily on so many things."

Boadicea turned sharply on him. So, unable to face up to the ordeal of admitting love for her, he was going to run from her. Oh, the mean-spirited dog.

"Ah," she said, "now you are hot for giving battle, after all. Yet in things that have to do with sweet life you are abject with cowardice."

"My mother, that is not true," said Cea gently but firmly. "I do not know what else you have been discussing but I do know you are confusing cowardice with compassion. Canis cannot order this battle tomorrow without being in concern for us, for he knows sweet life is dependent on its outcome. Is it not?"

"Cea, go back to your rest," said Boadicea. There was already too much of the woman about her elder daughter. For the first time she realised Cea was beautiful.

"Canis," said Cea, "I will pray for you to be invincible and for the queen to be cherished by Andrasta. In you and in her lie all our happiness and love."

"The sweetest and most peaceful sleep to you," he said and smiled at her. And Cea, who had touched no man since that day of horror, put out her hand to touch his as he went from the dwelling. Turning to speak a final tender farewell to the queen she found her mother in such incomprehensible emotion as to be almost unable to say a word. Her mother was more temperamental than ever these days. It was the war and this terrible conflict with Paullinus tomorrow.

But Paullinus was not Canis. Canis was twice him in strategy. Cophistus said so. Still, she could not rid herself of some anxieties concerning the battle. But how sweet it was to feel life warm again within her after so many months of self-pity and self-disgust.

Canis still loved her. He would forgive her her impurity and, when victory was won, speak for her and wed her, as he had promised.

Cea drifted into almost happy sleep.

It was late when Canis, having arranged for the army to march soon after daybreak, returned to the small timber and reed dwelling the villagers had offered him. Outside was Cerdwa, sitting on her heels, hands to her face and weeping.

"Lord," she wept, "I am to be given to the Druids."

"What folly is this?"

"There are to be three virgins sacrificed before battle," she wept, "and the queen has laid the sacred rite on unhappy Cerdwa. The night lies cruel in my heart because of this, for though I do not want to die a virgin either in battle or on altar, I would sooner it be in battle."

Canis, no believer in Druidism, was sure it would also have little appeal to Cerdwa. She would consider the sacrifice of her body very unrewarding from her own point of view. Indeed, she was weeping at the prospect, and few men ever heard a wood-witch crying at night.

"I did not think your end was writ this way," he said drily. Cerdwa stifled a sob but kept her long hair hiding her face. "I will see the queen and ask her to let you die in battle," he said.

"Alas, she will only scorn you, lord. She is very proud and must act as her moods take her, and I know it would go against all her desires to reprieve me, even at your behest. Though I love her fiercely, I know she loves me not. She frowns on my regard for you and so has named me for the Druids' knife."

"Is this all of it?" he asked. "Or are you taking the longest distance to bridge the shortest gap?"

"Do not go to the queen," she begged, "for she has retired to her bed in the fiercest of tempers and if you woke her up to speak for me I would fear for both of us. However, if you have the smallest feeling for me in your tenderness, which I know is often above your cruelty, though not too often, if you do have such feeling, which is unlikely, since you are akin to a god while I am only a miserable wood-witch with little beauty, though it is said I own a fine shape—"

"Come at the point quickly, scatter-tongue, or I will put my foot on your miserable wood-witch neck."

"Lord," she entreated, on her knees, her head bent, "if you have any liking for Cerdwa, be it only a little, will you not save her from the Druids? Will you not let me lie with you this night so that I shall no longer be a virgin at dawn? Then the Druids will reject me and I will be spared to join you in the battle. The Druids will not demand your head, lord, for we will say I was despoiled by a villain called Ceffwyn as I lay bemused with sleep. They will kill Ceffwyn for robbing the altar of me, but he is a man of the most minor account, lord, who does not know one end of a spear from the other and constantly plants the wrong end on his foot."

"Cerdwa, you are the most witchlike of wood-witches and the most persuasive of virgins. Is this Ceffwyn expected to go happily to his death for a deed he will not have committed?"

"Lord," said the quick, liquid voice from the curtain of hair, "he has not the brain of half a sheep and will be in such pleasure at being accounted strong enough to ravish me that he will die laughing."

"Something might be done for a dimwit as happy as that," said Canis. He was beset with his own bitter problems but Cerdwa was a beguiling wench and the greatest of warrior maids. "I will do what you wish, Cerdwa, for you have served Boadicea as well as any.

And it is a night when, because of tomorrow, none should withhold love or tenderness from another.''

Cerdwa's eyes glowed, but with bliss was pain also. Canis was sad.

''Lord, be neither sad nor afraid,'' she whispered, ''for though I may die tomorrow, no Roman can destroy you. Every mountain and every forest in Britain will give life to you, for you will have given a forest maid life after death instead of loveless penance.''

''Cerdwa, you believe there is life after death?'' He was sceptical of all gods, cynical of all godly promises.

''With all my heart, lord, for how else after I have gone may I hope to see you and serve you again? Is it not writ that Cerdwa will stand in the shadow of Canis for all time?'' Her voice was murmurous. ''I will wait for you in the light, and in your sweet mercy, will you favour Cerdwa? Will you, when I have fallen, take up my axe and keep it always, so that when your own time comes you may bring it to me?''

''I will,'' he said, for there was a sweetness about his woodwitch now that was mystic and haunting. ''You are a strange creature, Cerdwa. Do you know if it is writ that Boadicea will die?''

Still on her knees before him, Cerdwa said, ''In time, lord, as do all mortals, but not by any Roman hand. Do not be in pain, for when you are Cerdwa is in pain too. Will I come to your bed soon?''

''In an hour,'' he said, going into the hut. ''I have a burden of thoughts that will take time to set aside.''

In the darkness the camp fires were dying, the army at its brief rest. But Cerdwa was alive, awake and glowing. She went to him at the appointed time. He was lying on his bed of soft skins. By the light of a single oil lamp she saw his eyes. He looked infinitely troubled. Tears sprang to her lids and she yearned to bring him to joy. She stooped to expunge the lamp, her naked body vibrant and gleaming, creamily reflecting the light before she put it out. Then she was beside him, stretching close to him. Her body was heated, yet when he put his hand on her she trembled and coldness seemed to strike her. Her smooth skin became sharp with goosepimples.

"It is nothing, lord," she whispered, "I am not afraid, I do but shiver with the joy of being close to you. You must know that this is a quite wondrously terrifying moment for me. All the same, I am not afraid."

"It is also a moment for tender deeds, not words, so bite on your tongue."

Cerdwa sighed, then shivered again. He would, in his way, do the deed swiftly and even cruelly. To be favoured, she knew, was not necessarily to be loved. But although his strength and hardness were so obtrusive that her shivering body suffused with confusing heat, she was wonderingly aware of a caressing gentleness. She sensed it was not going to be swiftly cruel at all.

Cerdwa's lithe, supple body burned from the heat of her racing blood.

So this was her lord who was also a god who was also a man.

Delight consumed her.

"Lord—"

"Stop your tongue."

For a while she was content enough to do this by biting him, but then she opened her mouth to cry out. At which he stopped her tongue with his own mouth. Cerdwa, gasps and cries stifled, vibrated at the wonder of it all, and when he finally did that which she so desired her blood ran like liquid fire. There was the strangest sensation of being unpardonably besieged, at which her mind laughed, for she was sure that her lord would be as accomplished in this as in all else. She cried out, a wild cry, but not even the sharp-eared foxes heard her, for the mouth of her lord was hard on her own.

At the end when she might have spoken she could not. Her tongue lay still. She held him that he might not go from her and he did not, but lay with her until her quivering body was as quiet as her tongue. In the darkness she saw only the pictures of her enraptured mind. His warm body withdrew. She turned and looked at him until his face came to her eyes out of the night. His eyes were open but unseeing, darkly still. Again tears sprang to prick her lashes, and she put her hot body against his and laid her head, with its soft crown of black hair, on his shoulder. Her mouth, shyly but in sensitive love, kissed him there, and he closed his eyes and after a while he slept.

"Lord," she whispered in a small voice, "I pinched you to wake you not because of my selfishness but because of my worry. I know so little of these things, are you sure I am no longer a virgin? I would not wish the Druids to have me after your great accomplishment on my behalf."

"In your knowledge as a woman and your shrewdness as a wood-witch," said Canis, his mind on so much else, "you know full well you are no longer a virgin."

"Can you not make me doubly sure? Canis, lord, will you do to me what you did before and so put my mind at rest and my body to sleep? In truth, I have not slept at all yet, and as I am to die tomorrow, as is writ, must my last night be so sleepless?"

He knew this to be artifice, not truth, but what was a man to do with so endearing a comrade as this one?

"Since you will chatter me from all sleep myself otherwise," he said resignedly, "I will do as you wish and in a way to remove all your uncertainty, I hope."

So he favoured her again and so convincingly that Cerdwa shuddered, blushed and bit ecstatically. It turned her mind upside-down, she thought she would never compose herself for sleep, but she did.

Before the first light of dawn had fingered the treetops Canis awoke. Cerdwa was by his side. He remembered, he sighed. At his ironic regard Cerdwa, who was herself awake, her eyes big and wondering, gave him a shy, nervous smile and over her face flew the colour of the sky at sunset. She pressed his hand to her round, warm breast, then drew it to her mouth and kissed the palm. Then came the sound of quick footsteps outside, the door of the hut was flung open and in the dim dawn light stood Queen Boadicea.

Canis, seeing her, felt a violent, woundy pain beset him, as if the sharp point of her dagger was deep between his ribs, for on the face of the queen was outrage on prior outrage, disgust on prior disgust and a fury beyond description.

Cerdwa gave a tragic cry and as the Queen plucked the dagger from her girdle the wood-witch slipped from the bed and with her body pearly in the faint light ran low to the door. With a cat-like movement and a strange sob she swooped under the dagger and out. From under the loose covering of skins, Canis up on his elbows stared ruefully at the open door and then warily at the queen. She stood there, one hand clutching her dagger, the other at her throat, her blue eyes frozen but her body trembling, and within the frame of her unbound hair her face was deathly pale. Her breath fought to free itself from tortured lungs.

It was not that a vigorous man was forbidden to have loving communion with a maid. As far as the Iceni were concerned it was the privilege of a maid or a woman to say aye or no according to her own wishes, providing no adultery was committed.

So there was no affront to the law in what Canis and Cerdwa had done, and no need, thought Canis, for Boadicea to look as outraged as this about it. Fury possessed her. Surely not because by his act he had frustrated the Druids? She had nothing in true common with them.

She found her voice at last. She sounded strangled.

"Licentious dog, you shall die for this!"

"My lady," he said placatingly, "this was not done in that way, I swear, but to save her from the Druids. She is too brave a warrior for their bloodstained altar, even though she is a wood-witch.''

"Lying jackal, what false tale is this?" she flung at him and never had he heard her so fierce with storm.

"Did you not command her body to the Druids' altar this morning? She deserves a better fate than that, my Queen."

The queen drew a choking breath and her hand around the dagger showed white so fierce was her grip.

"So!" She shook with fury. "So! You pleasured her to fool and cheat the Druids, but were fooled and cheated yourself! And by a wanton with a tongue more twisted than your own. I did not command her to any sacrifice, I did not even speak of it. What are Druids to me? What is she and her wishes to me? As for you—" She broke off, robbed of breath by her fury, her torment, her despair.

Canis rose, fastening a skin around his waist, and her burning eyes followed his every movement.

"Cerdwa is not to blame," he said quietly, "for by her virginity and her beliefs she was in distress, thinking that if she died unloved—"

"Your licentiousness is one thing," she hissed, "your treachery and deceit another!"

"My treachery?" he said in amazement.

"Aye, unspeakable treachery to me and mine! By your foul wood-witch you have betrayed Cea, and by Cea you have betrayed me! In deceit you have gone behind my back with Cea, you have told her you will speak for her, and because of this and other things you are the blackest and vilest dog in all Britain! This morning, only a short while ago, Cea came to tell me that because the battle today will mean either darkness or joy, she could not longer withhold from me that which has passed between you and her. I could not believe it true, I could not believe you sought to conclude your game of many years ago and so make a mockery of me. So I came at once in my anger and found you bedded with your wanton—oh, you are a shame and an offence in the eyes of all!''

"Am I so?'' he said and he had become a little grim.

"You are! You have dared to raise your presumptuous eyes to my sweet princess, you have bemused her and her heart with your flattering tongue. For that alone I might have you done to death!''

"This is the truth,'' he said evenly. "I did raise my eyes to Cea, but that which I said to her was at a time when the king lay dead and your house was being squeezed to death by Septimus Cato. All sweetness seemed to be going from Cea's life. She is young and sets great store by love and kindness—''

"Do I not know my own daughter?'' she raged, racked by a jealousy that gave her unbearable pain. "Who are you, you lackey, to instruct me on a girl I am mother to? Did you not tell her you loved her?''

"Aye, and I do love her,'' said Canis as the grey light of dawn reached in, "but this—''

"So!'' The queen, distraught, was suddenly haggard. "And you do not love me!''

"This is untrue,'' he protested, agonisingly trapped between what he must do for stricken Cea and what he felt for his suffering queen, "and I have said more than once—''

"What you have said more than once has been with the tongue of a fawning lackey or silver liar! You have used that tongue to bemuse me too, to blind me to what obtained between you and Cea, hoping that I might fall in battle so that when you wed her she would be queen!''

His hard brown face took on a pale harshness and the bitterness of his eyes pierced her, so that her heart cried out. She looked wildly at him, the pain she felt overriding everything but a passion to put him in greater pain.

"My lady," he said, "to put me to death is your queenly right but to destroy me is to set yourself up above the cruellest gods."

"Have you not in your treachery concealed from me your purpose with Cea in order to keep yourself in my good graces?"

"I have never been in your good graces," he said harshly.

Her hands to her throat, her eyes dark and enormous, Boadicea gasped, "You have lain with your odious wood-witch, and her smell is still on you! You have betrayed Cea! And made a mockery of me! I brand you liar and dog!"

He looked sadly at her outraged pride. She could not hide the mortal wound she felt and he would have gone to her and eased her hurt in whatever way he could. But as he put out a hand she withdrew as if from a contagion. Perhaps history would have taken a different course had he persisted, had he taken her into his arms and kissed the agony from her eyes. But she was still the queen and he was still in his trap.

"My lady," he said, "is this how we must arm ourselves for battle today? With your anger and my errors paramount? If I have unforgivably offended you let it be registered and I will take the consequences later. But for the moment no more unqueenly words, I beg you. The important conflict is not the one between you and me, the real issue not my folly concerning Cerdwa or my guilt over Cea, but with Paullinus and only with Paullinus."

"Oh," she said bitterly, "you shall enter the battle with your shame and villainy branded to the skies!"

Canis let sudden dark anger ride across his face.

"Have done with this, I say," he said.

"Ah," she whispered, new anger shuddering through her, "so we are to put aside your treachery and let you raise your detestable voice against your queen—"

"Have done!" he thundered, and she stood incredulous at that, her breast heaving, her eyes wide and misty. "We have to march, we have to contrive, we have to fight. Make as public as you wish the weakness and frailty you find in me, but do this when all else is over. We will put behind us for the moment all loud voices and dire threats concerning matters which, in truth, have nothing to do with our people and freedom, only with you and me."

"And Cea," she whispered, "and Cea." She put her hands to her eyes for a second, then said brokenly, "Oh, Canis, you stand more bravely against me than any other man would dare, yet you have betrayed me in a way no one else would. Because of this I would have kept you shackled to a waggon today to await the outcome. But this would shame your father, who has always been as honourable and as loyal as any chieftain. So, for his sake, you shall for the space of the battle today still be my general. But in name only. You shall not have the honour of deciding how it shall be fought, for this you do not deserve. Instead, you shall lead the assault under my command. This is the last favour I will grant you. In leading the assault you will be able to die proudly and without shame on Roman swords, and my warriors will not know there is anything amiss. In this way I shall have honoured the general who dishonoured me."

His sadness was such as Cerdwa had discerned. It tore at the heart of Boadicea. They looked at each other. His eyes were lonely, bleak, hers full of pain. And her mouth would not be still.

"If I said you spoke unqueenly words, then I wronged you," he said quietly, "for you are always true to your concepts and never less than proudly generous. It shall be as you say."

"Oh, you will disarm me yet," she whispered, "so speak no more words like these." She went to the door. She turned, trembling. The glitter in her eyes was not of anger. "I had always thought," she said, her voice breaking, ''that you were more than any other man, despite all your conceits. A woman might have known you were not, for a woman knows that all men will deceive her, but a woman who is a queen first does not expect to be deceived by any except her enemies.''

Then she was gone and Canis, bitter in his helplessness and ravaged by his grievous mistake, stood there in infinite loneliness.

16

THEY MARCHED AN hour after daybreak, all seventy thousand of them, combatants and non-combatants, to the rumble of their waggons and the music of their songs. They were turbulently joyful, for today they would see their invincible queen destroy Paullinus. Before the sun went down he and his army would be slain to the last man. Boadicea was at her proudest and most tempestuous. Aye, she was strangely tempestuous.

Cerdwa rode beside Canis. She found him bitter and this made her sad. She had brought him his morning food but he said no word, only looked at her in a way that brought fear and anguish to her. Even now he would not suffer her to say a single word. They rode some distance behind the queen, and this at least pleased Cerdwa. To come under the queen's eye was, she knew, to risk instant death.

At midday scouts reported the host of Paullinus massed in front of them and not long afterwards the two armies confronted each other. Canis clipped his lower lip savagely with his teeth. It was as he had suspected. Paullinus had secured himself well. His army was drawn up in a defile, a thick wood at its rear screening it from attack there, its flanks protected by steeply rising banks lush with trees, bush and tangled thorn. The only open ground lay in front of the Romans. Moreover, there was a gradient, which meant that every assault by the Britons would be uphill all the way.

The Roman centre was so formidable as to be almost impenetrable, its heart comprising the Fourteenth and Twentieth Legions, both greatly experienced. Paullinus had other troops of quality and masses of auxiliaries and levies. Although his total force was numerically inferior to Boadicea's, it was of considerable strength indeed when viewed in the light of the position it held and its superiority in armour, weapons and discipline.

Though Canis grimly weighed up the inadvisability of attacking on such a restricted front, Boadicea viewed the Roman host with more than her usual fire.

"There stands our final enemy," she said. "There will be no arguing about tactics, there is no need." She spoke more to Cophistus on her left than to Canis near her right. "We are twice their strength and will go against them in all our might."

"Aye, there is no better way, O Queen," said Cywmryn next to Cophistus.

"If we are to die today," she said, "then let us die boldly, not cautiously."

"My lady," said Canis urgently from his chariot, "my lady, we cannot and must not attack. This is what Paullinus wishes us to do, he has fashioned the block on which he aspires to hammer out victory for himself. This is his field of battle, not ours. We can attack only his front and will be encumbered by our weight."

"A lark twittered," said Boadicea loudly and her chieftains looked at her in some surprise. There was that about her to make a man pensive. She seemed like a queen newly scourged. "What say you, Cophistus?" she asked.

"I am for your resolution, O Queen," said soft-voiced Cophistus, "and for your general's strategy."

"I heard Canis say we should do nothing," said Boadicea shortly. "Is that strategy? What say you, Cywmryn?"

"I say," said Cywmryn boldly, "that there is no Roman army which can stand against you, my lady, here or anywhere. Indeed, here you can crush them to death. You have the cause, you have the warriors. They have only their shame."

"Romans are not born to any shame," said Canis,

"only to an awareness that to be Roman is to be honoured by the gods."

Boadicea laughed a little wildly. There was the noise and commotion of her host deploying behind her, awaiting orders, and of the waggons rumbling up in the distance. The troops of Paullinus were quiet.

"I would not think Romans dealt in honour," she said, "but perhaps this is because honour does not mean to others what it means to me."

She was in suppressed emotion and because of it Canis knew she was also in folly. He sensed the danger.

"My lady," he said, meeting her contemptuous eyes, "Paullinus considers Roman honour to have been fiercely savaged by us and he will exact his revenge as determinedly as we have exacted ours."

"What, is he so determined that he has cowed you before a single blow has been struck?" she cried, and she laughed again. It was obvious to many that Boadicea was strangely out of humour with her general. Though she often twisted his ear in a manner of speaking, she never mocked him as she was doing now, nor would she allow any man, whether highest noble or most redoubtable captain, to give him anything but the respect she considered was his due. It was odd, therefore, to see her turn from him and hear her invite all to offer counsel. Usually, once Canis had spoken, she would listen favourably to none of them.

Having been invited they all spoke at once. She smote the rail of her chariot to quieten them. She nodded at Cywmryn. He always had the boldest and strongest voice.

"I am for your strategy, O Queen," he said, "for there is not one warrior here who does not wish to have done with Paullinus as quickly as we can contrive. Let us go against them as you have said. If we cannot envelop their flanks in this valley, then let us ride at them and over them and bury them."

"Aye, aye!" shouted several.

"So be it," said Boadicea.

"My lady," said Canis with more urgency, "I beg you, let us stand off. Time is still with us for a week or so. Paullinus cannot be made stronger than he is now. We can hold and command every approach. Or we can withdraw one half of our army as if we have a commitment elsewhere. Although he will not lightly forsake this position he will become uneasy. In the end he will wish himself able to leave. But we shall be the stopper in the jar he occupies. He has a forest protecting his back but will worry about this too. In the end he will attack or count himself there to be starved out. And when he attacks we will bring back the rest of our force."

"You are in contradiction of yourself," said Cywmryn impatiently, "for if he loves this ground as much as you imply he will stay on it far longer than we can afford."

"We have another ploy," said Canis, observing that the queen resolutely refused to look at him. "Not only will we starve him, we will deprive him of water, harry him by night, burn his stores and his tents, take out his guards and destroy all we can of men and materials. My lady, Paullinus thinks he has us, but in truth we have him, by his throat and belly."

"There at last you speak some sense," said Boadicea, while her army grew restless behind her. "We have him indeed and will crush him not in a week, not in a month, but today!"

"You cannot believe this," said Canis and she turned to show eyes glittering dangerously out of her drawn, pale face.

"You are outside the limits given you this day," she said.

He shook his head sadly. He surveyed again the Romans solid on the upper reach of the valley, he saw the martial, unmoving disposition of the thousands of armoured and helmeted Romans, the heavy cavalry on

each flank. He manoeuvred his chariot through the ruck
until his vehicle touched hers and he was able to speak
to her alone. His face was grey, his voice desperate.

"Before the eyes of the gods you cherish, before the
light of the sun, take this new fire from your heart, my
lady, for it burns needlessly. Boadicea, heed me. It was
kindled by no true cause."

She had a hand to her throat and was looking blindly
at him, and a hundred eyes were looking wonderingly at
her. Cacchus was nearby, and Callupus, and both these
men knew what had disturbed her heart for so long.

"Canis, oh Canis," she whispered, "stand away, do
not disarm me more, do not—"

"They send a galloper!" shouted a captain, and
turning they saw a Roman riding purposefully towards
them down the valley. The herald was a centurion,
flanked by two cavalrymen. He rode up to the host of
Boadicea, halted and sat his mount confidently, his
helmet bright in the hot sun, his face proud and his eyes
fearless as they sought the queen.

"Greetings from Caesar's august and Imperial
Governor, Suetonius Paullinus, to Boadicea!" His
voice was clear. He did not seem perturbed by the size of
her army. "Will you come before me to receive
ultimatum?"

There was a buzzing and a murmur. Ultimatum?
Iceni and Trinovantes looked incredulously at the
herald and then all who had heard his words broke into
ribald laughter, saving only Canis and the queen. And
Cerdwa.

The queen rode slowly forward and looked coldly
into the face of the centurion. He had never seen her
before and found himself gazing at a proud, handsome
countenance and into icy blue eyes. Her burnished hair
was like a sunburst.

"Speak, Roman," she said without a tremor.

He spoke.

"From Suetonius Paullinus, commander and governor in the province of Britain by authority of Caesar, to the widow who presumptuously styles herself queen of the Iceni. You have in your wanton pride engulfed your own land and other lands in fire and rebellion, you have put wilful hand on that which is Caesar's, you have slain his soldiers and his people, and you have shamefully destroyed the sacred temple of Claudius at Camulodunum.

"Hear the words of noble Paullinus," continued the centurion loudly. "Unless you and your ignoble army lay down all arms and surrender, you shall be hurled into the dust this day. If you have wisdom above folly and agree to surrender, then you, Boadicea, with your daughters, will by Caesar's clemency vested in his Imperial Governor not be harmed but taken to Camulodunum where, in penitence and humility to Caesar for the outrages you have committed, you and your daughters shall serve the rest of your days as slaves in the household of a Roman official."

In this way did Paullinus offer Boadicea the most subtle punishment his malice could devise, knowing full well that while such clemency might irk Nero it would surely be unbearable to Boadicea.

"Speak on, Roman," she said, while Canis bowed his head. Tears came to the eyes of Cerdwa to see him so cast down.

"And if you do not surrender," went on the centurion, "but make further war against Rome, you shall be hurled into the dust, as has already been said, and at the end your daughters shall be consigned to a house of harlots, there to pleasure the comrades of men you have barbarously slaughtered."

Boadicea turned white, then shook with fury. But she did not speak, she only looked, but with such fire in her eyes that the centurion's pride at last retreated and sweat stood sudden upon his brow. And through Iceni and Trinovantes close enough to have heard those words passed a surge of almost uncontrollable rage.

"As to yourself, Boadicea," said the centurion in less clear tones, "you shall first be given for sport to comrades of those you have slain and then you shall be taken to Rome, where you will walk in chains so that Romans may have sight of your shackled wantonness before you try your boastful skill on lions in the arena. And all your people will be put to the sword, every man, woman and child, save one man known as Canis the Wolfhead who, because he has dared to raise himself like you above Caesar's will, shall be crucified before our ruined temple in Camulodunum. So speaks our noble and august Imperial Governor!"

A great shout of fury went up from the foremost warriors, but Boadicea made no outcry and gave tongue to no speech, for her body was aflame with rushing blood and violent tremors besieged her. Then they were stilled, the flame turned to ice, and her voice came chillingly.

"Quote me to your so noble governor in this wise. Say first to him that you yourself are a dog to bring such message to a wronged queen and to let such infamy lie on your tongue. Say next that august Suetonius Paullinus is twice a dog to send you on so contemptible an errand. Say that in my mind regarding him was only the thought to give him true soldier's death on our spears, for it is not our custom or part of our culture to drag defeated queens or defeated generals in chains through our cities to be mocked and reviled. If it be the custom of Romans to do so, it is the vilest custom, and if Romans would take two innocent princesses and so defile them, as indeed you have already done, then you and Paullinus and Caesar and all your kind will surely stink in the nostrils of your own gods."

The centurion quivered. He set his face in a stony mask.

"Say to noble Paullinus that you, as his emissary, are a mockery in the eyes of all true warriors.

"Say to Paullinus that he, proud servant of Caesar,

speaks brave words for one who has spent so much time running from me.

"And say that Queen Boadicea, because of the infamy and vileness of Rome and Romans, will this day make a bloody and bitter end of Paullinus and all his army!"

And with that the queen seized a spear and hurled it before the feet of the centurion's horse, and such was the strength and fury with which she flung it that as it struck the ground the iron head broke from the shaft. Cerdwa drew a hissing breath at this portent, while Canis looked at his tall, defiant queen with a love that was immeasurable. The centurion, biting his lip, wheeled his mount and with his escort galloped back to Paullinus. Boadicea, eyes suffused, watched him go, then turned to Grud.

"The dogs, oh the infamous dogs! Grud, go and bring the princesses to me."

"Must this be?" asked Grud.

"Obey me!" she shouted, and Grud went, springing from the chariot and hastening on his bow legs through the path warriors opened up for him.

Canis dismounted and went to the queen. She watched his approach with wild eyes, her breast heaving because of so much that was unbearable. He had a greyness about him.

"My lady," he said, looking up at her, his deep voice compassionate, coercive.

"If you come to speak of more compromise, of waiting or withdrawing, then do not," she burst out. "I have said you will command nothing today but your own self. So do not seek to divert me, for now I am doubly resolved to crush Paullinus. Go from me. Canis, go." She ended on a sob.

"Aye, I will, but first hear me. What is your intention concerning the princesses?"

The sun made a glory of her hair as she flung up her

head and eyed first the distant Romans and then her own assembled might.

"My princesses," she said fiercely, "shall help me put the fire within me into the hearts and stomachs of every warrior here, and with that fire we shall utterly destroy the Romans."

Guessing her exact purpose he spoke resolutely.

"My lady, you know this is neither needful nor kind. Do not parade them, for it would hurt them as nothing else can and bring back to them much which they are learning to forget."

"Who are you to say what I must or must not do? Return to your foul wood-witch, who has cunningly managed to avoid me. Commune together in your deceit!"

"Hear me, you must," he said desperately. "Paullinus gave you no true ultimatum, only deliberate provocation—"

"Provocation has been my lot since they scourged me," she said, "and Paullinus will die for it as have others. I will heed no man, only my gods, who cry on me to avenge my daughters and my scourging. Aye, in that matter perhaps you remember how you left me to the whip that day?

Ah, she had wounded him with that one, as she had wounded him earlier with another. Her eyes grew bright with wild laughter to see how the blood left his face, but then, at the look he gave her, unendurable pain gripped her and her legs so trembled that she had to clutch the chariot rail for support.

"Aye, I remember, my lady," he said, "it was my bitterest day." And he turned and left her.

The Roman host waited. Grud came with Cea and Dilwys, Cea quiet and Dilwys unhappy. They mounted the chariot to stand one on each side of the queen. With her army hushed to expectancy, her daughters pale, Boadicea rode slowly up and down to exhort her warriors with these words.

"Hear me! You are Britons all, Iceni, Trinovantes, Brigantes and others, and all of you belong to proud peoples. I know this is so because I have lived among you since our struggle began. In peace you are content, in war you are brave. Today we will end war, today we fight our last battle against the evil that is Rome. Today we will conquer or perish.

"My people, my friends, my allies! As you love me so do I love you, and if you die I will die too. I am Boadicea, queen of the Iceni. Look upon me! Here with my daughters I am before you on this great day, and I ask of you one thing only. Victory!"

There was a roar.

"Boadicea! We will give you victory!"

She continued to ride slowly and to speak loudly and clearly.

"These are my daughters, look upon them!"

Dilwys bent her pale, unhappy face to look at her feet, while Cea's desperate eyes sought Canis. She had not seen him all morning and had been haunted by the tragic, suffering eyes of her mother. She could not see him now, perhaps because she could not clearly see anything, but Canis saw her, paraded before the host. He suffered for her and for the extravagant emotionalism of the queen.

"You know full well, my people," cried Boadicea, "how vilely the Romans used my innocent maids. Now you shall know that Paullinus has threatened, if we are defeated, to use them even more vilely, to cast them into a house of harlots!" At this Dilwys staggered in the slow-moving chariot and clutched in shame and terror at the queen's cloak. Cea turned white. A moaning sigh came from the Britons, followed by a shout of fury that matched the tempestuous mood of the queen.

"Look upon my innocents, blasted by Roman lust that has grown so unspeakable it leaves nothing undefiled. Can there be any among you who would wish to spare a single drop of Roman blood?''

The answering roar took thunder to the skies.

"Oh, Cea, Cea,'' whispered the shivering Dilwys.

"It is cold for so bright a summer day,'' said Cea in a queerly high voice.

"My people!'' Boadicea was as fiery as the sun itself. "Shall we make war this day with all our might?''

"Lead us, lead us!''

"I will, I will!'' she cried. "This day we will throw down the last Roman army, we will free all Britain of the scourge of Rome and in such a way that none shall attempt this land again for a thousand years. Follow me!''

"Lead us!''

Grud helped the princesses down and gave them into the charge of loving warriors, who led them back to their waggon. Dilwys was weeping but Cea walked with a strange remoteness. Boadicea took a spear and held it high over her head, on which Grud now placed her battle helmet. The fire reflected by the helmet was more than matched by the fire in her eyes.

"Advance my host, my every warrior!'' cried the queen. "There are the Romans and there we will give them death!''

"Oh, blind gods, the folly,'' groaned Canis, but mounted his chariot with Cerdwa. She cast back her raven hair and touched his arm.

"It is on us, lord, and will be a cruel fight,'' she said amid the clamour of manoeuvring thousands, "will you not speak one small word to Cerdwa before we run upon them?''

"Ask your gods to speak to you, I cannot,'' he said harshly, wheeling to bring the chariot free of milling foot warriors.

"You are my god,'' said Cerdwa.

"Then I am the only god witless enough to be fooled by a wood-witch.''

Above the roar of the forming host he heard her sob.

He glanced to see the tears brimming in her eyes, the woe undisguised on her wild beauty. He sighed. What was the bitterness to do with her?

His chariot was impeded. He gritted his teeth, for although Boadicea advanced slowly to give her army time to form into cohesive array behind her, such was the fire she had indeed put into every heart that disorder was already prevalent. Captains shouted as foot warriors jostled with the mounted in their desire to be in the van of attack. The chieftains were all concerned with bringing their own companies first into the fray.

"Cerdwa," said Canis, "shed no tears. Think only of the joy you have in your bright axe. Today you shall use it as never before. It is all and everything for the queen now. We are to lead the way, you and I, and it will be bloodier for us than it has ever been. I will forget how you fooled me and remember only your sweetness. You are a beautiful comrade and I have not known a doughtier one."

"Lord, I will follow you onto a thousand Roman swords," she whispered, and as he drove forward over trampled grass she was in joy, for he had called her beautiful and said he would remember only her sweetness.

Meanwhile Suetonius Paullinus had listened icily to the reply his centurion brought back from the queen. There were impudent words that galled him but in the main her reply indicated he had goaded her beyond discretion. If that meant she would throw her whole army at him, he would not be displeased.

He addressed his army calmly, pointing out that they alone could hope to finally defeat the rampaging hordes of Boadicea. He made no mention of the wrongs suffered by Boadicea or of her outraged daughters, nor did he explain why it was that her army, of which he spoke so slightingly, had won its victories. But he did touch on a point which rankled in the hearts of his troops.

"You have heard," he said, "how these barbaric

people use women to fight for them in battle, and now that fact is before your eyes. But you will not let their presence bemuse you as it has bemused others, you will remember there are no warriors of any nation who can ultimately triumph over men who fight for Rome. Least of all shall shameless, uncivilised women intimidate you. You will slay them without quibble.

"You will stand firm and not yield the smallest ground. You will stand firm for Caesar, for Rome and your own honour. When they falter and seek to draw back from our iron front their great numbers will be a hindrance not a help. At the right moment you will receive the order for the counter-attack, when you will advance as a wedge in the customary way and cleave them apart. Because of their barbaric affront to great Caesar you will put all to the sword, all, saving only the widow, her daughters and her general, a man called Canis. This man you will take alive for the greater glory of Rome."

It was a calm and confident address, different in every way from the fiery exhortation Boadicea had indulged in.

Under the bright sun the Iceni queen ordered her host into battle. She halted her advance into the valley, turning to look back at the thousands of warriors, at the chariots and the cavalry streaming behind her. The horns blew. She heard the thunder of the horse, the singing cries of war, and she felt the fervour and the fire. The valley began to echo to the noise of the advance.

Canis rode through the van and his appearance brought forth a roar of delight. There under the clear sky in the valley of green stood the warriors' proud queen and her wily general. He edged forward until his hub scraped her wheel. The blood ran heatedly beneath her skin and the singleness of her mind and purpose fevered her glittering eyes.

"There is your redemption, Canis," she said,

pointing to the Roman front, "there is where you may win yourself brave quittance of life and of me!"

"I will run onto it," he said. "but in the name of sanity, you cannot order your cavalry and your foot warriors to attack together."

"All will engage, all!"

"Sweet Queen, you will commit your army and yourself to suicide."

She shuddered, her eyes clouded and closed. She opened them and they swam in mist.

"I thought I knew a man who was to be my life, but he was no man, for he emptied my life. Canis—" Her voice broke, the mist deepened, Grud looked at the sky and Cerdwa looked at Canis. Boadicea looked blinded. She said despairingly, "Lead us, lead us; and may your quittance be a merciful and honourable one—lead us—"

She could say no more. She faced the Romans, she raised her spear, pointed it and drew it back. Eagerly, ardently, her warriors awaited her signal for the massed onslaught. Perhaps at this moment the inevitability of a final conflict forced itself like a palliative into the queen's unhappy mind. Paullinus had to be engaged and now was more opportune than tomorrow. Postponement must favour the Roman, for there was always the possibility of rushed reinforcements arriving from Gaul. The battle had to be. It was unavoidable, it could not be refused.

Yet for seconds that seemed an eternity she held back, her poised spear rigid. Then with a compulsive sweep of her arm she hurled it upwards and forwards. There was a tumultuous shout, a turbulent roar and again the horns brayed. Her chariots broke from the van, her cavalry charged and her massed infantry leapt forward in the wake of the mounted. Warriors ran rapturously in advance of the queen as she whipped up her pair. The warrior maids sped fleetly upwards over the slopes, laughing to see that the first man into the attack was their beloved Wolfhead, with his blackhaired Cerdwa of the axe. They ran easily and swiftly at his wheels, calling his name and singing their war cries.

The Britons bore weapons of every kind, swords or spears, javelins or cudgels, daggers or axes, staves or sickles. Some were armoured but many, in especial the women, wore little armour at all. Behind the climbing, bucketing chariots and charging cavalry the foot warriors swarmed in jostling thousands, spilling and fanning out over the width of the valley. They were like a flowing, rolling river of brightness, the light dancing on their myriad weapons as on shimmering waters in flood. Those on the flanks ran close to the rising slopes, brushing bracken and bush, with each warrior treading or riding hard on the heels of another.

The horn trumpets blew. Upwards the host charged, on to the thick Roman array of brass and bronze and iron that blocked the upper region of the valley. Swelling the music of war were the sounds of the rushing chariots, the galloping cavalry and the reverberating beat of countless feet. The earth shook to the weight of this human tempest and to the roll of waggons bringing thousands of Boadicea's people to watch her annihilate Paullinus and his whole army.

The Romans waited while the thunder grew. They stood shoulder to shoulder, solidly armoured in helmets and leather cuirasses, shields clamped one to the other, their short and heavy throwing spears poised for flying discharge before swords were brought into play.

Paullinus had placed his cavalry on the flanks. His centre consisted of his two experienced legions and on either side of these were his numerous auxiliaries, many Belgae among them.

Canis did not run in on the enemy with suicide in mind. He had no intention of recklessly expending himself, despite his despair. He drove with the grim certainty that any warrior who flung himself heedlessly on Roman swords would be of no help to the queen today.

A thousand foremost Britons on horse and foot hurled themselves at the Roman line. Canis was there, the joy of battle like wild laughter on the face of Cerdwa as he skilfully slewed his chariot to run sideways on. The Romans narrowed their eyes as they saw the warrior maids, tunics colourful, limbs bright and faces exultant as they leapt to smite.

From the iron front came the first volley of hissing pila, and because the Britons came in such numbers and such recklessness, many of them fell pierced. With a shuddering, clamorous shock the armies engaged. The Romans buckled a little but did not yield. The second rank, standing steadily, discharged its pila, the first rank presenting locked, unbreakable shields and stabbing with short swords. On came the Britons, masses of them, chariots tangling with infantry, cavalry bunched, and heedless of their fallen comrades some broke through the unbreakable to bring down Romans and to be hacked to death themselves. Immediately the Romans made their front whole again.

The Britons were fighting for space to fight, coming on shoulder to shoulder and elbow to elbow. Boadicea, endeavouring to manoeuvre, to ride up and down as she loved to do, also found herself starved of space at a distance of a hundred paces from the locked fronts. She saw her swarming van spill and break redly against the Roman brass and iron. Spears, javelins, daggers and swords smote ringingly on Roman shields, but the Britons were impeding each other in their fire and fervour, and the stabbing Roman swords pierced the bunched targets. Canis and Cerdwa found themselves not within the reach of Romans but amid the surging tide of Britons.

The queen saw in that moment the folly and tragedy of her tactics, her army filling the valley, with no warrior giving another room to move. She saw the helplessness of hemmed-in chariots, her hampered cavalry, her host of bunched infantry, and she cried out.

She tried to whip up her pair, to force her way through the tightening mass.

"Oh, my warriors, my people—stand off! Make space, draw back, stand off from those in front—Grud, the horns! Have them blow for withdrawal!"

"Withdrawal?" Grud made himself heard by putting his mouth close to her ear. "Can you turn your army's back on Paullinus now? That will make tigers of his Romans."

She shouted at her jostling, surging warriors, but they could not hear her in the rising clamour. They surged upwards and onwards, so that continually the foremost were carried onto the bossed shields and the short swords willy-nilly. Yet it was not wholly impossible everywhere. In places some units were either stronger or more adept than others, winning room to smite and kill. But elsewhere they pressed forward too eagerly, too recklessly, and though they found the enemy they found no space. They were squeezed on all sides and they trampled on their fallen and in the blood of the dying. They fell and as they fell their comrades behind came on. If their impetus was accelerated by the constant pressure behind them, this was not unwelcome to them in their ardour, for it brought them quicker to the Romans.

The men died bravely, the warrior maids with blood choking their laughter. One woman, brought to her knees by a violent surge of warriors behind her, saw death in the glint of a thrusting Roman sword, but even as the weapon stabbed at her she smote simultaneously with her short spear. The Roman screamed and she died laughing at the soft-bellied fool.

The Britons were having to climb not only the valley but their mounting piles of dead now. And the Romans yielded not a yard.

Cerdwa was in anger at the stupidity of warrior crowding warrior.

"Lord," she cried above the din, "how may we smite

for the queen in such a sorry mess as this?''

"And how may we die for her except under the feet of our own warriors?'' Canis returned savagely.

In his awareness of impending tragedy he forced his chariot cruelly hard through his Britons, breaking out on the seething right flank to roar at the nearest warriors that they were to turn and hold back the advance of others. But those who could hear could not obey, for they could not even turn. Try as they might they were at the mercy of the rolling weight behind them. Canis descended from his useless vehicle, Cerdwa with him, and began to thrust and shoulder his way through. Cerdwa clung to his belt, desperate not to be divorced from him in this milling confusion.

Miraculously Callupus appeared. The old wolf understood his son's purpose and with a number of his tribal warriors roared and smote with the flat of his sword to make others understand also. And warrior maids came surging to do what they could for Canis. He made it savagely clear they needed space to build a wedge and drive it into the Roman front, anything that would break that unyielding barrier of armour. They kicked heedless ones aside, they formed a perimeter of the stoutest and hardiest men, creating a barrier of their own around which oncoming warriors spilled because they could not go through it.

It was not a moment for the weak as Canis attacked not the Romans but his own Britons, laying about with him his round shield. With Callupus, with Cerdwa and with the strongest and most merciless, he literally savaged out sufficient room to manoeuvre. Now he reached the ears of his father and other warriors with a rallying call.

"Come, better to die with a purpose in mind than out of hotheadedness. Let us see if we can dig a hole or two in the Roman's ribs.''

He led them, with Cerdwa at his side, and she shook her hair back and kissed her axe. They formed the

suicidal apex of the wedge as they advanced to pierce the
armoured line. Clamped, bossed shields confronted
them and a legionary's sharp sword thrust. Canis smiled
at the man, a harsh, savage smile, turned the thrust
aside and countered with his long, heavy sword. The
man's eyes rolled inward, he coughed and dropped. His
comrade planted a firm right foot, picked his spot and
then reeled as an axe smashed his shield violently aside.
He had a momentary vision of a glossy-haired warrior
maid laughing as she smote again. The axe clove his
face.

Using shields against the short, darting swords, Canis
and Cerdwa fought in fierce, inseparable union, long
sword and bright axe becoming red with blood as they
thrust and smashed their way in. Now the Romans here
found themselves squeezed and the British wedge slowly
drove in. Its sides were beset fiercely but hurriedly,
crowdedly, and the resolute Britons gave better than
they got. At last they had room to fight. And although
Canis and Cerdwa, lodging the wedge deeper, were
harried by determined Romans, these met warriors who
saw to it that none could get at the backs of the inseparable pair.

They were quick, formidable, Canis savagely clinical,
Cerdwa devastating. The fierce joy on her face held a
man nerveless and Roman after Roman died from that
crashing axe without making a thrust. It was enough to
turn other men cold to see how that red, flashing axe
dealt death, and to watch the sword of Canis turn aside
a blow, feint and then sink deep into leather and flesh.

Here the battle took a dangerous turn for the
Romans, but such was their strength in depth that
although the British wedge bit deep and forcefully it
eventually became locked in static conflict. And
Paullinus sent orders for no more ground to be conceded there.

Elsewhere his troops, despite losses, held their
positions against the self-encumbering weight of

Boadicea's assault. The battle raged on but the Britons were dying in struggling, frustrated fury as they spilled in still crowded confusion against the long wall of bossed shields and sharp swords. Had they drawn off cohesively, had they given themselves space in which to fight and time to take in the orders of chieftains or captains, they would at least have died less foolishly. But only Boadicea's emotional address governed their feverish minds.

The queen, her chariot beleaguered by the constant, shifting mass of surging warriors, looked at the tumbling, tragic confusion of her army, and her blue eyes were frozen, her face white.

"Oh, Grud," she cried, "what have I done this day? This is no battle, this is only confusion and death! Oh, Grud, why will they not draw off?"

She shouted, she shook her spear, but the roar of battle drowned her words and the gesturing spear seemed only a further exhortation to those who saw. Her army surged on, the dead and dying pulled from the ruck in front by warriors who were concerned not so much with compassion as getting at Romans.

"Oh, Andrasta, you have turned your face from me and my people."

Paullinus had no such reproaches to make. He was more than satisfied with the way the battle was going. The Britons were in hopeless, disorganised attack still, and unless they untangled themselves the situation could only get worse for them. Apart from the gap savaged in their left flank by the one cohesive unit of Britons, the Roman front stood firm. Sometimes it swayed or buckled before the pounding fury of frustrated Britons, but always it straightened again as men stepped quickly forward to take the place of the fallen.

Paullinus did not miss the fact that Boadicea seemingly had no other idea, no other tactic, than that of rolling her army ceaselessly forward. She had engaged her complete host and to the point now where she would find it impossible to disengage without causing worse confusion.

The clamour of the conflict was an unceasing roar and there was an acrid smell of blood and carnage. The fervour of the Britons remained unbroken, but so did the resolution of the Romans, each side knowing it had all to lose. Iceni and Trinovantes advanced through blood and over bodies to hack and smite for Queen Boadicea, and they died more in frustration than sorrow. The sun began to withdraw in appalled retreat to the west.

Its heat blackened the oozing scarlet.

Paullinus could not yet accept that Boadicea and her renowned general had no other tactics in mind, though he had planned and hoped for such an assault, and had also provoked it. With their great waggons crowding and blocking their rear they had not even left themselves room to fight an orderly retreat, and indeed if the Roman counter-attack was effective enough it would crush any retreat against those waggons.

Meanwhile, Canis fought with cold savageness. His wedge of fiercely smiting warriors was as unyielding as Romans, but for all that they were held in the gap they had hewn. How they would have welcomed a diversion, a crushing onslaught by Boadicea's famed wings that would have brought a cracking and a yielding of the Romans in front of them.

But there were always more Romans. From time to time Canis and Cerdwa drew back within the centre of their formation, taking short respite while the wedge shuddered around them. During one such interval Cerdwa, breast heaving, her limbs and tunic spattered with blood, looked at him in despair. They both knew this was the last battle. The grey shadows stared from the brown of his face, but strangely he smiled.

"You are a beautiful warrior, Cerdwa."

"And you my most beloved one," she said.

The hours slipped by on a cascading tide of blood,

until Paullinus at last was sure the Britons would never disentangle themselves from the web he had spun and in which they had enmeshed themselves. And so he gave the order to counter-attack at a moment when the frustration and confusion of the Britons were as bitter as the blood of their slain. The order required the unyielding iron lines to form into a huge wedge-like ram that could split an enemy host clean apart. The Roman infantry began the manoeuvre and the solid phalanx changed shape. That which had been a wide front of clamped armour became, by disciplined skill, a pointed ram bristling with the teeth of sharp swords. Slowly, remorselessly it moved to bite into the massed front of the Britons, and the blood of Boadicea's army, already thickly staining the ground, began to run like the first lazy flow of an incoming tide over a mangled beach.

Furiously the Britons resisted, but the slow-moving iron wedge gouged into them, pressing them into tighter masses. The rearward Britons, long conscious of the chaos in the van, now retreated in an attempt to form a defensive force, only to realise they would be pinned against their own waggons. And in these waggons men, women and children began to wail, striking fear into their warriors.

Boadicea, tragedy stark upon her, tried desperately to get some part of her fighting force to withdraw and re-form, but this had been an impossibility from the moment she clashed with the enemy. Grud looked silently on the uselessness of it all. The throng about her chariot, about all the immobilised vehicles, was wild and fierce. But this was not because of defeat, it was because the sight of the queen made the Britons as ardent as ever. They still believed in victory. It was only a question of contact, of each of them getting to grips with Romans, and so they struggled and fought to reach a place where they might smite for the queen. Tumult became torment, rage embittering scores of Britons as the Roman ram squeezed them tighter, restricted them further. Death was less unbearable than helplessness.

Canis fought on, his gashed shield diverting thrusts, his long sword slipping in. The gap he had cut out had dissolved when the Romans had changed formation, and now with Cerdwa, Callupus and others, he sought to carve out a new one, to strike hard into the side of the creeping iron dragon. Cerdwa, teeth showing, lips drawn back, struck in fiery rage. Side by side with Canis she fought, breaking in, crumpling the side of the Roman wedge.

But the pressure was momentous elsewhere. Along the sides of the valley warriors found themselves tumbling against bramble and gorse, and in the rear they were spilling back against the bulky waggons, wherein women and children were crying and despairing. Some jumped down and ran all ways in hysteria.

The queen's strong oak, iron-grey Callupus, died from a flung javelin, not far from his tall son. Cophistus died from one more sword-thrust that in his exhaustion he could no longer evade, and Bograt, his faithful servant, from a lunging Belgic spear. Cywmryn, teeth agleam, forced himself furiously into the Roman ram, slew one man with a stroke that severed his windpipe, another with a gigantic thrust that buried his sword deep in leather and flesh, then died from a dozen swords in his own body. Cacchus the elder threw off his mantle, drew the sword he had not used for many years, and followed by Lygulf went forward from the waggons and entered the battle.

Grud took the reins from the frozen hands of his tormented queen and attempted passage through struggling warriors. He rode over trampled ones, for he knew that come what may the Romans must not take Boadicea.

"Oh, Grud," she whispered, in icy horror for her dying army, her doomed people, "forgive me for I have brought you and all my brave Iceni to death." Grud did not hear.

She saw the hopeless turmoil of her army, warriors flowing in jumbled torrents that lapped darkly at the wooded slopes, the movements constantly changing shape as many fell not from wounds but from the pressure spreading fatally from within, as a ripple spreads over a lake. Agony was in her eyes and she fought with Grud to bring her chariot round to face the Romans.

"Turn!" she cried. "Turn back, accursed old one!"

"My lady," shouted Grud, "you shall not be trapped, you must not be!"

"But, Grud," she panted, "only see how my poeple die! Put me not with my back to the dogs of Rome, for all my warriors still face them."

Grud would not turn or temporise. He lashed at the horses. But the chariot was impeded, the horses rearing in refusal of the human barrier. Grud and his queen could only watch her warriors die. And they still died bravely, the warrior maids no less courageously than the men, as they fell with their long, graceful limbs broken and bloody. Incredibly, the Britons still tried to attack, humming and buzzing at the enemy like angry wasps squeezed from a vast nest. The Roman ram, slow, deliberate and resistless, moved over a thick carpet of dead and dying, gathering power to split wide the struggling army of Britons. Warriors dropped, the scarlet gushing from gaping wounds and lay with life running swiftly from them, their bodies trodden into the outraged earth.

"Draw back, lord!" shouted a sweating warrior, seeing the haggard, grey face of Canis and hearing his harsh, labouring breath. "Draw back, Cerdwa, rest a space—we will contain them here a while. But draw back so that you may come at them again, draw back!"

So Canis and Cerdwa once more took respite within the protective body of their grim band. Cerdwa sank to her knees, each gasping breath coming from her lungs like a great sob. She lifted her head to gaze in distress at her lord and a faintness took her to see the bitter resignation in his eyes.

"Canis, lord," she panted, "tear not your heart so. You shall win free, aye, and Boadicea also."

"Witch!" he hissed. "Do you think me so blind that I cannot see all is lost? Will you seek to fool me yet again and on a day as bloody as this? With all lost Boadicea cannot win free!"

"The queen shall win free of Romans, this I swear," gasped Cerdwa, her eyes wet and beseeching. "Lord, look not so upon me, do not break my heart as you have broken hers."

Amid the hideous tumult, within the shuddering ring of the mercilessly beset Britons, Canis, bloody and terrible, looked down at his wood-witch with everything of life and death in his expression. He smiled a strange, rueful smile, and put his blood-stained hand to her thick, tumbled hair.

"No, I will not break your heart, Cerdwa, for there is that in each of us which is like one to the other and calls us both. You have fought a greater fight than any of us today. So hold fast to your axe and let us give final quittance for Boadicea."

He helped her to her feet. Cerdwa gazed at him, her great eyes swimming. She pressed his hand to her wild heart. He kissed her, and for Cerdwa there was a second when there was no hideous tumult, no conflict, only joy. Suddenly came a violent surge of movement as the ring of protection was newly squeezed and Cerdwa was almost torn from Canis. She gave a wild cry, regained his side with a frantic leap, and they struggled through to engage once more with the bristling ram.

Boadicea's host was splitting apart. Yet every warrior who could still hailed her bravely, still struggled bravely, seeking to strike at least one blow for her.

The queen could not believe her gods so pitiless as to see her proud people meet such an end as this, squeezed to death by that iron dragon of Rome. Yet it was not the gods who had brought them to this, it was herself. She looked around in an agony of despair, seeking at last the strength, wisdom and comfort of the only man who could give her these things. But she saw only the advancing ram and her suffering, dying army. There was a sickly heat rising from the ground, from the slaughtered, and the smell of death was the bitter smell of defeat. Above the battlefield the winged scavengers were already gliding and waiting.

Oh, my peoples, to what have I brought you? And oh, Canis, my strong beloved, to what have I brought you and myself?

Her warriors were dying in their scores, their hundreds, the sundering Roman ram a glittering, bristling instrument of division and death. Grud turned the queen's chariot again and again, edging into a gap here and a space there, while Boadicea gripped the rail in unbearable despair.

Although she could not see him, Canis was not all that far from her. He and Cerdwa fell back again, exhaustion greying them, Cerdwa's axe wavering at last, her breath tortured and sobbing.

"Mithras in his mercy," groaned Canis, "make not the end so cruel for Boadicea."

"Go to her, lord," gasped Cerdwa, "go to her, for you alone can make it less cruel."

He fought his way through and Cerdwa went with him. Their ears were stunned from the ceaseless roar of the battle, and sweat ran to impede their vision. But they saw the queen, standing above the turbulence in her chariot, and they hammered and thrust to get to her. Boadicea saw him then and cried out to him, and with Cerdwa he reached her. Amid the ruck of her tumbling army, amid broken, overturned chariots, slain horses and all her tragedy, she leaned to touch him, huge tears in her eyes. In them he saw the stark intensity of a battle lost and a nation destroyed.

"Go, Boadicea!" he shouted. "Take her from this, Grud, take her by any means, but take her!"

"I will not go, I cannot!" cried Boadicea. "I will not leave you or my people." Her helmet was off, her richly bright hair all about her, and although she was in her agony of despair there was a wild gladness to see him before her. "Here I will stay and here I will die. Oh, Canis, my sweet cruel Wolfhead, that this should be after so much that was joy!"

"Take her, Grud!" he shouted again, and Grud sought yet again to whip the horses into the river of reeling Britons. The pair sweated and rolled their eyes. Canis put aside his exhaustion and leapt onto the chariot. Boadicea saw his bitter despair for her and more than that. She could not find voice, for surely it was a look of great love he gave her. Heedless of all else, she caught his right hand, and in a wild, husky voice she spoke.

"Canis, I thought to shackle you only to keep you near me, for you left me seven long years ago and so when you returned I thought never to let you leave me more. But now I will let you go. Because of your regard for me you shall find my heart with your dagger, because my heart is yours and always was, from the very first. Canis, you shall keep me from the Romans and give me sweet death. Do this now."

And she plucked the dagger from his richly-studded belt, her own gift to her general, and put it into his left hand. But he shook his head. She repeated her wild request, but again he shook his head and very tenderly he said, "How may a man kill that which he loves beyond anything else, even on such a day as this?"

Boadicea drew sobbing breath.

"Now I will die in some content," she whispered, but Canis shook his head yet again, his eyes wet, and he thrust the dagger back into his belt. He smiled at her in great tenderness and then he smote her in a way he knew so that she sagged senseless against him. He lowered her gently to the chariot floor, then commanded Grud to take her where she might escape Romans, to take the princesses too.

"This I will attempt," said Grud, "but heed me, Wolfhead, you must follow as soon as you can. She is too great a queen to die alone and uncomforted."

"I will follow if I can," said Canis and stepped down from the chariot.

He seemed drained of all further purpose as he watched Grud forcing the chariot towards the waggons. Tears spilled from Cerdwa's eyes as she saw him fumbling to adjust his belt, which needed no adjusting. But he was not as remote from practicalities as she thought, for he unbuckled the belt and reversed it to hide its studded glitter. Now the Romans would not be able to pick him out by reason of his general's belt.

"Come," he said brusquely, and Cerdwa went with him to help him rally the Britons. He did rally them at a point where the valley floor sloped upwards to the higher level of trees and bush, where the Britons for once had the incline in their favour. Hundreds of men and women warriors were resisting fiercely here, beating and hacking Romans to their knees, and as Canis and Cerdwa appeared such were the shouts of welcome that it was as if the queen's general only needed to make his mark on a Roman shield or two for Paullinus to cry quits. They attacked with greater zest and stood their ground easier, squeezed though they were, because the slope favoured them. All the same, they still dropped, they still died.

"When the gods can show me Romans able to stand undefeated against the warrior maids of Britain," Canis had once said, "then they will show me invincibles."

He had said this to put heart into Cea, but now his rejected gods were showing him such invincibles, the disciplined Romans of Paullinus.

Even so, against invincibility Canis and Cerdwa

fought as an indivisible twain. Romans still coughed
and sagged from the countering intrusion of sword, still
toppled and crashed under the cleaving stroke of the
axe. The Roman ram lost many bristling teeth at this
place as Canis, Cerdwa and their hacking comrades did
all they could, but new teeth sprang, every breech
closed, and still that iron dragon gouged resistlessly. It
tore the very heart of Boadicea's army apart.

Canis and Cerdwa stood in blood, fought in blood,
went back step by step in blood, the Romans desperate
now to destroy these two. The melee at this point grew
fiercer. Grey exhaustion seeped into Canis again and the
axe of Cerdwa no longer split shields or smashed them
aside. From within the moving, battering wedge a
weighty javelin flew. It struck Canis a violent, glancing
blow on his temple. Blackness rushed and he fell.
Cerdwa gazed down at him in terror and heartbreak.

"Lord, do not leave me, do not die!" she cried. The
Romans moved to trample him, to pierce him, at which
she gave a wild shout and bestrode his body. Long-
limbed, gory with Roman blood and terrifyingly protective, she swung her axe with renewed fire and strength at
those who would have hacked her lord to pieces.

Canis lay there, hearing nothing and seeing nothing,
his coppery-brown hair dipping thickly into the river of
blood oozing in sickly dark scarlet from dying men.

He came to, the noise of battle a dull, aching thunder
in his head, the smell of slaughter obscene. Above him
were blue skies and the soft bosoms of drifting clouds.
He felt a great inertia and a sense of unbearable
desolation. His legs seemed clamped to the desecrated
earth and with an effort he came up on one elbow. His
aching, smarting eyes slowly took in the curious picture
of a Roman who lay over his knees. The man's eyes
stared sightlessly upwards and his arm hung by bloody
tissues from his shoulder. Over the legs of this Roman
lay another, his head half-severed from his body, and
close around lay three more, all smitten to death in

similarly violent fashion. And there were slain Britons
lying in grotesque heaps, the sprawling limbs of warrior
maids linked obscenely with the limbs of men. He
turned, painfully and stiffly freeing his legs from the
weight of corpses.

"Canis . . . lord . . ."

The weight was gone. With eyes that burned his lids
he looked beyond the disordered litter of dead to where
the battle still continued, on each flank and around the
distant waggons, some now burning. Groups of Roman
cavalry were in action against remnants of mounted
Britons, and vast tides of surging Roman infantry were
rolling over units of struggling British foot warriors. He
saw how complete final defeat was to be. Over the valley
there was no place not thickly covered with dead,
Romans and Britons alike, and his leaden heart knew
the bitterest pain that so many warrior maids should lie
so starkly still, their bright limbs, their flowing hair and
their vivid tunics hideously dark from drying blood.

Who had spoken from this great field of dead?

"I am here . . . lord . . ."

The voice was faint but so yearning. He turned his
head and saw her. She was not far from him. She lay on
her back, her head with its lustrous mantle of raven hair
turned towards him. The dead weight of a slaughtered
Roman pinned her by her legs.

"Will you come to me lord? I cannot to you."

He knelt by her side and saw the javelin head that
pierced her ribs, the shaft broken, the cruel point deep
within her. Blood trickled slowly, dripping into the pool
below.

"Cerdwa? Has it come to you at last?"

Her violet eyes were huge and feverishly bright, her
lovely face pale and her hair lay in tangled strands.
There were smears of scarlet on her forehead, on her
face, on her bright, beautiful limbs, and her right arm
which had wielded her formidable axe was wholly
stained. He thrust the dead Roman from her to give her

some ease and saw others who had died under her deadly blade. They lay twisted and huddled around her.

"Did I not say . . . it was writ so?" she whispered, her velvet voice husky.

"Aye, but not that you should die for me," he said, knowing why these Romans lay so dead.

She regarded him in sweet, sad mourning.

"At the end," she whispered, "when it came to me . . . although it was writ . . . I so wished it would not . . . because of you . . . for I did not know the joys of love . . . nor the ways . . . until last night . . ."

Despite all, despite a despair that tore at him, he smiled down at her and Cerdwa fought fiercely to stay with him as she looked up into his pitying eyes.

"Cerdwa, you are no wood-witch," he said, putting his left hand, less bloody than his right, on her forehead and gently sweeping back her sweat-dampened hair, "you are a true forest maid and sweet. Aye, and brave and dear and strong."

She tried to smile at that, struggling against the drowsiness of oncoming death.

"I would have lived if I could . . . I so desired to . . . so that I might serve you all my days . . . asking only a little . . . that sometimes you would smile on me—" She broke off, shuddering, and her teeth bit sharply on her red lip. Canis, grieving so much for her, saw the great yearning in the violet eyes. The sounds of ebbing battle meant nothing to either then as he gave her love for love.

"In every way, sweet Cerdwa, your presence would have been dear to me," he said, and his tender smile brought the faintest answering smile from Cerdwa. "I have had only joy from you and though you are no wood-witch I will take your axe, as promised, as would any man for so great and beautiful a warrior as you. Go in love, Cerdwa, go in love."

Bliss touched Cerdwa's dying face, then feebly her hand sought to take his. He laid his fingers within her own. Her look changed and he saw anguished plea in her eyes and felt it in the clutch of her hand.

"And, lord," she gasped, "will you take Cerdwa also . . . oh, will you? Leave me not for the carrion . . . but take me . . ."

"Never doubt," he assured her, though how it was to be done he did not know. "I will take you, Cerdwa, and you shall sleep beside a forest oak, I promise."

"Then I shall sleep in peace," she whispered, "but first . . . there is another promise . . . will you also kiss me?"

"Aye, Cerdwa, for this was a promise that encompassed love."

He would not raise her for fear of bringing pain to her, so he bent low and kissed her lips, thinking to find them cold with imminent death, but they were warm and passionate, leaping into last sweet life for him. He felt the joy she had of this moment.

"Truly, now I go in love . . . and you must go too . . ." Her voice was weaker, each word costing her more. "To Boadicea, who loves you more than any man . . . you shall help her win free . . . as you must . . . for you love her above any other woman . . . as Cerdwa has always known . . ."

How dear was his bright, beautiful warrior maid to him then.

"Go your way, brave Cerdwa," he whispered, infinitely tender.

Battle was gone from them, they heard none of the still clamorous discord, they were remote from all human conflict, for Canis dwelt in the eyes of Cerdwa and the eyes of Cerdwa held him and drew him deep into her heart.

Her heavy lids fell again, opened again, their brightness dimming under the glazing film of death, and he would have given his soul to pluck her from the clutch of the dark ones. Because of her spirit and her yearning

she was still conscious, still fighting to stay with him
who had brought love to her.

"Lord?" Fainter yet.

"Cerdwa, be not afraid, I will take your axe and in
time come for you, so go your way, go in sweet peace
and with all my love," he said, his heart stirred beyond
the telling at the way she strove to resist pain and death.
Another shudder shook her, once more her eyes closed,
and her voice came as a sighing murmur that was
breathlessly sweet.

"I did so love you . . . and none could stand against
Canis and Cerdwa . . . none . . . but take me when you
go, for I would rest where you . . . not Romans . . . put
me . . . and where I rest you shall lie forever in my
heart . . ."

The dark ones reached. He took her hand and kissed
the bloodstained fingers, and Cerdwa's eyes opened for
the last time to caress him in wild, wanton adoration.
Then she coughed and the blood came.

In this way did Cerdwa, whom many called a wood-
witch, die for Canis the Briton, who was her lord, her
god and her beloved. And the wind came to stir the
banking clouds and bring a plaintive, murmurous sigh
as if a distant forest sent forth its whisper of mourning.

"Oh, blind blind gods," Canis said in bitterness.
Palls of smoke drifted from burning waggons. A
riderless horse plunged towards him, eyes rolling and
ears pricked in fright, and he caught it, checked it,
gentled it. He was far from the isolated pockets of conflict but it needed only a chance spin of the wheel to
bring Roman cavalry down on any who rose from a
heap of corpses.

He stripped a dead Roman of helmet and cuirass and
put them on. He lifted Cerdwa, placing her lifeless body
over the horse. About to mount he remembered her axe.
It was there, she had lain with it beneath her. He took it
up, thrust it into his belt, and with a pain in his head like

the hammer of Vulcan he mounted and rode from this field of battle and tragedy.

His Roman helmet and cuirass came first to the eyes of those who spared time to glance at him. So none sought to impede him. He skirted rearguard groups of Britons locked in wild but unavailing conflict with masses of Romans. Over the bodies of slain women and children he leapt in his savage endeavour to win free. Leaving carnage behind he encountered looting Romans. Some he scattered with the violence of his gallop and others he smashed aside with murderous blows of Cerdwa's axe, for in his compulsive determination to bear his dead warrior maid away and to find Boadicea his renewed strength was like that of a man possessed.

Bearing Cerdwa he rode to the queen.

17

FOR AN HOUR he galloped the sweating, straining horse.

The hammer beat at him. He discarded the helmet, then the cuirass.

The way was full of doomed, fleeing people who turned to cry on him for news. He stayed to give no answers, only shouted at them to leave the road and make for the forests. He had pity for them but no time. He could think only of lifeless Cerdwa and of Boadicea in torment.

He passed people who sat exhausted and weeping, he passed wailing women who begged him for help, but he stopped for none of them. At the end of an hour he turned off the road and galloped over a rough track into the quiet heart of green land. Cerdwa's body shifted and jolted. He steadied it. It was still warm.

The unhappy day was oppressive now, the sinking sun obscured by heavy cloud. He rode mechanically, seeing only the pictures of his tortured mind. But guided by his heart and the necessity of bringing Cerdwa to her resting place he reached at last the village around which the queen's host had camped the night before. In the brooding light not even a chicken scratched and no eye came to view the final act of great tragedy, save only the eye of the ageless one.

Grud was there, not far from the dwelling of the village elder. He looked at Canis and the horse and dead Cerdwa without emotion, for such was his way.

"You are late," he said, "but not too late. Go within and speak to the queen, and speak to her in a way that will lay no more grief on her. You know what she must do. It cannot be else. I will wait here. You have little time. The dogs of Rome will have her if they can. Yet first clean yourself.''

There was a wooden bucket of clean water into which Canis dipped his hands and arms. He laved his face, he washed the blood from himself. There was a large livid mark on his temple, and this he could not wash off, nor could he remove the hammer that pounded inside his head.

"'Where are the princesses?'' he asked as he dried himself on the linen Grud handed to him.

"We will speak of them later,'' said Grud expressionlessly. "Go to the queen.''

Canis went into the cottage. She was there, sitting on a crude chair. She was quite alone. Her eyes were on the door as he entered, they lifted to his and showed darkly, inkily blue. Her hair was bound with fillets of fine gold, there was cleanness upon her, her cloak and tunic had been changed for new, which were brave with colour and richness. Her mouth was touched delicately with rouge, and her shadowed face was softly, hauntingly beautiful. Only in her eyes did the dark sadness show, for her countenance was gentle with smile. On the rough table stood a flask of wine and two silver cups.

"So,'' she said softly, "you have not failed me, you have come.''

"Aye, my lady,'' he said just as softly.

"I knew you would be here,'' she said, "and so I waited not too impatiently. I have waited for you so often, Canis, and always you came in the end.''

She rose and put out a hand and Canis took it and bent his knee and touched her fingers to his forehead. She said nothing but a great sigh came from her, and when he straightened she looked into his eyes. She saw his pity, his tenderness and also his grey, sad awareness of what she must do.

"You pay an undeserving queen sweet homage,'' she said quietly. She was controlled for the moment. Only in her expressive eyes was tragedy clear.

"I know nothing of any undeserving queen," he said. "My lady, we have had so much that has been sweet until now."

"Our quarrels? They were the sweetest, were they not?"

She trembled suddenly and he said very gently, "Where are Cea and Dilwys?"

Whiteness pinched her mouth and she closed her eyes for a moment.

"Dilwys is dead and so life for her is mercifully gone," she whispered. "I do not know where Cea is, only that all who saw her said she walked away going from side to side as if without sight. So I have sent all who are still alive and loyal to search for her. They are to bring her to you, Canis, for you are the only one she will cleave to now."

She turned and began to pace the floor, shivering as she walked until he went to her, when she caught his hand.

"Speak me true, Canis, speak me true."

"I will," he said.

"All my days since I first saw you," she said in a low, unsteady voice, "since first you ran in the forests with me and hunted with me and put laughter into the eyes of my women, since the day you came to my house with laughter in your own eyes, I have loved you, though I knew such love was wrong. Oh, Canis, you gave me such sweet words earlier, when I was in agony for my people, but because I am a woman I have put myself in doubt, thinking perhaps you spoke them only to comfort me and ease my agony. So will you now truly speak your heart? Canis, do you love me?"

Canis pressed her trembling hand. He looked into the darkness of her torment.

"Sweet Queen," he said in a voice that hid all his desolation, "I have a love for you that has been a pain in my heart since the day I first saw you, and though I went seven years from you the pain went with me. As you could not love any other man but the king, so I could not give you my love. Am I to say again that you are beautiful? You are more than that, you have the beauty of all women. It is in your spirit and your brave heart, it is in your way of life and in your love for your people. It is in your eyes, it is on your mouth, it is there whenever I look upon you. It is a magic you have for men. I know not what magic, only that it has haunted me and always will. You are my incomparable queen. You are my one love, my single love, my only love.''

Boadicea gave a sob. She closed her eyes and pressed her fingers to her trembling mouth that would not be still. She fought the anguish in her heart as Cerdwa had fought the anguish of dying.

Then she whispered, ''I had you whipped and banished. In my frustration I had you whipped, for I thought to break your pride and make you humble so that I would not love you so much, because I have no regard for humble men. But it did not make you humble and in my further torment I offered you Bodulga. Canis, had you taken her I would have slain her in the night. I did not know what I was at, I only knew nothing could be as I desired, and in the end I lost all my senses and commanded you to go. And you did go and my heart broke, for oh, Canis, I did not think you would.''

Canis put his hands to his eyes. How much pain, how much sadness, how much grief, you blind uncharitable gods, can you put upon a single woman?

''Boadicea,'' he said, ''you have always been and will always be my most beloved queen.''

''And when you finally returned,'' she whispered, as if all must be told, ''you do not know the joy I felt, or the burning impatience I suffered because as a widow I could not speak for a year and a day of all that I wanted from you. Oh, Canis, if I am your most beloved queen you are my heart and my eyes, my life and my death. Do you love Cea because she is sweet?''

''Because of that and because she is of you I love

her," he said, "but it is not the same love I have for you. I could not hurt her, nor did I think I would so hurt you concerning her, for I did not dream I had Boadicea's love."

Her pale, shadowed face and her tragic eyes smiled for him.

"Oh, you have been a sweetly cruel man," she said, "and I love you above the stars, the sun and even the gods. I so hungered for you during seven long years, and when you returned I would in due time have made you consort and king. I would have had no pride, I would have demanded and commanded you to wed me, for you are a man to make any queen yearn to possess you and then to give you all that she has. Did I not rage to keep you away from all risks in battle? Oh, my heart, I died a thousand times on this account. But see, you have given me love now and I know you have spoken true. You have made my bitterest day my sweetest one also. Within me is that which I know is finality, but there is so much joy too, so much. Canis, will you not put your hand on me, will you not look at me and feel and see how I love you?"

"O my Queen," he said huskily, "do you not think I know now every reason and every cause for so many things? Do you not think I am in wonder because of your love?" But he did as she wished. He put his arm around her and felt the trembling of her proud, handsome body. He put his other hand on her breast and discovered her warm, beating heart. And as he touched her, there was, in her darkly blue eyes, all the magic and mystery with which the gods endow women. It is the magic and mystery of giving heart and mind and body. It is not within the compass of man to fully comprehend such giving, for the gods, in their own mystery, have designed man to be the plunderer.

Boadicea raised her mouth.

They kissed.

He felt immeasurable sweetness. His iron bitterness

dissolved. There was warmth, peace, beauty, and so much else. And he knew, as he had always known, that to kiss the mouth of Boadicea in love was to lift a man to both joy and pain, for joy of such kind is lapped by pain as laughter so often is lapped by tears.

He lifted his head. Her eyes, like Cerdwa's, were in wonder, mist softening their darkness. She wound her arms around him, gave an agonised sob and, at last, Boadicea wept. Distraughtly, brokenly, she wept, her head on his shoulder. He held her close to comfort her.

"Canis . . . you are dearer to me than all my kingdom, and yet in my anger and pride I have brought you and my kingdom, and Britain, to this shameful end. I have wept few tears, I have wept but twice, once on the day I banished you and once this morning when I thought you had given your heart to Cea and bitterly betrayed my love. And now I weep a third and last time, for all that now is and must be, for you and Cea and dear, loved Dilwys, for all my slain people and for Britain. Oh, Canis, in your love, forgive me, forgive my pride and wickedness."

"Boadicea, you are a queen, you have lived like one and fought like one, you have done nothing that was not of your true heart and faith. You repaid the Romans tenfold for the evil they did you and not even their great victory today can purge them of the bitter defeats they suffered at your hands. There is no ruler in all Britain who could have led and inspired a people as you did yours, nor any who could have gathered such a mighty host as you."

Boadicea held him fiercely for a moment, then turned and groped her way blindly to the chair, where she sat to let her tears run unchecked.

"But nor could any ruler have so betrayed a people as I betrayed mine today," she wept. "In my pride, in my anger, I led them to such cruel, undeserving death. Oh, Canis, what great wrong I have done them. And Cea and Dilwys, even my daughters.''

He went to her, stooped, took her hands and looked into the anguished, swimming blue.

"Boadicea," he said, 'there was no one who did not want you to do other than you did do. Paullinus, by his dark herald, laid such provocation on you that you could not refuse battle. Do not torment yourself so, for what happened was governed by gods long divorced from justice and compassion. Every warrior fought fiercely because of love for you. Do you think any of them laid blame at your door? Never. Not one, my heart.''

"But you did not want this battle," she cried despairingly. "I wanted to listen to you but would not, I was in such terrible hurt. Yet in the end when you urged your last caution on me, my heart broke because of your sadness and I would have commanded our army to stand off as you advised, oh I would, I swear. But then came that unbearable ultimatum from Paullinus, which put me in so much greater anger that I did what you begged me not to. Before Paullinus sent his vile messenger I would have turned back, I would!''

"But Paullinus delivered his infamous provocation and so it came to what it did, and it was inevitable, sweet Queen.'' He lifted her hands and kissed each trembling palm. "It will be said and remembered that the army of Queen Boadicea died under the sword to save the shame of dishonourable surrender, that there was great pride and courage in so dying. And never doubt my love, it is a love of your pride which you miscall and your beauty which is my joy. There was no folly, only a brave, defiant spirit. But now we must go or the Romans will be on us. Come.''.

He brought her to her feet. She flicked the tears from her long lashes. She was very pale as she closed her eyes and prayed to her gods for a moment. Then she was as calm as she could be.

"You are to go, Canis, for you are now all the life and hope left to my people. You are the only man who can lift them from their sorrow, you must look to all who are left and be their strength and protection. The Romans will seek you but not in the same way they would seek me. They would raze the whole land to find me. Canis, you must live, fugitive or no, and you must take Cea to wife and let her bear your children, or the house of Boadicea will die. This is my wish—oh, more than my wish. In love of Cea you will be in love of me. Live for her, live for my people, or none will survive."

"You must survive," he said, harsh in voice now because of emotion, "for how can I wed Cea with you in my heart?"

She looked at him in great longing.

"Oh, that I might go with you," she said, "for I have spent so many years wishing and dreaming. But I cannot and this you know. If the Romans took me, how could you endure my shame? Did you not weep when they scourged me? Could I let you die a death each day they hunted me? I could not." She took his hand, held it to her breast and went on in quiet resolution. "Grud has mixed me a different potion this time, one with no pain to it, only peace and sleep. Do not look so bitter, my heart, you know this must be done. It is in your eyes as much as in mine. I will not let them take me and I will give you time to escape them. Come, help me in this." She tried to smile but new tears sprang. She shook her head and they flew from her. "But first, hold me for one sweet moment more so that you will know all my dreams will be of you. Then let us drink in token of a queen who in her folly destroyed a proud nation."

"I will not drink in such false token as that," he said. He hid his pain, he took her into his arms. In love Boadicea lifted her mouth and kissed him yearningly, passionately, her slim beautiful body arched to give and his hard body poised to take. He held her, enfolded her,

laying his mouth on hers in emotional communication
of all the love he had always had for her, and for a brief,
rapturous moment she put aside the desolate emptiness
that lay ahead for her. Although the proudest of queens
she was also the most passionate of women, and the
moment was of such fulfilment that the emptiness
became a sweet, ecstatic certainty that she would sleep
in eternal peace.

Canis took his mouth from hers. The pain savaged
him then. She was smiling.

"Oh, my heart, be strong for me," she whispered.

"Am I to smile and bring you the potion myself?" he
said. "I cannot. How can any man bring death to that
which is his life and smile on it? I will let you go because
of what I know the Romans will do to you—but,
Boadicea, sweet and majestic Queen, will you not make
one more throw, take one more chance and come with
me?"

"Would you have me hunted, taken and made
hideous sport of?" The mist was a soft glimmer. "Help
me in what I must do, there is no time for anything else.
Help me go in sweet peace." She smiled again, then pale
but calm went to the table and took up the silver cups, in
which the red wine shimmered.

"Take this," she said, handing him a cup. "Therein
is my heart, for it has belonged to you from the very
first. And I will drink from this other cup." She looked
into the wine and the finality was as much in her eyes as
in the liquid. "In this I will pledge you my love now and
for all time, and in yours you shall pledge love for me,
which because it is the love of Canis for Boadicea will be
constant and eternal."

And she looked at him over her cup, as proud and as
courageous at this moment as she had ever been. He
knew what was in her wine and he could not, for a
space, conceal his anguish. But then he gave her a smile
to match the bravery of her own, for whatever else may

be said of Queen Boadicea and Canis the Briton, they both had the strength and spirit to shame the blind gods of their time.

He lifted his cup.

"You are sweet life," he said in deep tenderness, "and will always be so. You are my enduring, undying queen."

Again the mist clouded the blue but she did not tremble or delay, she lifted her own cup.

"You are my heart and my reason," she said in her richest and sweetest voice.

She drank. She held the cup steadily to her lips until she had drained it. And Canis drank his own wine to the last drop. Boadicea's cup fell from her hand and Canis threw his down. He went close to her.

"Canis, oh Canis," she said, her hand to her throat, her voice breathless. "Canis, wait. Almost I forgot. Take this." The poison was upon her as she pulled fumblingly at the heavy gold ring on her finger. "Take this, it is yours . . . it is of me. Canis, my life, come close to my heart. Hold me . . . Grud has mixed it well . . . there is no pain . . . only do not put me down . . . hold me . . . oh, my beloved, do not let me fall."

"Never," he said, his eyes wet, and he took her within his strong, compassionate arms and Boadicea looked up at him with a strange, fixed smile. Canis, as great in spirit as she was, gave her his own smile, the smile she so loved. Her darkness was gone, her eyes were summer blue, giving him all they could of warm life and infinite love, for she was a true Celt and all things to do with life could be read in her eyes, even in death.

"Canis . . . it has been so sweet . . . so sweet . . ."

"Boadicea, remember in your rest, I love you beyond your death."

"Then I am content, so content." And so on her feet and in the strong but anguished arms of her general, Boadicea, queen of the Iceni and the beloved of her people, died. And in death she was as majestic and beautiful as in life.

He could not believe her great spirit had gone, had slipped away from him. In grief that ravaged him he held her close, her deadness no less dear to him than her life. Then he stooped and lifted her, and her proud head hung limply, but her face was at peace and the echo of her last smile seemed to still touch her lips. He carried her to the door and Grud came.

"So," said the young-old one emotionlessly, "it is over and not before time. She has gone beyond us and the Romans too. Aye, and braver queen never lived. She did not wish to die because of her love for you and she was, therefore, braver in her moment of death than any man or woman. What is your purpose? It must be swift for soon the sharp-toothed Roman dogs will be on us. They are hunting all who fled. Do you not hear them?"

He heard them. They were the cruel whispers that came murmuring over the reddening land as the tragic day gave up its light.

"Come, Grud," said Canis, "you have been the queen's loyal servant and friend, so you and I will find her a burial ground safe from Romans. Aye, and brave Cerdwa too, for they both deserve to lie in safety and peace."

"We have no time," complained Grud, "and the Romans may give her proud burial themselves."

"The Romans would give her to the dogs, and Cerdwa also."

He carried the dead queen in due line with distant Venta Icenorum, leaving the village and crossing the track. In the stillness of brooding evening, the sinking sun again obscured by ponderous clouds, he went on until he reached a tall oak standing at the edge of a forest. He marked the spot in his memory for years to come. Behind him toiled Grud, bearing the body of Cerdwa which, during his wait, he had in his sense of what was right cleansed of all blood. They laid them down, the bronze-haired queen and the raven-haired warrior maid, and between the oak and the forest they dug deeply, cutting back thick turf with axe and sword, turning the rich earth quickly and without words. In one grave, with her feet pointing to Venta Icenorum, they laid the dead queen, and Canis knelt to fold her hands over her still breast. He touched her lifeless lids and silent lips with his mouth. He looked at her.

She was in peace.

In the other grave they laid sweet Cerdwa, her feet turned towards the heart of the forest, for in another such forest she had lived in joyous freedom until she left it to fight for her queen. Between her hands Canis put a sprig from the oak and then, because she had placed so much importance on the kiss of love in death, he put his mouth to hers.

The forest whispered.

Her lips, which should have been chill, were still warm.

They covered the bodies with earth so that in the end Boadicea and Cerdwa passed from the eyes of men. Over the earth they carefully replaced the grassy turf they had cut, pressing it flat and erasing all marks so that none would know that here lay proud queen and bright warrior maid, buried too deeply for even the wolves to scent.

And at the last Grud thrust a strong reed deep into the head of the queen's grave so that, as he said, although she was gone from life she might still breathe its sweetness.

The wind came, sighing and unexpected, bringing murmurs to the quiet of this lonely place. The heavy, darkening sky broke restlessly and suddenly where there had been only an oppressive greyness, light appeared as banked clouds separated. Here and there in the east was a flushed blue, but in the west was the glory of uncovered evening sun. It flooded the earth with colour and marked the graves with red-gold radiance.

Grud muttered and shifted as Canis spoke in final homage to his queen.

"What is the earth if it is not full of life? What is a queen if she is not full of majesty? You have gone in great majesty but you are not beyond us, for though I believe in no gods I believe in Cerdwa, who spoke of life after death. If such life is not for all it must be for you, sweet Queen. If it is not then the earth and the sun are an illusion and a mockery. Be in sweetest peace, Boadicea, for you were loved by us all."

And despite Grud's grumbling urgency he would not go without speaking in tenderness to Cerdwa too.

"I will secure your axe, Cerdwa, and bring it to you when my own years have reached their end. This you desired and this I will do. But do not run wild while you wait, for come what may I will in the ultimate place it in your brave right hand again. You were loving comrade and beautiful warrior. Look to the queen, sweet Cerdwa, you are worth your place beside her."

They went from the place as the clouds coalesced to mask the radiance, and the soft wind mourned their going. And over the ground wherein Boadicea and Cerdwa slept in peace the green grass stirred and sighed.

They returned to the silent, deserted village. There Canis buried Cerdwa's axe, marking that spot also in his mind. The sounds of hunting Romans were murmurs of warning now. He began to collect precious relics, placing them carefully in a coarse sack. Grud shook his head impatiently, departed and then came back.

"Be quick," he said, "for you have had all the time this day can give you. Go your way now, for you are to help the people as the queen wished. I go to search for Princess Cea. There is that about me which will keep me from Roman revenge and bring me to her, soon or late."

Cea? The hammer began to thunder again.

"I will look for her with you," said Canis.

"You may look where you will but not with me. You

must go alone. That is how each of us will best achieve. I give you farewell.''

And silently, swiftly ageless Grud was gone. Canis took up the sack and left that sad place, then remembered the most precious relic, the ring, which he knew he did not have. He heard horsed Romans, even the jingle of their equipment. He ran back to the cottage and searched in quick haste in the grey gloom, while his hammer beat. He found the ring, on the floor, though how her golden gift had got there he could not say. He put it on his smallest finger and again left the cottage. As he did so four mounted Romans rode at him out of the gathering gloom. One slipped quickly from his horse and approached with drawn sword and uncompromising look.

"Speak, dog, else your death will be painful. Where is Boadicea? This far we have traced her, so speak, or I will strike bits from you little by little.''

An officer came clattering over the trodden ground, dark eyes weary, anxious, but keen. He saw the tall Briton, he peered and a small sigh escaped him.

"Stand away, Rufus,'' he said to the dismounted Roman, while the other three wheeled about in search. Canis looked up to see Julian. Julian showed no triumph, only sad regret, and he winced for the desolation and bitterness of the Briton. He shook his head in sorrow.

"It was a bloodier finish than either of us looked for,'' he said quietly.

"It was,'' said Canis, the pain in heart and head thickening his voice.

"Where is the queen?'' asked Julian and Rufus glowered to hear the defeated widow given this title. "This I must know,'' added Julian with soft emphasis.

"She is dead from a potion gifted to her by a man called Grud,'' said Canis.

"Lying dog,'' said Rufus, and heedless of Julian he

smote Canis over the jaw with the back of his heavy hand. Canis merely turned remote, incurious eyes on him. Julian urged his horse forward and, leaning, spun Rufus sideways.

"Did I not say stand away?" he said. He dismounted, he went to Canis and the Briton gave him a weary smile.

"It makes no matter," said Canis.

"It is a major matter," said Julian, then spoke softly for the ears of the Briton alone. "It has cost me every argument and device to head the pursuit of the queen, to reach her before anyone else. I had to be in advance of others, for I love Boadicea too well to allow Paullinus to shame her. If she is truly dead, I will not deny I am glad. I would rather that than see her taken. Where is she? Show her to me." He paused, then added, "I must see that she is dead, Canis, and if you will take me to her I will save you from the wooden cross."

"I will have the wooden cross," said Canis, haggard but enduring, "for I cannot show her to Romans. She is at peace, she is for no eyes but those of the sun, for only the sun came to see her at rest. I will not uncover her."

"Canis, I am desperate for you," said Julian. "You know I have only had admiration for your queen. I saw her scourged, I loved her for her pride and courage. I know her people loved her too, for she had a beauty and a dignity which no honest man could deny. Will you not show her to me? Then I may truly report that she is dead. My word will not be questioned and I also have some influence with Paullinus. If you will show her to me, Canis, then no matter where she lies I will give no knowledge of it to anybody. This is what you will wish, this is what I swear."

"I will show you," said Canis, "and because your men must stay here I will not escape you on the way."

"Wait here," Julian ordered his men and they looked askance to see him go by himself with the tall, hard-faced Briton.

It was dark now but Canis walked with him. He cast frequent glances at the silent Briton. He kept his own silence. The only sounds were of a whispering forest that loomed darkly ahead of them.

"Wait," said Julian at last, affected by an eerie tug at his heart. He put out his hand, took Canis by the arm, and they stopped. "She is nearby?"

"She is here," said Canis and went on until he reached the oak. Julian stood by his side. The quiet was infinite and yet it was not quiet. There was a sense of haunting majesty entirely disturbing.

"I will keep faith," said Julian, his heart squeezed, "aye, and more than that. Do not uncover her. I know she is here. I know this because of you and because her spirit has already made its mark here. May all the gods protect her and look to her. We will not turn her earth back with any Roman sword, not even mine. I loved her well and envy you the place you had in her life. But Canis, while I know you for a compassionate man, by your deeds you have made it incomparably hard for Romans like Paullinus to be compassionate with you."

Canis was silent. She was there in the darkness, all about him. And he knew there would not be a day in all the years left to him when her spirit would not be close to him.

He had let her go by Grud's painless gift on her bitterest day.

He answered Julian calmly. His grief was his alone.

"Compassion," he said, "is not in deeds, it is in the heart and the mind. But I understand you. And for what you have done now, for me and for Boadicea, you have my friendship, though in my present circumstances it is worth little to any man."

"It is worth a great deal to me," said Julian. They had neither of them moved, they stood there by the oak and Julian had a strangely warm awareness that he and Canis were not alone. "Canis, even Romans have heard that Boadicea loved her general. If this is true, then despite your present circumstances you cannot say you have had less than other men. You have had far more. But what made you come against us so wildly and foolishly today?''

"We came at you with our hearts and left our heads in our waggons," said Canis, and his voice was so deep with tragedy that Julian impulsively put his hand on the Briton's shoulder.

"Let us return," he said, "but slowly and with dirt on our swords and feet, so that it will look as if we have opened the queen's grave." They walked away, the silence behind them yielding to night whispers. "Canis, it is better that she is beyond the vengeance of Paullinus, and I have heard her daughters are dead too. So there is only yourself. Do you know you are condemned to die on a wooden cross before our ruined temple at Camulodunum? From this I will save you as twice you saved me from a most bloody end. But it will still be hard for you and you will need the spirit of your queen to endure. My house stands high with Paullinus, a close friend to my father. My father, I regret, died fighting your warriors."

"This is how some fathers die, but we still grieve."

"Paullinus will not refuse me a favour," continued Julian, dark grass warm to his feet, "even though it goes against his nature and desire. However, there is the law to be invoked in the matter, for you are the legal slave of my sister Lydia, who purchased you by favour of Septimus Cato. This Paullinus might set aside, but not if he knows it is my earnest wish that he does not. I will prevail on him to uphold Lydia's claim on you and give up his own claim. That is why it will be hard for you. You will be Lydia's property. But you will live and perhaps find the time to write the true story of your queen. You will be in my house, and though your life or death will be at the whim of Lydia, I do not think she will ever break you. Will you agree, Canis, will you surrender yourself to me and accordingly to Lydia?''

Canis seemed to consider it. But his thoughts were almost wholly on his queen. Her being was so strong in the darkness. Warm, embracing, undying. With an effort that made the pain in his head more violent, he brought Lydia into his mind. And the alternatives.

"If I were to escape you, Julian, I would be hunted down?"

"Aye," said Julian, "and I warn you, if Paullinus has to hunt you he will, when he has taken you, crucify you without more ado. He has had trouble enough from you."

They had reached the village. The humble dwellings were burning, Julian's men, with others who had arrived, destroying with fire the place that had sheltered Boadicea and her general for a night. But they could not destroy the haunting intangibility of her stay, the nights would always whisper of it.

Julian spoke to some of his men, telling them that Queen Boadicea was dead, he had seen her dead, and though they could not understand why he named her queen, they were satisfied. Julian Osirus was a man of integrity, and what he had said he had seen he surely had. Boadicea, who thought to rise above Caesar, had paid the price of her colossal arrogance. And so had her people.

Rufus came to bind Canis, for Julian was first to deliver the Briton to Paullinus as captive. Canis, the sack slung and tied over his shoulder, offered submissive wrists to Rufus, then dealt him a blow so unexpected and violent that it put the Roman senseless on his back.

"Get to him!" Julian shouted as he saw Canis slip away, making for the darkness that called beyond the light of the flames. "Let him not escape for his own good!" They galloped after him, three mounted men, and caught him as he ran for the shelter of the forest. He turned, slipped under a blow, and reached to pull the man from his horse, only for the flat of a second man's sword to smite his temple, where the hammer beat. The light went from his mind and he fell as limply as his sack.

They leapt from their horses, all three of them, and beat him into deeper unconsciousness.

18

There is blue on the water in summer days
There is silver on the land in winter
There is forest so deep its heart is night
Where the boar runs fierce and wily
There is a spirit I know
And a heart I know
And the spirit is strong and the heart is sweet
There is a life I know
A life that is gone
To a river that is blue and a forest that is deep
To where the blue on the water and the silver on the land
Are mist in the eyes of my love.

HE LIVED THROUGH many dark days, when his mind ran confused with noises and dreams, when he saw again the flashing axe of Cerdwa, the joy in her eyes, the wild beauty of her face, when he heard her velvet voice and the whisper of her warm body. Many times she was there in his dreams and always she asked the same question.

"Where is my axe, lord? Do not let it lie too long in cold ground, for you have much to accomplish and it will kiss Romans as sweetly for you as for Cerdwa. Do not be desolate for those you have lost, for I lived in joy and the queen in proud splendour. You will achieve, the queen will wait and I will serve."

In his fevered sleep his dreams were not tormenting. They were the bright adversary of darkness in which Boadicea lived again for him. He walked with her in the sun and wind, he hunted with her in the green forest, she with her face radiant and her eyes brilliant. Her murmurous voice reached to him.

"You are my lord, you are my love, my life and my heart."

And sometimes she would come not out of the sunshine but out of the night, indefinable and shadowy except for her glowing eyes and her caressing voice.

"Do not deny me, O my love, do not deny me."

And in the dream her warm mouth would come to lay haunting sweetness on his lips.

One morning he awoke, the illness and fever gone from him. He was lying on a rude couch with shaggy, worn skins over him, in a room which was small and indifferent. There came faintly to him the moist sharpness of autumn wind, the forest scent of wet leaves it brought, and faintly also the dying, bitter-sweet fragrance of tragic summer gone. For a while he was wholly detached from dreams or reality, and then the unbearable sweetness of all dreams brought pain and through that pain unchallengeable reality stabbed at him.

Someone else was in the room. He turned his head and saw Lydia, the Roman woman, sitting on a stool by the side of his couch and regarding him with smilingly malicious satisfaction. His brown hair was unkempt, his chin bearded, his face thin, but as long as he was here, alive, she did not care how he looked.

"You have kept me waiting many days, barbarian," she murmured, her green eyes hungry, "but the physician said you would return to life today and you have. Did I not say such a day would come, a day unfortunate for you but happy for me?"

"More than once," he said and though his voice had for the moment lost its resonance it did not sound troubled by whatever she implied. There was no day and no happening in all the years left to him which could give him greater pain than that which he had suffered on the day of Boadicea's defeat.

She was alive with greedy, consuming joy. How impatiently, how burningly she had awaited this moment. Now it had come and she savoured it to the full.

"For you," she said, "I would have waited a thousand years, but because of my many offerings to Diana she has delivered you to me now. You are my slave, my especial property, and will sweat and groan for the rest of your days. I would have lost all other slaves and not blinked a single eyelash as long as I did not lose you. On you, beater of women, will fall the full measure of my vengeance, and because you are more of a dog than a man I will pleasure myself in making less of both until you are nothing, nothing."

"I have heard hard names before, but spoken by a more endearing tongue than yours," he said, and though there was the instant stab at his heart for the memory invoked, yet there was also the content of knowing he could bring his queen close to him by all manner of things, even the most casual of words.

Lydia knew whose tongue he meant.

"Oh, you were in fine company with that harlot widow," she sneered, but to Canis that was so much weak water thrown against the hardest wall. He smiled, for not Lydia, not any man or woman, could take from him that which he had been given. The heart of Boadicea.

"Aye," he said in the husky voice of illness, "we came upon the Romans and spitted them like cattle. They died bellowing."

She leaned forward, her body stirring in anger beneath her white robe, and lightly but spitefully struck him across his bearded mouth.

"Do you know the lowly station of a slave, barbarian?" she murmured. "You will learn that yours is in the dirt and in humble silence. You will cast down your eyes in my presence and lift them never above my feet. You will speak only when commanded to. Soon, slave, you will pant and groan. It will be sweet music to my ear, never doubt."

"You are a child," he said.

At that she was in vibrating fury and, had there been a dagger to hand, might have killed him. But no, that was not the way in any event. It would not satisfy her at all to give him sharp, quick death. He was to be destroyed first, turned from a man into a dribbling animal and then given slow, tortuous death.

He recovered quickly from that day on. Soon he was well enough to leave his room, which was part of a terraced dwelling built for the slaves at the rear of the house wherein Julian, now deputy fiscal procurator of Calleva Atrebatum, lived with Lydia. Early one morning the Briton found himself one of a long line of slaves and Lydia was up to see them marshalled outside their quarters by Dilpus, her steward, who was half-Roman, half-Greek. Dilpus, for all his proud antecedents, had a mind as small as his little wet mouth. Lydia, clad in a green robe, with her dark silky hair fashionably bound, smiled to see the one she had come especially to see. Canis stood half a head taller than any other, though he looked gaunt because of his illness. He had done what he could with his untrimmed hair, binding it in the Gaulish way at the nape of the neck, but he had done nothing with his beard. Dilpus, by order of Lydia, denied him that with which to trim it and pumice with which to smooth his chin if it had been shorn. His tunic was as it had been on the night they had taken him, dark and stiff with Roman blood. All other slaves wore the white garment of their station.

"Barbarian," called Lydia softly.

Canis did not move, but said to his neighbour, a Belgic man, "Is it you she calls, friend?"

The Belgic man rolled a warning eye at the new slave. Being Belgic the presence of Canis did not arouse much in him beyond curiosity. He had heard of Boadicea's general, but what was the fellow if not a typically stiff-necked Iceni more above himself than the rest?

"Stand forward, barbarian," said Lydia to Canis.

"You are to stand forward, friend," said Canis to the Belgic man, and the Belgic man appealed silently to the skies, begging them to bear witness that it was not his intent to become involved in the provocation of so sharp-tempered a mistress as Lydia.

Lydia took the whip of short thongs from her steward and deftly flicked the chest of Canis.

"It was you I addressed, offal," she said. "Stand forward."

Canis stood forward from the line.

He did not seem perturbed by what she might have in mind for him, his grey eyes were as remote as if he did not even see her. Frustration fingered her spite. She had spent long days and even longer nights thinking up a thousand different ways to humiliate him and now that the moment was hers in all its triumph his attitude was such that she could not think of any.

There must be something that would make a happy beginning for her.

"There is dirt beneath my feet," she said.

The tiled surface on which she stood shone clean in the misty light of early morning. It was always kept so.

"This dirt," continued Lydia, "you shall lick up." She pointed to the floor with the whip. "You shall clean every tile with your tongue. You shall spit the dirt into a bucket and what you cannot spit you may swallow and so dirt shall go to dirt."

Almost there was pity for her in his expression.

"This I cannot do," he said, "since while you have a thousand tiles I have only one tongue."

A sigh came from Dilpus the steward. He knew all the pretty arts for bringing pain to slaves without affecting their usefulness.

"Cannot?" Lydia's mouth curved in her greedy, libidinous smile. "Is it then your wish to invite groaning death so soon?"

"This is your wish, not mine," said Canis, "and if you put me to death then you will slit your nose to spite your face, which is no uncommon thing among childish women.''

There was another sigh, this time from the slaves. Boadicea's general had surely brought himself to slow death. Lydia's sulkily beautiful face contorted in hate. She gestured and Dilpus, with the aid of two brawny slaves from Gaul, seized Canis. He offered no resistance as they forced him to his knees. They ripped his tunic to bare his lean brown back. Lydia struck again and again with the whip, uncaring that no Roman master or mistress ever did such work, then she flung the whip at Dilpus.

''Do not spare your arm, Dilpus, it grows too fat as it is. When you have sufficiently bled him, give him the lowest work to do.''

She left her steward to it and Dilpus obliged. But no sound came from the Briton. He closed his mind to the pain by thinking of Boadicea under the scourge. Though he had not witnessed her agony he knew she had not uttered a single cry under lashes far more cruel than these.

''I will live for your people, my lady,'' he said to himself, ''and easily, for by the scourge and standards of Bilbo, the whip of Dilpus is no more than the kiss of a mouse.''

*   *   *

He did not live in squalor, he would not. He kept his room clean. He knew why Lydia had quartered him separately from all other male slaves. His rations were the merest, his duties the meanest, but he suffered most in that while all other slaves wore the clean tunics of the house and were allowed to bath in the public washing-place for slaves, he was allowed neither clean linen nor any bath. Not even water with which to wash. But other slaves frequently stole water for him and he made the best use he could of the cold liquid pittance.

Daily Lydia put other humiliations upon him through Dilpus, and always her eyes were greedy to mark how great was his fall. Yet always greed gave way to frustration, for though she had him in the dirt, as she had promised, he was quite indifferent to her vindictiveness. He did not dwell on his misfortunes, his mind was forever full of life's offering. He dwelt on green and purple heathlands, on the warm forests of summer, the silvery stillness of Iceni waters in winter. He dwelt on the beauty of a laughing or angry Boadicea, on the richness of her voice.

So it was that Lydia would often come upon him, gloating to see him sunk so low, his ragged tunic an offence, only to experience a wild, furious suspicion that her vengeance was not proceeding as agreeably for her as it should. Kneeling, perhaps, in the wet chill of her garden, using no tools but grubbing with his hands for that which was unwanted in her soil, he would look up and see her. And she would feel that he did not see her. She burned and craved to discern an awareness of his miserable lot but all she ever saw in his grey eyes was an infinite remoteness or a darkness that was like a forest swept by winter rain.

Her desire for satisfaction was far stronger than any desire to be circumspect or modest. She did not know she could hate any man as she hated this one. It would rage through her body during her worst moments, when his indifference to her malice soured the sweetness of her revenge.

"Oh, I will break you, insolence," she told herself one day, "I will break you and put out your detestable eyes that mock me by not seeing me. I will have you crawling at my feet and pleading for death. Oh, and death I will give you in the end, as I have sworn, a death to avenge Paulus and my father and my house."

At every provocation he gave her she had Dilpus score his back with the whip, and she liked to be there to see it done. Nothing gave her more pleasure or satisfaction than to see how bloodily her steward marked the Briton.

Julian had little opportunity to lighten the burden for Canis. The Briton was his sister's property and she would not brook the smallest interference with her obsessive purpose. Her brother came upon her one day when Canis was collecting the dung of horses from the stables with his hands. Lydia in her blue robe and her spite stood on the terrace by the side of the house, watching.

"This, by Jupiter," said Julian in angry disgust, "I will not permit."

"Then," said Lydia calmly, "I will give up the barbarian to Paullinus, who still feels cheated, I imagine, and waits only a word from me to claim him."

Julian looked at his sister in cold contempt.

"Lydia, you are as consumed by hate as was Medea, so that your mind is possessed only by evil. Do you not remember we owe this man our lives, not once but twice?"

"I remember nothing save that he brutalised me, that his wanton widow slew my father, that he killed Paulus and destroyed the temple of Claudius. I remember nothing save that he burned our towns and slaughtered our people."

"This was in war which we ourselves provoked," said Julian, "which he fought bravely for his queen. You know this. Can you not see that in using him as you do it is yourself you will destroy, not him?"

"I can only see he is a barbarian," she said, "and I will reduce him to nothing, nothing! This I will do for my slain father and for Rome. Also, I hate him, which for my own purposes is enough."

Julian, shaking his head at her blind vindictiveness, said "We put seven times ten thousand to the sword when we defeated Boadicea. Is that not sufficient revenge? Lydia, think of his great loneliness. He has lost all he cherished, all he loved."

"How come you to such sweet charity in defence of a

mortal enemy?'' she said, coldly regarding a jewelled ring on her finger.

"Will your eyes never open?'' Julian turned for her and called to Canis. "Canis, will you come and speak with me?''

Canis wiped his hands on straw and approached. He was leaner, his face sharp with the thrust of strong bone, but his eyes were almost serene as he smiled up at Julian from the ground below the terrace.

"Stand off, offal,'' said Lydia, hand to her nose, "you have a vile smell even at this distance.''

"It comes only from that which is of your house,'' said Canis.

Julian almost felt the quiver of hate which rushed through his sister and he hastened to put a question before she could put new malice on Canis.

"What is your life now, Canis?''

"I think,'' said Canis reflectively, "it is of that which I have seen and that which I have learned. It is within me. It is here.'' He touched his forehead. "It is here.'' He touched his heart. "I have seen the ways of many peoples and believe in many, I have heard of all gods and believe in none. I have lived in the light of the sun and have known a greater brightness than any sun. I have lived in many houses and known a richer one than Caesar's. I have seen the death of the bravest warrior and the passing of life's brightest light, but it is only bodies which grow cold. With this knowledge I am in wonder at what has been and in curiosity at what is to come. Therefore, in my own way, I am content.''

Who, thought Julian, could have lost so much and still call himself content?

Canis turned to go back to his work. There was much dung to be fed to the earth of Lydia's garden. There was a cold bite in the air, for winter was here, and the chill breeze stirred his brown hair, which was still thick and showed no touch of grey. He was in his thirty-fifth winter.

Sharply Lydia called him back. "Do you not know how to take leave of me, how to address me, dirt?"

His eyes were gone from her. He heard the chiding voice of his queen, calling him back to bend his knee.

"Aye, I know how to address you," he said, "I call you Roman."

She called in outrage for Dilpus, she called again, and Dilpus came at a trot.

"Dilpus, take the barbarian," she said venomously, "and put his head into vile water. Hold it there for one minute each time until he calls out, 'My lady, I beg sweet mercy of you.' "

"I will not call you or any Roman woman in that way," said Canis evenly.

In bitter helplessness, Julian looked at Canis, then at his sister.

"You are a shame in my eyes and in the eyes of all who love true Rome," he whispered, "and never will you break him, only yourself."

He went into the house, loathing himself for his helplessness. Lydia turned her spiteful eyes on Canis, then said to Dilpus, "Take this toad in the guise of man and do to him as I commanded until he calls me my lady as he should. Let me know when it is done."

Dilpus returned to Lydia thirty minutes later. She sat on her couch in her heated room and her eyes snapped to see his uneasiness. She knew this presaged more frustration.

"Mistress," he said, "countless times we have held his head face down in the vilest water, but it is nothing to him, he holds his breath with ease, no matter how long we hold his head, and each time he comes up he is smiling. But he will not say one word and the only consequence is that by the minute he smells viler than the water."

"Bring him to me on the terrace," said Lydia. They brought him to her where she waited in a warm cloak. The Gaulish slaves thrust him down to his knees, his head dripping, his hair lank, his odour as vile as Dilpus had said.

"Lift his evil face, Dilpus," she commanded and Dilpus seized the Briton by the hair and jerked his face upward. Lydia saw his eyes, clouded, his mind closed to every action of spite. It made her hatred uncontrollable. "This, then, for your vile tongue which will not give me respect!" And she struck his mouth with the back of her hand. "And this for Paulus, who was proud Roman and my friend!" She struck again. "And this for your harlot widow!" She struck a third time and one of her rings drew blood. He said nothing for a moment, then addressed his feet.

"We are better off in the stables, for there we have avoided the questionable benefits conferred by a child who wishes to be called a lady."

Lydia uttered a sound almost like a scream, then cried frenziedly to Dilpus, "Mark my words, steward! Keep your eye every minute of every day on this spawn of filth and see him fittingly punished for every fault, every provocation and every insolence, for anything you consider not in accordance with his state. Knot the long whip for him. Give him no food except that which the dogs leave."

Which made the days even harder for Canis. Dilpus never found it difficult to find offence in him. A slave could be in offence merely by standing upright sometimes. Many of the bonded Britons lay fierce-eyed at night because of what was done to Boadicea's general, and women wept tears that were hot. They despised Lydia for her malice, and especially they despised her for her attempts to humiliate him in front of all her slaves.

She would say something like, "You grow fouler each day in your stinking tunic, barbarian, but since this is only in accord with your mind and habits it is acceptable to you, is it not?"

If he remained silent she would shout at him, and

Canis, looking at the sky, would say, "Infant birds with ruffled feathers are noisier than a flock of offended eagles."

It maddened her that he did not seem to care what cruelty his arrogance aroused in her. Again and again she felt uncontrollable desire to slay him, but could not rob herself of the pleasure of gradually reducing him to filthy ignomiry. She did not care how long this took. If it took years they would be years of sweet satisfaction. And there was always the joy of dwelling on how she would eventually have him put to death.

Returning one day from the house of Valeria, her close friend, she heard the sound of the knotted whip coming from the tiled courtyard. Her green eyes flickered and she ran her tongue over her lip, for she had a happy sense that under the whip was her especial property. She entered the courtyard and saw she had not been mistaken. His hands were bound to a nail above the door of his room. His sundered tunic hung like a collection of sadly-sewn rags from his waist, and down his now scarred back the blood from fresh stripes oozed.

The sultry mouth of Lydia curved in her spiteful smile as she looked at the battered barbarian. He turned his head.

"You come a little late, Roman," he said mildly, though his breath jerked at each lash, "for the best is over. Dilpus has grown so womanish I can feel his panting more than his whip."

Lydia bit her lip. His eyes were clouded with a strange pain that she sensed was not because of Dilpus. She saw his scarred, bloody back and the mockery of his expression, for he was even smiling at her. Smiling? Aye, as a man might when bearing indignity to indulge a spoilt child. And of a sudden a wild faintness took her and she could not get her breath. She put a hand to her throat, a sickness there, and then deep in her heart a tiny smouldering that had been fretfully disturbing her recently, though she had not known what it was or why it was there, burst into a flame so fierce that she knew it to be inextinguishable. With a choking cry she ran over the tiled floor to snatch the whip from Dilpus and lash his astonished face with it.

"Breeder of swine!" she cried. "Who gave you leave to flog your mistress's property!"

"But, my lady Lydia," he stammered, putting his hand to the weals she had raised on his face, "I have that leave by your special command—"

"Then you did vilely mistake me," she panted, "for the barbarian is my own particular concern and is to be punished only by me!" Dumb, bemused, hurt, Dilpus fell back from her temper. He saw her catch her breath as she looked again at the Briton's scored back. "Did I wish you to kill him, dog?" she cried.

"But, mistress—"

"Monster! Out of my sight!" As Dilpus hastily departed she shouted at his servants, the two Gauls, to cut the Briton free. Because of her strange wildness they used the knife clumsily and drew blood. Lydia cried out and lashed them from the place. Then, in tormented agitation, she spoke to Canis, but with averted face.

"I—" She swallowed. "I will get the physician to you."

"To speedily restore me?" Canis sounded almost amused. "You have a spirited way of enjoying life. Have you no friends you might invite to share these pleasures?"

Her nails dug into her palms, her colour came and went. His mockery was an abomination, putting her into such straits that she felt herself shuddering. He was quite divorced from her malice, his world so remote from hers that even the most spiteful facets of her vengeance could not affect him. He was simply indifferent. Her new emotions so tortured her that she thought she would go out of her mind. She turned from him.

"I am not wholly cruel, not wholly unmerciful," she gasped.

"You are only a girl finding it difficult to grow into a woman," he said.

"Oh, how vile you are!" she cried wildly. "You are insulting, insufferable, unspeakable! I have long been a woman but no, you still call me child or girl. I am not a child! See, this is how you have always treated me and made me hate you, you have never tried to understand me."

"I am a careful man. I do not attempt the impossible."

"Oh!" Lydia could have wept. "Oh, it is not be be borne that any man should have a tongue as hurtful as yours." She swallowed again, then said unsteadily, "Your back—it is cut—does it pain you?"

"I have known worse," said Canis. Winter cold assailed the courtyard and his scourged flesh. "I think I will live for your further indulgence."

"Is not my indulgence of vengeance justified?" she cried, turning this way and that but never to face him. "Did you not use me brutally, shamefully? Did you not murder my friends, my father and my people? I risked the anger of our Imperial Governor in robbing him of you, yet in return you mock me still. Oh, you have deserved far worse than you have had from me!"

"Do not lay your weakness for tantrums at my door," said Canis, "for that is assuredly the way of a child."

"Child!" Lydia swung round, her face white, her eyes dilated. "Oh, you are beyond any clemency, any forgiveness! Call me child again and I will be your death! Oh, I will break you, slave, slave—and then kill you, kill you!"

With that she ran into the house, where she stood trembling and aghast. Distractedly she dismissed Suella, her servant girl, but called her back and told her to summon the healer. Then she stood before her square crystalled window, seeing nothing of the chill landscape of winter. It was not possible, it was not! Did she not hate him more each day? Was he not the most detestable of all detestable Britons?

No, no, no!

O Diana, sister to all women, aid me, aid me, for I do not know what has come upon me. When I saw him under the whip I could have died in shame of myself, and this cannot be, it cannot!

Diana, Great Protectress, take this torment from me, it is not to be borne—

My heart pounds, my blood is on fire, yet I am icy cold.

O Diana, you know full well how truly I hate him, for did I not pray unceasingly to you to deliver him to my vengeance—

This day I will give him up to Paullinus—

No, no, no!

Lydia threw herself down on her couch and over the luxurious fabrics she spilled wild tears and bit at her knuckles with fierce teeth. She started up as she heard the physician arrive. She dashed the tears from her eyes, then crept silently through the house to look out at the courtyard. All she saw was the physician and the slave who led him to the room occupied by Canis.

Lydia shivered and fresh tears flowed. Would he thank her for summoning the physician? No, he would not, except in some mocking way. Was he at least a little thankful that she had housed him in his own room instead of herding him communally with the other male slaves? No, he was not. Because he knew that such comfort as that poor room had was only a symbol of her own mockery. Such had been her thought when Julian had brought him to her in fevered illness. How rapturous she had been. In company with Julian she had used every wile and argument to persuade Suetonius Paullinus to concede her claim to the Briton. She had succeeded. In her triumph she had been ecstatic with joy and wildly grateful to Diana.

'Where had gone that joy?

She went back to her room to lie shivering on her couch.

Dilpus came to her next day as she sat at the pale green window overlooking the terrace. He bowed low. She looked at him contemptuously, while he wondered at her unusual pallor.

"Well?" she said sharply.

"In the matter of your own especial property, my lady Lydia—"

"Dilpus," she breathed, "is it not enough that he should mock me? How would it do for Canis to give you a taste of the whip you have used all too eagerly on him? Aye, it has not escaped me that you have flayed him as if he were your property and not mine."

He thought she must be going from her mind but did not say so.

"Mistress, I swear I thought only to do as you commanded."

"Will you argue?" She was close to agitation. She calmed herself. "What else have you come to irritate me with?"

"Concerning the barbarian, the physician has seen to his meagre stripes—"

"Meagre?" she cried, suddenly beside herself with pitiful unhappiness. "Did you not see his wounds, his blood?"

"Mistress?" he stammered, amazed she should trouble herself with such minor matters.

"Let him rest this day, see that he is not disturbed." Then in some excuse for her concern she added, "Do you think I want him to die and so escape me?"

"But, my lady, he has gone—"

"Gone?" Lydia leapt to her feet, she turned white, she trembled. Wildly she cried, "Gone? Oh, I will have your flesh in strips for this!"

"No, no, mistress, I mean he has gone from his room

to rub down the horses. He will not continue cleaning the stables, he says his back is too stiff today, and because of what you said yesterday I do not know how to deal with his whims, and so I came to ask you—''

"Leave me," said Lydia, "go about your duties elsewhere."

When he had gone she wrapped herself in a woollen cloak and went to the stables. Canis was there, the day bitter, his face a little drawn. He was working on a big black horse which constantly sought to nuzzle his shoulder, and she guessed from his movements how sore his back was. Dilpus had been savage yesterday.

"If your back is so stiff," she said, "why do you do this? There—there is no need, I have told Dilpus you may rest today."

"There is more relief to be got from this than from lying on my stomach," he said. "Also, it keeps my mind from my scratches, in the matter of which your physician was competent, in the matter of which I am grateful."

She ran hot then.

"Oh, detestable," she cried, "for by that I do not know whether I am thanked for bringing the physician or the whip to your back, which is always the ungrateful way you use your tongue!"

"Mistress," he said, which was as much as he would call her, "you are too high and I too low for you to give my tongue serious consideration."

"You are low indeed," she flashed, "and could not look the part better! Your rags are disgusting—ah, it is like you to insult my house in this way, by wearing garments unfit for the filthiest beggar. From now on you are to wear the house tunic, you are to rid yourself of those stinking tatters. Oh, very dog, look at me when I speak to you!"

How strange he was. He turned and his eyes were full of light, his expression one of indefinable warmth. Her breath caught in her throat, only for fret to take her again, for although he was looking straight at her she knew he did not even see her.

Then he smiled a little and said, "Sometimes, mistress, you have a way of using words that remind me of another."

"My words are my own," she said, "and you are to take notice of them. I have told you before that your rags are unworthy." She knew she had never told him this, for she had meant him to wear his tatters until they dropped off. "Do you hear me? Go, speak to Dilpus, tell him he is to give you house garments clean and wholesome. I will not have you put shame on us by looking as you do and being as odorous as you are."

Canis put his hand to his mouth, then said, "My odour is by reason of yourself, since you have forbidden me the baths and even the smallest amount of water."

"If I have," she said, her heart wrenched, "it was only ever because of your arrogance—oh, I have never met such obstinate arrogance as yours."

"Ah," he said as if that solved all.

He smiled again. Lydia's newly sensitive heart tumbled over and drowned in a well of foolish, incredible tears that seemed to flood her whole body. For in all the wretchedness of his attire, in his unkemptness and his fall from triumph to tragedy, he still looked a man of quiet pride and courage, untouched by the indignities she had forced on him. She knew now that what she saw so often in his eyes was a great and inescapable loneliness, that whatever she might do for him to ease his lot she could not give him that which would take his loneliness away. What was it that would?

He had told Julian that in his own way he was content, but in such loneliness he could not be content until he was dead.

"Go," she said in a choked voice, "go to Dilpus and say I command you to be bathed at once—within the house—and then to be fitted with clean linen and tunic. And—and take your beard from your chin so that you may look yourself, for at this moment—'' She stopped, swallowed, turned her back and said, "Go, do you hear me? Go at once.''

"In truth," said Canis, "this is the sweetest chaity, sweetest mistress, for what you have commanded me to command of Dilpus is better than Caesar's supper.''

Sweetest mistress?

Oh, Diana!

She watched him on his way, gazing after his long, striding figure until it was blurred by the wetness in her eyes, and then she fled back to the house and her room, there to weep bitter tears and choke on her sobs.

*   *   *

Dilpus was dumb, his little mouth falling apart as much as it could when Canis advised him of the latest impossible whim of the lady Lydia. He stared at the Briton like a man to whom news has been brought of the overthrow of Jupiter.

"You lie, barbarian dungheap," he wheezed at last.

"Then go to your mistress, steward, and say so," said Canis, "but go on your toes so that you shall be ready to fly from her when she comes at you tooth and nail.''

Dilpus scowled, but uneasily, then knew it was as the dog had said. If this was not proof of the incomprehensible moods of a woman, then what else was it? He took Canis and gave him into the charge of the servants of the bath, and Canis wallowed long and luxuriously, although the water came sharply to his sore back. Then he trimmed his beard and scraped the bristles with pumice stone until his chin was smooth again. Dilpus moodily brought him clean linen and a white tunic embroidered with the blue emblem of the house of Osirus.

He was given new duties. No longer degrading, they were mainly to do with supervising other slaves in the conditioning of the Osirus horses. Dilpus was in a constant turmoil, for Lydia was fierce in ensuring her steward gave the Briton no task she did not approve. Once, seeing Canis kneeling in dirt to apply salve to a mare's tender fetlock, she flew hissing at Dilpus and left the red, angry marks of her clawing nails on his well-fed face.

"Dog," she breathed in fury, "the dirt is for others, it is not for him! I will see you in it yourself if it happens again!"

Dilpus could have told his temperamental mistress that the Briton was, by reason of her lack of reason, becoming virtually his own master within his circumscribed limits. But he held his tongue. In her present moods, all of them impossible, she would not lack to have his tongue slit.

Dilpus might regard him malevolently, but in truth Canis went about in quiet and inoffensive fashion. Because of his way with people and his gift for speech and song, he brought some pleasure to the other slaves at the end of each day when they gathered together in their quarters.

"Tell us of Boadicea," they would say, for although only a few were Iceni the exploits of the queen were of great interest to all of them.

"She was a queen. She lived like a queen and died like one. She had sweet life, brave death and is in the hearts of all who knew her."

And that was all he would ever say of Boadicea, but it was sufficient in its way and perhaps everything unsaid could be read in his eyes by those who loved him enough.

He did not wear Boadicea's ring. Slaves owned no property and he would not in any case put the precious ring at risk by disclosing it to the curious or covetous. Julian had generously taken charge of his sack of relics and returned it to Canis, and only Julian knew what it contained. Among other things were a neckchain, a clasp, two silver cups, two brooches, the cloak she had worn in her last battle, the ring and two gold fillets. The fillets would, he knew, bring to him the scent of her rich, honey-bronze hair if he did no more than lay them in the palm of his hand. But in the quiet of his room he did not disturb the sack or its contents. Except for the ring they belonged to her people. He did not need to take them out to bring her close. In the darkness he reached for her spirit and it was all about him.

It did not matter that Lydia had him at the moment. Though his body was shackled by his bondage, his own spirit was free. A moment in time would come again for him.

19

LYDIA WAS LIKE a woman at odds with reason, wholly unable to comprehend why Diana allowed her to be in such unhappiness.

She did not go near Canis, she dared not. If she saw him she hastened away. To be near him, to have to speak to him, brought on emotions that threatened all her self-control. She tried to convince herself that she only had to wrest him from her sight to remove him from her mind. But she could not. She might successfully keep him out of her sight for days but she was always aware of him, and always her mind was feverishly obsessed by thoughts of him.

There was one solution. She could hand him over to Paullinus.

She froze at what Paullinus would do to him.

Frequently she left her house to visit her friend Valeria, or go on some purposeless ride or take herself off to the market. She avoided Julian as much as she could, though she could not avoid taking supper with him. She did not speak to him of her especial property, nor did she affect any interest whenever Julian mentioned him, though her heart turned painfully over at the sound of his name.

"I am not disposed to discuss him," she would say, "he is of no great interest to me, after all."

In her room each night when Suella, her Dobunni servant, had been dismissed, Lydia could neither rest nor sleep. She tossed and turned on her couch until flame became a hot fever, consuming her like a burning sickness that could never be eased. Because she was strong-willed she thought to tear it from her. She only

307

needed other things to think about. But again and again as she lay weeping in the darkness she was confronted by the vision of her own heart, which fiercely refused to be divorced from that which possessed it.

Sometimes during the day the sickness would take her suddenly, making her hot, breathless and faint. It would take her in the street if she saw a taller man than usual, with something about him, however insignificant, that the Briton had. And to her mind his image would instantly leap, she would hear his voice and see the clouds in his eyes.

Whenever she returned to the house it was always in nervous agitation, her blood running hot and cold in case he appeared, although he seldom entered the villa since she herself ensured his duties lay elsewhere. Only during the evenings when he was in conversation with Julian was he within her four walls. But to hear him talking to her brother, his deep voice a murmur from Julian's room, so distracted her that she would fling herself down and use cushions and fabrics to smother her ears against every sound except that of her pounding heart.

She did come across him one day. As she hastened along the flagged path from the gate he appeared, carrying a bridle. Numbly she looked at him. He ventured a smile, for he did not think much of the law which forbade this human impulse, and he even accorded her a gesture that may have been a friendly greeting. But he gave her no word and would have gone on his way to the stables, except that in her incurable torment Lydia simply would not have it.

"Oh, insolence!" she cried. He turned back to her in mild surprise. That did not help her, either. "Am I to be looked through, walked over and not given proper respect? Am I not your mistress, your owner, your keeper, your life and your death?"

Canis reflected on this loud, angry outburst. There was little any man could do for a maid at a moment when she was experiencing all the moods and confusion of turning into a woman.

"You are my owner, mistress," he said, "and the arbiter of my speech. What is your new indulgence concerning me? Is it that you wish me to hail your comings and goings? And if so, am I to hail you in a loud voice or respectful one?"

Oh, the cruelty of him. To mock her when she had been so charitable for so many days. And to look at her, as now, as if she were only some kind of curio whose value was governed by demand or fashion, how could he?

"Oh, if there is any man less deserving than you," she breathed, "great Diana would strike him dead."

"Ah, great Diana," he said, "there is a goddess for women indeed. She has more moods than all of you put together."

Lydia waited for a hundred arrows of fire to pierce him and when nothing happened she said passionately, "Worshipper of false gods, defiler of the true, know that it is my undeviating vow to break you and destroy you, and this vow I will pursue until you are miserably dead!"

"Mistress," he said calmly, "such idealistic pursuance of a vow like that is the purest form of obstinacy. Life with all its wonders is just beginning for you. Why do you not enjoy it?"

Lydia cried out in bitter protest, then ran blindly to the refuge of her room, where she beat the cushions of her couch in despair and frenzy. Tomorrow she would have him in the dirt again, under the whip again. Aye, she would. Tomorrow. Or the day after.

It was the day after when Valeria, a likeable and uncommonly fair Roman woman, accompanied Lydia home from an outing to gossip with her in the comfort of the warm villa, heated by underfloor piping. At the door to her room Lydia saw Canis in conversation with Suella, a girl with a pretty daintiness who had a way in

dressing her mistress's hair and enhancing her beauty
that pleased even the imperious, moody Lydia. Lydia
perceived instantly the brightness on the girl's face and
the smile that Canis had for her. And Lydia's heart felt
pain so cruel that anger just as cruel burned her.

"So," she said, reaching them, "this is how you idle
when your mistress is out of sight. Go about your work,
you lazy wench." And she smote Suella's smooth cheek
stingingly. Suella cried out and seeing Lydia's expression, fled. Lydia turned on Canis. His hard-faced
disapproval of her treatment of Suella shattered her.
"As for you, you repay my kindness by creeping about
my house, which is forbidden you! Go, do you hear,
go!"

"By the order of Dilpus," said Canis, indicating a
sheaf of evergreen sprigs he held, "I brought these to
Suella, who was to arrange them for you. I will leave
them with you." He put the sprigs into her arms with a
care that mocked her. Her body shuddered at his nearness. Her pride was so beset, her pain so intense, that
she flung the sprigs childishly at his feet.

"Barbarian," she cried, "do you think me as low as
you, to handle stuff that crawls with wet winter bugs
and has dirt on its leaves? Take it up, I do not want it.
And do not come within the house again unless I say
so."

Behind her Valeria had come to witness the scene, to
look at Canis with a curious but not prejudiced eye.
Valeria was of equable disposition and judged all
people, Romans or Britons, slaves or free men, as she
found them. She thought Lydia strangely passionate
about something she herself would have dismissed with
a smile.

Valeria knew this was the Briton who had been
general to the confederated armies of Boadicea, and
that by the unusually generous dispensation of the normally unyielding Paullinus he was now slave to Lydia.
This was the first time she had seen him close, and he

did not have the wild, Celtic face she had imagined, nor did he show barbarous. His features were hard but finely expressive, holding a gentle irony for the follies of the world. Nor had she ever seen such compelling, haunting eyes in a man, wide and deeply grey, reflecting all the subtle shadows of life. Sensing her regard as he turned to go from the trembling Lydia, he glanced at Valeria and smiled at her as if he knew her for the woman she was, and Valeria felt a quick, hot melting within her.

Oh, Venus, she thought, this is no barbarian, this is not the man Lydia speaks of, this is not a man she even knows.

Canis went, taking the unwanted evergreens with him. And because she had wanted them, Lydia could have run at him and frenziedly beaten him.

"I did not think him to be as comely as he is," said Valeria when she and Lydia were reclining comfortably in the room overlooking the terrace.

"Oh? Who is this you mean?" asked Lydia with careful indifference.

"Your slave, Canis."

"He is as wolfish as his name," said Lydia abruptly. "He is as sly and treacherous as a wolf and as cowardly, and only a mockery of a man. Do not speak of him, I detest him."

"You have said so before, Lydia. Might I then purchase him from you?"

Lydia thrust her hands into the folds of her robe to hide their trembling.

"I would not inflict him on any of my friends, least of all you," she said. "Oh, believe me, Valeria, I know his cruelty and his insolence. Whip him and he laughs at you."

"You have had him whipped? This man?" said Valeria in astonishment.

Lydia's face suffused with her agitated, suffering blood.

"You do not know him as I do," she said, "it is because I detest him that I made him my slave." Seeing Valeria raise her eyebrows she added hastily, "It was to cure him of his arrogance."

"Ah," said Valeria, smiling in a different way then. "That would be the last reason to make me purchase a man. But, Lydia, I have heard you say hard things about him before, and yet he has a strangely sweet smile."

"Aye," said Lydia darkly, "as a snake has just before it swallows you."

* * *

IF THE DAYS were hard for Lydia, the nights were well-nigh unbearable. It was at night when she wept for what her traitorous heart was making shamefully obvious to her strong mind. Not until she was physically and mentally exhausted could she find sleep. Julian commented on her pallor one morning and was angrily told his eyes deceived him as, she added, they so often did.

"In what matters?" he asked drily.

"In all matters."

"In especial, a barbarian?" he suggested.

"Aye, him among other things," she retorted.

"Who is the more deceived, I wonder? Lydia, you no longer find him degrading work, you are kinder to him. Why do we not give him the comfort of the house each evening? He is an interesting man to talk to."

"Am I to approve what I already know obtains?"

"I should simply prefer it to be done openly, that is all. We owe him a great deal and to offer him a little civilisation each evening would not be much in return. I might ask him if a man may safely wed a young woman called Fabia, who has a sweet aptitude for making a man laugh."

Julian had recently met the dark-eyed daughter of a tribune.

"How might he answer this when he has no understanding of women?" said Lydia in some passion.

"I think he has some understanding of you, sweet sister," said Julian with a smile.

The red blood rushed to Lydia's face and her mouth trembled.

"What has he said of me, what has he said?" she asked, and she could not contain the violent beat of her heart.

"Only that you are beginning to grow up," said Julian slyly.

Lydia gave a cry.

"Oh, you are contemptible to let a vile slave speak of me in such a way! To say that about me when—oh, he is undeserving of any kindness, he is the cruellest of men, the—"

"Lydia, Lydia," said Julian soothingly.

"He is! He is the cruellest man I know and is entirely forbidden the house! Oh," she cried, "never will I let him set foot inside it again, and do not sneak him in or I will give him to Paullinus, who still wants him!"

"Paullinus?" Julian was shocked. "Paullinus, Lydia?"

Lydia was white, desperate, shivering.

"No," she gasped, "no—that is, I meant I do not want him in this house."

"You will relax this in time," said Julian, "for he is right. You are growing up for all your tantrums. It is in your face, Lydia. Why do you fight it so?"

"Go about your business, go!"

When he had gone she sat there still shivering, still burning.

An evening came when she was so racked and desolate that she could no longer sit and wait for the hour that saw her to bed. She had been listening to a murmur, a haunting murmur with faint, sweet song to it. She knew it came from the slaves' quarters and something about it tugged at her aching heart. Fastening a cloak about herself, she stole on slippered feet from the house and across the lamplit courtyard, her mouth dry, her heart thumping, irresistibly drawn. She entered a dark passage and saw light and heard sound issuing from the room which housed the male slaves. The sound was of softly-plucked string and deep haunting voice, and the pain within her put her in great and over-whelming longing. Silently, tremblingly, she stood by the open door and because it was dark in the passage and her robe was also dark, she saw into the room without being seen herself.

There on a stool sat Canis, with a wooden lyre musically strung, and around him sat or stood the slaves, men and women. In the light of the oil lamps their faces were still, with shadows upon them, and there were shadows also on the face of Canis. His eyes reflected that which had gone beyond return and the song he sang was this.

There is blue on the water in summer days
There is silver on the land in winter
There is forest so deep its heart is night
Where the boar runs fierce and wily
There is a spirit I know
And a heart I know
And the spirit is strong and the heart is sweet
There is a life I know
A life that is gone
To a river that is blue and a forest that is deep
To where the blue on the water and the silver on the land
Are mist in the eyes of my love.

The tears were huge on her lashes and her heart was drowning and she could not get her breath. Nor could she see. And when she could Canis was standing before her in the dim light of the doorway, stooping a little because of its lowness.

"Mistress," he said, "what is there any of us might do for you?"

What? Oh, she thought in weeping despair, let one of you strike me dead, and let this one be you since your cruel eyes found me where none else would.

She drew back, shivering, hiding herself in deeper darkness.

"I heard noises," she said, her voice throaty, "and came to discover the cause. It is forbidden for slaves to gather together and disturb the house."

"Is it? I thought we sang as softly as nested birds," said Canis, while the other slaves silently wondered about her. Then she saw Suella and was almost glad to feel the raging jealousy, for it came like a fiery antidote to her suffering.

"So," she said, stepping to the door but keeping her face shadowed by the hood of her cloak, "this is where you loll, lazy wench. Did you not hear me call?"

Since she had dismissed Suella an hour ago, wanting to be alone, there was a nervous bewilderment on the girl's face at this capriciousness.

"Mistress, I cry pardon, I thought—"

"It is not your place to think but to obey my call." And Lydia turned abruptly, almost running as she crossed the courtyard in her agitated flight. When she had reached her room Suella came hesitantly to attend her.

"Well?" said Lydia, throwing off her cloak to uncover a robe of green.

"My lady, did you not say you wanted me?" said the girl, in further nervousness at the strained, intense look on her mistress's face.

"Did I? Well, what I wanted you for I cannot now remember," said Lydia. "Wait outside and when I have remembered I will call you." She saw Suella's nervousness and was conscious of a spasm of self-disgust. To her own astonishment she found herself speaking kindly. "But no, it is of little importance, Suella. I have my mind on neither one thing nor another tonight. Go, return to your friends and say they may sing."

Suella, confused now, thanked her breathlessly and made for the door. Lydia put out a sudden hand.

"Tarry a moment, Suella." Then, with affected casualness, "I only wished to say you are a pleasing girl in your minding of my needs and I should not want you to be unhappy. Do you—do you sometimes think me unkind, Suella?"

"My lady," said Suella as bravely as she could, "you are only high-spirited and I do not mind this."

"You have put it in a sweeter way than I would," said Lydia. The colour deepened in her cheeks. "I cannot think why in your sweetness and prettiness no man has spoken for you. Is—is there such a man whom you would like to?'

Suella became more confused.

"There is not, mistress," she said.

"Why, is there no one who looks admiringly at you, Suella?" Lydia began to pursue the point which now had her by the heart and throat. "Have I not seen affectionate smiles between you and Canis?"

"Canis is not for me, mistress," said the girl in a low voice, and looking down to hide her face.

"Why? He is not above you. You are his equal here and he is not to consider himself better than you."

"He is not for Suella, mistress," said the girl quietly.

Lydia swallowed and with an effort continued to speak lightly.

"Come, Suella, what he was before has no significance," she said, "and he has looked at you and smiled at you, has he not?" Her nails began to gouge the damp palms of her hands. "Is he afraid I will have him whipped if he raises bolder eyes to you?"

Suella lifted unhappy face to her mistress, begging with her eyes to be spared all this embarrassment.

"My lady Lydia, Canis belongs to no woman save one, so do not speak to him of Suella, I beg."

"Save one?" The deep colour fled, leaving Lydia pale. Her nails dug cruelly. She simulated a careless laugh which even to her own ears sounded like the croak of a husky frog. "Which woman is this, pray, who has won such mighty esteem?"

Suella hesitated, then said, "I do not know, mistress."

"You do know," said Lydia a little wildly. Suella dropped her eyes again and Lydia was sure the girl did indeed know but would not tell. A fiercer jealousy than all others gripped her and she conjured up the image of a woman she would surely kill if she could find her. "Go, then," she said in a suppressed voice, "but send Canis to me."

Unhappy Suella fled in relief and in a while Canis arrived. He stood on the threshold and she turned so that he could not wholly see her face.

"Mistress?" he said and she trembled at the sound of the voice she had so hated and which now haunted her.

"I would speak with you, Canis," she whispered, and it was the first time she had called him by name.

"I am here," he said.

"I heard your song and thought it pleasant but so sad. Can you not sing more joyful tunes?"

"Aye, on joyful occasions," he said.

"Oh, I know you have come to a sad turn in life," she said quickly, "but I have not been too unpleasant to you lately, have I? There is no need to be quite as sad as you have been, is there?"

"Not for myself," said Canis, "for Dilpus. He has lost the gold from one of his teeth and could not be in more grief if he had lost his supper."

Her steward's liking for his evening victuals was well-known. But the allusion held no amusement for Lydia, balanced dangerously as she was on the over-sensitive edge of emotion.

"Oh, will you never cease to mock me?" she said passionately.

"A trifle of light gossip is not mockery, mistress." Canis spoke quite gently. "You look so often for it that you frequently find it when it is not there. All maids are sensitive. Also, many of them, like you, are sometimes of one mind and sometimes of another."

"You—oh," she cried, "in no other Roman house does any slave have the temerity or license to speak as you speak to me! You are intolerable!"

"But is this not why I am your especial property?" And he was mocking now. "Was it not my intolerable self you desired to acquire above all else? Is it not your undeviating vow to reduce me wholly, until I am nothing?"

She could have died at cruelty as merciless as this.

"You are ingratitude in its meanest essence," she whispered, aghast at the feel of tears trembling precariously. "You know I have left you in peace for many days now. If—" She halted, frightened by her weakness. "If I gave you great unkindness at first it was no more than human, for you hurt and shamed me when we met—oh, you cannot deny that. And did you not become a terrible scourge of my people? I am no more and no less than any man or woman. If you rose up in wrath against us for the wrong you thought we did you, is it not my right to rise up against you for what you did?"

"In the world as it is," said Canis, "it is your especial Roman privilege."

She took a nervous step towards him. He saw how pale she was. But all her spite and petulance seemed gone and despite her paleness she was beautiful beneath her crown of glossy black hair, the richly-bound tresses adorned by jewelled clasps.

"Canis, you make it so hard for me to be kind," she said unsteadily, "but I will be if you will only understand me a little. I—I cannot deny Julian any longer. He has a great regard for you. Although, as you know, I find you cruel and unfeeling, I will make some amends for my unkindnesses by saying you are free to come to the house each evening. Then you may discuss politics with Julian, which are an obsession with him and so many men, which is why men bring so much grief to women."

"Why, mistress," said Canis with a smile, "that is the first sound observation I have heard you make."

"That is because you have never been in sympathy with me," she said, "and even now I expect you will only mock me for my charity. Also—" Here she drew a breath before she could go on. "Also, I believe there is some woman you have a regard for and if you will name her and it is within my power I will—I will purchase her for you so that you and she may be together—"

"Purchase her?" he said and in a way that put fear into her, not for her body but for the violability of her heart.

"Oh, do not mistake me," she gasped, "I did not mean it to sound like cold, bloodless commerce, only that if I could help you in any way with your wishes or desires then I would—willingly."

Willingly? Had she herself said that when she was only burning to find out which woman it was?

Canis looked thoughtfully at her. Then he smiled and her heart breathed again.

"By this offer, which I will not forget," he said, "I am rebuked for much I have said to you."

Not forget? Then there was—oh, Diana, no! No!

"Who is she?" Lydia, white and fierce, flung the question in anguished cry.

"If there is any rumour which has reached you," said Canis quietly, "put it from you, for it is only rumour. But for your kindness I am grateful."

A sudden incredulous thought smote her, seizing her heart as well as her mind.

"Hear me," she said breathlessly, "and know that if such woman be Roman and you are afraid of what might befall you for lifting your eyes to her, you need have no worry, I swear. If she is Roman, speak her name—perhaps that is what she so wishes, to hear you name her—I will be sympathetic—"

"There is no woman, Roman or otherwise, whom I have set my eyes on in love since I came to your house," he said evenly. "I bid you sweet dreams and peaceful night, mistress."

He turned to go.

"Will you never show me respect, will you never regard me?" she cried. The strange clouds darkened his eyes and she knew he was gone from her. Beside herself she said furiously, "You have some harlot among the women and are hot to go to her!"

"Mistress," he said in a resigned way, "you take one step forward, then one step back."

At this and his unbearable indifference, Lydia ran wildly forward and smote his face with a violent hand, then stared in terror at the mark of her blow. His grey eyes showed only pity for her utter foolishness. She seized with her left hand the hand that had struck him and pressed it to her hammering heart, and anguish so darkened her world that she cried words she had never before spoken.

"Forgive me, oh forgive me!"

"Readily," said Canis, "and will you now bid me go?"

"Help me, oh help me, I beg you," she gasped and dropped to her knees, shivering and hiding her face in her hands, the blue-black of her coiled hair glinting in the light of the lamps.

Canis looked down at her bent head, his mouth twitched and he smiled.

"So this is it," he said. "Well, it comes to all of us in

time and makes us in many ways not more than we are but less. However, it is not so bad for you as it is for the godless. For you it is merely a question of involving the aid of your goddess of love. And if she fails there is, particularly for you, always Diana. Are you so much in love, mistress?''

She lifted her face, her tears brilliant, her mouth quivering.

"Canis, I am dying of it," she wept, "it consumes me and burns me. Oh, will you not be merciful? Will you not speak me kindly, sweetly?''

"This is folly in one so proud and strong," he said. He stooped, took her by her elbows and brought her to her feet. Lydia, at the touch of his hands, shivered anew as if in fever, then fire took its hold and her blood ran with heat even after he released her. "None can die of love, mistress," he said, "only for it. You are in so much confusion that you have forgotten you are a woman with all a woman's ways of resolving the matter. Have you not thought to close his eyes and mouth with kisses?''

"Aye, I have," she whispered through her glittering, green tears, "every minute of every day, every minute of every night. I have kissed him in my thoughts and in my dreams, and when he has been standing before me I have kissed him with my eyes. But he neither sees me nor acknowledges me, neither knows me nor understands me. Oh, Canis," she cried, "it is you, it is only you, am I not making it shamelessly plain? Has it not been in my heart and my eyes for many days now?''

"Mistress, you are in even worse confusion than I thought," said Canis gently.

"Oh, no, no, no!" She was sobbing, distracted, pleading. "I am only in pain, and in such pain as I never dreamed. I am so in love, it takes my breath, I cannot eat, I cannot sleep, nor think of anything or anyone but you. I know I have been so unkind to you and have been in such shame over this, but forgive me, do not turn from me or I will surely die. See, I will give you anything you wish, anything, if you will only give me just a little love and call me Lydia.''

He seemed sad and the thought that this was all he could feel, that the most she could arouse in him was pity, distracted her more. Her eyes begged him, beseeched him, and her tears implored him.

''This cannot be, you know that,'' he said quietly. ''You are a proud, rich, patrician Roman and I as a slave barbarian even less than a free one.''

''Barbarian? Oh, no, no, no!'' she cried again, and remembered how he had come upon her and the wounded Julian in the sun-reddened forest and how he had looked more bitter and formidable than Mars.

''Because of so much that has happened,'' he went on, ''you must believe you are much more in confusion than love, that you are experiencing emotions inescapable to emergent women. You are feeling all a woman's pain and hunger. Perhaps your erstwhile petulance does make you unhappy, but we all grow up, mistress, we all experience painful regret for youthful impulses. Because you are now a woman you would be kind where before you were wilful. Is this not the heart of it?''

She was incredulous. She had asked for sweetness, for love, and he had given her a lecture.

''It is not,'' she wept, ''for you speak as if I have only just become aware of the world. You have never seen me, you have only ever looked through me. Do you not think I have fought my love for you? I have, I have. But it has grown worse each day. Oh, I did not dream love could be like this, you do not know its pain. I had never thought to speak of it, but tonight, oh my heart is breaking tonight. I know you are proud, but because of this do not reject me or I shall be in torment always. Unless I can do for you all that I might, then I cannot ever find joy or undo the wrong I committed in using you so degradingly and mocking your queen so shamefully. Oh, forgive me, forgive me in that I hurt you so much concerning her, and do not look through me, but see me, see me.''

See me.

The words of majestic beauty.

The eyes of Canis were shadowed, masking his own pain. Lydia. The woman who had spat upon his queen. Nevertheless, he spoke very gently.

"It cannot be, mistress."

"Do not call me mistress," she pleaded, "do not think of what divides us, for I will do anything to change this, give you anything."

"My freedom to go among my people, those who are left, and help them?"

"Willingly, more than willingly, if you will only take me with you and love me."

"That I cannot do," he said.

She could not believe him to be in such calm finality. Distraught beyond words she sank to her knees again, sobbing piteously for a while, and then she said, "You have miscalled me in many hateful ways for my cruelty to you, but now I know you are far more cruel."

"Mistress," he said, "it will be better if you sleep on this and come to different conclusions. I will wish you sweet dreams and peaceful night."

Sweet dreams? Peaceful night? Did he know what he was saying? Was he as unfeeling as that?

"Aye, go, go! " She rose to her feet and through her hopeless tears spoke fiercely. "Since you can only be pitiless, I will be pitiless too. In my rejected love I will be more bitter than in my hate. Go, go, and from now on I will have Dilpus make every day as unbearable for you as you make each one unbearable for me! I will tear you from my heart, I will have Dilpus lay your back in stripes, so that as I suffer in my way you shall suffer in yours."

"You are indeed a woman," he said ironically, "since though you may derive some satisfaction from my suffering, you know I will derive none from yours.''

He left her and Lydia collapsed over her couch, sobbing in heartbreak.

But she did not instruct Dilpus as she had threatened. She could not have endured seeing Canis under the whip again. His body was not for any whip, it was for her, for her. If there was another woman, oh, if there was, she would find her and kill her. She did not care how long it might take, she would ensure Canis looked to one woman alone. Herself. He could not permanently reject her, he could not.

But for the moment she did not know what to do or how she lived through the next days, hungering and crying for his love and remembering the touch of his hands on her. She went each day to the small temple of Diana, making great offerings to the goddess and praying that some concession, however small, be granted to her in this matter of her breaking heart.

She prayed to Diana because Diana was truly omnipotent and the only one who could give Canis to her in love because she had been the only one to give him in vengeance. Some called Venus the dispenser of favours where love was concerned, but Lydia considered Venus too inordinately vain a goddess to be genuinely concerned with other women, especially mortal women. It was possible that Venus thought it an offence for any man, mortal or immortal, to love another woman in advance of herself.

Diana was great. Diana was understanding. Diana knew how she loved him, how she had always loved him, which was the reason why she hated him when he contempted her so. Now she understood the intensity of her feelings that day she had first seen him and why his mockery had so embittered her. He had shocked her into angry resentment with one glance of his eyes, looking at her not as if she were a beautiful young woman (which she was), but as if she were a wayward child (which she was not).

Oh, Diana, help me, give him to me.

But Diana appeared not to have heard, for nothing changed. Canis, whenever she contrived to be in his path, was as remote as ever, his smile an abstraction that desolated her.

So after fruitless days of misery she summoned her litter and was carried cloaked and hooded to the unostentatious dwelling of one Scythia, an ancient votaress of Diana who aided many worshippers of the goddess with various charms she knew the magic and mystery of.

It was dim in the unprepossessing room and Scythia, a gaunt old crone with a weakness for imported figs, dipped long bony fingers into a dish of them as she sat behind a drab, semi-opaque curtain and listened to Lydia, whose hood concealed her face.

"It is always a matter of a man," grumbled Scythia through a mouthful of juicy fruit. "Am I to know his name and under which star he was born?"

"I cannot," said Lydia.

"Ah," said Scythia, "it is almost always thus. Then is he soldier or official?"

"Neither. Mother, can you not just give me a simple herb to help me become what I wish to him?"

"If the herb were as simple as that, daughter, I should be more than the goddess herself. Is he dark or fair? Does he have brown eyes or blue?"

Lydia drew a deep breath and within the hood her eyes glowed.

"He is perhaps darker than fairer, yet he is fairer than any man and more cruel than Mars and more commanding than Apollo. He is tall with the tallness of Jupiter, so that all look up to him, aye or no, and oh, Mother, he has such eyes with all the world in them so that when he looks at me my heart drowns in hot tears and I cannot speak."

"What colour?" mumbled Scythia through another succulent fig.

"The colour of the sky before the sun breaks, the colour of a lake in the shadow of a mountain, the colour of the sea on a winter day, the colour of a cloud in a summer storm, the—"

"Folly," interrupted Scythia, "they are grey, so say so. What would you do for this mortal, grey-eyed god?"

"Love him, comfort him, take his loneliness from him, serve him, be his life, his rapture, his being. Oh, Mother, make him love me a little at least."

"More folly," muttered the old one, "for a little love is worse than none at all. Do you want aid in love or desire?" she asked bluntly, and Lydia answered in a breathless voice.

"Mother, I want him now and forever, wholly and completely."

"Hm," murmured Scythia. "Tall, perhaps darker than fairer, with grey eyes that bring tears to a woman. Hm." She mumbled on, then took a dull, battered silver dish and emptied some fine ash into it and scratched about in it with a sticky fingernail, muttering over it. Then from a small satchel depending from her waist she took a tiny vial and, pushing the curtain aside a little, gave it into Lydia's eager, grateful hand. "It is not to be swallowed to bring you satisfaction from a small flirtation," she said, "but to bring you a true love, if you are capable of true love. It is enough for two takings. And because it cost me much to come by so must it cost you much to acquire. In gold."

"Is this enough?" asked Lydia, handing the old woman a gold brooch inset with lapis lazuli. Scythia took it grumblingly, pawed it, peered at it and, with her brown teeth, bit on it. Satisfied, she tucked it into her satchel and helped herself to another fig.

In a voice wet from chewing she said, "It is to be taken in wine just before sleep. Shut tight the door as you go for there is an icy chill in the air today that catches my every bone."

The night could not come too soon for Lydia. She had Suella bring her wine, then dismissed her. Her heart beat almost painfully. Never had she thought she would seek help from a dispenser of charms. How, she had always asked, could any pensioned votaress give what a goddess withheld? But then she had never been in the desperate need she was now. And it was not that Diana had withheld, it was that inexplicably she had not heard. Moreover, Scythia was, after all, a votaress of long standing and highly recommended.

Lydia carefully poured half the contents of the vial into her cup of wine. She held the cup between prayerful hands and meticulously spun it until the amber liquid from the vial was mixed well with the wine. She prayed, then she drank the mixture down.

She retired to her couch, arranged the rich draperies about herself, then sat up in the dim light of the single lamp she had left burning and waited for what? She did not know. She felt no different except for the warm comfort the wine had given her. No wondrous change exhilarated her body. Nor, for the matter, did Canis, spellbound, come amorously in to cast himself at the foot of her couch and beg for her love. Tears sprang to her eyes. This was unendurable. She had never known true tears in the past. Now she was always weeping. She fought the weakness and waited. She sank back and waited.

She waited.

She slept.

She dreamed.

There was a woman there, one with a wealth of bright hair, sweet wide mouth and strange, glowing beauty. If only her eyes could be seen Lydia thought she would know her, but there was a mist before them, hiding them. In rich, musical voice she spoke to Lydia.

"You are Roman."

"I am," said Lydia proudly.

"And spilt his blood."

"Never, not one drop, I could not, would not!"

"Did you not scourge his back with whips?"

"This I had forgotten and put behind me, for I could not bear to think on it."

"I too had him scourged," said the woman, "so you must let him go, as I let him go."

"I cannot!"

"How might you bind him to you when I myself could not?"

"I will bind him with my love, which is greater than my life," cried Lydia.

The mouth of the woman curved in a proud, bitter smile, but the mist deepened.

"All who truly love must suffer."

"I do love and I do suffer!"

"You suffer only the sulks of selfish and unrequited desire."

"If he never comes to my bed I will weep for his neglect of me, but even this I will endure if only he will take my hand and cleave to no other woman."

"That is only foolishness," said the woman, her red mouth mocking, "and is also untrue. What woman who desires fulfilment will ask only for her hand to be held? You are no more than a spoilt child, striving for that which you cannot have and do not deserve. You do not feel true love, only wanton desire."

"Who are you to so contempt me?"

Again the woman smiled and though the mist still drifted and wreathed to hide her eyes, there was radiance about her.

"I am his heart, his mind, his strength, his purpose. I am his life and his death, as he was mine."

"You are wicked to so possess him!"

"Roman," said the woman of the mist, "I never possessed him, so great was my love. I sent him from me. You must do the same."

"I cannot, I will not! Can the earth exist without its

sun, the night without its stars? Who are you to so command me?"

"Once who waits for him."

"I will never release him to you or any woman, never!"

"What content will it bring you to imprison his body and lose his heart? You are your own folly and own defeat."

And the woman laughed, and in her dream the sound of the laughter was to Lydia like the flow of a soft, murmurous river on a summer night and the whisper of the wind above the trees of a forest.

20

LYDIA AWOKE. It was bright morning. The chill of winter had overnight passed and was in flight from the caressing warmth of spring. Yesterday had been bitter. Today was gentle. She thought this a propitious omen and rose eagerly, quickly, reaching for her shining mirror. It reflected the rosy softness that came from deep sleep, deeper than she had known for a long time. Her eyes glowed with health. The dream returned vividly but she put it from her, for she was not concerned with dreams of that kind. It was life which called. And surely the potion had given her life in place of misery, surely her reflection showed new beauty to enchant even the most indifferent beholder? Was this the magic of Diana's dispensation?

She called Suella and the girl helped her dress with more than usual care, binding her thick, silky hair with artful skill, so that when her toilet was complete Suella could not hold back her admiration.

"Mistress Lydia, surely you are a picture to delight the hearts and eyes of all men today."

All men? There was only one. Open his eyes, Diana, make him see me.

Lydia touched Suella's cheek with a kind hand.

"You are a sweet child to say that," she said, although she was only two years older than the girl. "We will have some early blooms cut to grace the house. Ask Dilpus for Canis to do this, for though he is a hard man he has an understanding way with tender stems. He is to bring them to me when I have eaten."

She ate little. Then she waited, looking often into her mirror, anxiety at odds with hope. It was seven days

330

since she had distractedly declared her love to him, and as much as he could he had avoided her since.

He arrived. She may have been different because of Diana, but he was unchanged. He was still, to her, more compelling and more commanding than any man. Her hungry eyes caressed him and he smiled as if there was no embarrassment between them. He placed a basket of new, crisp-looking blooms on her mosaic table but she did not even glance at them.

"Canis," she said, fighting the weaknesses already besetting her, "I had you bring me sweet blooms to show you I bear you no ill will for the unhappiness you gave me seven days ago."

Canis regarded her glowing beauty a little warily.

"Since Dilpus had no ill will, either," he said, "I felt you had none yourself, mistress, despite what words there were. You are in sweetness today."

"Am I sweet, Canis, am I?" she asked like a young, breathless girl.

"There is sweetness in all women," he said, "although it is more difficult to find in some than in others."

"You would not find it difficult to discover in me," she said longingly. She had wanted to make progress slowly, but her weakness and desire made her rush on. "Oh, do not shake your head, but look at me. Many men have said I am beautiful and though I do not know if any have said this merely to indulge my vanity, I do not think I am wholly unbeautiful, am I? Tell me, am I not just a little pleasing to your eye?"

He regarded her in a way that warmed her, excited her. There were no shadows, no indifference. For the first time his eyes were smiling, seeing, searching.

"More than a little," he said.

Her blood rushed, her knees trembled and her eyes shone.

"Then surely," she breathed, "surely you will not

turn from me but come to love me—only a little at first—I will not ask for more, not at first. Oh, you do not know how desperate I am to have you sweet to me."

Impulsively she put her hand on his arm. The contact brought flame to her body and because of self-confidence and because she could no longer deny herself sweeter contact, she flung herself against him, pressing close to bring to him the scented allure of her beauty and the power the potion had surely given her. She lifted her face and beckoned his love with the appeal of her vivid, trembling mouth. Above her great longing to possess him leapt an even greater longing to be possessed.

But Canis put her gently from him and Lydia went white with shock and pain.

"Mistress," he began, but in wounded temper she would not listen to him.

"So," she cried, her voice noisy with her pain, "I am so sweet and beautiful you cannot even bear the touch of me!"

"You are Roman, born for another Roman of as high a status as your own," he counselled her, "and between us there can only be such friendship as you in your exalted position care to bestow on me from one day to the next. Mistress, will you not come at this matter with your head instead of your heart?"

"I am a woman," she said emotionally, "I am not a man, a man of cold, selfish indifference, who has no heart at all—oh, where are you going?"

"To my work."

"I am ugly in your sight," she said bitterly.

"You are not," he said kindly, but she did not want kindness that stemmed only from pity.

"I was right," she stormed, "you do have a harlot among the women, and I will discover which one it is and kill her!"

"Now you are in confusion again," he said, "but it will pass."

She turned to seize the basket of flowers and hurl it at him, but before she could do so he had gone.

Despair returned. She had never envisaged love could be the agony it was. She had striven to reject it when she had first become incredulously aware of it, but it could neither be rejected nor extinguished. It asked, demanded, fulfilment. She went about distraught, thinking that the gods put no anguish on a woman that was more unendurable than unrequited love. Julian would not stay quiet, so changed was she and so woeful.

"Come," he said kindly one evening, "you are in more than ordinary trouble, Lydia, say what you will. It is so long since I heard you laugh, even in spite, or had any sensible word from you, that I am beginning to worry about you."

"It is nothing except a headache," she said.

"Then it is a headache of unreasonable duration," he said, "and I will have the physician call to dose you."

"I will not see him."

"Then it is no headache," said Julian. "What is it, Lydia? Something exceedingly strange, I judge. Once you were the most exacting of mistresses with your servants. Now you are less exacting than any."

"It is nothing you need concern yourself over," said Lydia palely, "and as for my servants, I am indifferent to every one of them."

"And what of Canis? Has your vengeance run its full course at last?"

"To him," she said in a low, bitter voice, "I am more indifferent than any. I care nothing for what he is about or where."

"Then I will have him for my servant," said Julian in some pleasure, "for he is scholarly and will be of great use to me."

"Then take him," she said in her bitterness, "or I will end by killing him as I have always said."

"You blow hot, cold and hot," said Julian. "Let me speak to him on your behalf, for he is a man of ex-

perience and may do for your headache what you will
not let the physician do.''

''He would not concern himself with me, no, not even
if I were dying,'' she said, impulsively betraying herself
so unhappy was she. ''Indeed, it might even please him
to have me die. So do not bring him to me, he will only
mock me with his hateful smile and hateful eyes.''

Julian stared hard at her, then said very soberly, ''So
this is the heart of it. The tiger you unleashed has turned
on you. Lydia, you brought this on yourself, for when
you let your tiger run in such unchecked passion its fury
died of exhaustion, as it was bound to. And now it has
turned to claw you in a way you did not expect but
should have foreseen. You love him, this I have suspected for some time now.''

Lydia raised eyes full of angry repudiation of such a
vile, unthinkable suggestion, but there was only sympathy in Julian's expression and even a little sadness.
The tears welled up from her heart and blinded her.

''Julian, oh Julian,'' she sobbed, and he went to her.
She laid her head on his shoulder and wept there.
''Julian, what am I to do? I am going out of my senses.
I have told myself he is cruel not to return my love, but I
know I have been so unlovable that how could he? I
behaved so shamefully, so unforgivably, that he will
never give me tenderness. He is especially cold to me for
all I said about his people and his queen—''

''Especially his queen,'' said Julian a little grimly.

''But all this was because of the way he treated me.''
Her sobs were heart-breaking. ''The day I met
him—Julian, he did humiliate me, he did, and it hurt me
bitterly, and I know now it was because I wanted him to
love me—and instead he put me in the dust. Yet I would
not see why I felt as I did. I made him my slave and
degraded him, and because of this he will never love me.
I am in such suffering I will die.''

''I cannot deny he may let you die,'' said Julian, ''for

he is sometimes the hardest man. Also, as the son of a
great Iceni chieftain he is a proud one too. But Lydia, if
you truly love him, do you not understand him? He is
grim when he has to be, but never would he withhold
pity from the deserving. He has his own understanding.
Do you think he condemns you for your acts of
vengeance?''

"Oh, he does," said Lydia miserably, "for when he
looks at me he does not even see me and this is worse
than any spoken condemnation. I have become nothing
to him, nothing. Julian, I swore that it was he who
would become nothing but it is I who have become so
and you do not know the torment I am in.''

"Do not add unnecessarily to it," said Julian con-
solingly, "since I am sure he understands what you did.
The day he put you in the dust he knew there might
come a time when it would be your turn to cry triumph.
But that thought did not stay his treatment of you. If a
man sought to weigh the far-off consequences of his
every deed he would never put a foot from his bed. I
would only say your way of revenge is, alas, your own.''

"But had I not made him my slave he would have
been crucified." Lydia shivered and her brother felt
something of her anguish. "Julian, he gives me no
sweetness, no kindness, he accords me nothing,
nothing, and I cannot bear it.''

Her overflowing eyes were pools of melancholy.

"What is it you most want from him? Love, kindness, gratitude?''

"Julian, I want him!''

"Are you sure? Or are you perhaps only in need of a
diversion? Has he become a toy you cannot have? Do
you want him simply because he does not want you?
You have had diversions in the past, Lydia, and other
whims and fancies.''

"Oh, you are vile to say this!''

"But realistic too," said Julian. "Come now, confess

it, you have had many moods concerning men, and when did any mood or any man last longer than a month?"

She stared in horror and incredulity at him, aghast that her own brother could be so hurtful when she was in such misery. She could not even remember which men he meant. What men were there apart from Canis? She could not think of any.

"Oh, that is even viler!" she gasped. "Oh, that my own brother should rub salt of this kind into my wounds." She restrained herself. Her brother was often able to put her on shifting ground. She went on more quietly. "In any event, you know that Canis is not like other men. You knew this even before I did. But he understands my feelings no more than you do. He says I am merely in confusion. He says that because I am patrician there can be nothing between us. But I say to you, Julian," she added passionately, "that if he were to speak me only the smallest word of love I would forswear Rome herself and go with him."

"Would you die for him?" asked Julian quietly.

"Die?" A strange look came into her eyes, then she said fiercely, "No, I would live for him, live! All his friends and all he loved have died for him already, and that is why he is so lonely. Oh, Julian, he is the loneliest man in the world and he will not let me comfort him."

Julian thought back to a dark, tragic night and two men who went to turn back a grave but did not.

"Aye, he is lonely," he said, "but he will endure."

"Julian," she said in some anxiety, "have you heard of some woman he loves? Suella said there was such a woman, but Canis said it was only rumour."

Julian's smile of reassurance veiled his knowledge. He would not destroy her hopes by telling her Canis could love no one but his dead queen.

"I have heard of no such woman in this town," he said, "nor, you must agree, is Canis in a position to go calling on any."

"Tell me," she said sadly, "if I set him free will he leave us?"

How changed she was, he thought. She had been so restless, always seeming in petulant search of the unattainable, giving no thought to those she hurt. Now she was a woman rejected. His heart went out to her, for he felt that in Canis she had come upon the wholly unattainable.

"Lydia," he said, "you must let him go. Only then will he come to love you."

"I cannot," she cried, "I cannot. If I let him go I will never see him again."

"Canis was not born to be a slave, least of all to woman," said Julian sternly. "Your peace of mind or your anguish is in your own hands."

*   *   *

BUT SHE WOULD not let her especial property go, she could not. She made him a house servant so that he could be useful to Julian, so that each day he would see her and note her beauty and her kindness and her undemanding heart. Undemanding? Oh, Diana! But he would give her a little love in time. He would not let her endure her torment forever.

Often she came silently upon him, seeking to steal close so that he might see her dark beauty and friendly smile. And indeed he would return her smile, but be as far from her as ever, the clouds in his eyes or the dark grey shadows. It was not her world she saw there, it was a world she could not enter. It made her weep within herself and then wait for a new moment on another day, for each day had its fresh hope and promise for her aching heart.

She went with Suella one day to the house of Valeria. Valeria greeted her with warm, affectionate smile, then frowned to see her dark-eyed, wan look.

"Lydia," she said, when Suella had skipped away to

the servants' quarters, "you are as colourful these days
as a pale moonbeam. Come, what ails you?"

"I do not sleep well," said Lydia, allowing herself to
be led into Valeria's favourite room, where the muted
green of draped couches and the soft light induced a
sense of restful comfort.

"Then I will have my new servant mix you an infamous and heady draught," said Valeria. "It tastes
vilely of unnameable things, but it will put you to sweet
sleep for a full night and day, if you so wish. You shall
let me know before you go. And I have a further new
acquisition, a girl with such eyes and the sweetest voice
who is called Cerdwa. I will have her sing for us."

She clapped her hands. A servant appeared. Valeria
asked for Cerdwa to be fetched and in a while there entered a maid with her hair as dark as Lydia's own, with
soft brown eyes, sweet mouth and sweet smile, and the
look of one far away. With her came a bow-legged man,
with ageless face and round innocent eyes, who carried a
lyre and gave it to the maid. The maid sat on a stool and
looked before her in sweetness but at nothing.

Lydia was in sudden curiosity. It quickened, attacked
her heart and made her uneasy. There was a disturbing
familiarity about the maid, about her brown, faraway
Celtic eyes. Yet there was also something neither
familiar nor true. She had no eyes for the bow-legged
man who was regarding her unwinkingly, she had eyes
only for the girl with the lyre.

And Lydia knew. This was a girl she had seen before,
in the palace of Boadicea at Venta Icenorum. She had
seen her at the side of the Iceni queen on the day Septimus Cato had pronounced Caesar's will. The girl was
Boadicea's elder daughter, Cea. The unfamiliar and the
false were in the colour of her hair, which was black
where before it had been rich auburn.

With recognition came understanding. Understanding of what Suella had said and of the world of
Canis. Suella had said Canis belonged to no woman

save one, and this was the one. Cea was of her mother,
and Lydia knew that the only world which meant
anything to Canis was that which had been Boadicea's.
This was she who alone had survived from his lost
world.

Valeria had never seen either Boadicea or her
daughters. If she had known this girl was Princess Cea,
or if Suetonius Paullinus knew it, then perhaps that
would be the end for Cea. And Canis would indeed have
lost all he loved.

"Will you sing for us, Cerdwa?" asked Valeria.

"If you wish, mistress," said the girl in sweet,
musical voice.

Cerdwa? Why was she called Cerdwa? To keep her
out of the hands of Paullinus for one thing, but
Cerdwa? And there leapt into Lydia's mind an evening
in a grim forest, red under the dying sun, a badly
wounded Julian, a savage hunt and Canis, hard and
bitter-faced, with death in his eyes for all Romans but
two. And riding by his side a wild, beautiful forest maid
whom he called Cerdwa, who bore a glittering axe and
had eyes only for her lord.

And it was a forest maid of whom Cea now sang, a
strange and haunting song of her love and her death.
When it was over Valeria sighed.

"Oh, it was sweetly sung, Cerdwa, but infinite sad.
She will not sing without Grud to keep her company,"
she smiled in a whispered aside to Lydia. "They were
taken as vagrant Belgae, I believe, and I am glad I had
the opportunity to acquire them, else they might have
been shipped to Rome because of the girl's looks. They
have been with me three days. The man Grud is a boon
about the house and is the one who will mix a potion for
you."

Lydia could not speak. She watched Cea as the girl
rose, gazing after her as she went smiling but unseeing
from the room, Grud with her. Confusion attacked
Lydia, but her panic was worse. Cea represented the

deathknell of her hopes, for if Canis found out she was alive he would hold fast to the substance of her survival. He would never look at another woman. Panic fostered the most desperate of thoughts, and her mind clung to it. She would not stay longer then, despite Valeria's surprise and disappointment at so brief a visit. With Suella she made her way home. There she summoned Canis.

He came.

Always whenever she saw him now her longing consumed her. The house tunic did not diminish him. How tall he was, how thick his hair with its glint of copper, how intimidating his quietness. It was as if he somehow knew that she now had the means to break him at last.

"Canis?" Her nervousness momentarily weakened her resolve.

"Mistress?" His voice was as quiet as his look.

"Canis," she said breathlessly, "I would not be cruel to you, but I have you in the palm of my hand and have but to close my fist to crush you."

"This is not new," he said, "this is how it has been since I was brought here."

"No," she said quickly, "I would not crush you with violence or pain. Such would crush me first. No, I do not speak of your body, Canis, but of your heart. I have it here." And she extended her hand, palm upright, and it was trembling.

"Do you find it a poor thing, as I do?" he asked.

"It is the greatest heart in all Britain, but I have it, Canis."

"In what fashion?" His eyes were not remote but stonily hard. "I know it is not your wish or purpose to deliver it to Paullinus."

"It is your body Paullinus would crucify, not your heart. He would have your body if he could, as he would have the body of another."

She saw the sudden naked pain on his face and her heart cried out, but she thrust the weakness from her in her desperation.

"Of whose body do you speak?" he asked.

"Do you not know, Canis?"

"All whom Paullinus wanted are dead, mistress, save only myself."

"So thinks Paullinus, but he is mistaken, for Princess Cea is alive."

He caught his breath and his hard face turned grey. He came close until Lydia could almost feel the sheer physical form of his body and her longing made her shiver. But she put the folly aside. There must be no yielding.

"You have seen her?"

"I have seen her and know where she is. But I alone know who she is and I will strike a bargain with you, Canis. I will keep silence always if, when I give you your freedom, you will take me to wife."

"Wife?" he said and both his eyes and his voice mocked her, reduced her and disclaimed her.

"Or, at least," she whispered, "if you will only love me."

"Ah," said Canis, and smiled. His teeth showed and it was no smile. "I did not expect your own body to be so much involved, mistress. It is a handsome body for this kind of trading, and some might say you could have asked for more than you have."

She crumpled before his irony, her face stricken, her eyes desperate.

"Oh, do not put it like that," she breathed, "that is not how I mean it—oh, do not look at me so—not like that—"

"I will respond as handsomely as I can," said Canis in merciless denial of her plea for understanding. "I will not disappoint you, fair Roman. Shall we put our sweet seal on the bargain now?"

He stooped swiftly, lifted her from her feet and carried her to her couch, setting her boldly down on its rich, sensuous comfort. She was numb with shame and terror, the terror not for any physical hurt he might give

her but for the wild hurt he could give her heart. He put
one knee on the couch and leaned over her, looking
down into her pleading eyes with a smile of cold purpose
on his face. He took her robe between both hands and
she cried out as she realised what he meant to do.

"Canis, no! I did not mean—oh, be merciful—"

"What is that to do with it?" he said softly. "I have
accepted the bargain and will do my part with loving
speed or loving deliberation according to your delicate
preference in so intimate a matter. For is it not agreed
that if I do this, Cea will not be delivered to your gentle,
forgiving governor?"

So saying he ripped both her robe and shift, parting
the sundered garments to reveal the curving beauty of
her body. Lydia cried out again. A wave of hot blood
rushed to suffuse her nakedness as she writhed under
the unbearable mockery of his eyes.

"Oh, Canis," she sobbed, "I have shamed myself
and you have shamed me more. Let me die but do not
do this to me, do not look at me so. Oh, if you have the
smallest mercy, forgive me—oh, forgive me, I beg
you."

He smiled again but in curiosity this time, his face
above hers. She saw his eyes investing her very soul,
searching her, reading her, and her writhing ceased and
she lay in hot, anguished shame.

Oh, Diana, I am betrayed by my own body, I am
wanton, for if I am to be possessed in this cruel way
even that is better than not to be possessed at all.

"You are a strangely reluctant presser of a bargain,"
said Canis. He stood upright, regarding her without
malice or mockery as with trembling hands she drew her
ripped garments together to cover herself. "Did I
mistake your terms or your earnestness?" he asked.

"Oh, you mistake me in every way," she wept, "for I
would not have done what I said, I would never have
betrayed your princess, never. It was a lie born of my
despair and need. She is the one you love? Is she?"

"She is the sweetest of princesses," said Canis sombrely.

"She is also the most fortunate—"

"That she is not."

"If she has your love," said Lydia in shivering distress, "then she is as fortunate as any woman could be. But I would not have given her to Paullinus, truly I would not. I sought only a way of bringing you into my arms. Oh, believe me in this, I would not have betrayed her."

"I believe you," he said, "and begin to understand you."

She sat up, clutching the torn robe to her. She rose to stand before him, raising her woeful eyes to his. Her tears spilled to lie quivering on her cheeks.

"Canis," she said, her voice catching on a sob, "I will take you to Cea and I will set you free, for if I cannot have your love as she has it, then I must give you to her. You have lost so much and I will do all I can to restore something to you."

He looked at her as if seeing her for the first time. He put his hands gently on her shoulders which, because of her torn robe, were bare, and because she was as she was and desperately in love, her blood ran heatedly and beneath her sorry shift her breasts rose taut and hard.

"Is this your true intent, Lydia?" he asked.

It was the first time he had ever named her and she closed her eyes for a moment on the heartbreak of sacrifice, then spoke in a whisper, the while her body burned to his touch.

"You are not my slave, Canis, but my reason for being. I would gladly go wherever you go, and be to you whatever you wished, but because of Cea I know you would not take me with you. My heart will die. But I will never forget you and I will pray to all my gods, especially Diana, to guide you and guard you. If you will sometimes remember me with a little sweetness, I will be content with that."

But she knew that if he left her she would know only emptiness.

"You are not completely of Rome, Lydia," he said, and he drew the drooping folds of her robe more securely about her in a gesture that equated for her his merciless rending of the garment. It made her burn again. "You are too generous and too forgiving."

When numbly and in a trance of heartbreak and misery she had changed her garments and repaired her looks, she called Suella and went with her and Canis to see Valeria again. Valeria, surprised, welcomed her with a smile nevertheless.

"Valeria, will you favour me in the matter of the girl called Cerdwa?"

"How might I do this? I will do whatever I can to bring back your smile, for by Venus herself you are more woebegone than ever in your looks."

"Canis—my servant, that is," began Lydia with an effort, then drew needed breath. "I think he has known the girl in happier days. If so, she is one he loves, and so I would buy her from you—if you would favour me—so that they may be together."

"May I not buy your tall Briton so that they may be together here?" smiled Valeria. "This I would frankly prefer. But no, I see your heart is not in that. However, must I lose Cerdwa so soon? Already I have a great affection for her."

"Valeria," said Lydia, mouth trembling, and Valeria took her hand, and that was trembling too.

"Come now," she said gently, concerned at what was surely despair on Lydia's face, "there is something deeper here than just a matter of two slaves. Let me help you with whatever is troubling you, for we have been friends for long."

Oh, thought Lydia distractedly, how can any mortal help me when I am dying? Has not even Diana, my own goddess, deserted me?

"Valeria," she said, "my trouble is only that I have a

wretched lack of sleep, and perhaps I will have your servant mix me the draught you spoke of before. Meanwhile, favour me and call Cerdwa. Do not think me unfriendly or strange, but will you allow her to meet Canis before my eyes only? Sweet Valeria, perhaps it is a little strange, but Canis is a strange man.''

''Also a little intimidating to a virtuous woman,'' said Valeria, not without perceptiveness in respect of Lydia's wan look. ''But there, it shall be as you wish. I will call the sweet one and you shall take her to Canis.''

So Lydia waited with Canis until Cea arrived, but Grud came first.

''So,'' he said, seemingly oblivious of Lydia, ''you are here, then. You have taken your time.''

''You knew I was in this town?'' said Canis.

''There is not one Briton, free or slave, who does not know that Canis, general to the army of Boadicea, dwells in Calleva Atrebatum as the especial property of one Lydia Osirus, high-born Roman woman.''

''Who stands here with me,'' said Canis.

''Aye, and who was here before,'' said Grud, turning his inoffensive gaze on Lydia and remarking her paleness.

''She will say nothing.''

''Will she not?''

''I say she will not because I know she will not,'' said Canis, and though they spoke almost impersonally of her Lydia gave Canis a look of gratitude for his faith in her.

Grud shifted imperturbably on his bow legs. He was in wisdom and warning as he spoke.

''I found her wandering, as you may suppose, by ways of danger many months ago, and the road has been hard and difficult ever since. Not in ministering to her, but in blinding the eyes of Romans as to her true identity. I stay by her side always, so that people must first look into my eyes, not hers, and when they have looked they go unsuspectingly on their way, for there is that about me which keeps them from looking too hard at her. I could have taken her to a forest where she would have been secure in the care of the hairy ones, but that is not her destiny. When she may come to her destiny, if ever, I do not know, however. For the moment she is happy in that she has put from her mind all that was, and each day, summer or winter, she dwells only in the sunshine of her dreams. And in her dreams she waits for you, Canis.''

Lydia went cold at the look on the face of Canis.

"I am here, old one," he said grimly.

"Aye," said the old one who looked so young, "but she will not know you, nor will she find her destiny unless she comes from her dreams. It is only in her dreams that she looks for you, it has nothing to do with reality. If, therefore, I am to fetch her, do not disclose yourself to her. This would bring back to her all that she has set aside and which you know of. It is her dreams that matter to her, Wolfhead, so do not bring trouble or grief to her. Deal gently with her. Also, she is now named Cerdwa, because of another who was also sweet, and she has black hair by virtue of my thought and ingenuity. Lastly, she considers herself only a simple forest maid, which is what we tell all Romans and now tell you.''

"Go, fetch her," he said fiercely, and Grud went. He returned with Cea. She came smiling into the room, dressed in the simple white tunic of a slave, and Canis drew his breath to see her Celtic charm, although her hair was as black as night instead of brightly auburn. He felt again the dagger of Boadicea, sharp and cruel, as he saw the sweetness of the mouth he had kissed long ago and the softness of the brown eyes that looked at him without recognition.

"You are tall," she said to Canis in soft, singing voice. And to Lydia, whom she did not remember from the previous meeting, she said, "And you are lovely. Am I to sing for you?''

"If it will please you," said Canis gently, "it will please us more."

So Cea took her lyre and sang the sweet but sad song of a forest maid.

A fair maid sighed in silvery grass,
Soft her eyes in summer's light
The flowers brushed her maiden cheeks
And petals kissed her lips
A man with question in his eyes
Came from she knew not where
Tall was he and proud and strong, and to him then she said
"What do you look for in this land?"
"I look for you," he said
And plucking at his sweet-strung lyre
He sang her song of love
She dwelt upon his eyes and voice for many fragrant days
And when his time had come to go this was what she said
"I waited long for you, my lord,
Through many hopeful years
And since you come to only go, I must wait again."
He went away, his eyes were blind,
And silvery grass turned blue
There came upon the maid four men
Whom afterwards they slew
And o'er the grass that now is red
The flowers weep their tears
And only trees can hear her voice and only sky her pain
"I wait for you to come again who are my lord and King
My eyes are stars that look for you to give me life, O King."

As she sang Canis stood unmoving, with a smile on his face for her beauty and her song, but Lydia saw the shadows that forever haunted him. She could not restrain herself from putting her hand on his arm.

"Oh, not all songs, not all life, should be so sad," she whispered, and he looked at her and her heart broke for all he had loved and lost. Then he smiled again at Cea, who was regarding him with the unaffected interest of a simple maid.

"What is your name, sweet one?" he asked her.

"My name is Cerdwa," she answered, "and I am a forest maid."

"What do you do with life?"

Cea looked at Grud.

"Answer with your heart," said Grud.

"I wait for Canis the Briton," she said, smiling.

"Who is he?" asked Canis.

She looked at Grud again, then at Canis, and her soft eyes glowed with the light of dreams.

"Canis is strong and gentle, cruel and cunning. He will come for me and I will go with him, and we will live where the maids of the forest will serve us and he will kiss me to sleep forever."

"Where is Canis?"

"He sleeps within the heart of another Cerdwa by the side of my mother under the light of the sun, but he will come for me. He is tall, even taller than you, and has a smile to woo all maids from their lovers and all women from their men."

"Who is your mother?" asked Canis.

"My mother is the daughter of the sun," said Cea.

"What is her name?"

"Her name is writ on the face of the sun, in the mist of the mountains and in the waters of the river. Shall I sing again?"

"Not now," interrupted Grud with gruff humour, "for we have petals to count on your flowers. Come, sweetling."

Cea rose, smiling softly at Canis and unaffectedly at Lydia, and went quietly with Grud. Canis was silent and still.

"Canis?" Lydia's voice was faint. He did not reply. She moved to face him. His eyes were dark with winter cloud. "Canis, I did not know it was like this."

"Come," he said in new bitterness, "there is nothing we may do here."

Obediently, as if their roles were reversed, she went

with him, forgetting in her suffering abstraction to say farewell to Valeria or to collect any draught. They returned home, and Canis would have departed abruptly, but Lydia drew him into her room.

"Canis, hear me a little longer," she begged.

"I could not do less, mistress," he said.

"You named me Lydia earlier," she said, "and it was sweet to my ears. But I will not speak wishfully, this is not the time. Canis, although your princess is not as she was, yet if you desire to be with her and the man Grud, I will set you free for this, and Valeria will favour me in the matter."

"I am to be bound to her house instead of yours?"

"Oh, no. I will purchase them from her, then give them their freedom and yours too."

"Will you give me my freedom outside of this, Lydia?"

"I will," she said bravely.

Out of his loneliness came a whimsical smile for her, to make her heart drown again in tears.

"You have come a full circle, Lydia," he said. "I will not distrub that which obtains between Cea and Grud, for only Grud can give her the time, the patience and the understanding she must have, and what is tolerable for him is not for me."

"I know you will leave me," Lydia said. "But I will not prevent you. You shall have your freedom. Where will you go?"

"Where each day leads me, but not forgetting that while Grud must look to Cea I must look to our people."

"But you will walk your land alone because although you may find a thousand of your people, you have lost the ones you loved. What do you seek, Canis, what?"

"Content, perhaps?" he said with the strangest of smiles.

The persistent tears squeezed from her lids. She shook them away.

"Content? Oh, how can you find content?"

"Love, according to a certain wood-witch, who was no wood-witch, does not belong to life alone," he said. "There is content to be had from that belief."

He took the tears from her cheeks with caressing fingertips so that Lydia was swept by new storms. Her heart cried out against her own Caesar for the destruction of his people and his queen. "You are a strange Roman to let your vengeance founder in seas of this kind."

She could not help herself, she caught his hand and pressed it to her heart.

"Oh, I am in such anguish for you—let me go with you so that you will not be alone—I will not trouble you in any other way, ask for nothing you cannot give me—only take me with you, take me with you."

"I would only give you hurt," he said, "and because I know you better than I did I would not wish you in hurt. There will be more in life for you than you think there is now."

She sank weeping to her knees.

"There is nothing without you," she gasped, "you do not know how much I love you. Oh, take me with you, let me be with you."

"It would only give you hurt," he said again, and he left her and Lydia felt life itself had ended for her.

But she would not go back on her promise and some days later it was done and Canis was a freedman. He was due to leave Calleva Atrebatum the day after and in the night no sleep came to Lydia, only an ocean of more tears. She lay in such despair that at intervals her sobs, however much she tried to muffle them, came racking and noisy.

Concerned, Julian entered her room to see what it was all about.

"Lydia, sweet sister," he whispered in the darkness, "must you be in such fret as this? Your woe has had me sleepless and groaning in my own bed. Is there nothing to bring you to quietness and rest?"

"Julian, oh Julian." She sat up, flung her arms around his neck and he felt the violence of her shivering woe. "Julian . . . if he goes I will open my veins. There will be nothing for me, nothing, so speak to him—he has a regard for you—speak to him, make him stay, or I do not know what will become of me."

"Hush," he whispered, holding her close. She was feverish, trembling.

"I am haunted, tormented—oh, forgive me for all I did—Julian, it was I who destroyed all that he loved—I and others like me—his queen herself haunts me."

"Hush," he said again. "The Iceni were the victims of the will of Caesar excessively implemented by Catus Decianus and our illustrious governor. They were the destroyers, not you. Remember, however, that the Iceni evoked their own dark spirits of self-destruction by their mercilessness, so that in the end it was either our extermination or theirs, for which there was blame on both sides. In all this you were only my wilful sister and I will not have you put yourself in such misery over it."

"I will die," she said in hopelessness.

"You will not. You suffer because you are in neglect of your goddess."

"She has forsaken me." Her arms slipped away and she lay back.

"It is the other way about," said Julian. "You have not been to her temple for days. So I have brought her to you. Take her, hold fast to her. Weep no more useless tears but pray to her."

Into her hand he put a small object, a figurine of Diana in gold. It lay warm and glowing within her cold palm. Julian tiptoed away. She clasped the precious image and after a long silence lifted it to her lips.

Great Diana, giver and protectress, boon to all women, help me, I beg you. Make known what I must do to enter his heart.

There was only silence.

352   *James Sinclair*

Eternal goddess, hear me, answer me. What must I do, what must I do?

Go with him, child. He will not reject you if you are strong. Will you weep forever and have him always put you aside?

There was an immutable silence then but so much warmth. And a sense of despair retreating and peace entering. She kissed the figurine, and it stayed warm in her hands as she turned over to sleep and dream.

21

THE NEW DAY was warm with sunshine. Julian stayed from his work that morning to say farewell to Canis. Lydia did not appear. Canis, in new tunic, looked much the same as when Julian and Lydia had first met him on the road to Venta Icenorum. He led a strong black horse, a gift from Julian which Canis, with a slight smile of reminiscence, had accepted. They spoke on light matters until Julian said, "Do you go to re-establish a kingdom, Canis?"

"I go only in the way of a man who is free."

"For my part," said Julian, "kingdoms and kings, empires and emperors, have lately wearied me. I begin to think the politics of a republic might give a man more peace."

At this time Suetonius Paullinus was still hounding the survivors and dependants of Boadicea's defeated host. Julius Classicianus, who had replaced the corrupt Catus Decianus, was dismayed by the Governor's harshness. So was Julian.

"The politics of a republic," said Canis in the light of the bright day, "will give you only fresh burdens, for a republic is fraught with far more politics than any kingdom or empire."

"I would have thought you a man to favour a republic," said Julian.

"You have not known majesty," said Canis. "In a republic your men of power are apt to purchase their votes, using either gold or promises. In a kingdom the bribery and rivalry which you cannot divorce from votes are non-existent, and a queen rules not by what she may purchase but by her due."

"What is a queen's due?" smiled Julian.

"That which is reciprocal. Love. By their might and heritage monarchs come to power, but that is not enough. They must inspire love in their people and return it. If they do not they are no monarchs, they are only republicans wearing a crown. But put aside your worries and doubts, Julian, for Rome will yet have a Caesar better than Nero."

"My worries and doubts are not in respect of Caesar, but you, Canis. Despite your brave words, under your queen you have lost all."

"All but love. That cannot be lost."

Julian looked into the sun, always softer in Britain than other lands.

"Well, go your way, friend, and may fortune favour you," he said. "Though I do not wish to interfere with whatever your purpose is, I must advise you I am not certain how the governor will regard your freedom. Now that you no longer belong to Lydia he may consider he has his own claim on you. If I were you, therefore, I would travel with discretion as companion to purpose."

"Julian," smiled Canis, "you are a man's friend before you are a Roman. I will heed your advice. In giving you my thanks and farewell, I will say Rome is well served by you, for you make friends where others make enemies. I would also like to say farewell to Lydia."

"That I would not advise," said Julian drily, "for Lydia is in more woe at your going than a thousand women have suffered together. She will drown us both with her tears."

"Tell her I will remember her," said Canis.

"A woman famished for want of love is likely to find little meat on that," said Julian, then raised an eyebrow, for Lydia had appeared. She wore a plain, practical robe, tightly woven, and her hair was unbound. Behind her came a servant leading a grey horse, on which was strapped a pack containing certain of her belongings. "What does this mean?" asked Julian, although he guessed.

"I am going with Canis," said Lydia, pale but resolute. She hid her apprehension and agitation, for Diana had shown her that this was the way.

Canis turned sombre grey eyes on her and Lydia quaked, not in fear of him but in fear that her resolution might not prove equal to his. She out-stared him and lifted her chin high. Julian rubbed his jaw.

"Should not Canis decide this?" he asked.

"He may decide where he will go," said Lydia, "but he cannot decide for me. I shall follow behind him. I am as free as he is. Also, if I do not follow him, then my life is without meaning or purpose."

"Your life belongs to Rome," said Julian, "and therefore has every meaning and purpose."

"I have come to believe," said Lydia, her unbound hair stirring in the breeze, "that Rome in all its might is not more important than what obtains between a man and a woman, for it is they who create, not Rome."

"You are now seeing too much where before you saw too little," said Julian.

"Lydia," said Canis, who wore a gold ring on his smallest finger, "you are not equipped to go where I go."

"Who are you to say how I am equipped?" said Lydia, putting her hand on the bridle of her horse. "It is for me to say if I have enough, and I have."

"Ah," said Canis. A little light entered the grey. She was haughty today.

"You are free now," said Lydia, "and may go where you wish. But I am free too and—"

"You have already said that."

The apprehension tightened into a knot. If he was in a pitiless mood she knew he would escape her, and easily.

"Nevertheless, I am going with you," she said. "I will not be a burden, I will ride always at a distance and each time you halt I will serve you." She spoke calmly.

There were no tears, only the resolution. "It is no use for you to argue," she said.

"Argument with a woman is man's most chastening pursuit," said Canis. He mounted his horse and looked down at brother and sister. "I give you both friendly farewell. Your house is a place of warmth, even allowing for Dilpus."

At a walking pace he rode on his way. When he had gone twenty paces Lydia mounted her own horse and began to follow.

"Lydia, this will only bring you hardship and distress," said Julian.

"Do not prevent me, for you know my heart," said Lydia and rode on. He went quickly after her, reached and took her hand, pressed it and relinquished it.

"O sweetest and most foolish sister, if the love you wish is denied you, find at least some content in what you do," he said.

She stopped a moment, reached to touch his hair and said, "Dearest Julian, today I am alive and very content." And she went on in the wake of her Briton.

They rode through the straight wide streets of Calleva Atrebatum, past the round temple of Jupiter, past the forum and the small temple of Diana, turning right towards the east gate. They rode through this without hindrance, turning north to pass the great stone amphitheatre, the man on the black horse, the woman on the grey, she always a score of paces behind him. He did not go far along the road before he left it, moving in easy, leisurely fashion over the undulating green countryside, lush with verdancy as spring beckoned to summer. The sky was of alternating blues and whites because of sailing clouds, so that sometimes the land was bright with sunshine and sometimes softly shadowed.

Canis rode without a word, Lydia behind him. Apart from the occasional rustling of the wind all was quiet.

There was only the land and the light. He did not turn
his head at any time to see if she followed. He could
hear her. When they had ridden for an hour he halted
and looked back at her. Lydia halted too, keeping her
distance.

"Come," he called, "I would rather you jingled at
my side than have you strike your everlasting refrain at
my back."

She rode slowly up to him, making no haste in case
too eager a response changed his mood. Her heart
breathed in sweet relief to see him smiling.

"You are as stubborn as any Roman," he said.

"It is true I came from Rome," said Lydia, "but that
was long ago. I am of Britain now. I will not miscall
Rome but she is not to me what she was. Here is all I
love, this is my sky and this is my land. And you are my
life. My children will be Britons, not Romans."

His eyes laughed at her.

"Pretentious one," he said, "you will wed a high-
born Roman and all your patrician children will be gifts
to Caesar."

"I will wed no man except you," she said, putting
aside strands of whipping hair, "and even if I do not
wed you I am to bear your children, for Diana has told
me so. I prayed to her, she answered and came to me in
my dreams also."

"A strange thing for a Roman goddess to do when
you have forsworn Rome."

"Her understanding is of women, not Rome," said
Lydia, "and because of what she told me I have left my
house to be with you. Among other things, how else
may I have your children unless I am with you?"

"Among other things," he said in irony, "your goddess, who does not enchant me as she does you, might
also have told you a woman cannot bear a man's
children merely by following him on a horse."

The red touched her face, her black hair danced and

blew, and for a moment she dropped her eyes. Then bravely she looked at him. His expression was unyielding.

"Even you cannot escape all the gods or defy all their meanings," she said, "and I will bear your children as Diana has said. They will not be gifted to Caesar but to Boadicea. And when I speak of Boadicea to them they will ask me who she was and I will tell them. I will tell them she was their father's queen and braver than any Caesar, and that all who knew her loved her so much that they followed her to death. Ah, and now I think I know what is in your mind, you are going to wander without purpose until death comes to you too. I will not let you."

She had the sun in her green eyes, defiance about her, and even pride, and with her hair as it was, wild in the wind, she reminded him of brave Cerdwa.

"Lydia," he said, "do not use the name of Boadicea to beguile me, do not ever use her name except in a context of truth, or I will give you a craving to return to your home at much greater speed than you left it, your other fancies notwithstanding."

"I am in truth," she said, "for I am not what I was, you know I am not. My eyes opened, my heart and mind opened. I know we did your queen a great wrong and it is not because of my love alone that I wish to be with you, but because of my feeling for her. I saw her scourged, Canis, and though I mocked her—and—"

"And spat on her," he said, and Lydia paled and seemed to shrink.

"This I confess," she whispered, "but did not think you knew."

"There is nothing that was done to Boadicea that day which I do not know of," he said in a hard voice.

"Canis," she said quietly, while the earth breathed under the sun, "although I did this to her yet I knew she was in great pride and courage, she shamed us all. I have asked your forgiveness for many things already, will you forgive me this too? Will you?"

"Am I to dispense forgiveness to a Roman on behalf of the queen?"

"You must," she cried, "for Roman or not, I now belong to you and to the cause of Boadicea, which is her suffering people. Deny me if you will, it will make no difference. I will be to you only what you wish, but I will never leave you, never, even though you deny me forgiveness and mock me and beat me."

"Beat you?" Perhaps it was rich amusement that chased away his shadows.

"Aye," she said, "you are cruel enough at times. But I will still follow you, always, until you are out of your loneliness and even then you will have to kill me before I leave you." She bent her head and her long, windblown hair fell over her face. In a low voice, in the way of a maid of Britain, she said, "You are my love and my lord."

He leaned close, he put out a hand and turned her face up to his.

"Lydia," he said, and if his voice was a little mocking his eyes were not, "you were more desirable in your wilfulness than you are in your meekness. I do not favour meek or servile women. Take your tongue from your cheek, humility from your address and subservience from your look. Be your true self. Come if you must, but ride with me and not at my back, and on your own foolish Roman head be your fate."

So Lydia rode by his side from then on, with a flush on her face and happiness in her heart.

*   *   *

"By all the gods," swore Suetonius Paullinus, when the rumour of the freeing of Canis the Wolfhead became a confirmed provocation, "I have been meanly tricked by the house of Osirus."

He would not countenance such effrontery, such at-

tempt to cheat him. The general of Boadicea belonged
to Rome, if not in one way then another. Canis, a dog
of all dogs, must not be free to go among Britons and
rouse them to rebellion again, as he surely would if he
were not apprehended and nailed to a wooden cross. So
Paullinus gave his orders and that day Roman soldiers
rode in search of Canis, to take him and to deliver him
into the cold hands of the imperial governor of Roman
Britain.

*   *   * >

Your name is Cea.

My name is Cerdwa.

*Cerdwa was a wood-witch. You are Cea, daughter of
Boadicea. Your frightened mind has shut out all truth,
you wear the image of cowardice.*

My name is Cerdwa, I am only a forest maid and I
know only a man called Grud who keeps me from all
harm.

*You are Cea, daughter of Boadicea. You do not
belong to Grud, nor to your foolish dreams, but to life
and to Canis.*

Canis will come for me when I die.

*He will not, for he has no regard for any maid or
woman who lacks a brave heart and a proud spirit, who
cowers from the truth and pain of life. He will not come
for one who at death will only be a pale ghost. You are a
child dwelling in an impossible world of dreams and
songs and flowers. You are pitiable.*

My name is Cerdwa, I am only a simple maid.

*You are simple in very truth. Will you live all your
days with your mind closed to your heritage and your
love? Will you let Romans take Canis and crucify him?
Child, you are no child, nor even a maid. You are a
woman, you are Cea. You are a princess. Look upon
me—do you not know your own mother?*

Cea awoke violently. She sat up in the darkness and

stared before her, and her heart raced and the blood ran wildly through her veins. Then she arose. Swiftly, silently she went to Grud who, by favour of Valeria, slept outside her door every night. She woke him up and drew him into her tiny room.

"Come, Grud, take up what we must and let us go."

"Go?" he said, ears twitching at the firmness of her voice.

"To Canis. The Romans have been sent to take him."

The ageless one smiled in the darkness.

"So, in bringing you here I made no mistake. You have returned to life and trouble, Princess, but that is how it should be, for no princess should forswear her destiny. We are slaves but what of it? We will go and they will not come after us until it is too late. The lady Valeria has looked into my eyes and she will be in no hurry to set the lictors about our ears."

"Do not waste time exercising your long-winded art of mumbling," said Cea imperiously, "but gather what we need and get horses. I know where we will find him, for she has shown me."

"Who has shown you?"

"The queen my mother. Make haste, old bow-legs."

*   *   *

Canis and Lydia had ridden in no great hurry. They had avoided all Roman towns and camps to escape questions and curiosity. They made a roundabout way north-east, towards the lands that had known the fiercest battles. Where they reached villages or encampments of Britons they were made welcome, and their journey was without incident or distress until they entered the country bearing the scars of those battles. Here there were few places which had not suffered from the vengeance of Paullinus after his defeat of the Iceni Queen. Farther north-east he had razed Venta Icenorum to the ground. Lydia could have wept for the waste of it all.

They changed direction to bear south-east for a while and at the end of that day reached a village which, like so many others, seemed to be inhabited only by the old, and these were Trinovantes. The elder came to greet them and to say to Canis, "We heard you were on your way, lord, and are proud to have you with us for this night. Distress and fire still lie fierce on our land and yours because of Paullinus, who cannot seem to stop raging to and fro."

"Old-beard," said Canis, "the shadow of Boadicea clings to his back. He rages to and fro to shake it off. It will be worse before it is better, for I am not intending to spend my days counting my fingers. You will rest us tonight?"

"All we have is yours. None shall know of your coming or going. Lord, will you pass my threshold? You and your woman are in time to sup with us."

When they had eaten the plain fare they were given a dwelling for the night. The elder showed them where they might sleep in comfort, at which the scarlet touched Lydia's face, for the one room and the one bed were not what she had expected. During nights of hospitality in other villages she had been housed with maids.

Canis, seeing her so pink, looked a little unimpressed.

"I should not have thought you as modest as that," he said, "but have no fears, I will sleep in the outer room."

"Which is full of fowls and dogs," said Lydia, "and no place for either of us. And it is not modesty which—" She broke off, her flush deeper. "You must know," she said, "that I am willing to be to you whatever you wish, to serve you outside of any modesty."

Her longing was hot in her body. During their days of unhurried progress she had known the joy of simply being with him and the frustration of not being able to touch him. Sometimes under the racing clouds, with the green earth and high woods seeming to belong only to them, there had been the sweet feeling of being alone in the world with him. But there was also an awareness of his reserve. They were together, yet not together.

He said, "It is service to look to our belongings, such as they are, and it is service to fetch water from a stream. It is service to keep a fire going. But it is out of all reasonable service to offer yourself. I will lie on the floor and you may have the bed."

He went out. She knew he would walk for a while in the darkness, as he often did. She looked at the bed. It was of rushes and skins, but at least the rushes were clean and the skins smelled fresh, as if they had blown long in the pure wind. She spread everything so that there were two beds. Fastidious, used to every luxury and to doing nothing for herself that others could do for her, she had applied herself to simple tasks uncertainly at first, then happily when she realised what satisfaction there was in the littlest achievements.

Now she prepared their beds, her heart thumping dangerously. Because of the smallness of the room she would lie within reaching distance of him tonight.

Diana, sweet goddess, make him love me a little, just a little.

She thought of the image Julian had given her. She had brought it with her. She took it out and prayed devotedly but shamelessly to it. It was warm, glowing.

Diana was beautiful and all-knowing and understanding.

Diana answered.

Lydia, heart beating faster, searched her belongings until she found a small vial, half-full of an amber liquid. There was only mead available and she poured a measure of this into an earthenware cup and emptied the contents of the vial into the honey brew. Why had she not realised that if the potion of old Scythia was to be truly effective, half of it had to be taken by the coveted man? It was because she had not prayed hard enough until now.

"To help you to sleep," she said to Canis when he returned, "for I know you often lie awake."

"Lydia," he said, "what is in your eyes is also in the mead."

"It is only my love," she said.

"When did love make a man sleep?" Whatever he had thought about in the darkness had brought the shadows back again, but he drank the mead and that which was mixed with it and Lydia's heart hammered so loudly she was sure he heard it.

Canis slept.

He dreamed.

She came to him, clear and hauntingly beautiful, as she had not come to him since his illness. There was splendour about her and magic in her eyes and she was wholly expressive of love.

"Canis, my strong foolish one, you are lonely yet."

"I am without light."

"Was I not without light for seven years?"

"Seven years was not forever."

"Sweet fool, I am a woman and every day was forever."

"Did I not return?"

"Aye, to give me more joy and more pain." She was warm, close, adoring. "But do not grieve so, do not put me in grief too. Have I not wept three times already for you? Must I weep more? I am witless to love a man who trifles with maids and torments queens. Is your will to achieve as great as your gift for inviting caresses?"

"My will is to free your suffering people and to destroy Paullinus."

In his dream her smile was a soft brilliance.

"Ah, you are in conceit again. That, however, is better than having you in grief. But deliver my people who are sorely pressed, do this for me who brought cruel death to so many others, and I will love you for all time. You have many a long year to run yet but, oh my heart, do not forget me.''

"Forget you? It would be easier to pull down the stars. I see you in all things, hear you in every whisper of the wind. You are my undying love.''

She was in glowing radiance.

"Then take happiness while you live, for in the end there will be only Boadicea and Canis, who are one and indivisible in the eyes of life and destiny. So do not grieve, my strong one, do not grieve more. See how you draw my tears.''

Her face was soft above him, her misty eyes caressing, and she laid her warm mouth on his in love and yearning.

He awoke but did not know if he was awake or not. There was darkness but no queen, only the sense that she had been there. His mind was bemused, his body drowsy. He lay dreamily for a while, then became aware that someone was close to him, someone who was cold and trembling. In the darkness his dream-filled eyes saw only the deeper darkness of her hair and the limpid pools framed by quivering lids.

"Wood-witch," he murmured, "are you here too, then? Are you still in curious uncertainty about yourself?''

"Oh, Canis, I am no wood-witch,'' whispered a breathless voice, "nor am I uncertain. Oh, be my love as I am yours, lie close to me, make me less cold than I am.''

"Wood-witch or not, you have put your spell on me. Come then, lie as close as you wish, but speak no wandering words. Either bite on your tongue or put your mouth to mine.''

She gave a cry like a sob, then came so close that her coldness turned into instant burning. She enfolded him

within the gift of her enraptured body, nor did she
forget in her bliss to offer up ecstatic thanks to Diana.

*   *   *

Canis rode with a frown on his face and his mouth compressed. Lydia rode in silence, casting uneasy glances at
his harsh profile. He had spoken but once to her all day,
and that had been in the light of early morning when he
had looked with thunder on her flushed nakedness and
said,

"To be fooled by a wood-witch was calamitous
enough. To be fooled by a high-born Roman witch is
beyond all my senses."

Nor despite her beseeching would he say any more,
either in companionship or rebuke, and so they rode in
silence all day. Beneath his grimness she sensed a bitterness at what he considered his own folly and
weakness, and she felt a little frightened at what he
might do.

Yet she could not forget the joy and bliss of the night,
his strong but tender investment of her body and the
wonder of their merging, so completely beautiful it was
surely bequeathed to them by Diana herself. He too had
found it so, had he not?

He must have, he must.

She glanced at him again. He was so remote it turned
her cold.

During the afternoon he became more distant. He
was in his own world, one she was desperate to enter but
which he denied her. He went on until by late afternoon
they reached the site of a certain village that had known
Boadicea in life and death. The Romans had burned
down every dwelling, leaving it a place of desolation.
His manner was strange as he brought her through the
wasted ruins to the bank of a small river that ran close
by. While he built a fire she tethered the horses and un-

packed what food there was, desperate for him to speak to her. He looked at what she had unpacked, his hard face expressionless, then shook his head.

"Tend the fire," he said, "while I find something better to eat than that."

Be strong. He will not reject you if you are strong.

"I am here to serve you," she said, "I am not here to be given orders."

The glint in his eyes promised anything but acceptance of her, and she was suddenly more than frightened. He would leave her, he would go and not come back. She could endure anything but that. Silently she went down on her knees, tending the fire, adding to it and coaxing it.

"Where will you find the food?" she asked, keeping her head bent.

"In the forest. There will be game there. It may take a while but I will find something."

"Do not be too long," she said, lifting her head. But his eyes were on the forest, he was gone already from her. Panic seized her, she reached and took his hand. "Canis, do not hate me for what happened, I did but do as Diana advised—"

"Then do as I advise," he said uncharitably, "and find yourself a different goddess. One as unworldly as that chaste virgin is likely to bring you to so many indiscretions you will be more of an embarrassment than a woman."

"Oh, Canis, you are cruel and godless to rebuke me as unkindly as that."

He turned at the brave reproach in her voice. There were tears in her eyes, a quiver on her lips, but she was not without pride and spirit. He put his hand to her hair and lightly fingered a wayward tress.

"Lydia," he said, "there are things within me that make me forget our circumstances are as hard for you as for me. But you gave me wine that took my senses, that made me think you were someone you were not."

"It is not that which has made you so bad-tempered," said Lydia, "it is the fact that you cannot forgive me for being Roman or yourself for—"

"For?" he prompted as she hesitated.

"For loving me as you did."

His faint smile was an acknowledgement of her argument.

"Will it help you to know that there is more to being fooled than mortification?" he said. "There is also sweetness."

She coloured in swift pleasure. She took his hand again and pressed her lips to his warm palm.

"Canis, oh, you are so much my life that it is joy to hear you sweet to me at last," she breathed, "and I did not fool you, I only loved you. Go, then, but do not be long. This is an unhappy place and I am just a little afraid."

Her green eyes were vivid, her hair as lustrous as Cerdwa's. She was not in humility, only in intense desire to become inseparable from him and his purpose.

Canis smiled and said, "I will return for you, Lydia, since if there is a reckoning to face from a night's love you are not to face it alone."

She watched him go, her hands to her hot face because of what he meant.

Oh, Diana, return him to me.

Canis went to a spot by a razed cottage. There he dug up an axe. Its blade showed a soft sheen of brown rust, but through the rust the iron still glittered. He cleaned it, put it into his belt, then with a javelin in his hand made his way towards the forest by the failing light of the westering sun as it dipped behind clouds. Though he could not yet distinguish the oak tree he knew his route as if it had been cut out step by step for him.

He came within seeing distance of the oak. The wooded depths beyond were calling to him. Her name was in every rustling murmur and she herself was alive in this green place beneath the evening sky. Her invisible hand squeezed his heart and he walked encompassed by her possessive spirit.

He heard a faint cry. He froze. It came again, bearing his own name over the haunting whispers.

"Canis! Canis!"

And now the whispers and the murmurs drew back, and the silence returned.

The cry again.

"Canis!"

It was her voice, full of Celtic music, singing and vibrant. The forest, wild with evening colour, echoed the cry so that every leaf and branch was murmurous with the sound of his name.

It came yet again.

It was not possible. Could any spirit, even one as deathless as Boadicea's, rise to give such voice except in dreams? Could his lost world, his lost love, live again in so silent a place? His mind rejected, his heart hammered.

"Canis!" So near, so joyful.

He turned and his unbelieving eyes saw the vision. A maid, clad in a loose cloak that whipped and swirled to disclose her short tunic, was flying towards him. Dark hair tossed and flew about her head, her limbs were supple and gleaming, her voice singing.

"Canis! Oh, Canis!"

She had not come from the forest but from the west, yet she looked like a fleet and elusive forest maid, she looked like Cerdwa of the wild black hair, and momentarily a coldness seized him. He carried her axe in his belt and she was flying to receive it from him. She ran and ran, she stretched out her arms, and he glimpsed at a distance behind her a bow-legged man leading two horses. She came nearer, in laughter and joy, and the sun broke through to put the flame of Boadicea in her

hair and to touch her face with the radiant magic of
Boadicea.

"Canis!" And even her voice was of Boadicea.

"Cea! Oh, Cea!" The flame reached his heart and the
bitter iron melted and he held out his arms, for she was
the spirit, the flesh and the blood of his queen.

"Canis, oh my love, my heart!" She was in his arms,
warm, panting and triumphant. "You are safe, you are
here. Grud did not know but I did."

She kissed his hands, his javelin, his tunic, his lips.

"Cea." He stopped her wild wanderings to turn her
face up to his. Cea looked completely and breathlessly
pleased with herself. "Cea, you are in sweet life again."

"Oh, more! I am Cea." She made a pronouncement
of it. "Canis, I have been living in the world of a
frightened child, but I have come from it at last and my
heart sings and I do not mind what hurt or trouble lies in
store, for I will be with you. Oh, I have finished
counting petals but tonight I am quite likely to ask you
to find me a moonbeam to dance on."

She shook back her hair, she laughed, then flung her
arms around his neck and pressed herself in love to him.
He kissed her and she clung to him, without reserve, and
Canis felt with deep, abiding relief the return of her
outraged body to the quick, eager healthiness that is the
joy of any maid in love.

"There is no time for this kind of foolishness," said
Grud, coming up to them, "for the Romans are
searching high and low for you, Wolfhead."

"I did not think Paullinus would prove as agreeable
as Lydia," said Canis, "but are his men so close?"

"They will be," said Grud.

"I had thought to stay here the night."

"Aye, to mope and mourn," said Grud, "for I know
this place. But who can say if so restless a queen as
Boadicea is here now?"

"One day," said Canis, arm around Cea's waist and

she kissing him in all the places she could reach, "I will stretch your tongue and sew it to your foot, Grud. Meanwhile, go into the village. There you will find Lydia Osirus, the Roman woman, tending a fire by the river and making a proud fuss of it. Scatter the fire and bring Lydia to us here."

"Leave her," said Cea in new-found imperiousness, "and when the Romans come she can go with them."

"Bring her," said Canis. Having experienced the imperiousness of a queen he could withstand that of a princess. "Bring her, for she wishes to serve us and our people. Bring the horses too, while I take charge of yours."

"I am not one to go here or run there except by my own inclination," grumbled Grud.

"Go, old goat, or I will hammer you senseless."

Grud went.

"Why is Lydia Osirus to come with us?" asked Cea, so much herself again that she was almost more than imperious.

"Because we have dealt too much already in anger and vengeance," said Canis, "and must cherish any who wish to help us, Britons or Romans."

"That need not mean we must especially cherish Lydia," said Cea, "and especially you are not to. You are to cherish me alone."

"Be a princess if you will, but be a sweet one," he smiled. "And, for the moment, remember the queen your mother. It is there—just there, by the oak—that she lies."

He showed her the green ground that lay between the oak and the forest, where Cerdwa also slept. Cea's eyes filled with tears as he spoke his final homage.

"Boadicea, here is your earth, here is your sky. Here rests your body and here lives your spirit. You will make something more of this place than it was, something more of yourself than cold bones. You were our most majestic cause and our bitterest day, for we let you die in heartbreak.

"Look to the queen, Cerdwa, for she was our head, our heart and our inspiration, and the gods, such as they are, owe her much more than dark earth. And you owe her your tongue, which she would have had from you but refrained. Without your tongue even you would not have gone joyfully to your forests.

"Dwell in light, sweet Queen. You are our bright day, our cherished night and our hopeful dawn. Rest with all our love."

"Canis, you loved her dearly." Cea spoke with her tears running.

"Aye, so dearly that I went seven years from her. She could not have given me that which I might have asked for and which I did not in any event think I could command in her. Do you know what you have given me, Cea, in returning to face life?"

"I give you myself."

"And a world I thought gone."

"Did not the queen my mother say and say again that you belonged to our house?" whispered Cea. "Did she not say you belonged to us? Oh, I know of your love for her, but do you love me dearly too?"

"I love you," he said, "as I have always loved you."

To Canis she was precious because she was of Boadicea. To Cea he was the first and only man. She raised her lips for his kiss as the setting sun tinted the forest with fire. And the forest stirred in the red light. There was movement, a movement they heard but could not see. It was around them, above them. The grass sighed and the sky breathed. They heard a far-off jingling, the distant noises of muted hoofbeats and muffled armour, the murmurous clash of spears and the rumble of mighty waggons. It became the clamour of a cavalcade marching and riding over the roof of the forest, the whispering music of fifty thousand voices floating across the reddening sky and calling to them from a world they had yet to find.

Thus did Cea and Canis hear again the mighty host of Boadicea.

* * *

And what happened to them after further battles against Rome, and to Lydia whose love for Canis gave her so much joy and torment, is another story.

But if you look hard enough at the people of the western mountains you may discover among them the descendants of Canis and Cea, and also of Lydia, who turned her back on Rome to go with Canis and the people of Boadicea, although she never wholly forsook her goddess Diana. They are distinctive, these descendants, and you will find them where the slopes of the mountains are green. They are as rich in their capacity for life and argument as their heroic forebears, but then so they should be, for Lydia gave up all she had in favour of sweet life, Cea was the daughter of her incomparable mother and Canis the most enduring of men.

He was also the life and death of his Queen.

HISTORY LACED WITH ROMANCE
The finest in Historical Romance from Berkley

THE BARBARIAN PRINCES   (03701-0 —$1.95)
  by Laura Buchanan

THE GOLDEN LOCKET   (03769-X —$1.95)
  by Juliana Davison

A HERITAGE OF STRANGERS   (03668-5 —$1.75)
  by Pamela D'Arcy

INDIGO NIGHTS   (03629-4 —$1.95)
  Olivia O'Neill

LUISE   (03767-3 —$1.95)
  by Dawn Stewart Field

MARIE LAVEAU   (03727-4 —$2.25)
  by Francine Prose

ROMANY PASSIONS   (03672-3 —$1.95)
  by Alexandra Ellis

CARDIGAN SQUARE   (03837-8 —$1.95)
  by Alexandra Manners

STAGE OF LOVE   (03879-3 —$1.95)
  by Cecily Shelbourne

DESTINY'S BRIDE   (03996-X —$1.95)
  Diana Stuart

Send for a list of all our books in print.

These books are available at your local bookstore, or send price indicated plus 30¢ for postage and handling. If more than four books are ordered, only $1.00 is necessary for postage. Allow three weeks for delivery. Send orders to:

      Berkley Book Mailing Service
      P.O. Box 690
      Rockville Centre, New York 11570